THE
WINTER
VOW

AVAILABLE FROM TIM AKERS AND TITAN BOOKS
IN THE HALLOWED WAR SERIES

The Pagan Night
The Iron Hound
The Winter Vow

BOOK THREE OF THE HALLOWED WAR

THE WINTER VOW

TIM AKERS

TITAN BOOKS

THE WINTER VOW
Print edition ISBN: 9781783299522
Electronic edition ISBN: 9781783299539

Published by Titan Books
A division of Titan Publishing Group Ltd
144 Southwark St, London SE1 0UP

First edition: August 2018
2 4 6 8 10 9 7 5 3 1

This is a work of fiction. Names, places and incidents are either products of the author's imagination or used fictitiously. Any resemblance to actual persons, living or dead (except for satirical purposes), is entirely coincidental.

Visit our website: www.titanbooks.com

A CIP catalogue record for this title is available from the British Library.

Printed and bound by CPI Group (UK) Ltd, Croydon, CR0 4YY.

This one's for Joshua. Without his patient guidance and wise counsel, this book would barely exist, and certainly wouldn't be worth reading.

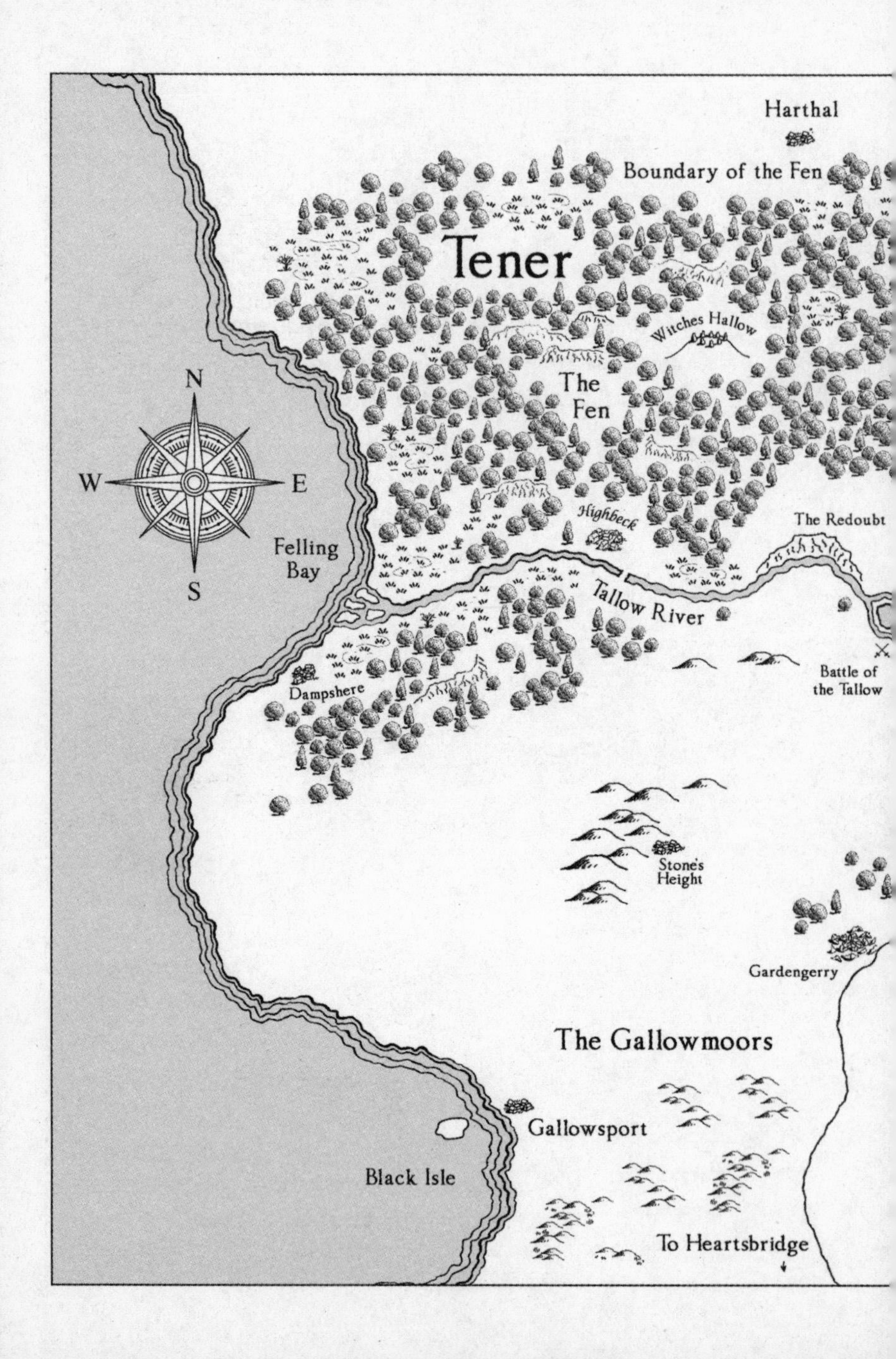
Harthal
Boundary of the Fen
Tener
Witches Hallow
The Fen
N
W
E
S
Felling Bay
Highbeck
The Redoubt
Tallow River
Dampshere
Battle of the Tallow
Stone's Height
Gardengerry
The Gallowmoors
Gallowsport
Black Isle
To Heartsbridge

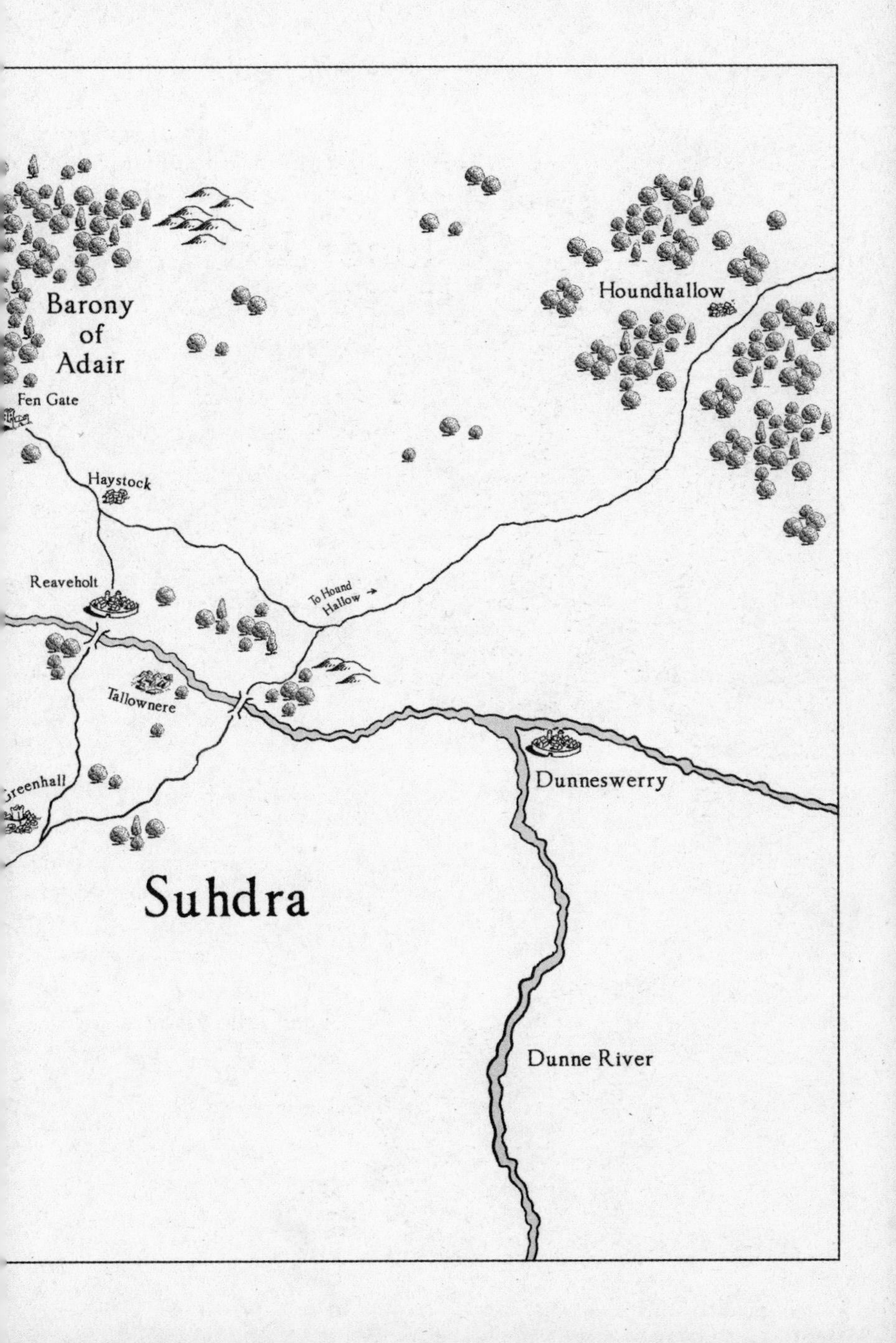

Barony
of
Adair
Fen Gate
Haystock
Reaveholt
To Hound Hallow
Houndhallow
Tallownere
Greenhall
Dunneswerry
Suhdra
Dunne River

PROLOGUE

THE BLESSED FORCES of the celestial church lined the field, banners flowing, rank upon rank of spear and arrow, joined by the holy cadres of inquisitors. The might of Cinder filled them. The glory of their god hung over them like a storm cloud.

"This will be a good day, Frair Voclain," the sergeant said. He was dressed in the black and gold of the church's livery, the mail of his coif as bright as moonlight. The rows of spear and shield stretched off in both directions, the men eager for battle, the priests chanting rites of blessing.

"It will be a day of judgment," Voclain answered, his stiff fingers going through the motions of the blessing without thought. He stepped to the next man, a child whose helm settled too low on his brow, and started the rite over again. "Judgment is sometimes good, and sometimes harrowing," he mumbled to himself. "But it is always necessary."

The soldiers ignored his words, their eyes turned to the bright fields below. The army of the rebel houses of Tener perched narrowly on the opposite rise, their thin ranks bolstered by the banners of a few Suhdrin dukes. The forests of the Fen hung black and forbidding in the background, and the Reaveholt loomed to the east. Voclain didn't see how Malcolm

Blakley could lead men to such obvious slaughter. The Suhdrin loyalists, commanded by Lady Bassion, duchess of Galleydeep, outnumbered Blakley's force nearly three to one. That was before the ranks of the army of Cinder were counted. Blakley's defeat was inevitable. Still, the man seemed determined to fight.

"Stubborn," Voclain said as he finished his prayers and turned to join his brothers at the core of the celestial contingent. He had met Duke Blakley once, at the Frostnight celebration nearly a decade ago. Houndhallow had seemed a reasonable man, faithful to the church and gifted with Cinder's reason. "The years change a man, I suppose. A pity."

A drumroll surged through the valley, calling the army to attention. Voclain took his place among the holy priests of Cinder. The gods' vengeance would be exacted on Tener. It was a tragedy that would take generations to mend. But there was no other way.

At the front of the Suhdrin army, a trio of priests climbed the stairs to a rickety platform to address the ranks. They wore simple black robes, but the glint of mail flashed at their hems, and their faces were buried in shadowy hoods. The murmur of steel and leather and the voices of nervous soldiers flowed like a tide over the army, and Voclain was worried that the priests' words would be lost to the wind. He watched nervously as the tallest of the three priests stepped forward.

"Odd that he wears no ornament," Voclain said. "It was the high elector of Cinder who led us out of Heartsbridge. I wonder where Dustasse is?"

"Probably transcribing Cinder's Only Law," Frair Delleux joked at his side. The two had been together since their investiture. Life on the road didn't agree with Delleux, but the smaller priest still seemed excited at the prospect of battle. “The old man always gets carried away with that.”

Voclain was about to answer when the priest on the platform started to speak. The words were strangely distant, as though they echoed from across the valley or from the clouds above. The babble of the army quieted as everyone strained to hear what the priest was saying. The silence was eerie. It was unnatural.

“What is happening?” Voclain asked, but his words died at his lips. He turned frantically to Delleux, only to see that the man was staring with horror down at his hands. Voclain grabbed him by the shoulder. Delleux looked up and started talking, but no words came out of his mouth. A black fog formed at his lips, drifting like smoke from a snuffed candle. The silence was absolute. Even Voclain’s heartbeat, thudding heavily in his chest, was muted.

Into the silence came a scream. Sharp, tearing, without direction but utterly terrified. Everyone looked up, but the sun still shone, the sky was clear. The scream died out, only to be joined by another, and another, coming from all around Voclain. Coming from his own mouth, passing through him like a wave and then on to Delleux, and the priests beyond. The force of it emptied his lungs, and when he tried to breathe there was no air to fill him. Voclain dropped to his knees.

Delleux fell by his side, tongue lolling, the blood of his heart pouring from his eyes. Voclain held his friend and watched him die.

The world rushed in with a crash, the sound of an army’s panic suddenly filling Voclain’s head. Someone stumbled into Voclain, a knight in full plate, treading on Delleux’s throat. There was fighting somewhere nearby, people dying, steel striking steel and flesh and bone. A boy fell down next to Voclain, his chest split open.

"What is happening?" Voclain asked again, his heart numb. The blood rushing through his head was a drumbeat. He stood up and looked around. People were dying. The army was dying.

At the head of the army, the three priests stood on the platform, their arms raised in prayer, their voices resonant. An inhuman chant rolled out of their throats, words meant to twist flesh and sunder spirit. Dark gods answered their prayers, tearing into the ranks of Suhdrin faithful.

Voclain got to his feet and ran.

Each step sent a jolt of pain down Voclain's spine. Something was broken deep inside his chest, but he pressed on. Gods help him, he had to press on.

It had been three weeks since the ambush, three weeks spent crawling through forests forsaken by god and man, eating whatever greenery looked edible and still getting sick half the time. Voclain tried eating some meat from a dead deer he found at the bottom of a gully, but the resulting misery ensured he would never do that again. The fact that he hadn't died could only be attributed to Cinder's will. Voclain was sure of it.

He paused on the rocky spine of a ridge. In the fading light of dusk, the dark towers of the Fen Gate loomed grimly out of the forest to the northeast. It wasn't where he wanted to be. But after the slaughter, Voclain had lost his mind, Cinder's reason fled. The horror still haunted him, waking and sleeping. Sometimes Voclain was sure the dreams were true, and this daylight ordeal of trackless forests and maggot-ridden meat was the nightmare.

A shadow flickered down the ridge, and Voclain flinched. The screams of his brothers and sisters lingered in his mind. The look on Delleux's face as his spirit left, his lungs starved and full of blood. Voclain had not been able to shrive his friend's soul, hadn't taken the time to usher the man into the quiet house. He wondered if anyone had. He doubted it. They were haunting him, these bound souls. Bound to him, for running. Bound to him, for his cowardice.

There was only one way to free himself from them. One way to give the souls of Delleux the rest they deserved. He had to get to the Fen Gate, to tell Frair Gilliam what had happened: that Blakley had used some kind of witchcraft against them, or that they had been betrayed, by priests still loyal to Sacombre, or by their own god. The thought chilled him.

"The Orphanshield will know," Voclain muttered to himself. "He will know what to do." He stumbled forward, shying away from the growing shadows along the ridgeline, refusing to look in their direction. The spirits of Delleux and the others. The spirits of the dead. "He must know. I must tell him."

"You mustn't, actually." The voice came from the shadows, drifting like fog through the forest. Dreams, again. Dreams among the living. Voclain was beginning to think he was going mad. Better to press on, to flee. But as Voclain hurried away from the shadows, something came out of them. A man, dressed in the glory of Cinder. "We will see to that, my friend."

Voclain paused and turned. The man descended from the ridgeline, grabbing at the trees for support as he slid down the steep incline, very like flesh and blood. Not a ghost. He was dressed in black robes and silver armor, and his hood was thrown back. When the setting sun peeked through the trees and found the man's face, it shone off golden hair and a nose that had been broken more than once. The man smiled at Voclain.

"You needn't look so surprised, frair," he said. "You made it much farther than we thought possible. Most of your compatriots went to Blakley for protection, or tried their luck south, hoping to reach Heartsbridge." He slowed as he reached Voclain, folding his arms into his robes. "Those who scattered into the Fen are dead. All but you. Frair Voclain, isn't it?"

"How did you know?"

"We still hold a stake in the realm of dreams. Cinder has left us that much, even those who have turned fully toward—" he paused, gesturing emptily toward the sky "—those who have taken another path. I am Frair Morrow."

"You are part of Gilliam's cadre? You look too old to be one of the Orphanshield's wards," Voclain said. "Take me to him. He must be warned."

"No," Morrow said. "He mustn't."

Morrow raised a hand. His palm was scored in black, like a wound that hadn't healed properly, and as Voclain's eyes lingered, it seemed to change. Dark lines crawled across the skin. They drew Voclain in, until he realized that he had unknowingly walked closer to the mysterious priest. Voclain shook his head and stepped away.

"What are you doing?" Voclain asked. The sun had set, and shadows filled the forest around them. "Cinder and Strife, what have you done?"

"What is necessary," Morrow said. And then the darkness of his palm filled Voclain's mind, and he fell.

1

THREATS AND REVERSALS

1

SHARP PAIN BURNED through Ian's chest. The wound was open like cracked earth, and the edges of his flesh were crusted with blood. Worked into his flesh, the fragments of the voidfather's amulet pulsed with malevolent red light. Streamers of fog danced up from the wound to tangle with the witch's fingers. Her eyes were closed in concentration. The only sound was the hum of her chant and Ian's pained groans. His sweat stained the sheets of the bed, and his fingers dug into the mattress. Finally, he could take no more.

"Enough!" Ian snapped, turning away. The spell broke, and the pain subsided. "It feels like you're yanking a fishhook through my ribs!"

"I don't understand," Maev said. Cahl had sent her when he had learned of Ian's wound, insisting she was the best healer the tribes had to offer, but Ian didn't think she was doing much good. "Your life energy is strong, but the wound resists me. You're not dying, though. At least not today."

"Very comforting," Ian muttered. He sat up, delicately running a finger along the edge of the wound. The flesh was hot, and as hard as baked clay. "I've always wanted an impressive scar, though this is not exactly what I had in mind."

"Women think less of scars than you might believe,"

Maev said. "It does little for your charm, and speaks to a life of violence and risk."

"That's not what I... Never mind. A pity Fianna isn't here. She was able to bring my mother back from the brink of death. I have trouble believing that this would cause her any difficulty."

"It's true, Fianna was skilled in water's gifts of healing." Maev stood and began packing her instruments. "Though considering it was her father who inflicted this injury on you, I don't know that I'd seek her aid, if I were you."

"So Folam really was her father?"

"Many whisper that she was to be the voidmother, when Folam set that burden down. If she knew of her father's betrayal..." Maev shrugged. "Anyway. She's not here, and I am, and I say that wound can't be healed."

"Thankfully it doesn't hurt very much," Ian said, but his mind was elsewhere. What did Fianna know of her father's sins? Was she part of it? Everything she'd told him about seeking the Hound, about following the old ways of Tener—had all of that been part of the deception?

"Good. Perhaps your southern gods can heal you. Now that Folam is dead, we may never learn what he did to you."

Ian sat quietly for a while, thinking. When he turned, the witch was gone, and he was alone in the room. There was a knock on the door. Sir Clough came in a heartbeat later. She wore a shirt of simple chain over her linens, but looked as ready for war as if she'd been in full plate. Her dark eyes took in the room, checking each corner thoroughly before resting on Ian. Clough settled into a stance of loose attention.

"My lord, may I have a word?"

"Does it have to be now?" Ian was trying not to blush

under the knight's steely glare. He barely knew Clough. They were nearly the same age, but her family was from much farther north than his. She had come to Houndhallow to petition for a place in his father's service shortly before the Allfire last year. So much had happened since then. "Didn't I leave you in charge of my sister's safety?"

"And it is of her safety I would speak, my lord. If I may—"

"Stop calling me lord. Malcolm Blakley is the lord of Houndhallow, and I'm not sure he would pass the throne to me. Not after…" Ian trailed off, remembering his father's words at the Fen Gate, the simple dismissal that sent Ian into exile. "This is not my throne to sit."

"You are the eldest Blakley present. There has been no word of Lord Blakley since he quit the Fen Gate, so in the absence of his authority, I must make my petition to you." Clough made the slightest bow, her face placid. "Whether you want it or nay."

Ian sighed, but the movement sent a jolt of pain through his chest, causing him to inhale sharply. Clough took a step forward.

"I saw the witch leave with a smug look on her face. Did she fix you, or did she make it worse?" she asked.

"No worse, thank the gods. But no better. It seems there's nothing to be done for me." Ian stood and nearly lost his balance, catching himself on the bedpost. "It will pass."

"Not everything passes. Some things only get worse," Clough said. "It's for the better that the witch wasn't able to help you. I don't trust these pagans."

"I would be dead without their help, and this castle fallen. They may not be the allies we expect, but they are the allies the gods have given us."

"I remember standing watch on this very tower at your sister's side as these same pagans swarmed the walls and crashed our gates. Odd behavior for allies."

"Not the same pagans, if Folam and his lot can be called that anymore." Ian grimaced as he belted on his sword. "The tribes were tricked into assaulting Houndhallow by Folam and his void priests. They lost as many honest souls to Folam's betrayal as we did."

"The souls we lost fell to pagan blades. Sir Tavvish held the door to this tower against the hope of reinforcement, and nearly died with a pagan spear in his gut. He's only now up and walking, and I swear the wound has changed that man. It was not this 'voidfather' who threw that blade." Clough's palm brushed the hilt of her dagger. "You can weigh your alliances in trickery and false promises. I weigh mine in blood."

"The weight of blood is more than any of us will be able to pay. Not in our lifetimes, at least."

"I am willing to make the effort," Clough answered, staring up at the wall.

"They are not the enemy, Clough. Not in this." Ian pulled his shirt back on, grimacing as the fabric pulled across the cracked flesh of his wound. "Folam would have us believe otherwise, but I am done dancing to the voidfather's dirge. I am no longer part of his game."

"Aren't you?" Clough asked. "Stories I heard out of the Fen Gate say you arrived in the arms of one of these witches, the same one taken south by the inquisition. And now we stand in the company of Gwendolyn Adair." Clough made a slow circuit of the room as she spoke. When she reached the door, she peered outside, then pressed it shut and lowered her voice. "I don't need to tell you what I think of House Adair."

"The Adairs were betrayed by our true enemy, Sacombre. It was the high inquisitor who started this war."

"First you blame this pagan, Folam, and now the high inquisitor. You make this hard to believe, my lord."

"It has been a complicated time. But Sacombre—"

"I have nothing to say about Tomas Sacombre," Clough interrupted. "You tell me he committed heresy, raised a pagan god of the dead, and murdered the Adairs. That he murdered Duke Halverdt and framed your father. You tell me these things, and that is all I know."

"You don't believe me?"

"If I did not believe you, we would not be having this conversation. But believing them and knowing them to be true are different things, my lord." The knight came closer, bending her head toward Ian. Her features were soft, more suited for a lady of the court than a knight, but she had murder in her eyes. "And what I know to be true is this: these people attacked your home. Call them 'pagans,' or 'the northern tribes,' or whatever you like. There are men and women wearing Blakley colors who are dead today because of them. Now they walk your hallways, and eat your bread, and shelter inside your walls, and why? Because of some story about this 'voidfather'?"

"You were there, Clough. You saw him raise a gheist, saw it tear through the pagans just as much as it tore through our people. You know what he was capable of."

"What I saw was another pagan, killing priests and good celestials. When you led us into battle, you claimed to ride for all Tenumbra. That's good enough. But you have to ride for your family first. They depend on you."

"And what am I supposed to do? Folam is dead, and his priests are fled. There is something in the forests, hunting any who dare leave these walls. Should I throw Gwen and her tribesmen into the forests, just as winter is falling, to be killed by feral gods? Is that what justice looks like to you?"

"Justice doesn't matter. Justice died with Folam, so we've no hope of that. What you need to do is protect your family. There has been no word from your father since Frair Gilliam drove him out of the Fen Gate. Gods know what became of your mother, or if she's even human anymore. Your sister is here, Ian, and she's depending on you. House Blakley, all these men and women wearing the hound and swearing to the hallow, they depend on you." Clough looked down at the bed, where some of the witch's tools remained. "What are they to think of their lord, keeping council with pagans, seeking a witch's healing? Are you even their lord, anymore?"

"My father is their lord. My father, who exiled me at the Fen Gate, and turned his back on the witch who saved his wife's life. My mother's life! These people shouldn't be looking to me for leadership."

"But we do. Because we have no one else." Clough took Ian by the shoulders and looked him square in the eye. "I swore a vow to your father, stood at your sister's side, would have died to keep her alive. And that vow descends to you."

"For my sister's safety, I thank you. But your vow should be to her. I am not ready for the throne," Ian said, pulling away. "My father will return. Until then, Houndhallow will have to see to itself."

Clough was silent for a minute, staring daggers at Ian. When she spoke, her voice held violence.

"What did they do to you, Blakley? Stories say you were

alone with the pagans for months, and when you returned, you looked more tribesman than duke's son. You've been running from your family ever since. So I ask, what did the witch do to you?"

"Fianna saved my life," Ian said, but even as the words left his mouth, his mind rebelled. *Why did she save you, Ian? To use you against your father? Against your family? She's Folam's daughter! Surely she knew.* He shook his head and continued. "She and Cahl led me through the Fen, and to my father's side. Without their help, that battle might have been lost. And my father thanked her by sending her south with the inquisition."

"Is Gwen Adair a heretic?" Clough asked suddenly.

"What? Yes, of course. By her own admission. But that's not—"

"And Sacombre? He is also a heretic, yes?"

"Yes. And a murderer as well."

"Murder in war is a difficult thing to judge. Sacombre has gone south, chained to the witch Fianna, to be judged. But Gwen walks free. Why?"

"Who are you to ask these questions?"

"A soldier of Tener, sworn to your house. I have fought fewer battles than you, my lord, but I have seen war enough. I have lost more friends to these pagans than I care to count. I have learned to be wary, especially of the enemy who claims to be my friend. So tell me, why does Gwen Adair walk free? Is her heresy somehow a lesser one than Sacombre's? Are the dead at her feet not deserving of life? Tell me, my lord."

"I don't know. That's not mine to judge."

"You are the heir of Houndhallow. We are in your halls, under your roof, surrounded by men and women who have sworn their lives to you. I have sworn my life to you. Your word is law. It is yours to judge, and no one else's. Unless you'd rather trust the inquisition to answer that question." Clough smiled mirthlessly and spread her hands. "Because I think we all know what they would decide."

"Gwen Adair and her tribes were just as much the victims of the voidfather as we were. They were tricked into this attack, and while I mourn the dead, I will not add to their number without reason." Ian drew himself up and faced Clough. "There is something more going on here. Whatever Folam planned, he wanted us to fight—Suhdrin against Tenerran, celestial against pagan."

"'Just as much the victims...'" Clough shook her head. "This is how *I* count, my lord: How many hundreds are dead? Suhdrin names, Tenerran names... dead at pagan hands. And you believe them?"

"It's not what I believe," Ian said. "It's what I know. I know Gwen Adair lost everything to Sacombre's plot, and Folam's blade. More than I have lost."

"Aye, Gwen Adair. Between her shaman and your witch, we all have a lot to lose."

"Her shaman?" Ian asked.

"Aye. Brute of a fellow, named Cahl. Looks like a rock most of the time, and talks less. He's the one who brought the Adair girl here."

"Did he?" Ian's voice grew distant. Cahl, whose witching wife was Fianna, the very man who walked by Ian's side through the Fen. *What was his loyalty to Folam?* "Did he indeed?"

Sir Bruler sat in a corner of the courtyard by himself, sharpening his blade. A crowd of Tenerran soldiers sat on the other side of the fire, talking among themselves and ignoring the Suhdrin knight. Bruler watched them out of the corner of his eye.

"Nearly had them," one of the Tenerrans said. He was a scrawny kid, with a scar that split his lip in two. "It was me and Master Tavvish, holding off the lot. Lucky for them Master Ian came back when he did."

"It was the heretic bitch who stopped the pagans, not you," his friend said. "Called them to heel like dogs."

"It weren't like that," Huck answered. "No Blakley soul owes their life to Gwen Adair. We held 'em back."

"Hell you did," another said. "Master Ian gave his word, then rushed off with his southern knights, and Adair gave the pagans the order to retreat." The man spat into the fire, his eyes passing briefly over Bruler. "Saved by Suhdrin blades and pagan whores. Better to have fallen."

"It was Suhdra what started this war, and pagans what kept it burning," Huck said. "There'll be no peace in Tener until they're both gone."

"Godsbless," they murmured as one, more than a few eyes darting in Bruler's direction. The Suhdrin knight laughed to himself.

"The only peace you'd have without us is the peace of the grave," Bruler said without looking up. "And if you're going to threaten your allies and speak poorly of the very men and women who risked their lives to save you, I would be happy enough to give you that peace." He paused in the sharpening of his blade, cocking his head in Huck's direction. "If you've steel enough in your blood, friend."

"Any man who draws steel against Sir Bruler draws steel against me." Ian Blakley appeared from the shadows. He was dressed in only a shirt and the thick leather of his riding breeches, but his hand rested on his sword. The crowd of Tenerran soldiers took a long breath to recognize him, then stood as one.

"Only words, my lord. You have our faith," Huck said quickly.

"Words are the sharpest blade, and the easiest to turn," Ian said. He walked past them, standing over the fire to stare down at Sir Bruler. "I would like to speak to this man in private, please."

The Tenerrans were gone in a heartbeat. Bruler folded his whetstone away, then leaned back, inspecting Ian's appearance. The young lord of Houndhallow looked sallow. His face was thin and puckered with pain, and the way he held his arm betrayed the wound hidden beneath his shirt.

"You're going to live?" Bruler asked.

"Today, at least. Unless there is a dagger waiting for my back tonight," Ian said. "The way this lot is talking, I would worry more about your back, Bruler."

"Children talk. As long as it stays that way, I'm not worried."

"I need something from you. Something only you can do."

"Someone killed? So you can blame it on the Suhdrin knight, and kick me out without losing faith among your subjects?"

"I hope not. But if I give this task to a Tenerran, it will certainly lead to a fight, and we can't afford that." Ian looked stiffly around, then lowered himself to the bench next to Bruler. "There is a shaman among the pagans, a large man. Cahl."

"Elder of the tribe of stones," Bruler said. "I know him. He's close to Gwen Adair."

"I need to know what he's doing. Whose counsel he keeps, and whose faith he holds."

"You have reason to suspect him?" Bruler asked.

"I don't know. Cahl was a friend to me, but he was close to Folam's daughter, as well. The deeper we get into this, the less I trust those I once called friend."

"And why do you trust me?"

"I don't. But you're alone here. You have no one else to trust, and much to lose in betrayal." Ian smiled thinly, then stood. "Let me know what Cahl does, who he talks to. If he means to betray me, or Gwen, I must be the first to know."

"I am a knight, my lord. Not a spy."

"And as a knight, you do as you are asked by your lord."

"I have sworn no vow to you, Blakley."

"We must pretend that you have. We must trust one another, Bruler. We have no one else, you and I." Ian glanced over at the crowd of Tenerrans who watched them still. "My own people don't trust me, though they obey my name. The pagans see the celestial in me; the Tenerrans look at my clothes and see a pagan. And both know my father's name, and wonder if I will live up to his story."

"And when they look at me, they see a Suhdrin fop. Always the enemy, even when alliances are forged." Bruler shook his head and stood, then offered Ian his hand. "A desperate business we're in."

"Desperate," Ian agreed. "But necessary."

They shook hands, then Ian turned and disappeared into the night. Bruler sat back down and continued sharpening his blade. Whatever this new task would bring, he would need a sharp sword and a clear head.

2

THE KNIGHT WORE the colors of the celestial church, black and gold, with Cinder's ashen moon on his chest. He rode unsupported across the churned mud of the field, bounding over the bodies of the dead. Lazy arrows fell around him. The line of spearmen at Malcolm Blakley's side wavered. They had withstood a dozen charges from the celestials, under the Reaveholt's watchful towers, but Malcolm didn't think they could handle even one more.

"Hold! Hold! Steady, and he will turn!" Malcolm wheeled his horse to face the rider, taking the measure of his intent. The loose column of celestial knights along the ridge milled about, as though unsure if they should join their comrade, or watch him die alone. The horn signaling their retreat still sounded beyond the ridge.

The celestial knight seemed intent on dying a hero. He made no move to turn aside, instead picking up speed as he approached the Tenerran line. The steel tip of his spear was aimed unerringly at Malcolm's chest.

Malcolm glanced at the spearmen beside him. They were weary from the battle just ended, dragging the bodies of their slain friends back to the Tenerran battle line, surprised to be back in the fight even as the enemy withdrew. Even one charging knight could break them. He looked back at the celestial guard, then unsheathed his sword.

"I will hold for you," he muttered to himself, then spurred his mount forward.

The field between them was littered with bodies and discarded steel. Malcolm gave the horse its head, trusting the beast to navigate the ground without his help. He held the feyiron blade of his sword in both hands, keeping his gaze steady on the rapidly approaching spear.

As the distance closed, Malcolm was able to hear the guard's voice, raised above the hammering of hooves and clatter of armor. He was singing the evensong, the dirge of daylight made rough by his battle-weary voice.

"To evening fall,
and ashes spread,
end daylight's call
in the black embrace of Cinder."

It was the first time Malcolm had heard the evensong since being chased out of Greenhall by an angry mob. It struck him as strangely out of place on the battlefield. The moment of distraction nearly cost him dearly. In the blink of an eye, the celestial guard was on him. The knight stopped singing, his voice twisting into a scream of rage and retribution.

"Cinder!" the knight howled. Their horses crashed together.

Malcolm swung his sword. He was aiming for the haft of the spear but instead the blade glanced off its steel tip. The spear's aim wavered, drawn off from Malcolm's heart, cutting instead into his shoulder. It snagged the rings of his chain shirt, popping links open like the burst seam of a wineskin. The two knights collided, the force of the impact sending Malcolm reeling in his saddle. Instinctively, his horse wheeled around, again almost throwing Malcolm to the ground. The duke of Houndhallow gripped the pommel, his left arm hanging loose at his side. The impact had numbed it, but a quick look showed no blood in the gap. His armor had saved him.

Malcolm's sword slithered down his mount's side, disappearing into the grass. The celestial knight wheeled to face Malcolm, dropping the shattered remnants of his spear and drawing an iron mace from his belt.

"Do you yield to the church's mercy, Sir Blakley?"

"The church has forsaken mercy, sir," Malcolm answered. His head was spinning. "I will not risk it, now or ever."

"Then be damned."

The knight spurred his horse, and it leapt toward Malcolm. With his good hand, Malcolm drew his dagger, the only weapon left to him. They met again, the knight swinging wildly at Malcolm's head, easily dodged, and then the backstroke skated across Malcolm's forearm. Their knees met, and Malcolm leaned into the contact, throwing his numb arm across the man's shoulders, fouling his swing.

Malcolm dragged his dagger across the knight's chest, the sharp edge grinding along steel and dancing off chain, finally catching beneath the plate protecting the man's thigh. The haft of the knight's mace caught Malcolm in the jaw, shoving his helm to the side, blinding him and pushing him back. Malcolm hung on to the dagger, driving the tip of the blade into the knight's thigh. Screams filled Malcolm's ears, his own and the knight's, and possibly more voices beyond. Malcolm pitched forward, crashed into the knight, his full weight on the dagger's hilt. There was half a breath of resistance, then chain links popped and the dagger drove home.

Screaming, they fell.

The ground met Malcolm with dark arms. His head buzzed, eyes swimming with colors, sweat and blood running down his face. He struggled to breathe. Still blinded by his helm, Malcolm wrenched himself onto his knees, doubling up as nausea swept through his body, biting back the bile in his mouth. With numb fingers, Malcolm twisted off his helm, throwing it aside.

The line of his spearmen washed over him, charging in to surround their lord. The celestial knights on the ridge had finally decided to join their comrade's lonely charge, and were even now breaking against the reinvigorated spear wall. The sound of their hooves thundered in Malcolm's head, shaking through his bones and chattering his teeth. The spears held, spitting any rider foolish enough to meet them.

One of the spearmen rushed past Malcolm to the fallen knight at his side. He drove his spear into the knight's chest, leaning on it until the screaming stopped. He turned to Malcolm.

"My lord, your blade!"

"Yes, I..." Malcolm struggled to draw breath. His chest was tight and his vision swam. "I lost it. Dropped it somewhere. Bloody thing."

"At your knee, my lord." Malcolm gaped up at the man, not understanding. The spearman knelt, scooping up the feyiron blade that was lying in the grass at Malcolm's knee. He offered Malcolm the hilt across his forearm, as though he were a king offering a commission.

Smiling wryly, Malcolm took the sword, then used it to stand up. The spearman remained kneeling for half a second, then scrambled to his feet and rejoined his comrades.

The skirmish rolled around them, until finally the knights tired of wheeling and broke back to the ridgeline. Malcolm gathered his spearmen, counted the newly dead, and signaled the retreat. They marched wearily back to the Tenerran lines.

Castian Jaerdin was waiting for him on the Tenerran battle line. The duke of Redgarden had waited calmly during the battle, receiving reports from the scattered bands of fighters who made up Malcolm's makeshift army. They had told him that when Lady Bassion's forces had been split up, betrayed by the priests of Cinder and the ranks of celestial guard, they'd flown in all directions. Some had found their way to Malcolm's line, others had fled into the woods, and the majority had run back to the south. The celestials had pursued, creating a confusing battlefield of small skirmishes, limited engagements, and sudden conflict. They had also told him that Malcolm's forces had spent the day rushing around trying to save elements of the shattered Bassion force while still avoiding a direct fight with the celestials. The betrayal of the priests of Cinder had thrown the entire battlefield into disarray, from unclear loyalties to murky battle lines, and it was up to Jaerdin to sort it all out.

"Houndhallow. What news from the front?" Jaerdin asked. He was still in battle armor, though he had exchanged his helm for a farmer's sun cap, and removed his greaves to better handle the maps and written reports.

"My only news is that the front's all over the bloody place. We engaged a small patrol just this side of the Tallow, but they were reinforced by mounted knights and a small cadre of archers." Malcolm accepted a bowl of water from a servant, drinking deeply before dumping the remainder over his head. Dirt and blood washed down his face. "They withdrew in short order, but not before one of their number decided to die a zealot's death."

"Another story for the Reaverbane's legend," Jaerdin said. "No wonder the Suhdrins fear you so."

"It wasn't my kill. I dropped my sword and very nearly my head. Had to be saved by some farmer's son."

"Then a story for that man's grandchildren, Godsbless." Jaerdin rifled through his reports, grimacing. "It's the same everywhere, Malcolm. Small battles, small deaths. We're staying away from the celestials as best we can, but sometimes the fight can't be dodged."

"What of Bassion's forces? Have any more sued for our aid?"

"Some," Jaerdin said. "It would help if their fellows would do the same—a few of them are still trying to fight us. Half these reports are of skirmishes fought between our men and Bassion's, with the priests of Cinder—the very ones who attacked them—watching from afar."

"Gods. We kill each other, and the wolf waits at the door. Has there been any sign of Lady Bassion? Or any of her command?"

"Not yet. A few knights have joined us. They tell of Lady Bassion falling back along the road, toward the Reaveholt. Perhaps Bourne offered her sanctuary."

"Not bloody likely. That man was as loyal to Adair as any in the north. I doubt he'll suffer Suhdrin guests at his table, not unless they force the door. We'll have to pray she lives. These Suhdrin knights: are they fighting for us, or merely tolerating our company?"

"I thought it best to keep them off the field, at least until the fog of war has passed. They're gathered in a tent, back in camp. The vow knight is watching them."

"Trueau? Very well. I should speak to them, before she poisons their minds any further." Malcolm slid from his saddle, landing with a wince. His legs and back were as brittle as dry wood, and just as stiff. "Godsbless, but war is a young man's business."

Malcolm made his slow way back to the makeshift camp. The sudden addition of Suhdrin rank-and-file from Bassion's shattered army had thrown the camp into disarray, and the once straight lines of tents and wagons looked like a game of scatterjacks now. Order would have to be reestablished if they were going to face the celestial army with a united front.

He was able to find the tent holding the Suhdrin knights easily enough. An informal ring of Tenerran guards circled it, none of them assigned to stand watch and yet all unwilling to allow Suhdrin nobility to roam freely through the camp. Malcolm nodded his way through their salutes, then ducked into the tent and closed the flap behind him.

The Suhdrin knights were gathered tightly at the center of the tent, holding a whispered conversation. They fell silent when Malcolm entered, turning as one to face him. The dim light inside the tent prevented him from identifying any of them. Malcolm tried to laugh, but managed only a dust-choked croak and a cough.

"Sirs," Malcolm said, "some of you I know from tournaments, some I have not had the honor of meeting." He threw his gloves down on a camp stool, then held out his hands. "I am Lord Malcolm Blakley, duke of Houndhallow, and by Strife's grace the commander of this force. I have—"

"We know who you are, Reaverbane." One of the inky shapes in the center of the tent stepped forward, resolving into a tall knight in simple armor. She held her helm in the crook of her arm, and rested a hand on the hilt of a northern-style broadsword. Malcolm didn't need to see her face to know her; he recognized her voice.

"Sir Tasse, we have not crossed blades since the Allfire tourney at Heartsbridge, three seasons past," Malcolm said. "I am sorry today's meeting is under less glorious conditions."

"Save your words," Tasse answered. "We want to know how you bent those shamans to your will, and how you snuck them into our ranks. The north has never stooped this low before. Killing priests! Summoning demons in open battle! I thought you better than this, Houndhallow!"

"I know less than you, Tasse." Malcolm held his hands away from his blade, though he needn't have bothered. The sound of Tenerran guards moving outside the tent was threat enough. "The first we knew of the priests of Cinder's attack upon their own army was when a group of your knights told us of it and threw themselves upon our mercy. It came as a complete surprise to us. They said the inquisitors themselves were using words of ancient power to kill."

Tasse snorted and turned away. Two other Suhdrin knights took her place. They could have been sisters, or even twins, but sported different tabards and had distinctly different accents. They wore their golden-red hair in thick plaits, and held their thin noses aloft, as though the air itself offended them.

"I am Sir Tabathe Hallister, sworn blade of the earl of

Dellspont, here to avenge the honor of Suhdrin sons and daughters, dead at pagan hands. Whatever happened out there, it was the work of gheists and pagan trickery. I have heard well of you, Reaverbane. But the hearts of men change, as well as their loyalty."

"You swear you had nothing to do with this?" the other woman asked. She wore two blades, each half the length of a regular sword. They were favored by captains in the navy, short enough for close-quarters work and fit for cutting ropes and heavy board without turning their edge.

"You have my word, and my heart, Sir..." Malcolm inclined his head.

"Sir Travailler. Gabrielle Travailler. I ride at the pleasure of Duke Bassion, though I am often abroad. I came home from two years at sea to find my beloved Tenumbra torn asunder. There are many who say I have you to thank for that."

"Sir Travailler, I am as sundered as our shared island. There has been treachery within the church, a betrayal that strikes at both Tener and Suhdra. We have all lost sons and daughters, sometimes to honest battle, sometimes to a knife in the dark." Malcolm paused, remembering Sir Dugan's possession and death. He shivered. "Sometimes worse. Now is not the time for accusation."

"And yet you accuse members of the holy church. When it was your man Lord Adair who betrayed us all!" Sir Hallister said, bristling. "Or do you deny his heresy?"

"I do not. But his betrayal is nothing compared to that of Tomas Sacombre. And now the high inquisitor's heresy seems to have spread. Your fellows report the attack upon your army came from the ranks of inquisitors, from your own allies. I believe that we are fighting the same enemy as struck down both Colm Adair and Gabriel Halverdt," Malcolm said.

"It was no agent of the church who raised the gheist in Greenhall. That was pagan work, and a pagan god," Tasse said from the side.

"You'll forgive me, but I was there when Halverdt died. I saw—"

"Not that," Tasse said, cutting Malcolm off. "I speak of the devastation of Greenhall. A god rose from the stones of the city, destroying buildings and killing untold innocents. It took all of Lady Halverdt's strength to put it down. The only reason she hasn't joined us yet is because she is still trying to secure her broken walls."

"I have heard nothing of this. How do you know it was pagan work, and not the same treachery that laid low the Fen Gate?"

"We are arguing distant treachery, when there is a knife at our throat," Sir Hallister said. She shouldered Travailler out of the way and punched her finger into Malcolm's chest. "How did those pagans get in our ranks?"

"They weren't pagans." This new voice came from behind the Suhdrin knights, low and quiet. Malcolm looked over Travailler's shoulder. There was a fourth figure, huddled on a camp stool. "They were my brothers. My friends. Or so I thought."

"My lady, you saw the attack?" Malcolm asked. The woman stood. She was a priest of Cinder, though her robes were muddied, and her face smudged with ash.

"Gods save me, I did," she said. "Priests of Cinder summoning pagan gheists, and using them to murder their brethren. A dark blade, turned against itself."

3

HE WAS A young man, barely old enough to shave, certainly young enough to be Gwen's age. He had the Tenerran look about him: dark hair, darker eyes, pale skin that was marred with grime from the prison cell. He was dressed in priestly robes, though not of the celestial church. Gwen could almost see her younger brother in his eyes, could see what Grieg might have become if Sacombre hadn't killed the boy, along with her mother and father.

She tightened her grip on the spear, then nodded to the guards. They unlocked the young man's cell and stepped aside.

Gwen knew she made a frightful sight. Her face and arms were slashed with the wounds sustained in the siege of Houndhallow, but the thin flakes of iron that had formed from her blood had turned to rust, disintegrating in the weeks after the battle. Her skin was stained red and black, especially around her eyes and the corners of her mouth. Even her hair had taken on the look of ruined iron. The priest looked unfazed, though. No doubt he had seen his share of horror in Folam Voidfather's company.

"Are you here to kill me, witch?" the priest asked.

"What is your name?"

"My name. So you can conjure with it? Put a curse on my eyes and wither my heart while I still live? No, I don't think I'll be telling you my name." He sat up, neck bent against the rune-inscribed iron collar, chains rattling. "But I know yours: Gwendolyn Adair, witch of the Fen Gate. Only, the Fen Gate has fallen, hasn't it?"

"Look, I need to call you something, so I'm going to go with 'idiot.' Is that okay with you?" The boy grinned and was about to speak when Gwen continued. "So, idiot, what brought you to Houndhallow? You haven't broken out, so you're clearly not one of those void priests we've heard so much about. You're too scrawny to fight, and too dumb to give orders. So why the hell are you here, idiot?"

"What do you know, witch? I could be one of the acolytes. Your shamans wouldn't have put these spellbound chains on me if you didn't think it was a possibility."

"The chains are for me," Gwen said. "They're to keep me from killing you. Idiot."

The boy's smile faltered, and one hand drifted instinctively to the iron at his neck, but he kept talking.

"Death is just another form of emptiness, witch. Another aspect of the one true god. You can't threaten me with that. I go where the voidfather has walked already." His smile deepened, confidence returning to his words. "I go where I was destined to go."

"Maybe. But I can make the journey there a hell of a lot less pleasant than you imagine." She dropped the tip of her spear down to the boy's throat, sliding the razor-sharp tip up his jaw, until it drew blood at the lobe of his left ear. "You're a zealot. I know the type. Anxious to die, not so anxious to suffer. Especially if none of your fellow zealots are around to witness your sacrifice. They're all gone, idiot. Your void priests, Folam, the pagans you lured to your service, and the priests corrupted by your heresy. All dead."

"Do you believe that? Good." He leaned gingerly back, avoiding Gwen's spear, until his head rested against the stone wall of the cell. "Rest safe in your bed, Gwendolyn Adair. I'm sure there's nothing to worry about."

"No, no, I'm not falling for that. I've figured out your type. Creepy and self-assured. I should never have trusted Folam, I see that now, and that other one... Aedan. The one who went to kill Sir LaFey and never came back. He was one of yours, too. I'm sure of it. I won't fall for that trap again."

"Won't you? You certainly weren't able to protect yourself from Folam Voidfather, or his witch-daughter. You weren't even able to protect your family from themselves, and here you are asking questions of an idiot, apparently not powerful enough to defend himself. Tell me, witch, why am I still alive? Why do you need me?"

Gwen snarled but didn't answer. The priest adjusted himself on the floor, sitting up a little straighter, smiling a little brighter.

"Because you don't know, do you? You don't know anything. Folam took you into his trust, then used you to strike at Greenhall. They blame you for that, by the way. You, and dead Sacombre, and all the priests of the celestial church. Suhdra is tearing itself apart trying to decide who is more responsible for their dead sons and broken thrones. And Tener can't field an army to defend itself without first being accused of heresy by the church, betrayal by their own brothers, or worse. Poor Malcolm Blakley has fled the Fen Gate..." He trailed off, seeing Gwen's reaction. "Surely you knew that? Your home is in celestial hands, witch. Our hands. What secrets will they find? What new heresies will the inquisition lay at your family's feet?"

"I care nothing for the church's condemnation, or Suhdra's trouble. They've earned their discord, and may the gods usher them to it. I am here for Tener, and the old gods."

"I am of the old gods, witch. Are we allies, then?"

"Whatever god you serve, it has nothing to do with the spirits of this world. Folam may have commanded respect among the tribes, but I've seen enough to know that he served a different kind of god."

"So sure, and yet so foolish. And you name me idiot." The priest stood, shoulders slumped under the weight of his chains, but as he shuffled toward Gwen she took a step back. "Do you think I'm alone, witch? I am never alone. Not here, nor in Heartsbridge, nor Cinderfell. Send me to any court in Tenumbra and I will count my brothers and sisters hidden in their ranks. The true faith is coming through."

"If you swear to the old gods, why do you kill our shamans? Why do you threaten the tribes? If we're both fighting against the celestial church—"

"There is no difference, witch. Your feral gods, and the bound gods of Heartsbridge... there is no difference. They are all just whispers before the shout. Lightning before the thunder, and in the end, emptiness." The priest laughed, then grabbed Gwen's spear. She twisted it out of his hands, swearing. He held up his hands, palm first, to show the blood she had drawn. "Threaten me all you want, but I am not your enemy. You'll see, in the end. You'll understand."

"This is all I need to understand: Folam betrayed me. Sacombre betrayed me. The tribes betrayed me, my family is dead, and my friends have abandoned me as a heretic. All I have left are these few who stand with me. So if you want to make threats, you're going to have to come up with something better."

"Look at your allies, witch. Ian Blakley, whose father led Halverdt to your gates, and whose army hunted you through the Fen. There are Suhdrins within the walls of your sanctuary, brought to Houndhallow by Ian. And who was it that counseled Ian in the wilderness, and brought him to the Fen Gate just in time to play the hero? The witch Fianna, and the shaman Cahl. Fianna, daughter of Folam. And isn't Cahl still at your side? It seems convenient that Ian and Cahl both survived the inquisition's hand, just to stand with you now."

"You will not have me questioning my allies."

"You're a stubborn girl. Join us, and be assured of victory. Be assured of your revenge against those who— Oh..." He looked down at his belly, and Gwen's spear protruding from it. "I thought we were talking."

"I am done talking," Gwen spat. The priest slid to the floor, staring up at her with eyes wide in pain and shock. "Bury this one with the horses, and see that his name is forgotten."

"I die in the house of my sword," the priest murmured. He grimaced, forcing the words out. "Forged under your nose, and—"

Gwen twisted the spear and withdrew it. The priest's belly came with it, spilling out across the floor. The boy gasped, eyes fluttering, then fell silent.

"Never mind," Gwen said. "Just burn the body with the rest of the shit. I won't have him poisoning my water."

"What did he mean, my lady?" the guard asked. Gwen

looked at him askance. He was one of Ian's bannermen, wearing the Blakley hound on his chest. "Dying in the house of his sword? What was that about?"

"Damned if I know," she said. "Tell your master I need to speak with him—if you can find him. Ian and I have much to discuss."

Cahl waited until the light from Gwen's torch was gone, then stood from his corner. The stone pulled away from him like a cloak, forming back into the wall that had concealed him. He had been on his way to question the priest when Gwen arrived, and barely had time to hide before the huntress of Adair was upon him. He went to stand over the dead priest.

"Your secrets go with you," he whispered. "But you have left poison enough behind. How is she supposed to trust anyone, with those sorts of lies in her ear?"

The priest didn't answer. Cahl grunted, then made his way to the door. It wouldn't be long before the guard came back for the body, and it wouldn't do for Cahl to be found at his side.

Cahl was troubled. Ever since Fianna had been taken by the inquisition, given over by Ian's father for the sin of saving his wife, Cahl had been on uncertain ground. As the elder of stone, Cahl was used to a firm foundation, but so many things had stopped making sense when Fianna had left him.

A troubled company filled the courtyard of Houndhallow. The Suhdrin knights had formed up near the stables, guarding their mounts and setting up a perimeter around their fires. Most had struck their colors, but a stubborn few wore the bright tabards of their sworn houses. Some had adopted the hound of Blakley, but the Tenerrans of that house clearly didn't trust them. Whatever their colors, the Suhdrins all watched the surrounding pagan host with nervous eyes, hands on hilts.

The Tenerrans were none better. The few remaining Blakley guards had no love for the pagans who only weeks ago had assaulted their walls and murdered their friends. The few Tenerrans of other houses at Houndhallow seemed to be always in armor, always peering over their shoulders.

For the pagans, life inside the walls of a castle was no more comfortable. They walked in anxious packs, sticking close together like pups trailing after their mother. The pagans spent as much time outside the walls as possible, but the woods were haunted by feral gods that answered to neither the shaman's commands nor the pagan's prayers. The fact that this castle belonged to Blakley, the first of the northern tribes to abandon the old faith and bend the knee to the Celestriarch, did little to comfort the pagans' fears.

It was not a settled company. Each faction had good reason to mistrust the others, and there were swords enough in their number to see everyone dead.

A group of clansmen from the tribe of stones stood around the entrance to the dungeons, keeping watch. Cahl joined them.

"The priest is dead. Gwen didn't get what she wanted out of him," he said. "None of us will, now."

"We tried to warn you she was coming," one of the pagans, a youth named Caern, whispered. "Did you learn anything?"

"I learned that Gwen Adair doesn't trust us. Doesn't trust anyone. Hard to blame her, the problems she's had."

"And how are we supposed to trust her, then? A lot of the tribes are looking to her to lead, now that Folam's dead, and the rest of the elders argue among themselves."

"May be better if she doesn't trust anyone. I'd have given Folam Voidfather my life, before he used us to set Suhdra against us. Gods know, Folam might have been in on this from the beginning. Might have been Sacombre's friend." Cahl grimaced, staring at a group of Blakley guards as they passed. *What if Fianna was part of this, as well? Folam was her father, as the priest said. What poison might she have laid in Ian's ears? She did talk a lot about grooming Ian to become the Hound of the Hallow, to reclaim his family's place among the pagan tribes. If she were working for these void priests...* Cahl shook his head, grunting. He couldn't start down that line of thought. He had enough enemies.

"Watch the gates," he said. "Worst thing that could happen is if they locked us in here, cut us off from the rest of the tribes. Cut us off from the gods."

"Those things in the woods are no gods of mine," Caern said.

"No. No, they're not. But keep watch."

"And where are you going?"

"Time I talked to Ian. We haven't seen much of each other since Fianna was taken."

"His guards are keeping him close. You won't be able to get within a hundred paces of his lordship," Caern said with a smirk.

"This is a house of stones," Cahl said, pushing off from the wall and heading toward the gate. "And I am the elder of stones. I will find a way."

* * *

Cahl didn't notice the eyes that watched him walk out of the gate. A group of men, wearing the hound and skulking in the shadows of the gate, signaled to each other. Another man, Suhdrin by birth but wearing the hound on a newly stitched tabard, came out of the gatehouse.

"I will follow him," Bruler said. "Stay here. Watch his tribesmen."

"Will you be safe?" one of the guards asked.

"None of us are. Not while that lot walks free through our gates." He shrugged and loosened his sword. "But I have my orders. Keep safe, and if I don't come back, see that Sir Blakley is informed."

4

WHATEVER FRAGMENT OF hope Frair Lucas harbored for finding aid from Sophie Halverdt was crushed by their first sight of Greenhall. The weeks since Tomas Sacombre's escape and untimely death had brought tales of Halverdt's zealotry, told by frightened priests of Cinder fleeing south, but Lucas knew of nowhere else to turn. The stories were enough to get Lucas to change out of his vestments and store them in his saddlebags, replacing them with a scholar's cowl and loose robes. The icons he stowed away in his satchel. His staff he disguised with leather wraps and a thick leather traveler's parcel. His sole companion, Martin Roard, the heir of Stormwatch, had no need for a disguise; he wore the same simple linen and tabard of red and yellow he'd donned when he'd joined Lucas's company.

Sacombre was gone, but his servants and fellow heretics were everywhere. If Sophie could separate her hatred for Sacombre from her fear of Cinder's priests, she would be a valuable ally. If not, a dangerous enemy. And all signs pointed to the latter.

At first, Lucas thought the city was burning. A thick cloud of smoke hung over it, drifting through the streets like a pestilence. Open flames flickered along the parapets. The walls of the city were hung with banners that bore the sigil of Lady Strife in her aspect of crusader, a red sun crossed by a burning sword. Another banner flew from the keep. From a distance it looked like the tri-acorn of Halverdt, crossed in gold, but as they approached the city Lucas was able to make out the details. The acorns were replaced with tongues of flame.

"Lady Halverdt has taken to the faith most strongly," Lucas said. "There were signs of this when we passed through, but it had not traveled so far."

"Nor so furiously," Martin said. He pointed to the former tourney ground, the site of the attacks that started this whole affair. The stands had finally been torn down, but their lumber was repurposed. Rows of x-shaped crosses lined the jousting field. Most were occupied, though their victims were long dead. Flocks of crows wheeled over the field, crying their joy. "She was always a zealot, as was her father. But this is beyond the pale."

"Who are they even killing? Most of the faithful of Cinder had already fled the last time we were here, and surely there weren't this many pagans hiding in the slums." They followed the slow procession of traffic going into the city, which swung in a wide detour, forcing all those who wished to enter to pass by the jousting field and its harvest of crosses. The smell of death disconcerted the horses. "We had better lead the mounts from here. I wouldn't want to crack my skull in Halverdt's court."

A group of men waited at the head of the crossrow. They wore robes of dirty white cloth, their chests emblazoned with the flames and cross of the banner that flew over Greenhall, done in cheap paint with little skill. All of them wore their hair short, though it looked as if their scalps had been burned clean, rather than shorn, and angry red welts traveled down their shoulders and across their faces. Their leader was a man of considerable age, the patchy stubble on his head and face as white as snow.

"A pox on winter, and spring eternal! The bright lady on earth! Light unending!" the man called to the passing travelers. He carried a dented censer, but instead of incense, the brass cage on the end of the chain was filled with burning coals. The man swung it precariously close to any who wandered near. "A crusade on winter! The true light of the celestial church is risen! This is the dawn, and we are the sun!"

"Gods bless them, but they're going to kill themselves with those flames," Martin muttered. The travelers around them kept their heads down, staring at their feet as they passed the zealots. Martin simply stared. "Has some madness gripped this town?"

"Madness, and the bright lady," Lucas said, glancing up just long enough to take in the rows of dead. "Though this feels like more than Strife's usual instability. These are peasants, killed for no reason I can see. We have to get to Sophie. We have to figure out what's going on here."

"I can tell you what's going on." The speaker wore the leather apron and calluses of a blacksmith, though her voice was gentle. "Sophie Halverdt has gone mad. She's changed Strife's hope into Cinder's terror. Gods know how this will end."

"Not well," Martin said. The zealots had turned toward him, noticing his stares, and were now preaching their crusade directly to him. He ducked his head and hurried forward.

"Surely Sophie is not allowing murder in her streets?"

"It's not murder if there are no courts," the smith said. "You'll not find a judge or inquisitor within a hundred miles of these walls. Not if they know what's good for them, you won't."

Lucas didn't answer, just pressed forward into the crowd. Their horses followed reluctantly, eyes wide at the fire and the stink of death on all sides. The guards at the gate paid no heed to Martin and Lucas.

Inside the gate, the crowds pressed close on all sides. Lucas was forced to slow to a snail's pace. The streets were piled with rubble, and many of the buildings were burned out or abandoned.

"Was there an attack here?" Lucas asked. "These people look like they've survived something horrific."

"And the buildings... We were just here, not a month ago. But I saw no signs of an army at their walls. No siegeworks, none of the ravage left by a besieging army. And yet there has clearly been violence." They came around a corner and caught sight of the old town. A crater lay at the center of the district, and the buildings nearby leaned toward it, like parishioners bowing to an altar. "A great deal of violence," he said quietly.

"A gheist," Lucas answered. "If I dared draw on the naether, I'm sure it would be obvious. But what sort of gheist can do this much damage?"

"We both know the answer to that. We were at the Fen Gate. We saw Gwen's manifestation, and the destruction that she wrought."

"Four decades I've been..." Lucas trailed off, suddenly aware of the ears all around, and the danger of talking about the inquisition. "What happened to Gwen was unusual. It was singular."

"And yet," Martin said, nodding to the crater. The road turned, bending toward the keep. Scaffolding climbed the walls, crawling with workers. "Even the keep was damaged."

"We need to figure out what happened here. And I'm willing to bet that our answers will lie at the center of that crater," Lucas said.

"Our plan was to go to the keep, to seek Sophie Halverdt's aid in hunting Sacombre's rescuers," Martin said. "Otherwise, why did we come all this way?"

"The plan has changed, young Stormwatch. I don't think Sophie would hear us, anyway. And I have no interest in being fitted for one of those crosses. This way," he said, turning down a side alley.

Lucas and Martin moved through the city like rabbits through a field, afraid of the hawks circling overhead. The streets were still crowded, though no one had the attention to spare an old scholar and his man-at-arms.

If the rest of Greenhall was in the throes of religious zealotry, the old town was held in a kind of hallowed tranquility, the sacred heart of silence. The crowds thinned, and the rubble by the side of the road took on a religious weight, as though these tumbledown buildings were the relics of some divine event, as holy as it was destructive.

Some survivors wandered the wreckage. Most were dressed in ragged linen robes, bleached white and bearing the tri-flame and cross. They were sifting through the rubble, searching for fragments of their former lives, or maybe relics of whatever new religion had settled on the people of Greenhall.

"Do you think they'll rebuild?" Martin asked.

"Not if it's holy to them. We never rebuilt Cinderfell, did we?" Cinderfell, the holiest site of the god of winter, was the place where Cinder descended to the earth to quench his flames in a lake. The lands around the lake were blasted for miles in all directions, the trees flattened and black.

"That's different," Martin said.

"I'm not so sure," Lucas answered. "The air here is humming... bright. Something happened here. But I wouldn't call it holy."

The geography of the city slowly descended, as though the earth collapsed in on itself. The closer they got to the crater, the more difficult the going became. They had to abandon the horses for the last part of their journey. Martin tied them up on a broken beam, behind the remains of a watchtower.

"Gods pray no one steals them," he said.

"There's no one here," Lucas said. "We haven't seen a soul in twenty minutes."

"No, we haven't," Martin agreed. He looked around at the broken buildings, suppressing a shiver. "But I can't shake the feeling that we're being followed."

Lucas didn't answer. His eyes were on the crater.

"Something is waiting. Has been waiting, for a long time," Lucas said.

"Should we continue? Is it safe?"

"No," Lucas said, then started scrambling down into the crater. Martin loosened his sword and followed.

The final descent was harsh, a steep slide into darkness. Halfway down, Martin wondered aloud if they'd even be able to crawl back out. Lucas didn't answer. They tumbled the last ten feet, landing in a cloud of dust and scree.

“What is this place?” Martin asked, rolling to his feet. Clouds of dust hung around them, and only a little light came down from above, even though it was nearly noon.

“I don’t know. But I mean to find out. It has a familiar feel to it,” Lucas said. He had brought his satchel of holy items, and took the time to unsling the staff of icons, using it to help him stand. He coughed into his hand as he peered into the darkness. “I have been in such a place before,” he said. “In the Fen.”

“You’re saying this is a hallow?”

“It was. Or something similar. But no, the witches’ hallow in the Fen wasn’t just a place of veneration. It was a tomb, a sanctuary. A place to hide the Fen God from the church.” Lucas raised his hand, and thin lines of purple light trailed from his fingertips. His eyes flashed once, then naether-mist began leaking down his cheeks. He inhaled sharply. “This feels different. Like a prison.”

“Why is there a pagan shrine underneath Greenhall? Gabriel Halverdt was strict in his faith. The man shrouded himself in frairwood, and had his own cadre of inquisitors, to keep the gheist at bay.”

“He may not have known it was here. The hallows used to stretch from shore to shore. Most of the holy sites of the celestial faith are just converted pagan shrines. Greenhall had a henge long before it had a doma. But this doesn’t feel like those places.”

Lucas gestured, and a shower of deep purple sparks fluttered away from him, spiraling through the darkness like fireflies. They landed on stone walls, the remnants of a dome, and a small shrine deep in the shadows. Their light turned the dust hanging in the air into gilt. Lucas grunted.

"This seems the core of it. Do you have a torch?"

Martin went to one knee, swinging his bag onto the ground. In moments he had a flame going, filling the chamber with orange light. Lucas motioned him toward the shrine.

It was small and black, made from some soft, lustrous stone that reflected the torch's light. The shrine was small, no larger than a wagon's strong box, but intricately worked. The base of the shrine was carved to resemble a man lying on his back, chest split open and arms thrown wide. A pillar of flowers erupted from the wound in his heart, the petals spreading wider and wider until they split into five parts, each of which descended to the edges of the shrine. Each descending arc landed on the supine figure, one on each hand and foot, the last on the man's forehead. Lucas bent to examine it more closely.

"More than petals," he muttered, running his finger over the pillar. "Blades and bones, a broken skull. All the makings of war. And look," he turned his attention to the figure's face. "He's crying. Joyfully."

"Do you know what god this represents?" Martin asked.

"The true god of summer." The voice came from the lip of the crater. Martin lifted the torch, though that only served to blind him. Lucas pushed the torch aside, peering up at the speaker.

It was a boy, or half a boy. He had a child's height, but one side of his head was covered in white, brittle hair, like an old man. When he swept the cascade of hair aside, they could see that half of his face hung in wrinkles and age spots, while the other side was smooth and young, if haunted. The hand on that side was thin, knotted with arthritis, the skin hanging in loose, spotted folds.

"I knew you would come," the boy said. "That is why he spared me. To be here, when you came, to protect the place of his birth."

"I have no interest in hurting a child," Martin said. He held his hands well away from his blade. "Don't make me do anything we'll both regret."

"The child has no interest in hurting you, either," the boy said, yet this time the decrepit half of his face was more animated, and his voice growled with the roughness of age. "But I have no such compunction."

"Tell us who you are!" Lucas shouted. The boy's wrinkled face smiled, but the young eye started to weep. Lucas turned to Martin. "Be ready to run."

"Where am I supposed to run?" Martin asked, looking around.

A crack of thunder drew their attention back to the boy. He was descending into the crater, his feet dragging along the scree as he floated down, arms wide, like the figure on the shrine. Burning petals spun from his open mouth.

Martin jumped onto the opposite side of the crater, scrambling for height. Debris tumbled around his hands and feet, starting an avalanche. The crater filled with dust once again. Shafts of light, thrown by the boy as well as from the sun above, turned the air into a hatchwork.

"You came to learn what I was, inquisitor. Why do you run even as I present myself? How can you learn as you flee?"

"I'm not running anywhere, demon," Lucas snapped. He threw his arms wide, sweeping his staff in a semicircle. A gust of wind flew from him, clearing the air. "Whatever you are, I will banish you. Wherever you flee, I will hunt you down."

"Then we will both die here. That is acceptable." The

boy touched down, balancing on one toe, the rest of his body held aloft by unseen forces. "I have many bodies. Many blossoms. More every day. This is very fertile ground."

Lucas didn't waste any more time talking. He struck, wrapping naether around his fist, punching toward the boy-gheist. The force of his blow scattered the carpet of flower petals accumulating at the boy's feet, but the dark lines of naetheric force broke against the gheist without moving him. Lucas set his feet and pushed harder. Stones flew from the ground, peeling away from the floor like dead skin, but still the gheist didn't move.

Exhausted, Lucas relented.

"Very good. A fine effort, but your lines are too straight, your reasons too just. I cannot be pushed so easily, moon priest. And now—" the boy swept forward, his wrinkled hand snapping toward the ground "—the form must be broken. All forms. All patterns. Your pattern is just another to be disrupted."

The ground where the gheist was pointing swirled like a troubled pool. It rose up, turning into a whip that struck at Lucas. The priest threw up a makeshift shield, taking the force of the blow but still knocking him off balance. The whip traveled on, digging a rut up the debris-choked incline and crashing into Martin. He yelled, rolled onto his back, and slid gracelessly back down into the crater.

"It is reasonable to defend yourself, priest. But I am not of your tribe. My elders are dead, my henges broken, and yet I remain. Because of people like this." The boy's wrinkled hand indicated the child-half of his body, then rose toward the lip of the crater. Thin shadows crept into the pit. A half-dozen forms rose above the crater's edge, all dressed in the tri-flame and cross. "Broken people. Dead people. People made holy by my touch."

"Godsbless," Martin muttered. He pushed up onto his feet, wincing as he stood. "We'll have to kill our way out of this."

"There's been enough killing," Lucas said. He clapped his hands together, letting the naether compress between his palms, breaking a hole in the mundane world and drawing the shadowform. His body started to dissolve. "Take a deep breath, Martin."

"What?" Martin asked, startled. He looked over at Lucas just in time to see the priest rush at him, faster than an old man should be able to move. The frair's arms encircled Martin, turning from flesh into shadow even as he ran, the force of the impact deeper than a hammer, lower than flesh, like a chiming bell felt but never heard. It swept Martin off his feet.

And then the world was gone. Martin's eyes were still open, but there was nothing to see, no light, not even the shifting darkness of nightfall. The air that was sucked through Martin's teeth was frigid, thick like water, cold as ice. His lungs gave out in horror. He started to shiver. A chorus of whispering voices sang through his head, terrified and yet calm, languages Martin had never heard. Lucas's voice came to him through his bones.

Patience. We are nearly done, Martin. We are nearly there.

Just as suddenly as the world had disappeared, it returned. Martin collapsed to the ground, sucking in huge gulps of air. Frost formed on his lips and in the tears streaming from his eyes. The ground under his hands burned like an oven.

Martin tried to call out, but there was no air in his lungs, and the only sound he could make was a stammering whimper.

He coughed, and then was able to breathe again. He went to wipe his eyes, but the sword was still in his hand, and he cut himself from cheek to ear. Martin dropped the sword with a yelp.

"What the hells was that?"

"The naether. I cannot..." Lucas's voice was shaky and weak. When Martin looked up, he realized that the frair was on his knees, shivering. Lucas's face was as pale as spoiled milk. "That was more than I am capable of doing. Gods, how am I..."

Lucas spilled forward, collapsing flat to the ground, like a sack of flour dumped out. Martin jumped to his feet, the blood and frost forgotten, and grabbed Lucas's shoulder. The frair was still breathing, though shallowly. Lucas's eyes fluttered open, and he moaned.

"We have to get to the horses. Where are we?" Martin asked.

"I don't... don't know. I just pushed through. I can't help you anymore."

Voices sounded, echoing off walls and through the rubble. For the first time, Martin looked around. They were in a narrow alleyway, the walls on either side collapsed onto each other, leaning together like drunk lovers. It didn't look familiar.

"We'll have to forget the horses, unless we get lucky and stumble across them. Come on," Martin urged. He pulled Lucas to his feet, throwing the priest's arm over his shoulder, then bending down to retrieve his sword. Lucas weighed next to nothing, even with his staff and bag of metal icons.

The two of them limped to the end of the alleyway,

looking around. The city's exterior wall loomed over them, shot through with cracks. The nearest tower lay flat across the ruins of several buildings. Martin stumbled toward it. He could hear the sound of hooves and horns coming from the keep.

"Summer light. Lumen," Lucas gasped. "In the air. I can taste... vow knights. Sophie's zealots have our scent."

"How close?"

"Close. Closer. They're coming. We need to fly."

"Then pray me some wings, frair," Martin said through gritted teeth. But Lucas's head lolled against Martin's shoulder. He became a dead weight. Martin hiked the priest up and hurried toward the collapsed tower.

The hooves were getting closer. Martin could hear them, no longer an echo. He twisted around and saw the vow knights charge past the mouth of the road, red and gold fluttering with the speed of their passage. They would come back. Any moment now.

Martin turned back to the tower and hurried on, bending his head to the ground, grunting with each step. So focused was he on moving forward under the burden of the unconscious priest that Martin didn't see the rider until it was too late.

The vow knight loomed over them, gilt-armor dented and worn, the tabard of the winter vow as ragged as a dishcloth. The knight's helm was dented, but the blade hanging over Martin's head was as bright and as sharp as the morning sun.

"Gods damn it all," Martin muttered. He took a step back, nearly dropping Lucas in his rush to draw his blade.

"Peace, child," Elsa said. She sheathed her blade and reached down. "Give me the priest."

"Sir LaFey?" Martin sputtered. "But you... you were..."

"Wherever I have been, I am here now." She grabbed Lucas by the shoulder and heaved him over the pommel of her saddle, then offered her hand to Martin. He hesitated. "Do you want to walk, Stormwatch?"

Martin stood dumbstruck for a heartbeat. Then he took Elsa's hand. With a strength that Martin would not have suspected of a bear, she plucked him from his feet and threw him onto the saddle behind her. As soon as he was settled, she pushed her horse on. They disappeared through the wall, and the horns of the mad vow knights followed close behind.

5

THE PRIEST SAT primly beside the fire, sipping tea from a cracked bowl. She was nearly Malcolm's age, and clearly more accustomed to the courtyard than the battlefield. But there was steel in her voice when she looked up at the ring of knights surrounding her and spoke.

"They joined us north of Greenhall, these priests who turned against us." She cleared her throat, then placed the bowl of tea in her lap and rubbed her eyes. "All familiar faces. Frair Laville came up through the ranks of Cinderfell with my son. At least half their number belonged to the inquisition."

"Frair Rhone—" Malcolm started.

"Ysella, please. I get tired of being called 'brother' all the time." The priest allowed a thin smile.

"Ysella, then. Why were so many priests of Cinder marching with Bassion's army? I did not think the church involved itself in these matters, especially after Sacombre's indiscretions."

"It was Sacombre's sin that brought me north, Houndhallow. Many of us were horrified by the high inquisitor's actions. We thought to gather him home."

"Frair Lucas didn't meet you on the road? He left here months ago."

"We missed him in Greenhall. Lady Bassion left Heartsbridge weeks before us. We caught her up at Lady Halverdt's court. Apparently Frair Lucas was there before us, but left in a hurry."

"Left?" Malcolm asked. "But why? And where did he go?"

"Lady Bassion made some sort of deal with the young Halverdt girl. Sophie wanted Sacombre's blood, and didn't care to wait around for the trial. Lucas sniffed it out, and fled before the noose could be tightened." Ysella took another drink from her tea, then shook her head. "As for where he went after that? Gods will know, but we must guess. There was strange news from Gallowsport, shortly after we arrived here, but it may be unrelated."

"And these inquisitors? The ones who joined you north of Greenhall? You say you knew them?"

Ysella paused, tapping her finger against her bowl.

"They were priests, true and sworn. But so was Tomas Sacombre. And we all know where that led," she said. "They claimed to be traveling south from Cinderfell when they heard of the massed army at Greenhall, and thought to join us. A particular frair led them, a name known to me, but not a man I knew personally. Frair Veureux."

"I know Veureux," Sir Hallister said. She hovered at Malcolm's shoulder, torn between protecting the priest and keeping an eye on the door. "He's no inquisitor, though he is sworn to Cinder. A man of books."

Ysella nodded. "Ensconced at Cinderfell, last I heard. Given his reputation, I was surprised to find him on the road. The others were more typical. A mix of thinkers and doers. They marched with a considerable number of celestial guardsmen."

"I thought that unusual," Sir Tasse said. "I rarely see the black-and-gold outside of Heartsbridge, or guarding the shrines. And these did not seem the typical guardsmen. Rougher. More familiar with the saddle."

"Perhaps mercenaries, then, enlisted to the colors," Malcolm said. "They certainly show a lack of discipline in their ranks."

"Either way, they joined in the slaughter," Ysella said. "Cutting down those they were meant to guard, sparing Veureux and his friends."

"And you saw them summoning gheists? Controlling them?" Malcolm asked. The Suhdrin knights grew tense.

"Yes," Ysella said. "At first I thought they were trying to banish them, that the spirits had risen up independently in our midst, and that these priests were defending us. I learned the lie of that when they turned on me. Veureux himself struck at us."

"And how did you escape?"

"I was with Lady Bassion's contingent. When Veureux came for us, her guards sold their lives to protect us. I ran, expecting Veureux to pursue me, but he didn't give me a second thought." Ysella closed her eyes. "He wanted Lady Bassion."

"Did Helenne escape?" Malcolm asked.

"For all I know, yes. Her guard died protecting her. The lady tried to stop them, even tried to charge Veureux's line unaided, but her knights knocked her from her saddle and carried her away. The last I saw of her ladyship, she was riding hard down the southern road, gathering banners as she ran."

"That matches my reports," Malcolm said. "We believe she has organized a resistance on the celestial's southern flank. It's the only reason they haven't rolled over us."

"If Helenne Bassion lives, I am sworn to rejoin her," Travailler said. "I should never have fled her lines."

"You should never have left your ship," Hallister said sharply. "Leave horse wars to dry knights."

"Bassion called every anointed blade. Do you doubt my right to stand at her side, sir?"

"Gods, Suhdrin honor," Malcolm swore. "Both of you, keep your blades dry. We need every knight we can muster. Neither of you is good to me dead."

"I will not fight beside Tenerran savages," Hallister muttered.

"You will. If the church asks it of you, and your lady commands, you will hold Tenerran spears and wash Tenerran feet," Ysella said. "And you'll consider it an honor to serve Cinder."

Hallister struggled to keep quiet, drawing a smirk from Travailler. It was Sir Tasse who broke the silence.

"We will fight as our lady commands. But none of us know our lady's will, not when she's fled the field of battle." She turned to Malcolm. "We thank you for your protection, Houndhallow, but I'm afraid Sir Travailler is correct. We are bound to return to Lady Bassion's side, if it is at all possible."

"My army could really use your blades," Malcolm said.

"Army? This is no army, Houndhallow," Hallister answered. "I would struggle to call this a militia. You are reduced to raiding and praying to be ignored."

"Our losses have been great," Malcolm said. "But fleeing our company will not improve that."

"Then let us add more than our own blades to your number," Tasse said. "Let us travel to Bassion, and offer her your peace. If she has managed to gather those who fled south, they will easily outnumber your ranks here."

"You're wagering on her listening to you, and being willing to accept my peace," Malcolm said. "For all we know, Bassion intends to gather her banners and keep riding south until she hits the Burning Coast."

"If that is her plan, it will take my word to turn her," Ysella said, standing. "She can't doubt the sworn testimony of a priest of Cinder."

"I will remind you that it was the sworn of Cinder who broke her army, and betrayed her ranks," Malcolm said. "She may trust you least of all."

"If her trust in the church has been lost, then there is nothing anyone can do."

Malcolm sighed, hooking his thumbs into his belt and gazing sightlessly up at the tent's ceiling. He didn't turn when the tent flap rustled, barely noticing the reaction of the Suhdrins.

"Husband? Is all well?"

Sorcha Blakley walked to her husband's side. She was strange to look upon. The injury given her by the witch Fianna, while saving her life, left Sorcha changed. Her skin glowed with unnatural light, and her veins pulsed brightly with the beating of her heart. Her eyes were the color of dark water, deep pits, clear and bottomless. Strangest of all was her hair, twisting as though she swam through troubled currents. Sorcha placed a hand on Malcolm's arm.

The three Suhdrin knights turned as one, drawing their blades and clustering around the priest. Frair Rhone stood slowly, making the signs of Cinder and muttering beneath her breath.

"What devilry is this?" Hallister snapped. "A gheist names you husband?"

"She was my wife long before..." Malcolm trailed off, grimacing as he turned to Sorcha. His wife stood unmoved, smiling at the Suhdrins. "This was done against her will. She is no gheist."

"But if she—" Hallister started.

"I am in the care of a priest of Strife, and guarded by a knight of the Winter Vow," Sorcha said primly. "If you worry for your safety, you will have to speak with them. As for whether or not I am a gheist..." Sorcha held out her hands, palms up, light from her veins growing. "I am holy. Whether that is of the church, or the gods, or something older, remains to be seen."

"There is nothing holy outside the church," Hallister said. "It is heresy to believe otherwise."

"I believe nothing," Sorcha said. "I simply am."

The Suhdrins stood awkwardly, on their guard and unsure. Frair Rhone cleared her throat.

"I will not accuse what I do not understand," she said. "But I think it wise if we leave your company. To protect against our own doubt, if nothing else."

"Agreed," Malcolm said. "Any of Bassion's knights who wish to travel with you are free to go. The rest can join my forces. My scouts can get you around the celestial army, at least as far as the Tallow. After that, you must rely on yourselves to find Lady Bassion."

"The gods will guide us," Ysella said.

"I pray that to be true," Sorcha answered.

Malcolm cleared his throat, then bowed and left the tent, guiding Sorcha by the elbow. As soon as the tent flap closed, he could hear the hissing whispers of the Suhdrin party.

"That was unnecessary, my love," Malcolm said.

"They must know who they stand with. And, more importantly, who they stand against. Their faith in the church and their fear of the pagans brought us to this war, Malcolm." Sorcha disentangled herself from her husband's grip and turned away. "Until our Suhdrin friends break themselves of old prejudices, we will be at risk of betrayal. Or worse."

"Worse?"

"We will be at risk of betraying ourselves," Sorcha said. "See that they reach Bassion, love. We cannot stand alone. But it would be better to fall alone than trust someone who hates us."

"There was a time when Helenne Bassion would have met me by a warm hearth, offered me meat and wine. Now this," Malcolm said. He sat on his horse in a copse of trees. Sir Doone sat next to him, her back stiff and armor blackened. Night was falling rapidly, and the chill of winter sat heavy in the air.

"Those times are past, my lord," Doone said.

"Never to come again, I fear," Malcolm answered. Doone didn't answer, but kept her eyes peeled on the trail ahead of them.

A single rider came down the trail, padded armor almost silent as the horse trotted through the mud. Doone whistled, and the rider stopped.

"The trail is as clear as I can see," the man said.

"But you can't see us, can you?" Doone asked. "Who's to say a hundred Suhdrin knights aren't creeping along the

Tallow right now, just out of your blunted sight?"

"I'd have smelled their perfume."

"Enough," Malcolm said. He kicked his mount forward, letting the horse pick its own way down the treacherous path. "If there's three or a thousand, we have to learn to trust them at some point."

"Any reason they can't learn to trust us, instead?" Doone asked. It was Malcolm's turn to not answer.

The riders, ten in all, trotted slowly down the path through the forest. They were near the Reaveholt, even within shouting distance of the celestial lines. It was a foolish place to meet, but it seemed neither Malcolm nor Helenne trusted the other enough to choose anywhere else. Farther north and the Tenerrans would be at the advantage, and to the south the Suhdrin rangers held the trails. So they met in the shadow of their mutual enemy. Perhaps fear would keep them honest.

The trees began to thin, until Malcolm was riding across open ground, broken only by distant copses and a scattering of tall boulders. Another line of trees lay on the other side of the clearing. As Malcolm's party approached, a figure stepped from the trees. It was the priest, Ysella Rhone, the woman Malcolm had dispatched to make contact with Lady Bassion. Malcolm reined in.

"Are you alone, frair?"

"No. They are here. But they asked that I speak with you first."

"They don't trust us?"

"I count ten among you," Ysella said. "We agreed to three."

"His lordship would be a fool to ride unaccompanied

through enemy territory," Doone answered. "And I'm sure Lady Bassion has brought her own blades, in case of treachery."

"A column strong waits behind us," Ysella said. "On the other side of this copse. Far enough away to remain hidden, but close enough to answer a shout." The priest glanced over her shoulder. "She told me not to tell you that."

"A first step toward honesty," Malcolm said. "And truthfully, we have a similar force to the north, waiting my word. So let us pretend everyone followed the rules. It's a convenient lie."

"Yes," Ysella said.

"Galleydeep wanted you to talk to me first. To what purpose?"

"She wanted to ensure your wife was not with you. Given events at Greenhall—"

"I would not risk my wife on this venture. More importantly, if I fall, she will take command of my army. And gods save you from her fury."

The priest didn't answer, turning her head as though listening to something behind her. Finally, she cleared her throat and faced Malcolm again.

"Stay here. I will fetch her ladyship."

Ysella disappeared once again, quickly blending in with the shadows between the trees. Malcolm wasn't sure if that was Cinder's magic or the failing light, but a shiver went through his spine. He turned to Sir Doone.

"If anything goes wrong, ride hellfire for the lines. If Bassion betrays us, my wife must know what happened."

"If Bassion betrays us, I will stay at your side, and die fighting. As is proper." Doone loosened her blade in its sheath, smiling. "Have faith in Sorcha. Your wife will know what to do."

"That's precisely what I fear."

Doone was about to answer when the sound of someone approaching through the woods reached them. They sat in silence as three mounted figures resolved from the shadows. One was the priest, riding a gray mare and holding her staff across her saddle. The other Malcolm recognized as Sir Hallister, fully armored. She had not bothered to blacken the steel or muffle the jangling chain of her hauberk. She watched Malcolm with piercing eyes.

Between them rode Helenne Bassion. The duchess of Galleydeep wore a large black robe, gathered in folds that fell across her legs and down the side of her mount. She seemed to have doffed her chain dress and steel helm, though her face was swaddled in shadow. When they stopped, Malcolm brought his horse a little closer, so he wouldn't have to raise his voice.

"Galleydeep, this is a dangerous place. Let's be about our business, before the celestials get wind of us. Have you gathered your scattered forces?"

"I have," Helenne said. Amid the folds of her hood, her voice was soft. "Though I lost many. Nearly half. Ysella tells me you had nothing to do with the attack upon them."

"I swear it on my father's grave. On Strife's bright blade, and Cinder's cold—"

"I will hear no more of the church from Tenerran mouths," Helenne said. She threw back her hood, and Malcolm's answer caught in his throat.

Helenne's face was marred. Across one cheek and through her eye, a twisting scar burrowed through her flesh, still raw. Whatever weapon had struck her, its blade had traveled across her ear, tearing hair and skin alike. Helenne tilted her head.

"Your gods did this to me, Tenerran," she said. "Who will answer for them? Whose blood do I have to spill to see Cinder's justice done?"

6

IAN WAS HAVING trouble sleeping. His old room at Houndhallow, situated over the grand hall and overlooking the keep's southern approach, held too many memories. Every time he closed his eyes, Ian heard his sister's voice in his mind, singing childish songs. He heard his mother offering words of comfort, or his father singing the evensong. Old voices, voices from his childhood. And yet not that old. A year past, maybe. A long and strange year, and everything changed in its passing.

Now, Nessie would not meet Ian's eyes when they passed in the hallway. His sister walked through the keep with a haunted look, jumping every time one of the pagans appeared around a corner. She locked her door at night, and took to carrying a tiny dagger in her belt. Ian sometimes caught her watching him with hooded eyes.

As for his father and mother, gods only knew where they were. But the last time they spoke, Malcolm Blakley had banished his son from the Fen Gate for daring to protect a pagan witch. And his mother... Ian wasn't sure what to believe about her. He had heard stories that sounded like myths: that the witch's healing had changed Sorcha Blakley, making her as much gheist as mortal. If the inquisition knew of her, they would likely burn her alive as a feral spirit.

None of them dead but all of them changed so much that their former lives might as well be buried. Sometimes Ian wondered if Gwen Adair didn't have the better lot. Her whole family murdered and their memories preserved. She would never have to watch her loved ones become strangers, become enemies, their love turned to hatred and fear. Perhaps that was better. Perhaps.

Instead of sleeping with these thoughts, Ian roamed the keep. This was no longer his home; the hallways were the same, the stones and the rooms and the furnishings, but all were foreign to him. Like a memory of a place he had visited long ago but no longer recognized. It didn't help that the Blakley guards who held the passages treated him like an interloper, and the servants hesitated whenever he gave an order. Ian wasn't comfortable carrying his father's authority, and he was pretty sure everyone could tell.

Ian climbed the stairs to the roof of the keep. The guard shifted his spear to block the way before he recognized Ian's face. Even then he paused for half a breath before raising the spear and bowing slightly.

"All is clear, guardsman?" Ian asked.

"All is clear. The forests teem with pagan devils, but the walls are safe." The man paused before continuing. "Whatever else the witches have done, they do keep the demons away."

"Some demons, at least. They have you up here alone?"

"Yes, my lord. Our numbers are thin. Most marched south with your father, and the rest died to pagan..." He stumbled over the words, remembering that Ian had come with the pagans, in their dress and with their blessing. "They died during the siege, my lord. We can't guard half the usual posts, and those we protect we must manage with longer shifts and fewer spears."

"Well, hopefully the worst of this battle has passed," Ian said. "Now that the tribes have come around to our side."

"My lord," the guard said, though his voice betrayed doubt. Ian sighed.

"I will watch this post for a while, guardsman. You may find another."

"Sir Clough said—"

"Find another," Ian snapped. "I wish to be alone."

The guard left without a word, though Ian heard him travel only a short way down the stairs before stopping. It would have to do. He turned his attention to the parapet.

The courtyard was crowded with tents, spotted with campfires and the restless shifting of sleeping animals. It reminded Ian of the Fen Gate during the Suhdrin siege. Here, though, pagans mingled with Tenerrans still loyal to the church. Beyond the walls, no army camped against them, but none dared travel through the gate. Something was in the forest, something that hunted and killed. It was safer during the day, but even then few ventured out. The witches and their shamans tried time and again to tame the spirit, and time and again they failed.

"I'm beginning to think we'll need an inquisitor," Ian muttered to himself. "And gods pray it doesn't come to that."

"I will join you in that prayer, hound," Cahl said, appearing from out of the shadows. The hulking shaman crouched on the parapet like a gargoyle.

"How'd you get here?" Ian asked. "Or should I ask that guard?"

"Your guards see flesh and blood, and this is a place of stone." Cahl glanced over at him. "You remember the Fen Gate. You know how I traveled here."

Ian did remember. Cahl had transported Ian and the witch, Fianna, through the stones and into the cellar of the Fen Gate.

"And how are my guards supposed to protect me if you can walk through stones, shaman?"

"There are ways," Cahl said. "Lost to your celestial priests, forgotten by the houses of Tener. Turn back to the true gods, and I will teach you."

"You know that isn't going to happen."

"And you know that I have to try." Cahl shifted, stepping down from the parapet, stretching his shoulders. "We have buried too many dead in this war for it to be that easy. But the question must still be asked."

"Is that why you're here? To try to convince me to betray my family and the church?"

"I am here to warn you. Gwen is losing faith in you, if she ever had it."

"Losing faith in me? Her family hides heresy for generations, betrays my father's trust, and then starts a war that may still tear this nation to pieces, and I must repair her faith in me?" Ian laughed. "What sin does she hold against me?"

"My friendship, and that of Fianna. Gwen doesn't know who to trust anymore. The void priest she questioned poisoned her ear."

"I heard about her questions. We don't kill prisoners in Houndhallow, not without a trial; I don't care who they are or what they've done." Ian turned angrily away. His people had brought him the body and Gwen's orders that it be burned. "And then she had the audacity to summon me, as though this was her castle."

"Count the spears, Ian of Hounds. This is her castle."

"Houndhallow is my home, the home of my ancestors. It will take more than pagan spears to change that. Did you come here just to taunt me, shaman? You never liked that Fianna rescued me from the river, or that she gave me such attention during the war. Now that Suhdra and Tener are rejoined—"

"Just because a handful of Suhdrin knights follow you in battle, Ian of Hounds, doesn't mean your petty war is over," Cahl said. "As long as it serves the purposes of the voidfather, Suhdra and Tener will be at one another's throats, with the tribes crushed between."

"Folam is dead."

"What little I know of the voidfather tells me this: Folam would not sacrifice himself lightly, or without reason. I will grant that you killed him. But I do not think that you defeated him."

Ian flinched away, unconsciously drawing his shirt tight over his wound. Few knew about his injury, or the true extent of its strangeness, but Cahl was aware. If Folam were willing to sacrifice his life to give Ian that wound, there must be a reason for it.

But what? Ian thought. *How could this serve his purpose? How am I being deceived, even now?*

"Are you all right?" Cahl asked, drawing closer. "You looked like you were about to jump over that wall."

"A quick solution," Ian muttered. *Unless that's what Folam wanted.* He shook his head. "What am I supposed to do about Gwen? What do you suggest? If she can't trust me, I who lost so much to defend her home, then who will she trust? You?"

"I think she may be losing her trust in me, as well." The big shaman shook his head. "As well she might. Fianna was close to me. And I'm the one who counseled Gwendolyn to trust the voidfather. My advice has done nothing but lead her into greater darkness."

"Then why should I trust you, either?" Ian asked.

Cahl paused, staring into the darkness beyond the wall and not moving. The shaman looked like he was carved from stone.

"There is something at the gate. Something beyond the wall."

"What? What the hells are you—?"

The stone of the parapet screamed and burst apart, spraying sharp fragments across the roof. Ian fell to the ground, his face and hands singing with pain. He rolled over onto his hands and knees, grappling numbly at his sword. Ian's ears were ringing. When he looked up, Cahl was wrestling with something in the darkness.

The door to the stairs burst open. The guard carried a torch in one hand and his spear in the other. The flame cast lurid shadows across the roof. A good portion of the parapet was missing, and the stones that lay around the roof were steaming. Ian blinked up at the guard and saw horror wash over the man's face. He looked back at the shaman.

A gheist spun out of the scarred stone, its body made of the wreckage of the parapet, shards of rock formed into a snake that danced like a cobra. A hood of sharp talons hid the gheist's face from Ian's view. It fought with Cahl, striking with the hooked claws of that hood, drawing blood and knocking the shaman back with each blow.

"Gheists in the keep! Betrayal! Murder!" the guard shouted. He dropped the lantern and ran down the stairs, still screaming about betrayal. The lantern shattered on the wooden planks, spreading a pool of burning oil over the roof. Ian rolled away from it, eventually coming to his feet and drawing his sword. He joined the fray, striking the gheist across the back of the hood with his sword. Sparks flew off the gheist's stony skin.

"Get inside!" Cahl shouted. "It's meant to kill you!"

"How can you know?"

Drawn by Ian's shouting, the gheist turned to face him. Like a cobra, the hood surrounded a cruel head.

Unlike a cobra, the gheist had Ian's face, worked in stone. It seemed to be pleading silently, eyes wide in misery, mouth open in a cry of lament. The talons of the hood flexed at seeing their prey, twitching like spider legs. It struck.

Ian fell back under the assault. The hood clapped shut like a mouth, hiding the stone face for a brief second before yawning wide, to strike again. Ian slashed at it with his sword, but the skin and talons were stone, and all he could do was scar its flesh without drawing blood. His own carved face watched the fight mournfully, immobile and horrified. The body of the gheist coiled and struck, coiled again. Ian danced back. Flames licked his ankles. He danced over the pool of oil and came down beside the door, putting the fire between him and the gheist.

The gheist slithered forward. As it crossed the flames, the stones of its body hissed, grinding over the wooden planks of the roof and turning them to splinters. Ian settled into a guard position, preparing to sell his life dearly to keep the gheist out of the keep.

Cahl leapt through the flames and tackled the gheist. It writhed in his arms, clapping the talons of its hood in the air as it tried to strike the shaman. Cahl screamed as fire singed his flesh and set his clothes aflame, but he didn't let go of the beast. Ian shielded his eyes as the flames leapt into the air.

"Beware Gwen! Beware the shadows!" Cahl shouted. Then bands of light sprang out from his skin, from the tattoos around his eyes and the fetishes woven into his hair and clothing. He rolled with the gheist against the stones of the surviving parapet, and a great inhalation of power filled the air. The flames changed from red to orange and then green, and a flash of light blinded Ian.

When he could see again, he was alone on the roof. The gheist horn sounded below, and the sounds of panicked shouting came up the stairs, but of Cahl or the feral god there was no sign.

Sir Bruler sat uncomfortably in the woods, peering into the darkness. He had followed the big shaman to this circle of runic stones, but then Cahl had disappeared into thin air. There had been no sign of him since, and Bruler was getting antsy. His hiding place was good, though. Bruler was sure no passing pagans would see him. He could only pray that whatever gheist was hunting these woods would miss him as well.

He could leave, return to the safety of the walls, and look for another opportunity to corner the shaman. But what little he knew of pagan power from the songs his mother had sung to him when he was a child, and a few hints cobbled from tavern-side limericks, suggested that a shaman always returned to his circle. Or maybe it was that shamans never used the same circle twice. Or maybe—

The gheist horn sounded behind him. Bruler stiffened and turned around. Flames danced at the top of the keep, and the shadow of a single figure stood against the light. Ian, unless he missed his guess. There was a flash of light, and then...

The circle of stones roared to life. Bruler whirled around, expecting to face an explosion, or a tide of gheists. Instead, Cahl stumbled out of the circle, wrestling something that looked like a bundle of scree. A thin wall of flame followed them, starting several small fires in the surrounding forest. The two figures twisted back and forth in the flickering light. Bruler was about to lend his aid when Cahl cried out suddenly.

The gheist dropped from his arms. When it struck the ground, it fell apart, bursting into a column of loose stone shards, completely without life. A face slid from the wreckage, cracking in half as it fell. The shaman stood over the stones, wavering back and forth, staring as if in disbelief.

Cahl turned slowly, facing away from where Bruler was hiding, and another figure stepped out of the shadows, dressed in black robes. *A void priest*, Bruler thought. *How long have they been there? Did they see me?*

"Elder of stones," the void priest said. "A pity it had to end like this."

"What have you... what have you done?" Cahl gasped. The shaman's voice was weak. He coughed wetly and lurched to the side, only keeping his balance by grabbing onto a tree. Bruler peered forward. There was a knife in the shaman's back.

"I have done as the void commands," the priest said. "As you should have done, if you wanted to stay true to the tribes."

"You're a traitor! A traitor to the tribes, and to your own people."

"I have no people," the priest said. "And soon, neither will you."

Cahl fell backwards onto the shattered corpse of the gheist. His fall pushed the knife deeper into his back, until the tip of the blade erupted from his chest. The void priest leaned over, touching the shaman lightly on the forehead.

"It is done," the priest said, and threw back her hood. She looked up at Bruler. "And as for you, heathen..."

Bruler turned and ran through the night. The shadows came for him.

7

THE LIGHTS FROM the inn were bright, and the sounds of music and laughter spilled out of the building. A pair of soldiers loitered at the doorway, passing a bottle back and forth, casting nervous eyes into the darkness. Every time a wave of laughter erupted from the building, the guards flinched. Other than the barn and a couple of outbuildings, there was nothing around but forest and the country road.

"Halverdt's men," Martin said, just a little too loudly. Elsa gave him a reproving look. He lowered his voice. "I didn't think her army would have gotten this far north." Their flight from Greenhall had taken them north, partly to get them away from Halverdt's zealots and partly to join with Malcolm Blakley at the Fen Gate. Lucas wanted to warn Houndhallow about what was coming. Stories of Halverdt's army, marching out of Greenhall days after Lucas's escape, filled the countryside with fear.

"This is not her army," Elsa said. Her legs and back hurt from days on the trail, trading saddle time with Martin and Lucas. "Only scouts. Though they scout in force."

"They drink in force, too," Martin said. "Every tavern between Greenhall and the Tallow must be filled with them."

"Celebration and wine are both aspects of Lady Strife,"

Lucas said. "They are perhaps a little overzealous."

Lucas's voice was terribly weak. Ever since she had picked the pair of them up in the ruins of Greenhall, Elsa had worried about the frair. Months in the saddle could not account for the shiver in his hands, or the tremble in his voice. Something had happened to him, but she couldn't get him to talk about it.

"Their zeal will help us," Martin said. "We need those horses."

"We don't have time to wait for them to drink themselves into oblivion." Elsa shifted in the bushes, backing away from the inn. "Stay here. I will distract them. When their attention is turned, you go for the stables."

"And what will you do once we are free?" Martin asked.

"Cease praying."

It only took a few moments for Elsa to backtrack to the road and recover her horse. The poor dear was exhausted from the journey. Without a spare mount, they had been forced to keep her constantly saddled, and even though Frair Lucas was hardly a burden, the endless ride had worn her down. Elsa walked as far as she dared, until they were nearly in sight of the inn, before she mounted. Every moment of rest mattered.

The guards turned to her as she approached, straightening when they saw her tabard of the winter vow. Elsa slid smoothly from the saddle.

"Strife's blessing," she called. "What news?"

"The sun will rise," the nearest guard said. "Do you come from Greenhall?"

"Points west. Word is spreading of an army of vow knights gathering under Halverdt's banner. I came to see the will of Strife." She looked down at their chests, and the sigils on their shields. Three tongues of flame, and the saltire. "I apologize, I mistook that for the sign of Greenhall. But I see it's not the tri-acorn at all."

"Oh, but it is!" the guard exclaimed, his drunken enthusiasm too much to hide. "Lady Halverdt has sworn to the lady bright. She is the chosen of Strife, and will work her will in the world."

"Then I suppose my search is at an end. Who is your commander?" A wave of laughter rolled out of the inn, followed shortly by a cacophony of breaking plates, and another round of laughter. Elsa raised her brows. "If he's fit to report, that is."

"Reports can wait until morning, and the light of dawn. Come in! Drink! Enjoy the warmth of the hearth and the blessings of Strife!" The guard offered Elsa his bottle, shaking it back and forth. "Hold winter off for one more night."

"Winter will not be denied with drink or hearth," Elsa said. "Go find your commander and bring him here."

The guard stared at her unhappily, then shrugged and went inside. His companion stayed, smiling idiotically at Elsa.

"You don't seem very happy, for a vow knight," the man said.

Elsa punched him solidly in the jaw, grabbing his jerkin to keep him from falling into the door. She laid him down and began waving frantically to the woods. Martin and Lucas appeared moments later.

"We don't have long. Hopefully their commander is reluctant to leave his fire and his ale. Take five horses and cut the rest free."

"None of them are saddled," Martin said.

"We don't have time for that. If we have to steal gear later, we will. For now we fly."

They disappeared into the stables. The sounds of disturbed horses and shifting gear followed. Elsa turned to the door of the inn and waited. It was only a few minutes before Martin came out of the stables, leading three horses.

"Let's go!" he called.

"They'll follow. You have to do something about the other horses."

Lucas muttered to himself, then closed his eyes and shifted his attention to the open barn door. The shadows inside coalesced. The sound of nervous horses followed. Seconds later, a dozen horses streamed out, rumbling into the forest.

"I hope you're happy," Lucas said. "They'll have nightmares for weeks. Now come on!"

"The commander will be out any second. Can't have him raising the alarm."

"Who cares if he does? We've cut the rest of the horses loose. They're halfway to Greenhall by now."

"You do your thing, let me do mine." The door to the inn rattled. Elsa tensed. "Here it is," she whispered to herself.

The door opened. Half a dozen soldiers stood just inside the doorway, but the commander was the only one looking out. The rest were talking among themselves and laughing.

"Hey, what are you—?"

Elsa struck, punching the commander and bowling him into the others.

Stoked on the fires of Strife's anger, the men grabbed their commander and threw him back out of the door. They came flooding after him.

Elsa waded into them with both fists, punching and strangling and throwing as best she could. But they were too drunk to understand how badly they were being hurt, and kept lumbering forward. Elsa slowly fell back. She looked over her shoulder at Lucas and Martin, who were just standing there, holding the reins of their stolen horses loosely in their hands.

"Get going!" she yelled. "I'll do what I can until—"

"This is nonsense," Lucas snapped. The old man raised one hand and breathed in the night's darkness. The air grew taut around him. "Get out of the way!"

Elsa grimaced, then rolled to one side. She was barely on her feet before a cone of black energy swirled out of Lucas's fist, bowling the soldiers down. Elsa dusted herself off, then went to take Lucas by the elbow.

"That wasn't necessary," she said. His arm trembled under her hand, and his skin was even paler than usual. "I had that."

"You did not. I expect that sort of nonsense from young Martin, but you should know better, Sir LaFey."

"What's that supposed to... Elsa!" Martin pointed at the door. More soldiers, scared sober and wielding swords, were pouring out of the inn. They stared down at the frost-skinned faces of their comrades, then looked up at Elsa and her friends with fury in their eyes.

"Okay, this I don't have," she said, then grabbed one of the horses and swung up onto its back, drawing her sword in the process. "Seriously, run!"

Martin helped Lucas onto another horse, then mounted the third. The old man hung over the courser's back like a sack of rice, but when the horse bolted for the road, Lucas was at least able to hold on. As soon as they were gone, Elsa turned to face the angry mob.

"For the bright lady! Get her! Get the heretic!" they shouted. They charged forward, heedless of her sword. She wasn't anxious to kill any of them, but when they rushed, she responded. Her new mount responded well to her commands, wheeling constantly, keeping its center still as it spun to keep from toppling its rider. Elsa slashed back and forth, trying desperately to stay mounted.

The soldiers fell back, bloodied and broken. Elsa stopped long enough to catch her breath. The light from the inn seemed wrong somehow. She calmed her mount and peered at the doorway.

Flames flickered inside. She could see nothing but fire, flickering across the tables and rushing up the rafters. The windows of the second floor turned red, and tendrils of smoke drifted through the roof.

"What in hell is going on in there?" she muttered.

"Strife has abandoned you, Elsa LaFey!" The voice came from the conflagration. A shadow stepped out of the doorway, pure blackness in the shape of a man. Smoke wreathed his head, and the tattered cover of his tabard was singed, but he wore the armor of a vow knight. "We wondered what happened to you, after Houndhallow. Now I see that you've fallen in with the heretics. It's no wonder Strife's flame has been snuffed from your soul."

"Sir Hollier?" she asked. The man's features were drawn tight, as though he were in constant pain, but his eyes glittered with joy. "What the hell has happened to you?"

"Revelation!" he shouted, then drew a sword of flame from his hip.

Elsa turned her horse and spurred it into the forest at a gallop. Wind and trees whipped her hair, and Hollier's laughter chased her through the darkness.

The forest was black, cut with shades of flame, as the trees reflected Hollier's bright blade. Elsa leaned close to her horse's mane and urged it on. The light on the trees around her grew brighter. She chanced a glance back and saw that Hollier had captured one of the fleeing horses and was giving chase.

"Faster, faster, faster," she whispered in her mount's ear. "Strife's wind, go!"

"Sir LaFey!" Hollier shouted. "You should not be running! Of all people, you know the futility of fleeing Strife's merciful flame!"

"Gods, shut up." The forest was ablaze with the man's flame. Elsa could feel it itching across her back, like a sunburn. The scars on her cheeks burned with the salt of her tears. "Shut up!"

The forest started to open up. Elsa dashed through a clearing, diving between two enormous trees on the other side, then through a loose copse of bristlewood. As she passed, the leaves on the trees started to smolder, then burst into flames. Hollier was nearly on her. She had to make a decision. There was no sign of Lucas or Martin. It was just her, and Hollier, and the flame.

In the next clearing she turned too hard, lost her seat, and tumbled from her mount. Elsa hit the ground and rolled, stumbling to her feet just as her stolen horse disappeared into the brambles. Sir Hollier rode into the clearing a heartbeat later, swinging his flaming sword like a banner.

"It always comes to this, Sir LaFey. The righteous hunt

down the wicked, and burn the evil out of them. I would not have marked you as fallen, Elsa, not in our days at the Lightfort, nor after your years of service against the gheist. But such things are not always clear." He did a slow circuit of the clearing, his expanding aura setting the tops of the trees aflame, until Elsa stood in the middle of a ring of fire. "So here we are. At the end of your flight, and the beginning of your redemption."

"I'm not the one who's fallen, Hollier," Elsa snapped. She drew her sword and settled into an easy guard, keeping the tip of her blade unwavering at the circling vow knight. "You've gone mad."

"I am holy, and you once were holy, LaFey. If you call it madness, that only speaks to your fall." Hollier slipped easily from his saddle, beckoning with open arms. "I will give you a choice. A peaceful death, and repentance. Or violence, and the mercy it requires."

"I have never chosen peace," Elsa said. She circled warily, trying to get between Hollier and his horse. If she could disable the man and steal his horse, she might still get out of this alive. "But I have no interest in hurting a brother in Strife."

"I have no such compunction," Hollier said. He swung his blade overhand, cutting a circle of flame in the air, spinning it down on Elsa. She blocked, and sparks of divine fire flew out from the contact. Elsa winced as the flames burned her face. Hollier spun, drew back, struck again and again. Each time Elsa retreated a few steps. A dozen lesser fires sprang up around the clearing.

"You will fight eventually," Hollier said. "A grand champion like you never goes out without a fight."

"I am fighting," Elsa puffed. "This is fighting, you idiot."

Hollier stepped back, sword casually in one hand, other hand held forward. "Come now, Elsa. We both know what you're capable of. I've heard tales of you, ever since you went north with that heretic. What was his name? Lucius?"

Elsa gritted her teeth and charged. Holding her sword in both hands, she crashed down on Hollier, swinging hard for his head. His steel sang loud against her blade; the blow forced him back. The sting of contact echoed through her bones, but it shook the fear from her. Her back swing nearly cut him in half. The only thing that saved Hollier was a fortunate tumble that sent him sprawling, so that Elsa's blade whistled over his head.

Hollier fell back, and Elsa pressed on. He scrambled to his knees, blocking her overhead swing with the forte of his blade, blow after blow until the sword skittered from his grasp. He rolled away, kicking at her knee, but Elsa sidestepped and buried her blade in the ground mere inches from his foot. Hollier's back was nearly to the flaming wall that surrounded the clearing.

"That's the legend I know," Hollier said, smiling weakly. "You have Strife's own gift with that blade. You seem to have bested me, sir."

"Relent, and I will spare you. I don't want holy blood on my hands."

"Relent? No, I can't. Strife does not teach surrender. But I wonder, Sir LaFey. Such skill with the blade, and yet you seem to be lacking a certain—" he held his hands out at his waist, palms up; light flared along the bloodwrought runes of his gauntlets, and tongues of flames arced up from his hands "—fire."

Elsa grimaced, then drew her blade behind her head and charged forward. Hollier waited for her, drawing her closer, then slammed his hands together. The sound was deafening, blowing cinders from the trees and shivering the trunks of the clearing. A wall of scalding heat hit her. Elsa pushed against it, leaning in, taking the brunt on her pauldrons, shielding her face with her arm, but it was too much. The relentless wailing of scorched air sucked the breath from her lungs. She fell back, back, finally tumbling to the ground. A wave of fire followed, washing over her, turning the ground to ash.

When she looked up, Hollier was walking toward her, slowly, hands smeared with soot. He scooped up his sword and smiled.

"Strife has read the sentence, and it is death. The bright lady has abandoned you. You have walked with heretics." Hollier raised his sword over his head, ready to cut Elsa down. "I claim your life, Sir Elsa LaFey. In the name of Strife's chosen champion, Lady Halverdt, of Flamehall."

"If you are what passes for holy in this age, then I will gladly name myself heretic," Elsa said. She stood, weary but unbroken. "Sophie is mad, and you with her. Kill me, if you must. Where I go, only the gods can judge me."

"As you will," Hollier said with a grim smile.

The ground under Elsa's feet turned black. With ash, she thought, but then frost chased the edge further out, and fell mists swirled up from the earth. At the border of the blight, strands of darkness twisted up, corkscrewing into the air. When Hollier stepped into it, his face turned red.

"Heretic!" he screamed. "Heretic! Winter shall die to summer's flame!"

The dark tendrils washed over him, latching onto his

arms, seizing his waist, pulling him toward the ground. Hollier fought, severing the shadow vines, channeling flame that turned the frost into charred flakes, spinning around as the darkness surrounded him. His words tumbled into an incoherent scream of rage.

"I can't hold him forever, you know," Lucas said from the edge of the clearing. Elsa spun around, saw that the frair was cowering under the boughs of a flaming tree, Martin at his side, holding a cloak up to shield them both from the embers that rained down. Lucas held his staff to the ground, and was channeling the naether through the earth. She turned back to Hollier.

"You were holy once," Elsa said. "I will find what demon corrupted you, and see your name justified."

"Burn in hell!" Hollier responded.

"My whole life," she said. Then Elsa stepped forward and brought her sword down on his jaw. Hollier's head snapped back, skull pivoting open around her blade, horror and then amazement twisting his features.

When he fell to the ground, the ring of fire that surrounded them drew in like a whirlpool, diving into his flesh. Flames crackled through his armor, burrowing through flesh and bone until there was nothing left but his shattered sword and the charred remnants of his armor.

Most of the flames went out, after that. A few pockets burned on, but night fell sudden and cold around them. Lucas and Martin walked up to Hollier's remains.

"What the hell was that?" Martin whispered.

"Judgment," Elsa answered. She turned and caught Hollier's horse; the creature had been too afraid to bolt. "Come on. We have dawn to catch."

8

THE BLACK HEAD of the iron hound stared down at Gwen. Flames guttered in its hollow eyes, the only light in the low-ceilinged shrine deep beneath the keep. Stained jaws snarled at her. Gwen was kneeling on the narrow bench that surrounded the icon, hands folded at her waist. The stones were cold under her knees. This was the ancient hallow of the Blakley clan, the totem that gave their castle its name and their crest its hound. When their ancestors forsook the tribes and swore faith to the celestial church, they had been allowed to keep the hallow as a mascot, if no longer a god.

But it was no icon to Gwen. She had seen the god, ridden its moss-covered back, bled into its fur and sworn to its creed. And then it had left her, shortly after the battle of Houndhallow. Shortly after Ian Blakley came home.

"He looks nothing like you, you know," Gwen said. The statue was silent. "I've never seen him snarl. Not at me, at least. And his teeth are bigger." She reached out a curious finger and brushed it over the iron jaw. The metal was pitted and rough. "Sharper, too. Ouch!"

Blood sprang from the tip of her finger. Gwen shook it off, then sucked at the wound. The hound watched her.

"Still hungry for sacrifice? The Blakleys haven't been following your rituals, have they? Is that why you came to me?" She stood and leaned closer to the head, running her hands over the worked fur, feeling the rough curves of its mane. The flames of its eyes singed the hairs on the back of her hand. She drew her knife and laid it against the palm of her hand. "Is that why you left?"

A horn cut through her thoughts, muffled by the thick stone walls of the keep. It was the gheist horn, sounding the alarm. Gwen stood still for a moment, hovering between sacrifice and duty. She sheathed the blade and turned away from the hound.

A guard rushed through the door. It was one of the tribesmen, a pagan ranger dressed in leathers and carrying an axe in both hands.

"My lady, there's been an attack! The Blakleys are mustering!"

"The void priests?"

"No, my lady, a gheist. One of the old gods manifested on the roof of the tower keep. Ian Blakley was there, and some others as well. All celestials."

"A gheist? Which one? None of the gods hold this ground sacred besides the hound. Was it him?"

"No, my lady," the ranger answered. The pagans had adopted the Suhdrin habit of calling her lady, even though the practice was forbidden among the tribes. Gwen couldn't decide if it was meant as an insult, or as a sign of respect, of setting her apart. "It was unknown. Some say it was of stone."

"Stone? And what does the elder of stone have to say about this?"

"Cahl cannot be found. We hoped... the elders hoped he would be with you."

Gwen shook her head. The shaman had been avoiding her since Ian's return, keeping to himself. Gwen suspected he was more troubled by Folam's betrayal than most. Cahl had been close to Fianna, Folam's daughter. Together the two of them had led Ian Blakley to safety in the early stages of this war.

"If Ian Blakley was attacked by a gheist, his people will blame us. We must lend our aid as quickly as possible before this escalates." Gwen brushed past the guard. "Find the other elders."

"They wait above."

"Already?" Gwen paused. The horn had only just sounded. "That seems odd. Never mind. I will speak with them."

Gwen hurried up the stairs that led to the crypts, and then the courtyard. The castle grounds were filled with clamorous activity. Soldiers of both Blakley and the tribes rushed about, securing rooms and putting on armor. Flames flickered at the top of the tower keep, and a dozen shadows darted back and forth against the light. The front gates were closed, and guards of both factions stood watch on the towers above, dividing their nervous attention between each other and the forest beyond.

The elders stood serenely in a half-circle, surrounding the entrance to the crypts. When Gwen emerged, the elders grew visibly tense. Morcant and Vilday, both old men, long in the service of the tribes, stood in the center. The newly appointed elder of bones, a young woman named Kesthe, was beside them. She wore her amber hair short and shaved at the sides, but her pale eyes looked almost Suhdrin. The ink of her tattoos scrolled nearly to her ears. Noel, the elder of the sun, and the only true Suhdrin among them, stood to one side. She looked worried.

"Elders, you gathered quickly. Or did you have some warning about the gheist?" Gwen asked.

"No. If any us were to know, it would be Cahl, and he is not to be found," Morcant said. The elder of tides sniffed loudly. "We thought you might know where he is."

"I don't. How did you come to gather so quickly?"

Morcant and Vilday glanced at one another, but didn't answer. Noel cleared her throat. "There are concerns among the tribes. About you, and where you're leading us."

"Astray, that's where," Kesthe said, grimacing. "Elder Judoc never trusted House Adair, and I won't be the first elder of bones to kneel at a Suhdrin altar."

"Elder Judoc was with Folam in his betrayal," Gwen said stiffly. "If you are going to follow his lead, we should put you in chains right now, child."

"Don't we have more pressing concerns?" Vilday asked with a sigh. "Blakley is sealing the keep. We're not far from drawn blades and bloody streets."

"In gods' names, why? What do we have to do to prove ourselves to these people?"

"Pray to the moon, and swear loyalty to the sun," Kesthe spat. "As Blakley did, and the rest of the traitors."

"Anytime a gheist appears in their homes, they are going to blame it on a witch. And we happen to have a lot of witches in our company," Vilday said.

"These fools wouldn't know a witch from a wash maid. One of them gave me a bucket to throw out as I passed by," Kesthe said.

“This is not about your spoiled pride, Kesthe,” Noel said. “We need to figure out what became of this gheist. Where it came from, who summoned it, and why.”

“I bloody well know why,” Gwen muttered. “There will be void priests behind this, I swear by any god you want to name.”

“Perhaps. Or it may be a natural—” Morcant was interrupted by a cry from the gate. The doors creaked, and the heavy windlass groaned as it started drawing up the portal. The elders turned to watch.

A trio of Suhdrin riders came through. One of them had a body across the back of his horse, and rode hard for the doma. As they passed, Gwen recognized the rough features of Sir Bruler. The Suhdrin knight’s face was pale, and blood stained his tunic.

“That’s trouble,” she said. Noel rushed after the rider, hand to her mouth. The other elders watched silently.

Just as the gates were about to close again, another shout went out. A tight group of tribesmen ran inside. They were carrying a body.

It was Cahl. The elder of stones was dead.

Gwen stood over Cahl’s silent body. The wound in his chest looked like such a small thing. She laid her palm over it, but there was no breath in his lungs, no beat in his heart. He was still.

“Did we find the knife?”

“Broken off in his back,” the scout said. “A Suhdrin blade.”

“For a Suhdrin knight. But why? What could Sir Bruler have against Cahl?”

"He's been following Cahl around, best part of two weeks now. Thinks he's smart about it, but he stalks like a lion among rats."

"And everyone knows he's at Ian Blakley's elbow at every council meeting," Kesthe said. "The boy ordered this."

"Ian Blakley ordered nothing. Cahl was trying to heal him. There's no reason—"

"As Fianna tried to heal Ian's mother? And what did that get her?" Kesthe crossed her arms angrily. "Why do we keep helping these traitors? They are Tenerran only by birth and brotherhood. They have betrayed their blood!"

"I will remind you, Kesthe, that you are only elder of the tribe of bones because your predecessor threw his lot in with Folam Voidfather. Together they betrayed us all, the gods and tribes alike." Gwen looked up from Cahl's body, careful to keep her voice even. "You are not so long in the position that I won't accuse you of the same, and be rid of you before nightfall."

"Careful, huntress," Morcant said. "You have no place in our council. The gods have gifted you, that is true, but you are no elder. You don't even belong to the tribes."

"I am of the tribe of iron. My family gave everything to protect the Fen God from the inquisition, only to be betrayed by the church and the tribes alike. Do not chide me on my place, elder."

"Enough of this bickering," Noel snapped. The elder of the sun had just returned, and now she stepped between them. "Word of Cahl's death has got out. Even now, our tribesmen whisper about Suhdrin daggers and Tenerran lords. If we don't interfere, something terrible is going to happen."

"Perhaps something terrible should happen," Kesthe whispered. They turned to glare at her.

"We will take up this discussion later," Gwen said coldly. "For now, come with me. Ian has avoided us long enough. Is he still in the keep?"

"I hear that he is praying in the doma," Noel said.

"Still faithful to Heartsbridge, that one," Kesthe said sharply. Gwen ignored her.

"Then we go to the doma. Elders, with me."

"You don't command us!" Morcant said to Gwen's retreating back. And yet, they followed, Kesthe trailing behind.

A steady crowd gathered around the elders as they approached the doma. Tenerran guards stood at the doors, watching nervously.

"Stand aside," Gwen said, waving her hand like the baron's daughter she was.

"This is holy ground, not to be trammeled by pagan hoofs," the guard said. He was a narrow man, with a hook nose and soft hands, and he spoke with a slight stammer. Gwen smiled.

"Are you a priest? Sworn to the holy orders?"

"I know more of the will of the gods than you, witch. That you haven't been struck down by Cinder is a mercy and a curse. If you try to force your way onto this holy ground, I will take Cinder's task in my own hands. I swear it!"

"Swear it, do you?" Gwen drew her blade cleanly, laying the forte against the guard's neck before he could move. "Do you swear it on your life's blood? Do you?"

"Gwendolyn," Morcant whispered, "this is not what Cahl would have wanted."

"Cahl is dead."

"And still, his will would not have changed." The elder

of tides eased Gwen's blade away from the guard's neck. "We only need to speak with Ian Blakley. We promise not to desecrate the shrine of Cinder and Strife any more than is completely necessary."

"Let them through, Hines," the other guard said. Throughout the confrontation, the man had hardly moved, even when his companion's life was threatened. Now he nodded to the doma. "They'll find what they need inside."

Hines quivered with rage, but slid to the side, bowing.

"If the gods spare you, we will have this conversation again, Lady Adair."

Gwen snorted and pushed into the doma. The elders followed, along with a good crowd of pagans. The door shut behind them.

During the siege of Houndhallow, after the pagans had rushed the walls and were breaking into the keep, much of the fighting in the inner courtyard had centered on the doma. Frair Daxter had led the defense, barricading the doors and sealing the calendar windows. Before the void priests and their plots were unveiled, the pagans successfully broke the doma's barricades and fought their way to the altar. They were turned aside only by the priest's unexpected prowess with the blade, and Ian Blakley's arrival.

The doma still showed signs of this struggle. The pews were in disarray, most broken or overturned, and many icons of the celestial faith had been burned. Soot stained the walls from the ensuing conflagration, though the flames had been extinguished in short order. Despite all that, the doma now held an air of serene peace. A handful of supplicants knelt throughout the space, resting on pillows as they faced the various stations of Cinder and Strife. Frairwood smoke drifted in thick layers, and the dozens of candles that lined the walls gave the smoke a silvery quality, as though the air itself glowed with holy light. Even in the midst of the gheist horn sounding outside, the doma seemed calm.

The pagans barged through the center, marching toward the altar. If Ian were here, he would be praying as close to the altar as possible, as was fitting for a lord of Tener. The priest stood behind the altar, watching them approach.

"Ian Blakley," Gwen said loudly. "Is he here?"

"What business do you have with the lord of Houndhallow?" Frair Daxter asked quietly. He was still frail from wounds sustained during the battle, but Daxter's voice was strong.

"Last I heard, Malcolm his father was still lord of this house," Gwen said.

"Ian is lord enough for us," Daxter answered. "And lord enough to see you thrown from these walls."

"Ian welcomed us in, opened the gates to us, even rode with us to battle," Gwen answered.

"And for that you thanked him by bringing your feral gods into our homes, and letting them loose among our children," Daxter answered. "Ian opened the gates, yes. But even lords make mistakes."

"You would cross his will?"

"I would enforce it," Daxter said. "Even if he doesn't truly know what his will should be. My brothers?"

The supplicants around the room stood as one. Their robes slipped away, revealing plate mail and steel blades.

"This doma has seen enough blood, frair," Gwen said. Behind her, the pagans were already standing back to back, drawing blades. "This doesn't have to happen."

"It already has," he said, then drew a wicked blade and lunged at her.

Gwen knocked him aside, twisting the knife from his hand and kicking the priest in the belly as he went down. She turned to address the closing ranks of Tenerrans when a startled cry of pain went up.

She looked down to see Kesthe kneeling over the priest. Her blade was slick and red as she pulled it from Daxter's belly. The elder of bones looked up at her.

"You would have sought peace," Kesthe said. "There can be no peace here."

"For Cinder!" some in the mob shouted. "For the frair, and Strife, and Blakley!"

"The hound! The hallow!" the rest of the mob answered, then fell on the circle of pagans, blades drawn and murder in their eyes.

9

THEY RODE NORTH. Elsa took the lead most of the way, with Lucas and Martin trailing behind, just out of sight. There were enough of Halverdt's scouts on these roads that Elsa didn't want to stumble across one and explain her inquisitor friend, and though they had a few close calls, they made good progress for the first week.

One night, long after Martin had drifted off to sleep, and Lucas and Elsa sat staring at the fire, the inquisitor asked the question they had been avoiding since Greenhall. Lucas cleared his throat, then looked his former vow knight in the eyes.

"What happened to you?"

"The same thing that happens to everyone in war. I got hurt," she said, ducking her head. She was twisting a stick in her hands, breaking off pieces and throwing them into the fire, one by one.

"I have seen the injuries of war, Elsa. I know what a sword can do to flesh. But you're not injured in that way. Tell me what happened."

So Elsa told him. About Folam Voidfather, and the battle under the walls of Houndhallow. Ian's charge, and her own fight with the priests of neither Cinder nor Strife. The wounds it left in her, and the god it took. When she was done, they sat in silence for a long time.

"I can't find Strife," she said finally. "The path is still there, but my feet stumble. I can..." She waved her hand in frustration. "I can see the house where she once lived, I can knock on the door, even walk its corridors. But there's no one there."

"Strife could not have left you, Elsa. She is still here, still working through the winter vow. Perhaps it's just the season. Winter is—"

"Winter is where I belong. I am a knight of the vow, Lucas, sworn to carry the light of Strife into the darkest days, yet I can't even kindle it in my heart." She threw the rest of her stick into the flames, staring at it as it burned. "What sort of darkness am I, that Strife herself can bring no light?"

"You mustn't think like that," Lucas said. "Whatever has happened, this isn't your fault. This voidfather must have done something to you, or his priests. I have seen some strange things since Sacombre's heresy, child. I no longer know what is possible, and what is merely myth."

"What does it matter? I can't draw on Strife. Without her, I am nothing more than an angry sword."

"You are more than that," Lucas said. He put a hand on her shoulder, smiling his grandfatherly smile. "You are a true and honest friend. We are blessed to have you at our side. If that is all Strife can do through you, it is more than enough."

"Hollier could have killed me. Would have, if you hadn't been nearby," she said, standing. "You are kind to say what you've said. But it's little comfort."

She turned and went to her sleeping mat, leaving Lucas

by the fire. The night was growing cold, but she went as far from the fire as she dared before setting her blankets down and wrapping up.

The next day, the number of Halverdt's scouts roaming the countryside tripled, clogging the roads so badly that Lucas and Martin rode with Elsa, to avoid being split up. They rode in silence, listening for approaching hoofbeats and scenting the air for campfires. What they heard were drums, coming from the road behind them.

"That's not a parade," Martin said nervously.

"Definitely not. Into that farmhouse," Lucas answered. "We'll just have to pray they pass us by."

The house seemed to be abandoned, so Lucas and Elsa dismounted and led the horses through the door while Martin inspected the rest of the house.

"Blankets still on the beds, and ashes in the fireplace. Whoever lived here, they went in a hurry, and traveled light."

"We'll worry about that later. Close the door and secure the shutters. Let's not give them any reason to get curious about what's inside," Lucas said, going around the main floor and closing every window and door. The horses snorted nervously in the middle of the room, their ears brushing the ceiling. Between the three mounts and the domestic setting, the scene was almost humorous.

The drums sounded again a short time later. Lucas and Elsa left one window open, covering it with a blanket that was thin enough to peer through.

"You might have been wrong about that parade, Sir Roard," Elsa whispered. Lucas shushed her, but through the cacophony there was little chance of them being heard.

The column that came around the corner was the living embodiment of chaos in motion. Marchers in motley uniforms followed a wagon of musicians, none of them playing the same song, all caught up in the rapture of their performance. The marchers were armed with everything from spears to pitchforks, halberds to blacksmiths' hammers, wearing armor drawn together from the three corners of Tenumbra and beyond. A small troupe of women waved multicolored flags, with swords strapped to their belts and marching boots under their ragged skirts. A cloud of children wafted around the column, carrying daggers and pitchers and clubs, whatever their chubby hands could find.

Behind the head of the column came another wagon, pulled by draught horses and festooned with banners of every color in the dawn. Shields hung along the side as if it were a Reaver raiding ship. In the center of the wagon was a throne, and on the throne sat a child. Or half a child. His other half was old and withered, with white hair framing a face that hung slack with age, or bright with youth, depending on which profile was facing you. He wore simple garments, and rested his hands, one young, one palsied, on a wooden sword. The half-boy stared straight ahead.

"Gods above, it's the boy. The one who chased us out of Greenhall," Lucas said. "How did he get north so fast, and with so many people?"

"That's not the half of it," Elsa said. She nodded back to the road. "Look."

After the wagon had passed the farmhouse, there was a gap, then the army proper started to march by. Rank upon rank of spears, followed by proud knights on their steeds and smart columns of crossbowmen. A solid corps of vow knights brought up the rear, each one still dressed in the ashen tree and sun tabard of their order, but with the addition of Halverdt's newly adopted sigil, the tri-flame and saltire, usually on one of their pauldrons or draped over their shields.

Sophie Halverdt rode at the head of the vow knights. She was in golden armor and cream, as neat and fine as you would expect from a Suhdrin duchess at a ball. There was a black mark on her forehead.

"She's taken the winter vow," Elsa whispered. "Gods, what is happening?"

"How can you tell?" Martin asked.

"On her forehead, the ashen brand. Not a brand, really, but harking back to darker rituals," Lucas answered. He glanced at Elsa, but when she didn't volunteer anything further, he continued. "All vow knights take it with their oath, wearing it through their first winter in Strife's service. I didn't know it could be applied anywhere other than the Lightfort."

"It cannot," Elsa said. "What new heresy is this, I wonder?"

"Gods know," Lucas answered. They watched as Sophie's army passed, keeping silent and counting their breaths. More men-at-arms followed the vow knights, and finally came the supply wagons. It was at least an hour before the last horse disappeared around the corner, and the last drumbeat disappeared into the forest. Dusk was falling.

"What do we do now?" Martin asked. "They'll surely have cut off the northern routes now."

"What I want to know is how they got so far north, so fast. We three have been traveling fast. It takes time to gather that kind of army, and longer still to get it down the road. Unless they left Greenhall before us—"

"Which we know they didn't, as we fled that terrifying child in the old town," Martin said.

"Right. So how are they making such good time?" Lucas asked.

"There is only one way to know," Elsa said as she opened the door and started the slow process of disentangling the horses from the furnishings. "We join the train. I can pass as a guard, and you two could be common soldiers."

"These old arms haven't carried a sword in decades," Lucas said.

"All the more convincing, given the company. Come on. We need to get there before they camp for the night. We won't go any further than the hangers-on, hoping for service. Unless Sir Roard fancies joining the dancing corps?" Elsa threw Martin a pack and smiled. "I'm sure his Suhdrin feet miss the ballroom."

"It would be impossible to find a proper partner in that rabble. Present company excluded, of course," he said, bowing stiffly to Elsa and presenting his hand, as though to promenade. "Would my lady care to saunter?"

Elsa shoved him away, ducking her head at his chortle. She didn't look up until they were on the road, and then only to give instruction. Lucas only smiled when she wasn't watching.

It was easy to get lost in Halverdt's train. Hundreds of desperate farmers, merchants, even whole families flocked to the army as it passed. They whispered about gheists haunting the fields and forests of the north, believing that only the true heir of Greenhall could keep them safe. That Sophie boasted a strong cadre of vow knights, and had herself taken the winter vow, lent credibility to this belief.

"These people have lost hope," Lucas muttered, several days after they had joined the train. The whole army moved at a snail's pace northward. "Foolish enough to put their faith in Halverdt."

"All else has failed them," Martin said. "Why are they fools for trusting the only true power they see in the north?"

"Power given by madness is not power. It's poison."

"Keep it down," Elsa said. "We've got eyes enough watching us without your muttering."

The three of them did stand out in this mass. There were soldiers enough in the train, hoping to be hired on to Halverdt's army, though few were willing to swear the oaths Sophie required. But no matter how much Martin slouched, or how little care he gave his armor, the heir of Stormwatch had a noble air about him. People were regularly calling him "my lord," and more than a few of the women in the train had taken to following him everywhere.

If Martin was conspicuous in his nobility, Elsa and Lucas stood out for different reasons. It was decided that each should play their opposite part, so Elsa had stripped off her armor and lent the few pieces that would fit Lucas to the frair. The rest, especially those pieces that identified her as a knight of the winter vow, were wrapped in burlap and hidden in sacks. But Lucas did not look comfortable in Elsa's massive chain shirt, and the sword buckled to his belt kept tangling in his legs or fouling in the saddle whenever he tried to dismount. And Elsa, even in linen, walking alongside her horse with a quarterstaff, could never be mistaken for anything other than a warrior. And of course, Elsa could not bring herself to part with her bloodwrought sword. It hung over her shoulder like a cross. Even wrapped in strips of cloth, it was clearly a great blade. She gathered her own following among the children of the train.

Despite this, no one marked them for what they truly were: priests of Cinder and Strife. Even when Sophie's vow knights rode by, none of them paused at the sight of these three strange travelers—there were simply too many people in the train.

In this humble and slow way, they traveled to within sight of the Reaveholt. The great fortress on the banks of the Tallow loomed on the horizon. As soon as it appeared, the army came to a halt, encamping on the same grounds where dozens of besieging armies had camped previously. The civilian train scattered into the surrounding woods, outside Halverdt's picket but within sight of her sentries. Lucas found a spot on a low ridgeline, on the very edges of the train. As soon as night fell and suspicious eyes were resting, he doffed his borrowed armor and huddled by the fire, shivering under a blanket.

"I don't know how you wear that all the time," Lucas said. "My shoulders are worn raw, and if I'm ever able to stand straight again it will be a godsdamned miracle. I can't even feel my hips!"

"There is comfort in steel," Elsa answered quietly. "I've spent the last week waiting for a blade to sink into my naked back. My skin itches in anticipation." She picked up the chain shirt that Lucas had cast aside, rubbing it between her fingers like fine silk. "A well-wrought shirt of rings, and plate above. No greater comfort."

"I would settle for a warm fire and decent bedding,"

Lucas said. "I think it's finally happened. I've grown old enough to hate the road."

"So what happens now, do you think?" Martin said, interrupting their reverie. "Will Lady Halverdt try to go through the Reaveholt? No army has taken that citadel in generations."

"No army has brought three score vow knights to the effort," Elsa said. "If that is the path she wishes to follow, I fear the consequences. You cannot ask people to trust a priesthood that has turned to reaving."

"The crusades were not peaceful affairs, Sir LaFey, and yet the north eventually took the faith. Time passes. People forget horrors," Lucas said. "And gods know what thoughts rest in Sophie's young head."

"No matter how fast she moves, she'll still have to go through the Reaveholt," Martin said. "There's no other way north. Not if she's making for the Fen Gate."

"Reaveholt or the blight. Or west to some port and then around." Elsa squinted at the fire, then gave Lucas a quizzical look. "Are you well, frair?"

"I'm fine. Truthfully, my shoulders feel fresh, and my hips..." Lucas paused, staring down at his legs. He hopped up. "My hips feel like a young man's."

"The grass is growing," Martin said. He leapt to his feet, bouncing from one foot to the other, as though he were afraid to touch the ground.

Elsa stood slowly, turning her eyes to the main camp.

"The air is warmer, and clean in my lungs. Fresh. The grass is growing, and our pains are eased." The tone of her voice changed, becoming a chant. "Cinder's House is closed. Winter's bite is cut. All sun's promise has been kept and moon's cold gaze is ending."

"The spring rite," Lucas said. He looked around. "Trees blossoming, the earth's frost softening, and our bones restored. What is she doing?"

"Bringing summer into the cold night of winter," Elsa said. She looked at Lucas, and her eyes were glazed over with tears. "As a vow knight must."

10

THE DOMA WAS a terrible place for a fight, and the elders had long outgrown the custom of battle. But the disgruntled mob led by Frair Daxter was not made up of the castle's finest warriors, and their weapons were scavenged from the scrapheap. Still, they fought with the conviction of hatred, swarming Gwen and her companions.

In the first heated moments of battle, Gwen grabbed one of her attackers and stripped him of his blade, drawing it across his throat before dropping him to the ground. The man's blood sprayed across her face, mingling with the rust-stain and soot that seemed a permanent part of her flesh. The others hesitated before swarming forward, giving the elders time to circle up.

"I was born in the sea, and I shall die there," Morcant said. He drew a ceremonial knife, forged to look like a conch shell, the whirls of steel that twisted around his fist shimmering in the dim light. "No crowd of peasants is going to change that."

"The gods do not always give us the death we demand," Kesthe said. The elder of bones held the stone-tipped staff of her station across her chest like a quarterstaff. Other than Gwen, she was the youngest of the lot, and the least patient with the Tenerran celestial faithfuls of Houndhallow. Gwen had no doubt she would die before giving way to Blakley's frair and his mob.

A heartbeat, and then there was no more time for talking. The rest of the Tenerrans closed the distance, jumping over their dead companion to attack. Gwen laid into them, slicing with the rust-pitted blade of her stolen sword. The hilt hummed in her hands, the tang loose and rattling, stinging her flesh with each blow. Blood started to leak around the hilt.

Kesthe proved her worth to the god of graves. The young elder smashed bones and shattered knees, sweeping her staff around her head in an endless dance of pain. The Tenerrans fell away from her, tentatively prodding at her defenses with their swords, holding her at bay without pinning her down.

For every skull that Kesthe cracked, though, three more waited among the pews. What they lacked in skill, they made up for in sheer numbers, and soon both Gwen and Kesthe were bleeding from a dozen cuts.

The other elders were of no use. Morcant growled and hissed, but whenever one of the Tenerrans got close, he would fade back, wincing. Noel, the Suhdrin elder of the tribe of flames, hid in the center of the elders' circle. She had seen her share of violence in the ruins of Greenhall, but never with blade or club. The few tribesmen who had followed them into the doma fought hard, but they were soldiers of the forest, accustomed to ambush and maneuver, not the pitched struggle of the city fight.

They were being overwhelmed. Morcant disappeared among the swirling robes of the Tenerrans, tumbling behind a broken pew. Kesthe screamed when she saw him fall, but there was no further fury in her attack; she was already fully committed, at the limit of her prowess. The dozen of their followers became single digits, and that was soon cut in half. Only Gwen and Kesthe stood strong, with Noel hidden in the wreckage. Dozens of Tenerrans lay dead at their feet, but it wasn't enough. It was never going to be enough.

The air began to howl at the center of the doma. Among the ruined pews, the swirling frairwood incense turned bright, and then ignited into fire. Smoke crisped in Gwen's nostrils. Noel stood from her hiding place, arms raised to the sky, eyes turned to light. Fire wove its way through her hair like glittering snakes. A slowing swirling nimbus of flames twisting beneath the domed ceiling, centered on the elder of the sun. The light from Noel's eyes cast harsh shadows among the pews.

"Enough of this! Enough madness!" Noel said. "I have suffered enough from betrayal and the zealot's hatred. Leave us! Leave, or face the fury of the gods!"

"You profane holy ground!" It was Hines, the guard from the door, shielding his eyes from Noel's fire. "The gods will deal harshly with you!"

"This is the harshness of a true god," Noel said. She motioned toward the cowering guard, and a lash of fire swept toward Hines. It burrowed through the prayer cushions and broken pews of the doma, turning wood and silk to ash. It swallowed Hines whole, enveloping him in tendrils of bright flame. His scream echoed through the chamber, cut suddenly short as the flames crawled down his throat. For a brief second, the man's flesh turned to kindling, and his bones stood stark against the flames, like the shadow of lightning. Then he was gone. Not even ash remained.

Noel withdrew her hands, her fingers trembling. She

looked around at the remaining Tenerrans. One by one, they dropped their blades, steel clattering against stone like hail. The surviving pagans slowly stood, looking around in shock.

"There is more mercy among the tribes than hatred," Noel said, lifting a hand to the collected Tenerrans. "You have forgotten your gods, but they can be remembered. There is no need to—"

"Noel!" Gwen shouted. The elder of flames looked to her. "Stop it, elder! Stop your burning god!"

As one, they turned to look at the spot where Hines fell. A knot of flame churned over the stones, digging into the floor and throwing sparks into the air. Noel tightened her brows, motioning to the flames, trying to dispel them with her will. The knot remained. It even started to grow.

"There is something wrong," Noel said. "The air... the earth... it is resisting me."

"Holy ground," Gwen muttered. "Worse, ground dedicated to Lady Strife, the very goddess of flames. Morcant!"

"He is fallen," Kesthe said. The young elder of bones stood slack-jawed, watching the flaming knot swell.

"Then raise him! Deny your god's hold on his soul, child! We need the tides!"

Kesthe snapped out of her reverie, kneeling by Morcant's side. The elder of tides was bleeding from the shoulder, his frail frame shivering as Kesthe ran her hands over him. He blinked unseeing at the ceiling.

"I am not a healer," she muttered. "I know nothing..."

"You know enough to keep him with us," Gwen said. "You must. It is necessary."

Noel ignored them. She walked closer to the burning

knot, bending her will in concentration, hands spread wide and eyes narrowed. The flames fluttered away from her, but the core of the knot burned brighter and brighter. Embers crawled across the hem of her robes, and her face flushed. Cinders floated through the nimbus of her hair.

"It is flowing… away from me!" she shouted. Her voice vibrated with the strain of holding the gheist. "Gwen! We need to run!"

"If we lose this gheist as we lost the god of flowers in Greenhall, we will lose all of Tener with it!" Gwen shouted. "The story that will be told is of witches destroying faithful castles with their mad gods. All of Tener will turn against us!"

"Good story, but we don't have a choice!" Noel's face was pale, the sweat running down her brow like a river. "It is no longer my god to bid!"

With a snap, the knot burst apart. Thin lines of burning gold splashed across the walls, turning the inside of the doma into a geode shot through with summer light. Tendrils of liquid flame crawled between the calendar windows, setting wood and rope to flame, burrowing into the domed ceiling like veins of fire.

"The Allfire, and Ides of Light," Gwen said. She followed the trails of flame, tracing the gheist's progress through the doma. "Summer Tide. All the way to the station of the Winter Vow. It is following the days of Strife. Gathering her power, maybe." As they watched, the gheist pooled around the calendar icons of the bright lady, flowing like liquid gold toward the western side of the doma. There, tucked into a nook, was the reliquary of the Winter Vow.

"What is happening?" Morcant asked, coughing. The

old man sat up, staring at the corona of fire that had settled around the grim altar to the setting sun. "Elder bones, what have you done to me?"

"Saved you from the grave," Kesthe whispered. "Now silence. Something is happening to Noel's god."

"No longer my god," Noel said. "The doma has claimed her."

The last of the scattered flames died down. The only light in the doma was the crown of flame that surrounded the reliquary of the winter vow. The fire turned from bright red and orange into a steady white, the color of the winter sun. The altar's carvings filled with silver, etching the story of Strife's mission to bring the light of hope into the desolation of winter, to remind those who suffered under Cinder's judgment of the promise of spring and the coming dawn. It was this aspect of Strife that guided the knights of the winter vow, those who walked with the inquisitors and hunted the feral gods of the north.

From the heart of the altar, a sword rose, carried by a hand clad in shimmering armor. A knight followed, towering over the crowd, its head brushing the ceiling of the doma. The black sun and twisted, burned tree of the knights of the winter vow stood stark on its chest. Eyes that burned with cold fire stared down at Noel, and the rest of the pagans.

"You are a corruption of truth," it said. Its voice sounded like the chiming of church bells, distantly heard. "Purify yourselves in sacrifice, or face the judgment of winter."

"I'd say the same about you," Noel said. "You're nothing but a reflection of the true gods. A fragment of the glory that was."

"Purify!" was the gheist's only answer. It rushed

forward, burning blade sweeping through the air in wide arcs, throwing embers when it struck.

Noel collapsed out of the way, the blade passing mere inches above her head. The sword's heat drove Gwen back. She shielded her eyes, staring down at the stone as the shadows passed. She could feel the holy energy of the gheist plucking at the wounds in her soul, the scars left by the Fen God, and later by the god of flowers. It felt like fishing line stitched into her bones, drawing tight.

"Morcant! Do something!"

The elder of tides groaned to his feet, leaning heavily on Kesthe and her staff of bones. Half of his face hung slack, the eye on that side swimming with black ink, but Morcant raised his arms and drew on the power of water.

The river that flowed at the base of Houndhallow was old and deep, its source far to the north, in the jagged mountains of the Elderspine. In time it fed the Tallow, and later the Dunne, finally finding its way to Heartsbridge to flow beneath the hundred bridges of that distant and holy city. Its waters ran from the crown of Tenumbra to the feet, gathering the rain and snowmelt of a hundred mountains, the blood of a thousand young springs. It was a river of ages, and at the will of the elder of tides, it rose.

Silver water appeared in the cracks of the stone floor, mingling with the blood spilled in battle, and the ash of the fire god's passing. Quickly these elements dissolved into pure water, as clean as rainwater and as cold as the ocean's depths. Soon frigid water lapped at Gwen's ankles, rising swiftly to reach her knees. The dead floated in the sudden tide, bumping limply against the walls. At the feet of the bright gheist, the water roiled into steam, hissing in clouds of mist that shrouded the burning figure of the knight.

Morcant drew his arms together, and the tide ebbed, gathering into a swollen pillar in front of the elder's frail form. The burning knight slashed at the pillar, but its sword passed through it without leaving a mark. As it struck, Morcant flinched back, the water's pain passing through the elder like a shockwave. Kesthe took his elbow.

"Steady, elder," she said. "I have faith in you."

"I will not die here," the old man said through clenched teeth. "Not so far from the tides."

"Gods willing," Kesthe whispered. "Now end it!"

Morcant motioned, and the gheist of water responded. The pillar rose up and arced forward, crashing into the burning knight in a torrent of cold water. The knight stumbled back, shielding itself with the forte of its blade, but the current washed over it. Sputtering flame flickered through the outflow, bits of burning steel and swirling embers quenched as it tore away from the knight.

The flood wrenched pieces of armor from the knight, exposing the bright light of its essence to the smothering stream. A pauldron tore free, clattering across the floor before crashing into a window, shattering it. Its flames winked out, leaving only a cold husk behind. The burning knight's flames were eroded, its form growing smaller and duller under Morcant's assault.

Finally, only a whisper of its essence remained, no taller than Morcant, no brighter than a candle. With a final rush, the gheist collapsed into the flood, disappearing like a snuffed torch. The doma was engulfed in darkness. Whatever holy force was keeping the pillar of water together withdrew. Gwen was once again awash in frigid water up to her knees. Detritus bumped against her legs.

"Light!" she yelled. "We need light!"

The door burst open, and the waters started to drain into the courtyard. Half a dozen pagan rangers, wielding torches and spears, stood in the entrance to the doma. The flickering light from their torches cast stark shadows across the surface of the water. The flood quickly receded.

"What the hell happened here?" the lead ranger, Deidra, asked. She was a tall woman, the sides of her head shaved, the rest of her hair drawn into long plaits that clung to her head like a ram's horns.

Gwen looked around the room. Bodies and broken pews, the damp ruin of pillows, and half the pagans who had first been ambushed. In the chaos of the gheist's attack, the Tenerrans had fled, disappearing into the castle.

Of the elder of tides there was no sign. The receding waters had taken him away, delivering Morcant to the depths.

"He went home," Gwen answered. "He died as he wished."

"Noel?" Kesthe asked hesitantly. The elder of the sun was staring at the altar of the winter vow, her face slack.

"I lost control," Noel said. "I lost the hand of my god."

"We never control," Kesthe said. "We only pray, and hope."

"Not even hope," Noel answered. "Not any longer."

11

THE THREE SUHDRINS were not alone. While Malcolm gawked at Helenne's ruined face, another half-dozen knights trotted out of the forest. They were a rough crowd, for noble blood, like a holiday party put off their celebration by bad food and a rude host. Their clothes, still finer than anything Malcolm owned, were wrinkled by weeks on the road and a lack of change. Their perfume did not conceal the stink of sweat, and many wore bandages under their silk. Sir Hallister sat calmly, her anger propping up her honor, never taking her eyes from Malcolm. Behind her rode a brace of knights from the Black Mountain, men sworn to Emil Fabron, whose head Malcolm had taken at the battle of White Lake. Sir Tasse waited quietly nearby, her head angled to one side, staring intently into the darkness.

It was hardly a welcoming committee.

Besides Sir Doone, Malcolm was joined by Grant MaeHerron, and several other knights he had grown to trust since the war started. The grim lord of the Feltower had appeared from somewhere in the days after Malcolm's rout, reunited with the Tenerran force and joining his gathered knights to the effort, an unexpected ally. Grant had grown silent since his father's death, the battle-joy lost in his dark eyes. He hovered at the edge of the meeting, cradling his axe and staring daggers at the Suhdrin knights.

The other Tenerrans were hardly better off. Franklin Gast still stood for the forces of Rudaine. That man was earning his way to a title, though Malcolm doubted if he did any of it for fame or glory. Lesser knights of Daeven, Swanston, and Thyber joined them, the only blooded names still in their company. Malcolm had ridden to White Lake in the company of dukes and earls, but the long grind of war left him standing with knights and common soldiers. There was more to nobility than blood, though. And these were all noble men and women, whatever their names held.

Only Helenne Bassion stood separate from the crowd. Her dark robe melted into the night air, and the harsh mauling of her wound turned half her face to black. She seemed to have aged a lifetime from the carefree and flirtatious noblewoman Malcolm remembered from his days in Heartsbridge.

"So," she said, when pleasantries and threats had been exchanged, and the conversation stalled. All heads turned toward her. "What of these gheists, and the priests who command them. What can you tell me of our enemy?"

"I would ask you the same," Malcolm said. "They rose from your ranks. Frair Rhone said they joined you on the road north." The priest made to speak, but Helenne silenced her.

"This is true. Traveling priests, stirred from their books at Cinderfell to join the war effort. When they heard we rode to face you, they could not hitch their wagons to our train quickly enough." Helenne stirred uncomfortably, glancing at one of the knights behind her. "Some of us know them better than others."

"We met them earlier," the man said quickly. His features

were sharp, and his beard narrowed to an oil-bright point. "My men and I were fasting at Cinderfell in preparation for the equinox celebrations when word of Lord Fabron's death reached us. We rode even before we broke our fast."

"And you are?"

"Sir Yves Durand, of House Fabron. I have the command of twenty knights, all holy men. We will see the end of this heresy, Houndhallow."

"And the priests came with you?" Malcolm said, ignoring the knight's burning glare. "The priests who killed your fellow knights, and wounded your lady?"

"They had just arrived themselves. There was some talk in Cinderfell at their coming—the inquisitors were not sure of the newcomers' place in the holy orders. Some of the new-arrived priests were known to Cinderfell; some were not. With Sacombre's heresy, the inquisition is asking a lot of questions."

"The inquisition is always asking a lot of questions," Gast said with a curling smile. "It's in the name. Perhaps you're just not used to having them directed at you."

"Only pagans fall under the inquisition's gaze," Durand answered, bristling.

"We have seen the lie of that," Gast said. "Unless you name us pagans? We can end this meeting quickly, if you like."

"Will this godsdamned argument never end?" Malcolm snapped. He stepped between Gast and Durand, both of whom had hands on hilts. "The enemy true has shown himself, and still we throw accusations back and forth like children at play. This fight is over! Neither Suhdra nor Tener will stand against this threat if we're going to be at one another's throats the whole time!"

"When I am about to fight a battle, and a dagger appears in my back, it is only natural that I look across the field at my enemy," Helenne said. "No one benefited from this betrayal more than you, Houndhallow."

"That is what you name me now? Enemy? Why meet with me here, if your only offer is a threat?"

"My lord?" Sir Doone whispered. Malcolm waved her off.

"Haven't you seen enough, Galleydeep? By your own man's admission, these priests of Cinder joined his party, and later turned the cloak. What more do you need?"

"They summoned gheists," Durand said, "the feral gods of Tener. Who but pagan witches can do that?"

"You're saying witches now walk the earth in Cinder's robes. Is that what you believe?"

"I believe what I've seen. A Tenerran army defending the heretic Adair, led by your hand. Tenerran gheists murdering my people when we march against you. And a Tenerran god nearly destroying Greenhall, to keep Sophie Halverdt from joining us here. How do you explain these things?"

"What happened at Greenhall?" Malcolm asked. Bassion paused.

"Pagan treachery. An unleashed god, unknown to the vow knights stationed there. It nearly destroyed the city." Helenne frowned at him. "This keeps happening around you, Houndhallow. Unknown gods defeating Suhdrin armies, and you as innocent as a dove."

"They're trying to keep this war between our countries going, Helenne. Surely you see—"

"If that was the case, why didn't they let us fight one another? Hm? Why stab me in the back when they could have simply held back and let us destroy each other? As I said, no one benefited from this more than you." Her eyes flickered to Sir Tasse, then into the darkness where the woman was staring. Bassion hesitated, then flicked her reins and rode into the forest, calling back over her shoulder as she went. "You can play the victim all you want, Malcolm. Your ink is on your face, and your guilt as well."

Hallister and the Fabron men sneered and followed their lady. Sir Tasse hesitated for a long moment, for the first time tearing her eyes away from the darkness to look at Malcolm. Then she, too, followed in Bassion's wake. Only the priest, Frair Rhone, remained.

"She is scared, Houndhallow. Scared and quick to accuse. You must give her time."

"Did she come here to betray me?" Malcolm asked. "Are her men surrounding us even now?"

"She was ready to act, if you attacked, but she wanted to talk. She still wants to talk, it's just..." Rhone struggled for words, finally shrugging. "She does not trust you. She does not trust anyone, anymore."

"I can't blame her. Still—"

Malcolm's voice caught in his throat. He was staring at Frair Rhone, the woman's pale face and black robes framed in the moonlight. The arrow in her throat was just as black, and spouting blood.

"To arms!" Malcolm shouted. The priest's horse bucked, nearly throwing the dying woman to the ground. Rhone was clawing at the shaft of the arrow, eyes wide, mouth gaping. A flight of arrows fell into the trees before them. Men and women started shouted. Rhone's horse finally bolted, darting back into the forest whence it had come.

"We must run!" Doone yelled. The arrows weren't aimed at them, but the distance was close. "Back to the camp, quickly!"

"Did you see that woman? The Tasse knight, who first brought the offer of peace from Lady Bassion? That arrow came from the direction she was looking in. She knew! She knew we were about to be ambushed!" MaeHerron snapped.

"Why would one of Bassion's knights shoot at Bassion's priest? No." Malcolm turned his mount. He could see the shadows forming behind them now, the trees of the distant copse bristling with spears. A section of horse came out of the trees and started trotting in their direction. "We must follow Galleydeep. There's no other way."

"She won't believe us," Doone said, but she spurred her horse and launched herself into the forest. The rest followed.

This copse was thin, not more than thirty feet of woods before it opened onto grasslands once again. Evidence of Bassion's supporting force was everywhere. The grass was churned into mud, and a handful of weapons lay strewn about. Looking more closely, Malcolm saw the bodies, torn and lying in the grass. The ground was thick with arrows, like a fletched thicket.

What remained of Bassion's force hurried up the hill. Most were mounted, but a few staggered up the incline, throwing down shields and swords in their haste. The rain of arrows stopped, but the rumbling sound of a great many horses trembled through the ground. When those on foot turned and saw Malcolm, they screamed and ran faster.

"We must speak to Helenne! She must know we had nothing to do with this!" Malcolm leaned low to his horse's neck, lashing it forward. He could hear Doone and

MaeHerron behind him. The Suhdrin party had quite a lead already, and the terror of pursuit sped them on. They would crest the hill long before Malcolm reached them. Then he spotted something along the ridgeline, and pulled up.

A small party of mounted celestial knights accompanied three riders dressed in dark vestments. They came over the ridge at a trot, as casual as hunters who have cornered their prey. The air around them was thick with mist and twisting shadows.

The lead priest raised his staff, and a flash of light crackled through the air. A wave of fog fountained from the staff and slowly rolled down the valley, sweeping aside the tall grasses and creeping toward the Suhdrins. It enveloped them in a heartbeat, shielding Bassion's retreating party from Malcolm's eyes.

Figures rose out of the fog. A dozen loping forms grew like tumors in the mist, larger and larger until they towered over Malcolm's head, taller on foot than the Tenerrans were mounted, arms bristling with sharp talons and gaping teeth instead of faces. Their flesh was pale, but the cruel edge of their claws glowed as bright as freshly fallen snow, and their misshapen bodies capered down the hill with liquid grace. Inside the fog, the Suhdrins began to scream.

"Into the gods! Spears into the pagan gods! For Strife! For Tenumbra!" Malcolm yelled. He drew the black steel of his feyiron blade. His knights gave a ragged yell, then they were hammering forward, their charge a panicked, tumbling gallop. Tendrils of fog whipped around their hooves.

Closer and closer, the silent gods risen from fog, and Malcolm's blade. Malcolm screamed his fury, but the mist swallowed them. They came together in silence.

12

THE SONG OF combat rang up from the doma, echoing through the stone walls of the courtyard like a struck bell. The crowds of Tenerrans and pagans rushing around in the wake of the gheist attack stood gaping at the noise. The sound of blade on blade was distinct, as were the screams of wounded soldiers.

"What in hell is going on down there?" Ian asked. He and Sir Clough stood in one of the many windows of the keep. The crowds in the courtyard were starting to realign themselves, pagans with pagans, loyal Tenerrans with others of the Blakley banner. There would be violence soon, no matter what Ian did.

"They were coming for you. Because of what happened to Cahl," Clough said.

"And what did happen to Cahl?" Ian asked. "I gave it to Bruler to follow the man, and now they're both dead. Is that coincidence?"

"Bruler lives, Ian. He was even now discharged from the infirmary."

"He lives for now. If this continues, few of us will see the dawn." Ian whirled on Sir Clough. The woman stood defiantly, hand comfortably on the hilt of her sword. "Did you have something to do with this? I saw Gwen and the elders pass into the doma. Did you arrange for them to be ambushed?"

"I arranged nothing. But someone has taken matters into their own hands." Clough shrugged. "Think of it as a gift. The question of what to do has been answered for you. The pagans must go."

"We only just saved this castle from one battle. It's too soon to be seeking another fight, especially among our extremely limited allies." Ian slammed his fist against the shutters, rattling them. "We have too many enemies already, Clough."

"The tribes should never have been our allies to begin with. It's their friendship that earned us the mistrust of the church."

"It's their friendship that kept this castle from burning to the ground!"

"Odd. I remember these same tribesmen swarming the walls and setting the fires. Perhaps things looked otherwise from where you were standing." She paused for a long moment. "Outside the walls."

"We've been through this. Either you accept me as my father's son and the heir to this castle, or you don't. It was the voidfather who waged war against us, the voidfather whom I killed. The tribes were his victims as well."

"I have dead soldiers who feel differently," Clough said stiffly. Ian shook his head.

"Zealots. The world must be burned clean and the enemy purged at the hands of zealots. How am I supposed to build a life around that?" Ian pushed away from the window, grabbing his breastplate from a nearby stand and starting the complicated process of strapping it on. "Help me with this, will you?"

"So you'll fight?"

"My sister is here, and my father's loyal bannermen. Whether I wanted this fight or not, it's here. If I can talk Gwendolyn down, I will. If I can't, then yes, I will fight."

Clough nodded and moved to help him, pulling tight on the straps that secured the plate. She reached for his greaves.

"There's no time for that. If it comes to battle, I won't be on horseback, and don't want to be hindered by that much steel. My shield and helm will have to do."

"Your men need to see you as a knight, my lord. For weeks now they've seen you in pagan leathers, and pagan company. You are not your father, but you must look like him."

"I do not need to be reminded of that, sir," Ian snapped. "The shield and the helm. If the men confuse me for a pagan, it will be their own fault, not mine."

Clough hesitated, but finally unhooked Ian's helm from the stand and handed it to him, along with his shield. She stood by the door while he finished.

"You should stay away from the doma. Until the deed is done, at least. You can deny having been involved."

"Or I can stop it," Ian said, pushing past her.

"My lord—"

"Enough with reasons!" Ian snapped, and hurried out of the room.

The halls of the keep were hectic with the efficient business of professional soldiers. Men-at-arms bustled from room to room, waking their comrades and spreading word of the fight below. Sergeants stood in doorways yelling while clouds of squires flocked around their knights, buckling on armor and soothing nerves. Everyone was too busy to notice Ian and Sir Clough, though a clear space opened up around the pair as they hurried down the hall. No one met Ian's eyes.

"Did I order a war footing?"

"No, my lord. But war has come to us, and these men are accustomed to its song." Clough stuck close to his side, weaving between obstructions. "As long as we hold this keep, we can hold the castle."

"Or maybe we can clear up this misunderstanding before it becomes a matter of siege." He pulled up short as a work crew spilled into the hallway. They were carrying a burden of lumber. "What in hell is this?"

"Barricades, my lord. The great hall has already fallen. Master Tavvish has us securing the approaches to the balcony, in case they choose to rush the keep."

"The balcony, you said? Then that is where we begin."

The way to the balconies that overlooked the great hall was strangely silent. Ian burst into the balcony with his shield up and sword in hand. He was nearly alone. The only Tenerrans on the balcony were cowering behind the balustrade, clutching crossbows and whispering nervously among themselves. Of Tavvish, or any other form of authority, there was no sign.

The great hall below was in chaos. Crowds of pagans milled about, talking angrily, calling for calm, calling for battle, calling for the gods. Many of them were still recovering from injuries taken at the battle of Houndhallow, row after row of cots crowded with the old and infirm. Those on their feet were mostly the families of the tribesmen, sheltering inside the castle against the coming winter. No more than a third were fighting men and women, all of different tribes, none of them shamans or witches.

"What is this?" Ian said. "I was told this room had fallen. There was no battle here." He raised his voice to address the pagans below. "Who speaks for you?"

"What have you done, Ian of Hounds?" The speaker was a tall woman, dressed in the camouflaged cloak and leathers of the rangers. Her hair was plaited into looping braids that clung to her head like a ram's horns. She stepped onto one of the long tables that ran the length of the hall. "We heard the gheist horns, but now we hear battle in the courtyard."

"I will find out what it means. For now, you should stay here and protect your families. I swear to you, they will be safe."

"As though we had a choice," the woman said. She nodded toward the doors. "We have been barricaded inside."

Ian turned to Clough, then to one of the crossbowmen hiding behind the balustrade.

"What are your orders?" The man didn't move, so Ian gave him a kick. "Your orders!"

"We are to hold the pagans here, until further instruction. If they try to leave…" The man paused uncertainly, his eyes darting to Sir Clough.

"If they try to leave, you are to shoot them down like pigs in a sty," Ian finished. "That will not happen. I will not have a massacre in my hall. Clough, see these men dispersed, and those doors opened."

"Whatever the reason for their imprisonment, it would be better if we did not strengthen the enemy's numbers. There is no harm in keeping them here."

"There is harm in thinking of them as the enemy!" He whirled on the crossbowmen. "Go down into the keep, see to the defenses, but do not shoot anyone." The men began to shuffle off, but Ian grabbed one of them. "And your orders. Who gave them to you?"

The man glanced at Clough before he answered. "Master Tavvish, my lord."

"And where is Tavvish?" No one had an answer for him, so he pushed them out the door. "Our first order of business is to find Tavvish and prevent him from starting a war. As soon as we get those doors open." He leaned over the balcony. "You will be free soon, my lady, though this may still be the safest place for you."

"Open those doors and we'll quit this castle immediately," she said. "I have had enough of narrow walls for a lifetime."

"Clough, stay here and ensure no one shoots these people," he said. The knight nodded shortly. "I mean it. No shooting, for any reason."

"You are the lord of this castle, and I will obey," Sir Clough said. "But remember your sister. If your orders endanger young Ness, I will be the first to ignore them."

"I will do nothing to endanger my sister," Ian said. When the knight didn't answer, Ian rushed out of the balcony and headed for the stairs.

The twisting staircase that led to the main level was already the victim of Master Tavvish's planned barricades. Barrels and twisted planks of wood cluttered the narrow stairs, and guards stood with spears protruding out of murder holes. Ian tore down the barricades and ordered the guards back upstairs, yelling the whole way. He got about halfway through the barricades before Tavvish found him. The master of hearth wore a chain shirt over his fine silk, with a sword strapped awkwardly to his hip.

"My lord, what are you doing?"

"Correcting a terrible misunderstanding," Ian answered.

"You are endangering the lives of every honest celestial in this castle, my lord! We must stop this fight before it gets out of hand!"

"Exactly what I'm trying to do, Tavvish. Who the hell gave you the authority to take these steps, anyway? Why was I not consulted on any of this?"

"Your father gave me the authority!" Tavvish said. The old man quivered with anger and old age. He had taken a wound during the siege, but instead of weakening him, the injury had hardened him. "I swore to protect these walls and your family, until Lord Malcolm returned. His wife would not take my advice, insisted on galloping off to his side, and look what happened to her. Look what's happened to you! I'll be godsdamned before I let the same happen to your sister."

"You gave orders to cut down the injured and aged, to barricade the keep without knowing what battle lies outside, to make enemies of the very people who helped save this castle with neither reason nor provocation!" Ian shouted. "How in hell does that make my sister safer?"

"You weren't here," Tavvish said. "You didn't see them come over the walls. I had to stand on this keep and watch the castle fall, had to stand beside your sister and assure her it would be okay, all the while knowing that every one of us was as good as dead."

"I was here. I ended that fight, along with the very people you are trying to have killed."

Tavvish tilted his head, listening to the sounds of battle rising from the doma, the screams and clashing steel.

"That fight does not seem ended, my lord. And I aim to win it, whether you will or not."

"Then I must relieve you of your position, Tavvish. You have served my family long and well, but this is an error I cannot overlook." Ian turned back to the barricade, pulling it down. "I will name another master of hearth."

"Only your father may relieve me, and he is not here."

"I am his heir, and the rightful ruler of this castle in his absence." Ian glanced over his shoulder. "And I will make peace in his name."

"You may have his blood, Ian, but not his authority." Tavvish drew his blade, and for a moment Ian thought he would have to defend himself from the old knight. The moment passed. Tavvish turned and trudged back up the stairs. "Hammet, Billes, Durant! Get over here. Start rebuilding this wall. Godsbless, we'll keep the pagans out, whatever the young lord asks of us."

Ian cursed under his breath, then pushed through the barricade. The lower half of the stairs was abandoned, but at the foot, a crowd of pagans milled about nervously. Ian recognized a young lad, one of the rangers who had ridden with him to kill the voidfather.

"Hassek!" Ian shouted. The pagan turned to him, the fetishes of bone in his hair clattering as he turned. Momentary recognition was quickly replaced with anger.

"This is not my doing, before you ask," Ian said quickly. "I'm trying to clear things up. Do you know what the hell is going on?"

"Traitors' blades fell on the elders as they walked through the doma, seeking you. We were told you were at prayer. For all we know, the elders are all dead, and Lady Adair with them."

"It will take more than treachery to kill Gwen Adair. They are still in the doma?"

"Yes. We're going there now, to free them."

"Take me with you. I still have some authority in this place."

"We'll have more need of your blade than your word, I suspect." Hassek looked Ian up and down with distaste. "But we'll take both. This way, my lord."

The last two words were twisted with anger, but Hassek trotted off toward the doma, and Ian followed.

13

THE FOG CLOSED around them, swallowing the sounds of battle. Malcolm charged forward, even as the mists hid the ground and shrouded his knights. The black blade of his sword cut through the fog like flame through snow. The mists peeled away from the feyiron. Malcolm slowed, wheeling his mount, searching for the rest of his troop. There was only fog and silence.

A pale figure lumbered out of the mists. It was taller than Malcolm and his mount together, its twisted shoulders even with the top of Malcolm's head, muscled arms raised high. Its hands bristled with talons, as many as the petals of a thistle, sharp thorns that glowed white as though they burned from inside. Its head was short, lacking any feature besides a wide mouth, full of teeth. Its skin sagged at the joints, as though its muscles were wasting away.

It caught sight of Malcolm and turned toward him. The gheist roared, but instead of sound, a stream of coiling mist poured out of its mouth. Malcolm wheeled to face the creature, flicking his sword back and forth to clear the mists.

"I have faced worse than you, mortal and divine," he said. "I will not be turned aside by clouds and palsied skin."

The gheist didn't answer, but charged forward, its loping

pace shaking the ground. Malcolm spurred his horse. The gap closed quickly, distances shrinking in the fog, and in a breath they were together. The gheist swung its mighty arms like clubs, the flanged thorns of its hands whistling through the air as it struck. Malcolm caught one of the fists on his shield, dodging the other. The blow shivered through his bones. The gheist's talons dug deep gouges in the face of his shield, snagging it and nearly pulling it from Malcolm's grasp. Malcolm struck back, hacking down with his feyiron blade, chopping into the gheist's shoulders. The creature howled and bit down on Malcolm's arm. Its rows of teeth clamped down on the thick steel of his vambrace, crushing chain into flesh and rippling the metal. He nearly dropped his sword, but instead punched with his shield, knocking the gheist's jaws free of its grip.

Malcolm wheeled away, cradling his arm as he retreated. Pain throbbed through his body, and his eyes swam with dark spots. The gheist stumbled away, silently howling, fog streaming from its wounds. It went to one knee. Malcolm clenched his jaw, testing his grip. Pain washed through him every time he grasped the hilt of his sword, but his hand seemed to be working. He guided his mount slowly to the gheist's side.

"Whatever god you were before the church got hold of you, I pray for a better sleep for you. And when you rise again, I pray a holier spirit will guide you." Malcolm raised his sword, then struck down at the stunned gheist. The creature's head split open. The wound traveled down its chest, flesh parting like a torn banner, twisting apart in pale streamers. Thick fog plumed across the ground, and then the gheist was gone. An area of clean air opened up around Malcolm.

The sky cleared, and for a brief moment Malcolm was staring up at the moon and its host of stars. Cinder's cold light bathed the valley, turning the fog into silver gauze. The trees in the valley below swayed like ghosts, animated by the movement of the celestial army through them. Malcolm enjoyed a moment of peace. The throbbing in his arm eased.

It was short-lived. The fog rolled in again, cutting Malcolm off from the sky and shielding him from Cinder's gaze. The pain returned, and with it the realization that he was cut off from the rest of his army, surrounded by gheists and unholy priests, not to mention Bassion's suspicions.

The fog thickened near him, resolving into another unusually tall figure. Malcolm was preparing to strike when he realized the figure was mounted. Moments later, Sir Doone charged past him, her horse sidestepping and bucking its way through the fog. Her shield was torn in half, and fresh dents shone brightly on her helm and the pauldron of her left shoulder. She discarded her shattered spear and drew her sword, whirling to face Malcolm as he approached.

"Hold, Doone!" Malcolm shouted. The knight froze for a second, then turned to face the direction she had come from. A second shadow had followed her. The gheist crashed into her, club-like fist banging against the remnants of her shield. Doone tangled her sword in the barbs of the creature's other fist, screaming as the force of the blow twisted her shoulder and nearly knocked her out of the saddle.

Malcolm paused for a heartbeat, watching in shock as Doone and her attacker stumbled past him, nearly disappearing in the fog. Then he charged forward, falling on the gheist from behind, cutting stripes out of its back. The gheist ignored him, pressing the assault on Doone, until Doone's horse faltered.

Knight and gheist and mount tumbled to the ground. Malcolm held back, afraid he would strike Doone.

Their charge led the trio out of the fog bank, leaving only the trailing streamers of mist from the gheist to obscure them. A scattering of shadows moved through the fog, and the sounds of battle rose into the air, strangely clear. Down the hill, in the copse of trees, Malcolm could make out a line of mounted shapes marching slowly into the clear. Even in the ghostly light of the moon, Malcolm counted dozens. They could not be his own people; the ones he could see did not look like Bassion's troops. They were cut off. There would be no retreat, not in that direction.

Malcolm's attention was drawn back to Doone by the sound of steel striking flesh. Doone had twisted free of her fallen mount, and was slashing down at the gheist, who was still tangled with the horse. Malcolm quickly dismounted, placing the tip of his sword at the center of the gheist, then leaning against it. The feyiron blade smoothly split the gheist open. In a final wave of choking mist, the spirit died.

"Watch the horse!" Doone shouted. The war-trained destrier was already scrambling to its feet. Doone snatched the reins and looked around. "Back into the mists?" she asked.

"We need to find Lady Bassion. Make sure she's safe. If the leader of the Suhdrin army is killed by a gheist while parlaying with us, it will be the end of our hopes for an alliance." Malcolm wiped ash from his sword, wheeling his horse toward the mist. "If she remains in the mists, we have no choice but to go back in."

Doone nodded and mounted smoothly. The wall of mists swirled like the surface of a deep pond, troubled by unseen currents.

"What of the priests?" she asked. Malcolm glanced toward the top of the hill. The small guard of celestial troops escorted the trio of priests over the ridge and out of sight. Malcolm shook his head.

"Let them go. We'll settle matters with them later."

A groaning roar came from the mists, along with the clash of steel and screaming horses. Malcolm urged his mount into the mists. The shrouded figure of Sir Doone followed close at heel. Once again, the fog swallowed all sound, leaving Malcolm deaf and damp in the chill air. He rode at a trot, straining into the murk, listening for any indication of the gheists, or the Bassions.

Instead, he found Grant MaeHerron, slowly dying. The lord of the Feltower was on his knees in the middle of a patch of churned sod, cradling his axe in his hands. There were other bodies around him, wearing the black and red of Fabron. Malcolm hurried to the man's side, dismounting and kneeling. MaeHerron looked up at him with cloudy eyes.

"Lord MaeHerron," Malcolm whispered, "what happened here?"

"It falls to my sister, now," he said. MaeHerron closed his eyes, tipping his head forward, but Malcolm grabbed the man's shoulder and shook him back to life. MaeHerron stared at him. "Why do you keep me from my father's hall?"

"What happened?" Malcolm hissed.

"The gods saw fit to—" MaeHerron took a gasping breath "—fit to see us dead. This lot, already fighting. I joined." He laughed, and blood bubbled onto his lips. "Should have let it kill them. Should have kept... kept riding."

"You were never the sort to ride past a fight," Malcolm said. "And neither was your father. But now—"

Horns sounded to the west. The mist began to thin, and Cinder's light revealed the terrain. The head of the valley was thick with flames, the flickering light of a thousand campfires. It was the celestial line. The sentry horns sounded again. At the top of the ridge, Malcolm spotted Lady Bassion and her escort, down to two knights, just as they disappeared out of sight. In the celestial camp, a column of riders stirred and started riding toward them.

"Their army marches. How in the hells did they know we were meeting Bassion here?" Doone muttered. "We'll be crushed."

Malcolm snatched MaeHerron's bloody axe, then mounted.

"The priests will collect the dead," he said. "Gods pray they give MaeHerron rest. He's earned it. Let's get out of here, before those riders catch sight of us."

Another horn caught Malcolm's attention, this one close and loud. Over the ridge that he and Doone had just crossed, banners bristled and armor flashed. For a brief moment, Malcolm thought they were ruined. Then he spotted Castian Jaerdin riding at the column's head.

"Redgarden!" he shouted. Jaerdin waved in his direction and rode closer. "You heard the horns?"

"A handful of your riders came to us, with the dying priest. I have brought what strength I can. Bit of a fight getting here, though..." Jaerdin's voice trailed off as he scanned the celestial line. "They've already cut off our retreat. We may get reinforcement from the camps, but it will be too late, and not enough."

"We must hold until they arrive, sir. Doone, see to MaeHerron's body. Jaerdin, with me. We must stand!"

14

A SHEET OF WATER rippled over the beaten earth of the courtyard, lapping against Ian's toes before sinking into the dirt. A crowd of pagans swirled around the entrance to the doma, their voices a confused jumble of panic and alarm. On the tower, the gheist horn fell silent. Ian grabbed Hassek by the shoulder.

"There were guards here. Tenerrans. What has become of them?" he asked.

"Any not of the tribes has fled, my lord," Hassek answered, again twisting those last two words in his mouth like a bitter herb. "Some few have converted to the old ways, but gods know if they can be trusted. Each will have to answer for their betrayal of the true gods, I imagine." He grinned at Ian menacingly, then twisted out of Ian's grip and rushed toward the doma.

As Ian watched, a ring of shouting men dragged a guard wearing the Blakley colors out from behind a wagon. They threw him to the ground in front of the doma, then started throwing trash and stones at the man. Ian stepped forward to intervene when a hand grabbed his collar. He turned to see Henri Volent, wrapped in a heavy cloak, his face mostly obscured by the deep cowl.

"You shouldn't be here, little hound. Neither of us should be."

"They have one of my men," Ian said. "I can't leave him to the crowd."

"Try to save him, and they'll have two gallows to raise instead of one." From behind Ian, the guard screamed as the crowd set on him with their boots. Ian flinched, but Volent pulled him closer. "Three, if we stay much longer."

"I can't leave him."

"You leave men in battle all the time, to save others. And there are many others to save here. If you hope to keep this castle, it will not be done here. Quickly!"

Ian clenched his jaw. The guard's screams had stopped. Stained glass shattered as someone threw a chair through a window of the doma. A line of pagans was dragging bodies out of the building, throwing the Tenerran dead into a pile while carefully lining up their own casualties. Soon after, a roar of applause went through the crowd. Ian turned to look. The doma was in flames.

"That is the house of the gods that they burn," he said. "My gods, on my land."

"Sterling wisdom, Blakley. Now come on. We have to get out of here before we're recognized."

Ian paused, pulling back against Volent's urgent tug. He stared at the flames spiraling up through the topmost calendar windows, their light as hot and as bright as a smithy's forge. How many had died in the doma? How many more would die, before this was over? He looked down at the doors to the doma, to see if any were still fleeing the burning building.

Gwen Adair stood just outside the door, her form limned by the flames inside. Even with her strange iron blood flaked away, Gwen looked fey against the firelight. She was dressed half in the Suhdrin-style armor of the nobility, and half in the camouflaged leathers of the tribes. She was a girl broken between worlds, bringing them together and tearing them apart. *Much like me,* Ian thought.

Gwen was looking right at him, staring him down. Her gaze pinned him in place. Would she call the crowd's attention to him? Would she march over and kill him herself? Neither. Gwen turned away. Ian pulled his hood over his head and turned to Volent.

"Let's get out of here," he whispered.

"Godsbless," Volent answered. The two cloaked forms scurried away.

What they found was chaos. The few Tenerrans outside the keep, whether they were still guarding the tower or the stables, or off duty in the barracks when Daxter and his renegades struck in the doma, had quickly found themselves overrun by angry pagans. Few knew why Houndhallow was falling to violence, either among the attackers or their victims. Once the blades were out, few questioned their need. They simply killed, to save themselves or to vent generations of frustration and anger.

"Like pigs to the slaughter. Tavvish will answer for this," Ian said. The hallway they entered looked like a battlefield. Overturned tables bristled with arrows, bodies littered the floor, and flames from spilled torches licked the walls.

"Tavvish didn't do this killing," Volent said. He threw off the cloak that enveloped him, revealing full armor underneath. Ian sometimes wondered if the man slept in that armor, so rarely was he without it. "The man did what he thought was right.

Gods know you haven't exactly been leading by example."

"What the hell does that mean?"

"It means that this has been simmering for weeks. You can't just name us all friends and expect it to be true. If it wasn't Tavvish, or some other faithful Tenerran, then it would have been the tribes who struck first."

"This is all Tavvish's fault," Ian said. "If he hadn't made those barricades—"

"If he hadn't barricaded the keep, there probably wouldn't be a living Tenerran inside the castle walls by now. Stop thinking like your father for a minute, Ian. There's no peace to be had here. Letting the pagans inside the walls was a mistake, but there's nothing to be done about it."

"I will not let Tavvish's mistakes, my father's indecision, or Gwen Adair's pagans take this castle," Ian spat. "Come on. We're going to the keep."

"And if Tavvish's soldiers try to stop us?"

"They are not Tavvish's spears to command. They are mine."

Fortunately, the men at the gate and the women watching over the approach with their crossbows all knew Ian, and allowed him passage, though they gave Volent a share of nervous looks. The fighting here had passed. There were no bodies, though bloody smears on the floor indicated their recent removal. Scared knights and children watched from the doorways leading off the main hall as Ian marched up the stairs, to the living quarters.

"Where is Master Tavvish?" Ian boomed. Those nearest looked away, though a few held Ian's angry stare with their own looks of defiance. "Where is the man who tried to take my authority from me, in my own house?"

"You took that name from me, my lord," Tavvish said, stepping into the hallway from one of the adjoining rooms. He carried a short bow and three quivers, and his forearm bled from being struck by the draw of the string. "For now I fight only to earn my honor, and to protect those I swore to keep safe."

"You have overstepped your bounds, Tavvish," Ian said. "You were set to slaughter those pagans, and look what it's bought you. Any of our people not inside this keep are dead, or worse. Gods know what's happening in the village, or surrounding farms. Where is your oath to protect them?"

"I saved those I could."

"No, you betrayed my trust, acted in secret, and abandoned any who would not bend to your selfish will." Ian leaned close to the man, but Tavvish did not flinch. "How does this end, Tavvish? How do we get out of this without all of us dead?"

"If we kill enough pagans, they'll surely break."

"Count the spears," Ian said, aware in the back of his mind that he was echoing Cahl's words from earlier that night. "Four pagans for every one of us."

"Then we'll kill four for every Tenerran that falls!" Tavvish spat. "Your father would do no less!"

"Do not bring my father into this. Malcolm Blakley would never arrange the slaughter of the innocent," Ian said. "You are not worthy of uttering his name!"

"You offend my honor, whelp," Tavvish growled. "Be careful of your next words. Men have paid in steel for lesser insults."

"Would you kill my sister for your honor? What of these children?" He motioned to the families at the end of the hall.

"These husbands, these wives? Do they need to die for your honor, Tavvish?"

"Your father would understand—"

"My father is not here; I am! My father is not in command of this castle right now. And neither are you, Master Tavvish." Ian gave the hefty old man a push, and was pleased to see him flinch away. "I am the heir of Houndhallow, and in my father's absence, I am its lord and commander. And I will not brook this insubordination any longer."

"What's it matter?" Tavvish said sharply. "Complain all you want. You would not act, so I did. You would not lead, so I did. You yell and you threaten, but the die is already thrown." Tavvish turned away. "This battle will be fought, and we will fall, or we won't. Our lives are in the hands of the gods. Take your comfort in that, child."

The blade went smoothly through Tavvish's bulk. The master of hearth stared down at the bloody tip protruding from his chest, blinking in shock. He tried to draw breath, but his lungs would only burble and rattle and wheeze. Ian whipped out the sword, and Tavvish collapsed to the ground.

"So to any who would take Houndhallow from the Blakleys," Ian whispered. "And so to you, Tavvish. I will pray for your soul."

15

THE SUHDRIN CAMP erupted into chaos. A growing tide of panic spread out from Halverdt's picket line; those closest to the main bonfire dropped whatever they were doing and fled. From their distant location, Lucas and Elsa weren't able to make out what was happening.

"We need to get closer," Lucas said. He snatched his staff off the ground and began unwinding the cloths he had used to hide the symbols of Cinder.

"Are you sure that's wise?" Martin asked. "Everyone else seems to be running away."

"Everyone else is a coward," Elsa answered. She already had her sword out of its linen bindings. "You have nothing to fear, Martin. You're not the kind of heretic these people like to burn."

"I'm not sure they'll take the time to ask," Martin said, but Lucas was already pushing through the crowd, with Elsa close behind. Martin gave their campsite one last look, then followed at a trot.

The fleeing camp followers and merchants made hard going, but eventually they were able to reach a low hill that overlooked the army's main camp. They looked down on ordered rows of tents that were interspersed with campfires, joined by braziers at every intersection and along the perimeter. A central bonfire cast long shadows. Elsa turned to Lucas.

"Something's spooked these people, but I'm not sure what it is. The flowering of spring seems to be all around us. But in the camp—"

"It's the bonfire. Or rather, the ritual occurring around the fire," Lucas said. He bent to the ground and started laying out a circle of icons around his legs. "I'm going into the naether. Guard me."

"I want to get closer. Martin, you watch the frair."

"Shouldn't you do that? I mean, I don't know much about—"

"Do you want to go in there?" Elsa snapped. Martin flinched back, but didn't answer. "Then stay here and watch Lucas. Keep anyone from, I don't know, lynching him or something. I'll be back."

Elsa didn't wait for Martin to answer. She ran down the hill, cradling her blade and keeping her eyes up. The grounds looked like an abandoned battlefield now that the crowd had scattered. Overturned carts, trampled tents, scattered possessions, and churned mud were all that remained of them. Under the influence of the sudden spring, grass sprouted up from the earth in unnaturally vital shades of green, and the occasional trees hung heavy with leaves and fruit as thick as hives. Even the clouds that hung low over the camp churned with greenish light, as though they would sprout a spring storm at any moment.

As she approached the picket line, Elsa slowed down. This was where the panic had started. And now she could see why. What she had taken as embers drifting from the bonfire at the center of the camp were actually glowing flowers. Petals of unearthly shades, as bright as lightning, spun lazily through the air. Where they landed, the ground turned to molten spring, boiling with growth and spewing clouds of pollen and light. More than one of these clouds hovered over dead bodies; civilians struck by the flowers, or children who had rushed to pick them up. Their flesh was green with viny growth, their faces locked in a rictus of joy as malevolent spring burrowed through their bodies.

A spinning flower drifted toward Elsa. She swung at it, popping it like a boil, and spun away. The burning pollen sizzled on her clothes. Coughing, Elsa brushed the last of it off before it could latch into her flesh. Her lungs filled with the scent of tilled earth and rain clouds.

Elsa grabbed a discarded blanket and threw it over her head, then ran for the picket line. The guard post was abandoned, and with it the frairwood brazier. The flames in the brazier hissed in the darkness, glowing brighter than they should, hardly throwing out any of the holy incense smoke that was their purpose. She rushed past.

Beyond the picket, the camp seemed in good order, if empty. Tent flaps opened into abandoned bivouacs, muddy lanes crossed through quiet regimental sections, guard posts remained unmanned. The deeper she went, the stranger it felt. Finally, she reached the center of the camp.

There was no bonfire. At the center of clearing, Sophie Halverdt stood in front of a column of flame that reached the low cloud roof overhead. She was flanked by half a dozen vow knights. The rest of the army, what remained of it, stood in nervous rows around the flames. They were all in full armor, carrying travel packs and torches of bundled frairwood. Sophie's voice carried over the crowd, exhorting them onward to glory.

Slowly, one at a time, the army was filing into the flame. When each man reached the coruscating wall of fire, his shadow sank into the light, like a body sinking into deep water. A cloud of spinning flowers went up, and then he would disappear into ash. Those who hesitated were pushed forward by vow knights. The flames consumed all.

"This is the gift of the bright lady!" Sophie was yelling. "Give yourself to her, and be reborn! We live not to fulfill the winter vow, but to end it! To end the need for it! So give yourself to flame, give yourself to fury, give yourself to summer and the war eternal! Rise, rise, rise!"

A cadre of mounted knights led their horses, blindfolded, into the flames. The smell of singed flesh filled the camp. Somewhere nearby there was screaming, though Elsa couldn't pinpoint its location. Slowly, she backed out of the clearing, hiding herself in the first tent she found.

A tangle of shadows in the corner of the tent resolved into Lucas's naetherform. He was a bare wisp of his usual self, merely cobwebs of darkness, almost in the shape of a man. If Elsa hadn't known him, she could have mistaken the frair for a trick of the light, or lack thereof.

"They're killing themselves," Elsa said. "Burning themselves alive in a column of fire. Gods, it's terrible. Even the horses!"

"I don't think so," Lucas answered. His voice was a bare whisper in her ear. "Those flames are not natural. Here, I will show you."

His hand reached out, tendrils of shadow melting around her shoulder, the touch as chill as the grave. Elsa's next breath was cold. She blinked, and was elsewhere.

"What is this?" Her voice boomed in the narrow space around her head. Lucas's hand tightened.

"Silence. This is no place for the living. See what the dead see."

There was a feeling of motion, and suddenly they were in the air. The neat rows of tents stretched out below them, bisected by a churning line of troubled clouds. Stick-figures swirled through the clouds, climbing higher and higher until they disappeared into the sky above. Lucas's voice reached through her bones and echoed through her skull.

"That is the column of fire. Whatever is happening to them, it is not death, though they are leaving this realm and traveling to another. The tomes of inquisition say nothing of this. I am at a loss."

As they watched, one of the figures strayed too close to the edge of the column and breached, tumbling out into the open air. The figure dissolved into a dozen smaller shapes, flowers lined with skulls, a petal of screaming mouths, a bouquet of grim teeth, falling down.

"The flowers," Elsa whispered as the dissipating figure drifted down to the ground. Lucas tightened his grip, reminding her to stay silent. She looked down at her feet, and realized her body was gone. The shock of it snapped her back to earth; she took a startled breath and fell flat on her back.

She was in the tent again. Lucas's naetherform hovered over her.

"You have to get moving. They're searching the camp for reluctant soldiers," he said. "Apparently not everyone was so eager to test the flame."

"What am I to do about Sophie? Can't I stop this?"

"If you had Strife's gifts, perhaps you could do something. As it is..." Lucas's shadowform began to unwind, disappearing into a knot of dark light. "Return to us."

When the inquisitor was gone, Elsa shook her head and stood up. The taste of frost lingered on her lips, and her head ached with what she had seen. As soon as she felt she was ready, Elsa crept out of the tent and started toward the picket, back the way she had come.

Three vow knights stepped out into the lane. Elsa froze, then straightened and shifted her sword into a guard position. Three more vow knights appeared behind her.

"There she is," one of them purred. "The lady bright said you would be joining us eventually. She could feel you in the train. She has been waiting patiently."

"And patience is not one of her virtues," another knight laughed. "Come now. There's no need to fight."

"There is always a need to fight," Elsa said. Before any of the knights could draw their blades or the power of Strife, she charged.

The three knights in front of her reacted well, as she knew they would. Even in the grips of whatever madness had consumed Halverdt's forces, no initiate of the Lightfort would be easily caught off guard. Elsa threw herself at the middle knight, using her sword as both battering ram and shield, blocking the knight's swiftly drawn blade before putting her shoulder into his belly. But Elsa wasn't wearing armor, and the chain and plate of the knight wrenched her shoulder. Together they tumbled to the ground. Elsa rolled, came to her feet, and took three unsteady steps toward freedom.

That's when the other two knights stepped in. They

hammered into Elsa's back, throwing her flat on her face, then kicked her sword out of her hand. She felt bones snap in her mangled hand and screamed.

"They always run," one of the knights muttered.

"That's what makes it worth doing," the other said, and all six laughed.

Elsa pushed herself onto her knees, cradling her broken hand.

A bolt of shadows shot out from the end of the lane, slamming into the nearest knight. Tangled darkness squirmed over him as he struggled. The other knights looked up.

Frair Lucas's shadowform crouched among the tents. He threw another bolt, then screamed into Elsa's head. "Run! I will hold—"

His sepulchral voice was cut off by a lance of flame. It came from the three farthest knights, their blades held together, summoning the full fury of Strife's power. The beam of light melted the naether that held Lucas together. He disappeared with a scream. On the distant hilltop where his body rested, Elsa could see a brief flare, and then a howl that cut through her soul.

"*Lucas!*" she shouted.

"Consorting with demons," one of the vow knights said. "No wonder the bright lady wants to see you." He swung the pommel of his blade into the back of Elsa's head. There was a blossom of pain, and then nothing.

She woke up hanging like a deer between two strong men, her arms and legs tied to a rail post, her mouth gagged. The pain was unimaginable. Her broken hand flopped loosely beneath the bonds, every movement grinding bone into bone. When she looked up, Sophie Halverdt was glaring down at her.

The duchess of Greenhall was much changed. Her gold armor, chased with cream and inlaid with the holiest runes of Strife, glistened in the firelight. Sophie's hair was shot through with streaks of brass and silver, and her eyes shimmered like copper pennies. Around her eyes, and running down her cheeks, were veins of golden light. Elsa's scars twinged at the sight of them. Whatever fire burned through Sophie's flesh, it didn't consume her skin, as it had Elsa's for so many years.

"I wondered when you would join us, broken one. Your spirit has lingered at the edges of my awareness for weeks now. I was afraid that if I pursued you, you would disappear into the wilds, never to be seen again. Thank the goddess you've come of your own accord."

"You have some strange ideas about free will," Elsa said, jerking her good hand against its bonds. "Are all of these fools here of their own accord as well? Or did you have to beat them into submission first?"

"Doubt must sometimes be tamed. It must be trained, turned inward. Cured." Sophie stepped forward, taking a ribbon of silk from her belt. She laid it over Elsa's broken hand and drew it tight.

The pain shivered through her arm. She tried not to scream, but the sound came through her clenched teeth, buckled her jaw, emptied her lungs. Sophie leaned down, putting her head close to Elsa's

"Just so," Sophie said. "Bones broken and set. Wills shattered, only to be aligned with the will of the goddess. Remember, Elsa, a stained-glass window was once nothing more than broken glass, and an artist's dream."

"You're fucking mad," Elsa growled. Bile filled her

mouth, but she swallowed it back, staring up at Sophie's placid face. "Worse than your father ever was."

"They always say that about prophets. Now, if you don't mind. It's time to put your faith to the test." Sophie straightened and signaled to the two men holding Elsa's post. They heaved her up, until her feet barely scraped the ground.

She thought the pain would knock her out again, but something else kept her awake. Fear. Horrifying, shivering, mind-breaking fear.

The column of flame sizzled in front of her. The heat that washed off it licked away her sweat and turned her skin into stone. With each step, pain echoed through her, as she got closer and closer to the fire. The flames reached out and singed her hair.

They carried her, screaming, into the fire.

16

THE FLAMES FROM the doma rose into the sky. Woodsmoke mingled with the sweet stink of burning bodies, turning Gwen's stomach. As the structure slowly collapsed, she faced the elders once again.

"I suppose you're going to blame me for this," she said. Kesthe smiled, a flash of humor before she set her expression again. The others didn't move. Their faces were washed in light from the conflagration behind Gwen. "Are your people done murdering farm boys and hanging lone guardsmen up by their feet?"

"We were attacked, Gwen. These people ambushed us."

"So it's natural to just kill everyone you come across, even if they had nothing to do with it?"

"They abandoned the true gods," Kesthe said. "They made their choice. I have no sympathy for them."

"A shocking lack of empathy from the elder of bones," Gwen said wryly. "Must I remind you that your predecessor betrayed us all, following Folam Voidfather in his deception?"

"No, but I'm sure you will," Kesthe answered. "You rarely miss an opportunity to hold that over my head. Thank the gods there's no blemish on your sainted soul, *huntress*."

"We must not argue among ourselves," Vilday said

shortly. "Whatever your sympathies for Ian Blakley, and the debt you owe his father for standing with your family, we cannot forgive this trespass. They attacked us. And they must pay the price."

"What price is that? Every one of them dead, and their tower burned? Would you salt their fields, as well? Murder the farmers that fill their granaries, and the farriers who shoe their mounts? And what of the other noble houses of Tener? Shall we lay siege to them all, and tear their names from the pages of history?"

"It would be a start," Kesthe said. Noel shook her head and stepped forward.

"There will be no peace in the north until this is settled. And no one will forgive us if we blot the name of Blakley from the earth. They are Tener's greatest name, and oldest family. Malcolm Blakley commands an army to the south, and those banners came at his word and in his trust. They would turn on us like fire turns on chaff."

"We do not need advice from a Suhdrin coward," Kesthe said. "Let Tenerrans rule the tribes, I say. We have plenty of witches of the tribe of flames."

"And I am their elder," Noel said. "Or do you no longer recognize the will of the gods who chose me?"

"This is what he wanted," Gwen said. She grabbed Kesthe by the shoulder and spun her around, locking eyes with her. "Folam Voidfather wanted us to fight, just like this. To be at each other's throats, rather than at his. And I will not fall in with his plans again. There will be no massacre here. Either of Blakleys or tribesmen. This ends. Now."

"Who are you to order such things?" Kesthe asked, her lip curled. "You don't command us!"

"Don't I?" Gwen arched her brow. Kesthe spat, but Gwen pushed her away and rounded on the other elders. "Don't I? Why else do you seek to correct me? Do I have no authority among you? I am no elder of the tribes, not even of a living tribe of Tenumbra. Yet you try to bend my ear, and my will with it. Why is that? Why do you think, Kesthe? Why haven't you done what you want, rather than talking to me about it first?"

"Because the gods have blessed you," Vilday said simply. The other elders tensed, but the old man shrugged. "It is true. You have held Fomharra, and the mad god of spring, and who knows what others. They grace you with their presence. Noel is right. We may argue among ourselves, but it is by the will of the gods that we rule. And the gods clearly favor you, Adair."

"They know true faith," Noel said. "And we must bend to their will."

"Do you all agree to this, then? I will lead this gathering of the tribes. There has been enough madness, enough bloodshed, enough treachery. I know what must be done, even if I don't like it."

"This is foolish. She was praying in a doma this time last year—" Kesthe was cut short by Vilday's upturned hand.

"What must be done, huntress?"

Ian appeared dazed, but unbroken. He stood at the doorway to the keep, hands folded over his belt, shoulders thrown back. He still wore the cloak of leaves Fianna had given him, though the rest of his dress was that of a noble of Tener.

"What is your word, Fen Gate?" he asked. Gwen had to smile at that.

"That title means nothing anymore," she said.

"It is still yours, if you would claim it," Ian said.

"I will not claim the title. But I mean to take the castle, if it can be won. There has been no word from its walls since the church drove your father out, but I have faith. The hallows must be restored, and whatever damage the inquisition has done must be repaired."

"Frair Gilliam is not an easy man to dislodge."

"And yet I will do it. It is the will of the gods," Gwen said. She looked around the courtyard. Her people had removed their things and returned what they could of normality to the surrounds. But there were still many dead, and many dying. "This was not. I am sorry."

"Not your doing. And Tavvish has already paid for his crimes."

"You are becoming difficult, Ian. Like your father."

"No. I am like myself. For now, at least." Ian glanced over her head at the loose mob of rangers waiting to escort Gwen out of the castle. "There are those in my council who think I should take you now, while I can. Lock you up, or execute you."

"The tribes would burn this place to the ground. Even the stones."

"Yes. But you would be dead," Ian said, smiling without humor.

"Is that what you want, Ian Blakley? To see me dead?"

"I'm not sure what I want, anymore. But it's not this. Not any of this." His face fell, and he glanced over his shoulder. "Go. My sister wants terribly to meet you, and I'm not sure I can prevent it much longer. Her anger, I cannot hope to assuage."

Gwen nodded. She remembered Nessie, from better days. It hurt to think such a child could hate her so much.

"Good luck here, Ian. The voidfather's plan is not done with you yet, I think."

"With either of us. I will say a prayer for you," he said, turning back into the keep. Gwen waited until the door was closed before she spoke again.

"And I will say a prayer for you. That the gods will not forget you, Ian Blakley, though you run so hard from their gaze."

She turned to her rangers. Deidra stood nearest, her cold eyes boring into the door. Gwen took her hand and dragged her away.

"Come. I want to go home. And when I am done there, we can return and purify this hallow. Whether Ian wants it or not."

17

THE SUN WAS just rising as Malcolm's force thundered up the hill under the banners of Blakley and Jaerdin. The column bristled with spears and the motley colors of shields and tabards of a dozen different names. Jaerdin had been able to gather nearly three hundred riders, mostly knights in plate-and-half, with more on the way. It was more than Malcolm could have hoped for, given the distance they were forced to travel so quickly. Still, it wasn't going to be enough to win this battle.

Malcolm didn't intend to win. He meant to fight, and may the gods have mercy and justice in equal measure.

The Tenerran column crested the ridge and slowed to a halt. Malcolm pulled up short, staring down into the valley with horror.

The Bassion banner flew at the center of the valley, surrounded by a small contingent of fighters, most of whom had lost their horses or been forced to dismount. The Suhdrins formed a shield wall around their banner, bristling with spears and halberds, while a small wedge of archers fired into the celestial forces swirling just out of reach. A column of spears, flanked by two blocks of archers, held the far side of the valley, cutting off escape to the south. A loose tangle of mounted archers wheeled in front of them, raining arrows down on the clutch of Bassion fighters. The original pursuers, mostly knights reinforced by mounted men-at-arms, were stretched in a thin line between Malcolm and Bassion's forces. Given time, the two lines of celestial forces would crush the Bassions between them like a vise.

"There are more than I expected," Jaerdin said.

"The odds were never good," Malcolm answered. "Though I see little hope of Bassion being able to withdraw. She's lost most of her horses."

"Not all. I can see the lady in their midst, still on her courser. If we can untangle her from that deathtrap, she may find her way home."

"Bassion will not leave her men to die."

"She must," Jaerdin said. "If there's to be any hope of victory in this war."

"Helenne Bassion believes we betrayed her," Sir Doone said. The knight rode a little forward, nudging past Malcolm and Jaerdin. "She means to carry word of that betrayal south, to set her army against us. If she were to die here..."

"I will not stand by and watch the celestials slaughter her," Malcolm said. "There is still hope. She may have gotten word to her ranks in the south. And our own camp is still mobilizing. All we have to do is hold them."

"Our full camp is not half this number," Jaerdin said. "And Bassion's ranks are still scattered. What few remain are too far south to do us much good. They may arrive, but only to see us properly buried."

"There is still the Reaveholt." Malcolm turned to peer at the fortress, perched on the banks of the Tallow. Its walls shadowed the head of the valley. "Sir Bourne still holds its walls, and there is some strength there. Surely they—"

"Sir Bourne holds faith with Colm Adair, even after the baron's death and heresy. A heresy you revealed, Houndhallow," Jaerdin said. "We cannot count on his help in this fight."

"Even if he rode out, gods know which side he'd join. The man may be desperate to prove his faith to the church. I can't imagine him fighting to keep Helenne Bassion alive," Doone said. She turned back to Malcolm. "Are we going to idle here all morning, my lord?"

"We are not," Malcolm said. He settled his helm on his head, ratcheting the visor shut. "Form up into three wedges, strongest in the center. We will split their ranks and crush them between us."

"Or splinter against their steel and die," Jaerdin said, then wheeled his horse around and trotted to the waiting knights. "May Strife's fury guide your sword, and Cinder's justice lead your soul to the quiet house, Houndhallow."

"And you, Redgarden. Sir Doone, I want you to lead the left wedge. I will take center."

"My place is at your side, my lord."

"You swore to keep my wife safe, and I'll hold you to that. Their numbers are thinnest on the left, and there is a clear line of escape. Once we're engaged and Lady Bassion is safely on her way, you're to break off and return to our camp. My wife must be informed if I fall. This is her army now."

"And if Bassion does not flee? If she decides to die here?"

"Then none of this will matter. Godsbless, Doone."

"The Hound. The Hallow," she answered stiffly, then rode off.

They came down the ridgeline at a gallop, horses surging like steel-capped waves, banners streaming behind them, the speed of their charge closing the distance quickly. The celestials saw their approach, and were wheeling to meet them, but Malcolm had the advantage of speed and the audacity of their attack. The celestial line had counted Malcolm's numbers and assumed he would wait for reinforcements. But Malcolm did not wait.

The Tenerran wedges struck like lances, shattering the steel of the celestial line and punching through. As soon as they were in the clear, the three prongs of Malcolm's attack came together, destroying the thin resistance between them. The celestial soldiers were surprised by the ferocity of the Tenerran assault, falling easily under their blades.

"They thought their priests had taken care of us," Malcolm said, wheeling. "Before they regroup! Again!" He charged back into the fray.

The long line of the celestial mounted forces began to splinter. Those closest to Malcolm's wedge peeled back, trying to get away from the Tenerran swords. The distant ends of the line curled forward, turning their face to Malcolm while denying their flank to the cluster of Bassions at the center of the valley. But the field of battle was too small, and their ranks too thin, to allow this. Eventually, both sides of the line had to expose their flanks to the huddled Bassion defenders.

Helenne Bassion saw her chance, and took it. Sounding the charge, the few remaining knights in her host broke free of their defenses and slammed into the western tip of the celestial line. Her dozens sent the celestial hundreds into disarray.

"This is our chance!" Malcolm shouted, rallying the Tenerran spears to his side. "Lances into the celestial line! Lances with me!"

Without waiting for a response, Malcolm spurred his mount hard into a charge, galloping over the uneven valley floor. The first Suhdrin blades he met scattered at his approach, and soon the thunder of Tenerran riders joined his side. They formed a long wedge aimed right at the heart of the northern half of the celestial position. Bassion's force struggled on the other side of the celestials, wheeling in tight circles to keep from being flanked and to protect the block of foot spearmen who were slowly marching west, out of the valley.

For a while, Malcolm and the Tenerrans were able to keep up the pressure. Their charge kept the celestial attention away from the retreating Suhdrins, though the threat of Bassion's knights prevented the celestials from committing fully to the attack on Malcolm. It was a delicate balance. A balance that could not be maintained.

Finally, the southern half of the celestial banners involved themselves in the fight. Other than the lightly armored archers, they had no mounted elements, and were forced to press the attack slowly. Rather than march directly into the attack, though, the line of spears at the southern half of the valley curled their flanks inward to cut off Bassion's escape route. Inexorably, they closed ranks with the northern columns, forming a pocket of celestial banners, with Bassion's force at the middle. The Suhdrins were stranded.

Once Bassion was no longer able to threaten the celestial north, they turned their attention to the Tenerrans. Malcolm and his cadre had been making some progress against the celestial forces, but that ended suddenly and completely. Malcolm found himself at the tip of a dissolving spear, his banners peeling away under celestial pressure. The three columns of the original Tenerran attack had fallen out of formation, crushed together into a single lance that was quickly blunting.

Malcolm lost sight of Helenne Bassion. She disappeared in a sea of waving spears and crashing horses. The banner of Galleydeep, held aloft throughout the battle, spun to the ground. He set his spurs and wheeled.

"Fall back!" Malcolm's voice was lost in the battle, but his command merely confirmed the retreat that was already happening. Those closest to him tightened around their lord. Sir Doone, theoretically in command of the left flank, pushed herself between Malcolm and the celestial assault.

The retreat was madness. Sensing the collapse, the celestials crashed forward. The knights of the celestial forces rode fast around Malcolm's force, joined by the mounted archers, while the ranks of spear kept the Tenerrans engaged to the front. They were trying to surround Malcolm, and they were succeeding.

Malcolm slowed. There was just as much resistance to the north as to the south, and lances of knights wheeled to either side. The Tenerran retreat stalled, and the shattered column was pressed into a square. Arrows rained down on them, and their numbers dwindled. Malcolm found himself on the ground, with Sir Doone dragging him out from under his dead horse. When he got to his feet, all Malcolm could see were rank upon rank of celestial blades surrounding them.

"You wanted a good death, my lord," Doone said. "You will have it."

"Bassion didn't get away," Malcolm answered. "I lost sight of her."

"She may survive. They may take her prisoner, for ransom, or leverage against the south." A sudden push of celestial blades drew her attention away, and for a handful of heartbeats there was nothing but fighting and the crash of swords on steel. When a lull came, Malcolm laid an arm on Doone's shoulder.

"This enemy has no interest in leverage. I don't know what they're after, but they have yet to show mercy. I expect none. But you must get away. You must beg whatever mercy you can, swear whatever promises they ask. You must get to my wife. She needs to know that this wasn't Bassion's betrayal."

"My blood will spill before yours, my lord," Doone said. "Your wife is Tenerran. She will know what to do."

A yell went up from the celestial lines. For a brief moment, Malcolm thought it was the final push, as the ranks of his enemy pressed forward. But rather than surging in attack, they were pushing against the Tenerran line in blind panic. A horn sounded over the melee, answered by another, and a third from the south.

The celestials fell away. The field cleared as the enemy line retreated, leaving dead and broken bodies in its wake. Malcolm was in shock. A riderless horse cantered past, and he caught up the reins, swinging into the saddle.

The Reaveholt's gates stood open, and a solid column of mounted knights was charging out. Dozens of banners, nearly a thousand spears, with the waterwheel of Sir Bourne flying at their head.

Another army formed up, much farther south. He could

see the colors of half a dozen Suhdrin houses, including the golden barque of Galleydeep. Bassion's reinforcements had come north, though they were too few, and too far away.

Bourne's attack, though, had turned the tide. He must have ridden out with the full strength of the Reaveholt, scraping the walls of every capable blade. The celestials melted before him; their attention had been on Malcolm's force and their flank was exposed. Bourne punched a hole through the celestial line, right toward the Tenerran position. As the celestials retreated west, Malcolm tried to get a glimpse of the Bassion force. He could see nothing among the collapsing ranks of the church.

"Hold this line. Don't pursue. Doone, you have the command!"

"Where are you going?"

"To see if Lady Bassion lives."

Malcolm charged off, quickly joined by a handful of knights who thought the rout was on. The remaining celestials avoided him. The church was in full retreat to the west, pouring out of the valley like wine from a spilled jug.

Where he had last seen Lady Bassion, Malcolm found only churned mud and the ragged remains of the Galleydeep banner. The dead were unrecognizable. Any of them could be Helenne Bassion. He wheeled back and forth, looking for some sign of the duchess of Galleydeep.

"My lord, there!" one of the knights shouted, pointing. Malcolm looked in that direction. A bare half-dozen knights in Suhdrin colors rode south across the valley floor, toward the approaching Suhdrin army. Helenne's black dress fluttered at their head. Malcolm let out a sigh of relief.

"Thank the gods. She may have her reasons to mistrust

us, but she can't deny our efforts on this field. She would be dead without us."

"We would all be dead without Bourne's intervention," the knight said, and Malcolm could only agree. As they watched, Helenne reached the advance elements of the Suhdrin army.

"We will need to set up a parlay. In the sunlight this time. There have been enough midnight meetings," Malcolm said. He turned his mount back to where Doone waited. "I will need to speak to Sir Bourne, as well, to thank him for risking his garrison. We all owe him our lives."

A scattering of horns sounded to the south, doubtlessly signaling the duchess' return. Malcolm was riding lazily north when the knight who accompanied him started swearing. Malcolm turned.

The Suhdrin army was wheeling, turning away from the battlefield, charging hard along the Tallow's northern bank. Malcolm's brow creased.

"What in hells are they doing?" he muttered. And then he saw.

As he watched, the Suhdrin army charged into the open gates of the Reaveholt, which was practically undefended now that Bourne's sally had stripped the walls. There was a brief fight on the drawbridge, but in moments the Suhdrin army had the gatehouse. The rest of the column fanned out, retreating slowly into the castle. Bourne's forces were fully engaged in routing the celestial army, and couldn't react even if they had noticed the betrayal. And Malcolm didn't have enough men to even challenge Bassion's claim to the walls.

Eventually, the gates closed. Shortly after that, the

Tenerran banners that flew from the Reaveholt's many towers started to fall one by one. The golden barque of Galleydeep billowed out from the main keep. For the first time in its history, the Reaveholt had fallen to Suhdrin blades.

18

SNOW TURNED THE black trees of the forest white, and muffled the usual sounds of beasts and wind. Ian's breath fogged the air in front of his face. He crouched by the base of a pine tree, its heavy branches brushing the top of his head, peering over the snow bank that surrounded the trunk. Other than his breathing and the hammer fall of his heart, there was only silence.

The gheist crept into the clearing on hundred-finger claws, so many joints and claws and pads that its paws poured like liquid wax over the ground. It was long and lean, a ribcage that flexed with every breath, backbone poking through fur as black as tar and just as smooth. It moved deliberately out of the trees, pausing to scent the air and touch its frilled jaw to the snow.

The bait lay in the middle of clearing, a child's toy by the side of a track in the snow, discarded as the child fled her nightmare. Or at least, that's the effect Ian hoped it left. The gheist buried its head in the lane, breathed deeply, then snorted. When it looked up, it was watching the trees to either side.

Ian held his breath, afraid that even the silky puff of his breath would give him away. The gheist stood frozen in place, the sinuous wave of its ribs as subtle as a breeze. It slipped liquidly forward, placing a prehensile tongue on the doll, leeching the fear off the dirty burlap bundle. Ian glanced down the line. The hunters were ready, coiled to spring. He raised his hand, then jumped out of his hiding place and threw.

A hail of spears joined his, springing out of the undergrowth with a *shush*, arcing down to bury themselves in the gheist's rippling hide. The creature howled, then leapt from the clearing, disappearing among the snow-capped trees. The forest canopy shivered at its passing, dropping snow in heavy piles from the branches. The gheist was gone in a heartbeat.

"That false trail isn't going to scare it away for long," Volent whispered.

"It doesn't have to keep it away forever. Just long enough for us to prepare. To secure the walls, maybe for a knight of the winter vow to reach us." Ian shook the loose snow from his shoulders and went to retrieve his spear. "It's just one gheist, Henri."

"There have been too many," Volent answered. "Even for winter."

The rest of the hunters squirmed out from their hiding places. None of them were trained to hunt gheists, much less kill them. But all their priests were dead, and Volent was right, there were more feral spirits stalking the woods around Houndhallow than Ian could ever remember there being. His people couldn't hide behind the walls forever.

The hunting party turned and made their way back to Houndhallow. None of them said what they knew to be true; that the gheists were following them, hunting them, waiting for them to slip up. They all visibly relaxed when they passed through the outer gate of the castle, even though Cahl had proved the walls were not proof against gheists.

"What are we going to do when they start coming inside?" Volent asked. "When they stalk our halls, rather than the forests?"

"One problem at a time, Volent."

The repairs to the doma were going well, though there was no priest to sanctify the grounds even if they managed to restore the sanctuary. But the work made the people feel useful, and that was better than nothing. So much in Ian's life these days was better than nothing.

"My lord," a messenger said as Ian dismounted. "Your sister asks to speak with you."

"Does she? Well, tell her I will be there as soon as I can," Ian said. Volent shook his head when the messenger went away.

"You can't avoid her forever," Volent said.

"No."

"Tavvish was her friend. Her ally. He kept her safe while you were gone," Volent said. "You can understand her anger."

"Yes," Ian said, but that was all. Volent shook his head again and walked off.

Ian rubbed at his chest, wincing as his fingers pressed against the hard flesh of his scar. It didn't really hurt, not in any normal way, but the wound left by the voidfather's pendant was deeply unsettling. It pulsed warm against his heart. Something else he would get used to, with time.

When he had marched south with his father to Greenhall, Ian never imagined it would be the last time he left Houndhallow in glory. In the months since, he had not given his home much thought, and now it seemed as lost to him as youthful innocence, even as he stood in its courtyard. This was not the home he had grown up in. Then again, he wasn't the child who once played in these grounds, or prayed in this doma. Perhaps it was best that they both changed with time. He looked around at the walls, the shell of the doma, even the keep and its barricades, all of them swarming with workers. They felt distant, as if he were seeing them from a great distance, or an even greater time later. Even the stones felt foreign.

That wasn't true of these people, though. With the exception of Henri Volent, most of the workers, soldiers, and servants hustling through the castle had lived their entire lives within sight of the walls of Houndhallow. Even his young sister, Ness, knew little of life outside their family lands. And now he was leading them, all of them.

This was not the life Ian had once imagined, nor the war he had spent his young life dreaming about. The glory his father had gained during the Reaver War, the legends of his forefathers during the crusades and the long-gone battles between tribes that came before... all of it seemed so distant. So impossible. Ian couldn't imagine his own tale ever being the stuff of legend. What had he done, other than disappoint his father and chase after spirits? And what was he to do now?

He walked up to the parapets that overlooked the front gate. The village below was abandoned, much of it ravaged by the pagans, and later the void priests. Now shadows stalked those once familiar streets, even as the villagers huddled inside the castle, praying for protection from an enemy against which stone walls and sturdy steel were no proof. How long could Ian hold out here? And if Gwen decided to come back and take the hallow, would he even try to stop her? Could he?

And where was his father? Gone from the Fen Gate, surely, and doing battle somewhere to the south. Ian should be there, but he couldn't bear to leave his sister behind, and didn't really have the strength of arms to matter. He could barely hold these walls against the cold, much less an army.

A spear of pain went through Ian's chest, and a great weight pressed down on him. The sensation passed as quickly as it had come, but when it was gone Ian couldn't help but feel that eyes were watching him from the abandoned village. He couldn't see anyone, or anything, but he ducked behind the wall and hurried to the keep.

19

FRAIR LUCAS HAD never felt such pain. It was as if his veins had turned to brambles, and each beat of his heart was slowly dragging the thorns through his body. The agony of moving was unbearable. He lay there, looking up at the sky and wondering what the quiet house would look like. If it would be cold, as he had always dreamed.

Martin Roard's face appeared above him. Lucas tried to smile, but the pain turned it into a grimace. Martin's expression was grim.

"We have to move you," he said. "They're coming around again."

"Whoever it is, leave me to them," Lucas whispered. "I've done enough in this life. Let me move on to the next."

"You're not even hurt, you fool. I swear, I haven't heard whining like this since my sister Bella lost her baby teeth. Now get up."

Lucas tried to protest, but Martin grabbed him by the elbow and hauled him to his feet. The pain didn't change, no better and no worse. Lucas blinked down at his body. No blood, no ash. Nothing to reflect the agony in his veins.

"Peculiar," he said through gritted teeth.

"What's peculiar is that you keep talking when vow

knights want us dead," Martin said. "Now let's go."

For the first time since his blackout, Lucas looked around. They were in a narrow clearing, tucked between tall stands of fir trees. The snow on the ground was brittle, and flames flickered through the tree branches. He could hear voices in the distance, along with the jangle of chain mail. It was difficult to focus on anything through the haze of pain. Martin reappeared.

"Come on, frair," he whispered. "They're just beyond this copse. I think they can smell you or something."

When Lucas didn't move immediately, Martin came over and took him by the hand and led him through the trees. The feeling of pine needles on his cheeks was refreshing, a sensation that wasn't pain, wasn't agony. Lucas closed his eyes and breathed the piney air.

"I always liked the forests up here. So much nicer than along the coast."

Martin glanced back at him with a worried look, but only shushed him before moving on. They passed through a dozen smaller copses, each broken up by snow-covered clearings. They scrambled up a ridge of loose rocks, Lucas struggling to keep his balance, Martin holding him up from behind. A rabble of stone rattled down, causing Martin to freeze and stare into the darkness.

"If they can smell me, it doesn't really matter, does it?" Lucas asked quietly. "We shouldn't even bother running."

"I've run too far with you, old man. I'm not stopping now."

When nothing appeared from the forest, Martin urged him on. They climbed a short incline and settled into a copse, burrowing together into a blanket of fallen leaves. Lucas was barely settled before he drifted off into restless, dreamless sleep.

Martin shook him awake. At first, Lucas thought the brambled pain was still with him, but as he slowly came to his senses, he realized he was simply freezing to death. Lucas pushed himself up to his knees, dislodging a thin blanket of leaves and snow, then blinked around.

"We're alive," he muttered.

"I wasn't sure at first," Martin said. "You were acting strangely back there."

"I must have been in shock. Every time my shadowform is destroyed, it's very disorienting. But I've never passed out before." He held up his hand. No scars, but every time he clenched it into a fist, there was a twinge of pain deep in his bones. "I'll be fine now."

"Well, I'm glad you're back to yourself. Best I could come up with was to hide in the snow, and that nearly killed us." Martin stood up and began stomping his feet, hugging himself tight. "I don't think I'll ever be warm again."

Lucas stood and stretched. The pain was definitely still there, but only an echo, scratching at his bones. It was most peculiar. The cold cut through him like a knife, though. The morning was clear and bright, the sun shining off the snow, and his breath puffed into small clouds. The remnants of unnatural spring lay dead all around them.

"I wonder what became of our pursuers," Lucas mused. "Hardly likely they just gave up and went back to camp."

"Camp's abandoned. The whole place is empty. Don't you remember?"

"I remember being in the naether, and seeing Elsa..." Lucas looked up sharply. "Where's Elsa?"

"She was in the camp, and you were shadowing her, and

then there was a bright light and you screamed and fell down. Shortly after that, vow knights started combing the forests, I assume looking for us. I carried you as far as I could, hid you in some trees, and went to watch." Martin knuckled his forehead nervously. "I thought about fighting them, but I didn't see—"

"You would be dead, and I with you. If they were able to capture Sir LaFey, then you and I would pose no true threat. There was something about a bonfire?"

Martin nodded. "I could see it burning in the middle of the camp. Went out shortly after we got up here. I haven't seen any vow knights since."

"Then we have only one choice. Into the camp, and hope the danger has passed."

"And if it hasn't?"

"Then we'll get to find out what became of Sir LaFey the hard way," Lucas said. He stood up, dusting the snow off his robes with shivering hands. "Maybe we'll find our horses, too. Gods only know."

Despite what Martin said, the camp was not completely abandoned. Many of the followers who had been trailing after Halverdt's retinue and had scattered during the sudden change in season had now returned and were going through the army's leavings. Most seemed to shrug off Halverdt's disappearance, treating it as a miracle, or a temporary absence. The whole camp had the feeling of ecstatic confusion, like disciples left in the wake of their unexpectedly absent prophet.

Lucas and Martin made their way through the camp and directly to the site of the bonfire at the center. There was a wide burned spot that covered the ground in ash. Lucas walked up to the edge and knelt.

"The fire was hot enough. There's no remnant of whatever they were burning, no logs or anything." Lucas paused as a clear image drifted through his mind, of people walking into the flames, their heads held high. He looked around. "No bones, or bits of armor. Very strange."

"It couldn't have been that hot," Martin said. He rubbed the ashes, pulling up chunks of green sod. "The grass beneath is unharmed. Even the detritus feels wrong. More like incense dust than bonfire ash."

"But if not a fire, what was it?" Lucas was having trouble focusing, the memories of the night before slipping through his fingers like ice. "What the hell happened here?"

"Was a miracle, of course," a woman said. She was pulling down a nearby tent, folding the linen neatly into a pile. She already had three or four reams of canvas on the mule waiting nearby. "Sophie Halverdt, the bright lady incarnate. Who would have thought we'd see days like this?"

"Who, indeed. Were you here last night?" Lucas asked.

"For a bit. Was trying to sell my wares when they closed the camp, hustled all the merchants out, and started that fire. Left some things behind, so I came back. No one at the gate, so I just walked right in. You wouldn't believe what I saw."

"You may be surprised at the depth of my belief," Lucas said. "Tell me."

"Whole army, standing around like they was in a daze, and Lady Halverdt, bless her, at the front talking like a priest. And then, one by one, they just walked into the fire. Slow as you pleased, eyes straight forward." She nodded smartly, then went back to her tent. "Ascended to a higher plane, to do battle with them moon people. That's what I think. Either way, they won't need these anymore, and it'd be a fool waste just to leave them here."

"Yes, that's right. I remember now. Elsa said the army was marching rank on rank into the fire. But..." Lucas looked around. "Where did they go?"

"We've been wondering how Halverdt got all these troops so far north so quickly," Martin said. "Maybe we have our answer. This woman claims they walked in slowly, eyes forward. I don't know about you, but if I was asked to walk into a bonfire, it would take some force to get me to do it."

"Unless you had done it before. Unless someone else showed you the way." Lucas nodded slowly. "Yes, I can see that. But how does it work? How is it even possible? There's nothing in the rites of Strife that allows this sort of magic. The pagans have similar powers, but I've never heard of any knight of the winter vow perform anything similar."

"The obvious answer," Martin started, then glanced over at the woman folding linen and lowered his voice. "The obvious answer is that Halverdt is under the influence of some kind of gheist. If the pagans can do this, and she just did it..." He trailed off with a shrug.

"I doubt all those vow knights were so easily fooled," Lucas said, then remembered the floating spirits he had seen at Greenhall, and the fountain of flowers spinning from the keep. "Elsa said there were flowers, falling from the sky. Yes, I think you're right. I think there's something of the pagan about this."

"Which means we can add Sophie Halverdt to our growing list of heretics, along with half the vow knights in

Tenumbra. There aren't many faithful celestials left. Where do you think they went?"

Lucas turned north, peering at the distant walls of the Reaveholt.

"I have an idea," he said. "Find us some horses, and maybe some supplies. No telling how long until we'll be in friendly territory again. But be quick about it."

20

THEY BUILT THE pyre far from the walls of Houndhallow, under the clear and holy sky. Since his witching wife was not present, Gwen laid the foundation for Cahl's pyre herself, stacking log upon log until it reached her shoulders. Then she stepped aside while the tribe of stone brought his body, wrapped in bark, and laid it on the pyre.

The new elder of the tribe of stone, an older man by the name of Wrent, came to stand beside Gwen, his bent frame and wrinkled skin at odds with Cahl's youth and strength. If Wrent had ever served in the rangers, his days of tracking and hunting were long behind him. The ink on his cheeks was blurred with age.

"Why do we not send him back to the earth?" Gwen asked. "Isn't that the appropriate home for your tribe?"

"For most, yes, but the elders must always go to the sky." Wrent's voice was high and thin, and when he talked his head shook with the effort. "It is the last honor. To separate souls from flesh, and let them mingle with the stars. I must admit, I'm glad for it. I have grown old fearing a tomb of stone and mud."

Gwen didn't answer, and Wrent seemed content to stare blearily at the flames as the attendants brought torches and set the pyre ablaze.

"I hardly knew him," Gwen muttered to herself. "Yet there is no one living I knew better. I owed him so much."

"And still do. He kept you alive in your early days with us. Aedan was not alone in his desire to see you dead." The elder glanced at her and shrugged. "Including me. I saw no reason to trust a failed huntress, so comfortable with Suhdrin ways, and Suhdrin gods."

"And now?"

"Now I see what he saw. A girl faithful to her tribe, even though they are all dead. And faithful to the gods, as well. All that remains to be seen is if her faith will lead her true, and us with her."

"I am no leader. The elders ignore me, the rangers mistrust me, and the witches despise me. Even the gods abandon me. Folam used my gift to destroy Greenhall, and the void priests betrayed us all." Gwen clenched her fists, remembering. "If Cahl trusted me, well, he trusted Folam Voidfather too."

"Cahl was a man, and all men fail." As though to emphasize the elder's words, a crash of flame swept through the pyre, lapping at Cahl's body. The fire burned away the bark covering and started on his flesh. The smell of burning meat filled the clearing. "If he trusted too much, it was Folam who failed him, and us. Not Cahl. Maybe his trust in you was misplaced. But that is not for Cahl to decide."

"Gods, you sound like Mother," Gwen muttered, and Wrent laughed. Gwen lost herself in the flames, wondering what Cahl would have thought of her decision to leave Houndhallow and try to retake her home in the Fen. She just didn't see what was to be gained in the slaughter. Ian had done what he could to keep his people safe.

A dissatisfied murmur went through the crowd that had

gathered to see Cahl into the next life. Wrent grunted.

"Having *him* here does not help your cause, huntress," Wrent whispered.

Gwen turned to see Sir Bruler standing at the edge of the crowd. The pagans gave him a wide berth, though more than a few rested hands on hilts and grimaced in his direction. Bruler was impervious to their hatred. Gwen admired that about him. She had been surprised when he had refused to stay at Houndhallow with Ian, and instead had joined her exodus. His wounds had been superficial, and Bruler had gone out of his way to convince her that he was innocent in Cahl's death.

"He answered my questions. Cahl's death was not at his hand."

"That does not make him a brother, or even Tenerran. He will always be Suhdrin. He marched north to war. How many—" Wrent fell silent at Gwen's impatient gesture. He sniffed. "If you want to win the faith of the tribes, you could go far by banishing that man. Or hanging him."

"That is always the solution with the elders. It's a wonder anyone survives your attention." Gwen raised a hand to Bruler, who nodded and came closer. She turned to answer Wrent's concerns, but the elder of stones had already shuffled away. Gwen smiled to herself.

"I have been less popular at parties, but that was usually due to my poor manner, and ill standing," Bruler said as he approached.

"This is the wake of the man you were accused of killing. Calling it a party is not the best way to ingratiate yourself," Gwen said stiffly.

Bruler winced. "You understand what I mean, then. I'm always putting my foot in it. What do you think? Will they wait until I sleep to string me up, or merely jump me as I walk back to the keep?"

"Keep this up and they'll take you now," Gwen said. "With my blessing."

"Bah. Cahl was a good man. No friend, but no enemy, either. You know I didn't kill him. And until we find who did, your people want my hide."

"Why didn't you stay in Houndhallow? I'm sure Ian would have been glad of your presence."

The Suhdrin knight shrugged elaborately. "I was called north for war, and found friends among my enemies. I wondered what I might find among even worse enemies, farther north."

"The Fen Gate is south of here," Gwen said. "And the best that you'll find is far from a friend. The elders want you dead."

"The elders wanted you dead, and here you are. So I think I'll stay close to you. So, we return to the Fen Gate? It is much changed from what you remember."

"That's right, you've been there more recently than I. What can you tell me of its defenders?"

"That they are friends of mine, some of them. Though LaGaere and his lot are just bastards, through and through. They were too eager to lead the battle against your father and Malcolm Blakley at the White Lake. It won't do you any good to talk to them."

"I wasn't planning on talking," Gwen said.

Bruler snorted. "Then what do you intend to do? Lure them out of the castle walls and hunt them, one by one? This is a fine army, Adair, but it will never be able to lay siege to a citadel like the Fen Gate."

"We took Houndhallow."

"With the void priests at your side, and treachery. Who inside the Fen Gate will you turn? What spirits will you bind to breach the walls? Remember that the Orphanshield sits your father's throne now, with a whole cadre of priests at his side." Cahl's pyre settled, and Bruler watched the shower of sparks twist up into the stars. "This will be a different business than you think."

"May aye, may nay," Gwen said. "Now leave me with my thoughts."

Bruler seemed about to speak, but instead walked off, disappearing into the crowd. Gwen didn't expect him to survive the night, not with the likes of Kesthe and Wrent watching his every move. But it had been Bruler's choice to come. She couldn't keep everyone safe.

One thing bothered her still. Bruler insisted that Cahl's murderer had dressed like a pagan, but no one in her company fit his description. This meant that there was another group of pagans out there, trailing them, needling them. Hunting them. Or might they truly be in Gwen's company, protected by one of the elders? It wouldn't be hard to hide one girl in this roving column of rangers, witches, shamans, and scavengers. Hell, it was days before Gwen had found out Bruler was with them, and then only because someone had tried to kill the man and Gwen had been forced to intervene.

Bruler was right. Gwen wasn't sure what she would do once they reached the Fen Gate. But she had to free it from the church's grip. She had lost the Fen God, and her family. Seeing Ian defend Houndhallow gave her new hope, and new determination. She would reclaim her home, and the gods long buried in its stones.

2
THE FICKLE FLAME

21

Sir Hammish Bourne was a bear of a man. He rode a draught horse instead of a destrier, ambling through the battlefield, laying waste with his double-bitted axe. When the celestials broke and ran, he watched their retreat like a lord watching the hunt from a distance, at his ease, unattached. Then he turned and rode toward Malcolm, who was with Sir Doone in the middle of the valley, among the ruins of the Bassion stand, surrounded by dead and dying soldiers. Most of them wore the black and gold of the celestial guard.

"Houndhallow," he said evenly. His accent was thick, even for a Tenerran. "You lost me my castle."

"I will add it to the list of grievances, Sir Bourne. Is there any hope of resistance inside?" Malcolm asked.

"Not likely. I didn't ride out sooner because I was gathering my full strength. Naught left in those walls but scullery maids and stable hands." Bourne hefted his axe, resting the bit on his shoulder. The runes of Strife ran down one edge of the blade, and the holy icons of Cinder down the other. Both sides were smeared with blood. "If Bassion wants to butcher that lot, she can manage it. Though it'll cost her a few dead."

"More than a few," Doone muttered, drawing a laugh from Bourne.

"Aye, more than a few." Bourne shook his head sadly, then peered at Malcolm. "I only rode out because I thought Bassion was your ally. From my walls it looked like you were fighting to free her from those damnable priests."

"We were. But only to correct a misunderstanding. She believed we laid an ambush for her, that we had something to do with the betrayal of Sacombre, and the rest of the priests of Cinder, those that followed the high inquisitor in his heresy."

"She still seems to hold that belief," Bourne said.

"May aye, may nay. At the very least, she can't doubt the sacrifice we made in winning her free of that battle. Or that the celestials fear our blade."

"How many in your force, Houndhallow?" Bourne asked. "I mean to retake the Reaveholt, if you'll lend your aid."

"These hundreds," Malcolm answered, waving a hand at the scattered forces wandering the valley, some of them still pursuing the celestial rout, others already searching through the dead. "And this number again, in camp to the north, protecting our supplies."

"I brought almost a thousand through that gate," Bourne said. "I hoped this was only a skirmish of your main force, not its bulk." The big man blew out his lips in frustration. "It's not enough to even harass the Reaveholt, much less lay siege to it."

"Well, you're welcome to join us in our battle, Sir Bourne. Sacombre's heresy has been laid bare, and his followers are out from the shadows. We fight for more than Tener, or the church. We fight for all Tenumbra."

"It feels as though all Tenumbra is fighting us,

Houndhallow," Bourne said. He wiped his axe against his thigh, then sheathed it before turning his massive horse away. "I will join you in prayers tonight. If you'll pardon me, I have dead to bury and costs to count."

Malcolm waited until Bourne was far enough away before he turned back to Sir Doone. She was watching Bourne curiously.

"Do you think his loyalty is still with Colm Adair?" he asked.

"May aye, may nay," she said. "He is certainly set against the Suhdrins, and whatever fragment of the celestial church follows Sacombre. But I have never known a more faithful man. To church and lord."

"That is what I know about him, as well. A better ally than an enemy, at least."

Doone didn't answer. She was watching a rider approaching from the field. It was a girl wearing MaeHerron's colors, though she was too young to carry a blade.

"My lord Houndhallow," the child said. "We have found Lord MaeHerron's body. If it please your lordship."

"It does not," Malcolm said. But he twitched his reins and followed.

Night brought funerals and the dirge. There were no priests of Cinder in their company, so Malcolm served to sing the liturgies of burial and memory. The few remaining members of MaeHerron's host carried their lord's body to the pyre, laying him among the dead in a place of honor. Malcolm spoke the words over Grant's body.

"He should have been buried in the Feltower, with his ancestors," Malcolm said. "We lost his father at White Lake, and him at the Reaveholt. The MaeHerrons deserve better than this."

"War does not give us what we deserve, my lord," Bourne said. "Strife gives us the fury for battle, and Cinder the reason to mourn our losses. Grant MaeHerron was a fine warrior, and a true son of Tener. May he find rest in the quiet house."

The ranks of Tenerran soldiers filed slowly past the pyre, dropping bundled twigs on the dead, some tied with strips of linen from their uniforms.

"Hammish, we need to talk," Malcolm said. The sparks from the pyres drifted over them, mingling with the stars. Malcolm took Bourne by the elbow, but the ward of the Reaveholt didn't move.

"Leave me with the dead, Houndhallow. You brought war to my lord, destroyed his house, and left his family dead." Malcolm started to protest, but Bourne cut him off. "It was not your war, and not your blade that ended them. I know this. But Colm Adair was your banner to protect, and you failed."

"I did everything I could, Bourne. Everything."

"It wasn't enough." Bourne held up his hand to keep Malcolm silent. "I know of their heresy. I spoke with Frair Lucas, and Sacombre, and I have made peace with the sin of House Adair. That doesn't change the love I felt for them. Strife teaches love, Cinder teaches justice. I will hold my love for them in one hand, and the justice they deserve in the other."

"As you wish," Malcolm said. "But we must decide how we are going to proceed."

Bourne nodded, his eyes still on the pyres. Malcolm

settled into a comfortable silence. The dirge floated through the night. Below them, Grant MaeHerron burned into the quiet house.

Their peace was short-lived. The celestial forces withdrew west toward White Lake, setting up a cordon between the Tallow and the Fen. With the Reaveholt in Bassion's hands, and LaGaere's Suhdrin garrison patrolling the roads to the north, Malcolm and his weary cadre were cut off from both relief and retreat. Their supplies were dwindling quickly, especially with the addition of Bourne's unsupported column.

As though the forces arrayed against them were insufficient, there were stark internal differences, as well. After their new allies were properly encamped, Malcolm called Sir Bourne together with Castian Jaerdin, the vow knight Sir Cass Trueau and the priest Catrin DeBray, to represent the interests of Strife. The other lesser lords were occupied with securing the camp and preparing for the inevitable celestial counterattack. They met on a hilltop, overlooking the camp, with the Reaveholt in the distance. Sorcha Blakley sat just over her husband's shoulder, the strange light that pulsed through her blood casting an eerie glow over the proceedings.

"Well, this is a motley council," Bourne said. He was perched precariously on a tree stump, leaning on his axe. Even out of his armor, Hammish looked fit for battle. "What is supposed to band us together, besides an uncommonly common enemy?"

"That isn't enough?" Malcolm asked. "The Reavers were threat enough for Suhdra and Tener to stand together, and this is a much graver threat than ever they were."

"Is it? Because my history tells me that Suhdra did not join that war until the Reaver prows cut through the Burning Coast, and followed the Dunne all the way to Heartsbridge." Bourne threw his arm wide, taking in the valley, the river, the fallen castle. "Yet this war is fought entirely on Tenerran land, with Tenerran banners falling to Suhdrin invaders. Whether they wear the colors of the church or some southern lord hardly matters. This is an incursion on our land. Nothing less."

"Not all your enemies are Suhdrin, sir," Jaerdin said sharply. "And not all your allies are Tenerran."

"Not all your allies, Houndhallow," Bourne said, addressing Malcolm directly, giving Jaerdin nothing more than a glance. "I have signed no alliance with southern cowards."

Before their argument could get out of hand, the young priest, Catrin DeBray, stepped forward. She was a mere slip of a girl, but her injuries at the hands of unknown assassins under the walls of the Fen Gate had turned her blood to iron. She addressed the council with a clear voice.

"The church would have us believe that our fight is between faithful celestials and pagan savages. But those of us who have met them directly know better. Sacombre was the holiest of men, but his actions were pure heresy. Some argue that his intent justified his sin, but that is not for us to decide. Cinder will judge, and Cinder—"

"I've had enough of Cinder," Malcolm snapped. "A god of dying and winter and bloody reasonable judgment. Cinder has never given me anything more than a reason to mourn and a loss to regret."

"That is hardly a fair assessment—" Jaerdin started, but Lady Sorcha stepped forward to interrupt him. Her unnatural appearance, from her slowly dancing hair to her eyes that looked like deep, still pools of water, silenced the council.

"My husband risked his place in the church to protect me from the inquisition, not out of heresy or pride, but out of love. It cost him the Fen Gate. He did nothing wrong, any man who has loved can see that. But to Cinder, his sin was unforgivable. And, Sir Bourne, was Colm Adair's sin any greater? Was he a bad lord? Did he do anything more than protect his people from Halverdt's depredations?"

"A great deal more," Malcolm said. "His family hid a pagan god for generations. Lied to his people, put them at risk from the inquisition, even lied to us, once the war had begun. What would we have done differently, had we known Halverdt's accusations were true?"

"A fine question, Houndhallow," Bourne said. "Would you have betrayed my lord? Would you have turned your back on your Tenerran brother, given Colm and his family over to Sacombre's mad inquisitors? Or would you have protected him, stood with him, hidden him from the inquisition—as you have hidden your wife?"

Malcolm stirred but didn't turn away. Sorcha smiled stiffly and looked to her husband.

"Yes, my dear. How far does your love go for Colm Adair? And for his children—his son, who was butchered by Tomas Sacombre even as he fled; for his daughter, Gwendolyn, who even now wanders the forests of the north doing gods know what?"

"Gwen can take care of herself," Malcolm said.

"We have taken this too far," Jaerdin said. "Our enemy is clear. Sacombre has corrupted the church, and twisted the teachings of Cinder to his own destructive means. Whether the forces lined up against us are true believers or merely truly deceived doesn't matter at this time."

"And what of Bassion? The duchess of Galleydeep has taken my castle, even as I was trying to help her win free of this celestial army." Bourne shifted, resting both hands on the pommel of his axe. "She is my enemy, if not yours."

"She may have retreated in panic, and would be willing to open the gates, if asked," Jaerdin said.

"She threw bodies from the walls, Redgarden. The bodies of my men."

"War makes strange allies, and stranger enemies," Malcolm said. "If you had told me I would be raising spears against the celestial banner, I would have called you a liar. Yet here we are."

"I do not recognize the church we fight against," Sir Trueau said quietly. The vow knight, who had witnessed the murder of her inquisitor at the hands of Catrin DeBray, had kept to herself during the troubles. But her words cast just as much of a chill as Sorcha's unnerving presence. "Cinder and Strife have always fought hand in hand against the dangers of the pagan north. And yet the betrayal of Sacombre, the actions of Frair Gilliam... I cannot explain it. I cannot believe it. But it is happening, and we must deal with it as best we can." She stepped forward, hands resting casually against the two thin blades on her belt. Her face was hidden behind a veil of white lace, the same veil that she had worn since the death of her inquisitor. "Summer is falling into winter, the season of culling, and the servants of Cinder seem to have gone mad. It is the vow of my sect that we will carry Strife's light into the darkness, to remind those who suffer under Cinder's judgment that the sun still rises, and spring will one day come. For years I thought that meant traveling into Tener, to cull the feral gods and restore hope in faithful celestials, ravaged by pagan spirits.

"Now it seems that the hope that must be restored is that of summer. Winter is all around us, in the season, yes, but also in the hearts of those who oppose us. They judge, and bring darkness, and offer hatred and condemnation. That is not for us." She drew her twin swords, crossing them in front of her, and the glittering light of the sun danced through the runes etched along the blades. "Our alliances are built not on judgment, but on hope. Not on the fear of night, but the promise of the light to come. I cannot heal the wounds that have passed between you, the promises broken and the dead you have buried. But I can offer this."

She lowered her blades, pointing one at Malcolm, the other at Sir Bourne. The two men grew wary, hands going unconsciously to their hilts.

"You have the promise of my light, and the hope of Strife. If we must burn down the church to save it, we shall. If we must turn all Tenumbra upside down to bring peace, we shall. And if that means standing next to pagans, arm in arm with heretics, we shall.

"Sacombre's heresy must be stopped, whatever the price. We shall pay it, in blood, in fire, in steel and flames. I swear it to you."

Malcolm looked around the room, his eyes lingering on Sorcha, then on Bourne. He nodded. "I bind myself to this fight. To end the heresy. It has cost us too much; family and friends and alliances we thought would stand forever. Will you stand with me? All of you?"

"To my last breath," Jaerdin said without hesitation.

"And I," Catrin said. "Strife stands with you, even if Cinder will not."

"You know you have our blades, Reaverbane," Franklin Gast said quietly.

They turned to Bourne, who had remained silent.

Slowly, the giant man shook his head. "This is madness. Cinder fighting Strife, Tenerrans standing with Suhdrins, even as southern lords reave our families. There is no loyalty to be had in this war." He stood, sliding the axe over his shoulder. For a brief second, it seemed he would swing. Malcolm braced himself for the blow, but it never came. "But war is often madness. I will fight with you. To restore Adair's name, and Tenerran blood to the Fen Gate. But know that my loyalty only goes so far as this battle, Houndhallow. If you turn on me, or on those I love, if you make peace with those who deserve execution, I will be the first to raise my banner against you."

"I can ask for no more," Malcolm said, extending his hand. Bourne looked down at it and sniffed. The big knight turned away, marching down the hill toward the camp. Malcolm watched him go.

"Not a ringing endorsement," Jaerdin said.

"No. But more than I hoped for," Malcolm said. Trueau came up beside him.

"We will teach you to hope again, Houndhallow. In Strife, if not in your fellow man," she said.

As the council dispersed, Sorcha took Malcolm by the arm and led him a small distance away. Malcolm watched his wife's face with concern.

"What's the matter, my dear?" he asked.

"I am. Or my presence, more precisely. I cannot stay here, husband." Sorcha lifted a hand, dismissing his objection before it left Malcolm's throat. "Bassion will never trust you as long as I am at your side. I will return to Houndhallow."

Malcolm paused, the pain of loss already swelling in his throat. Finally, he nodded. "You are right, of course. I will dispatch a guard to accompany you."

"You can't afford to lose the strength."

"I can't afford to lose my wife. Have faith, Sorcha. I will make due with whatever strength the gods see fit to leave me. You heard Trueau. We must learn to hope."

Malcolm smiled but it didn't reach his heart. He knew better than to hope.

22

THE WORLD WAS light and darkness. Flames twisted through Elsa's flesh, but they did not burn. She spent a screaming eternity falling through nothing, a garden of madness that churned like foam across her body. Whenever she thought it might be over, a wave of grief crashed through her. Whenever she thought she might die in this void, a ray of hope pierced her soul, lifting her into ecstasy. Finally it ended. Everything ended.

Elsa's first sensation was of tiny fans, as soft as silk, brushing over her face. The only light was distant, obscured by a rain of colors that blotted out her vision. Elsa felt like she was falling, but the movement was very slow, as though she were sliding down a shallow hill of loose sand. Feeling returned to her body, making her realize that she had been numb. She took a deep breath. The air smelled like flowers.

Elsa's heel struck ground, and her vision suddenly cleared. The feeling of falling ended. She opened her eyes (had they been closed? had she been blind?) and looked around. She was standing in a field of flowers, the bobbing heads reaching as high as her waist. The flowers were flowing away from her like a river, and as she came to herself, she realized that the current of the flower river was moving her.

She stumbled forward, heels bumping along the ground as the current carried her along.

She wasn't alone. The river was full of people, each one looking around in surprise, walking forward as though they were still asleep. The river, she saw now, was as wide as a lake, the current actually waves driving her to shore. Elsa turned around and stared. She nearly fell as her mind tried to wrap around what she was seeing.

The lake was being fed by a column of burning flowers, falling from a clear sky. They crashed into the center of the lake, washing outward in ripples. Closer to the column there was only the smooth, multicolored surface of the lake, but as it spread out, people appeared; first their heads, then shoulders, and finally the whole person stumbling along, just like Elsa.

A column of horses breached the surface, their riders bouncing smoothly into their saddles and whipping off the blindfolds that had let them guide the mounts into the flames. They spurred forward, heading to shore at a gallop. Elsa watched them with envy. They seemed so free. So happy.

The lake she was walking through (now up to her knees) was on top of a hill. A forest bristled along one shore, flowers lapping at its trunks, while ahead of her a valley stretched away. There was an army at the center of the valley, and another farther away. And anchoring the valley, standing tall and dark over everything, was the Reaveholt.

Elsa reached for her sword, but it wasn't there. She looked down at her hand. Something wasn't right. White lines stretched across the skin, like scars, but there was no pain in the hand. That felt wrong. She flexed her fingers, then remembered the pain of bones grinding against each other, breaking through the skin, the laughter as the vow knights goaded her forward. Sophie's ribbon over the wound, and the agony that followed. She looked around again as she reached the shore of the lake of flowers.

She was surrounded by vow knights, the army of Sophie Halverdt. No one seemed to be paying attention to her. Her bonds were gone, and her injury with them.

A few remaining petals worked free of her clothes as she ran, leaving a trail behind her. She bumped aside soldiers and knights as she passed, pushing down anyone who tried to lay a hand on her. Someone shouted her name, but she kept going. A hand grabbed her shoulder, twisting into the fabric of her shirt, but she spun around and punched the assailant in his throat, spinning away before she could really see his face. The crowds thinned. Elsa stumbled into the open.

Shock stopped Elsa in her tracks. The nearest army, the one camped at the foot of the Reaveholt, flew the colors of the celestial guard. Thick mists clung to the camp, and the army that held it was bound in shadow and darkness. Elsa sensed something terrible deep inside the camp, lodged there like an arrowhead festering in the wound. She took a step back.

As Elsa stood there, she realized what she was seeing. Even in this form, she recognized the god in the valley. It was the same as the one she had fought at the Fen Gate, and a splinter of it later in Harthal, when she and Ian had met Henri Volent. The god of death, Sacombre's corrupted heresy, and now it was here. She looked up at the army camped across the valley from it, preparing for battle.

"Houndhallow. Redgarden. The Drownhal and the Feltower," she whispered to herself, counting the banners.

"Malcolm Blakley's army. But what are they doing here? What are *we* doing here?"

A horn sounded behind her, and Sophie's army quickly formed up. Ranks of spearmen lined up at her side, and the cavalry she had watched gallop through the flowers made up the flank.

"Now do you see why we must all sacrifice? What sort of enemy we face?" Sophie asked. Elsa whirled around to see the girl standing beside the spears, most of whom were gawking at her in shock, and ignoring their formations. When Elsa flinched away, Sophie frowned and held out her hands. "I'm not going to hurt you. The opposite, in fact. How's your hand?"

"You healed it? I have trouble feeling grateful, considering it was your zealots who broke it in the first place."

"Your hand, yes. But that's not all that's broken about you, is it, Sir LaFey?" Sophie took another step forward, and Elsa matched it by backing further away. "Look at who you're running to. Do you really want to join them?"

"Malcolm Blakley will have me. I have served his son well."

"His son isn't with him. Ian is north of here, fighting for his home. The home Malcolm has apparently abandoned, and the church along with it. And I have heard tell that Malcolm Blakley has the blood of an inquisitor on his hands. So before you go running to him, consider that Houndhallow might not be the man you once knew."

"How do you know these things?"

Sophie gestured to the sky. "The sun shines on all things."

"That's such crock. I know how informants work. Does Malcolm know the vow knights at his side have sworn to you?

Does Ian? What other trusts have you betrayed, Halverdt?"

"They have not sworn to me, but to Strife. The true expression of Strife, not the pale candle clutched tight in the Lightfort all these years." Sophie folded her hands at her belt and smiled benevolently. "The Lightfort's flame can flicker and die. As you know all too well, Elsa."

Elsa scowled. "What do you know of me, child? I swore the vows before you were off your mother's lap. I walked the wilds of Tenumbra while you sheltered in a convent, praying to be safe, protected by people like me. And now you think to lead the vow knights? What arrogance! No wonder your father went mad."

"Do not speak so lightly of the dead," Sophie snapped, her pristine composure momentarily cracked. "If you and this inquisitor, this *Lucas*—" she spat the word "—if you had been better at your jobs, my father might not be dead."

"If your father wasn't so scared of the dark, maybe he could have learned to truly stand in the light, rather than cowering behind the cloaks of better men."

A column of mounted knights thundered past, deafening Elsa. She turned to watch them go. They rode down the valley toward Blakley's camp, flying the now-familiar tri-flame and cross that Sophie had adopted upon her conversion to the vow. Elsa shook her head. When she turned around, Sophie was close.

"Why are we fighting, sworn sister?" Sophie whispered in her ear. "We have a common enemy, and a common vow. You may not agree with my methods, but surely you agree with my goals. To rid Tenumbra of the gheists. Forever."

"It can't be done. The inquisition has been trying to do that for ages." Elsa shrugged Sophie's arm away. "The gheists can only be held back. I have fought that war my entire life. I should know."

"You should, and yet you don't. What if I told you there was a way? A way that you and I could do that, together?"

"I would say you're a fool, or mad. Probably both. And even if you had such a method, I would be no good to you." Elsa felt something break inside of her. "The goddess has left me. I can't reach her, no matter what I do."

"You can't reach your pale goddess, no, but that's not what I'm talking about. True power. Bright power." Sophie grew warm beside her, the heat coming off her skin making Elsa wince and step away. "The real power of Lady Strife!"

Sophie's skin had turned to golden light, and her cloak rustled ominously. The pupils of her eyes were tongues of flame. She drew her blade, and the steel sizzled with molten energy.

"I can restore you, Elsa LaFey. I can make you not merely a knight of the winter vow, but the will of the goddess herself. Join me, and wreak havoc in summer's name!"

Elsa was silent. But she did not run.

The vow knights camped under the open stars, lying with their feet facing one of the dozens of bonfires Sophie had conjured into flame, which spread outward like rays of the sun. After her talk with Sophie, no one bothered Elsa, or seemed to be keeping a watch on her. She could have left at any time. She didn't.

When she woke up the next morning, someone had brought replacements for her armor and returned her sword, newly sharpened and resting in a fresh sheath. The armor was mundane, but there wouldn't have been a point in wearing bloodwrought steel, anyway. Not since Strife had abandoned her. Still, Elsa felt strange settling the plain breastplate over her head, as though she were wearing a disguise.

As Elsa struggled to affix her pauldrons, a young squire stepped out of the crowd to help. She wore the tri-flame and saltire, but also a light gold band around her head, common with initiates to the Lightfort. She buckled the straps of Elsa's shoulderplate, then held it in place while Elsa adjusted the fit. Before Elsa could protest, the girl bent and started fitting the greaves.

"I do not need a squire," Elsa said. "I have spent years in the wilderness, donning and doffing my plate with nothing more than the verbal assistance of my inquisitor."

"Beg pardon, sir, but I think you do," the girl said. She worked efficiently around the greaves, laying them flat and then wrapping them over Elsa's knees. She glanced up briefly, catching Elsa in green eyes and golden hair. "Vow knight, eh? You don't look it."

"What is a vow knight supposed to look like?"

"You know. Golden armor, charred hair, zealous eyes." She stepped back, viewing her work, then knelt again to make adjustments. "Strife knows you have the build, though. Mistress LeViere says I'm too slight for vows, but what does she know, cooped up in the Lightfort like a chicken still scared of foxes."

"LeViere has been teaching initiates longer than you've been alive," Elsa said. "Nearly as long as I have been alive. She has been culling gheists and burning blood since my mother was a knight, and she'll be doing it long after you and I are gone."

"That doesn't sound right." The squire bounced up

again, looking Elsa over with a crooked smile. "Maybe she's changed. Poor girl just sits in her solarium and reads old books. She's lost the flame. Maybe that's what happens when you get old. Are you sure you're a vow knight?"

"I have distinct memories that lead me to that conclusion, yes," Elsa said. She picked up her new sheath and buckled it onto her belt, then drew the sword. The girl's eyes widened.

"That has to be the biggest bloodwrought sword I've ever seen! Gods in heaven, how do you wield that thing?" She bent close, running a hand over the fuller. "They've got us training with long swords and mercy daggers. Gentleblades, even. And these runes are so fine! Where did you get it?"

"The holy forge at Hollyhaute," Elsa said, and couldn't keep the pride out of her voice. "A season I was there, bleeding into the coals. The elector said he thought I would die in the effort." She turned the blade to catch the sun, letting the light play over the deep rust icons of the runes. "But I was stronger than he thought."

"I just don't see the point, though. Any bloodwrought blade will do, right? It's the might of Strife that kills the gheist, not the blade itself. So why such a large sword?"

"Northern gods take more than faith to kill," Elsa said with a frown. She slid the sword home in its new sheath, wincing at the rasp. "What would an initiate know, anyway?"

"I know enough to see that everyone here is afraid of you," she said. "Enough to see that you don't really belong with us. The other vow knights haven't welcomed you. The priests and their followers are avoiding you. Even the crazy little half-boy wants nothing to do with you."

"So why are you talking to me?"

"I'm curious what has them all so scared," she said,

then stepped forward and curtsied. "Morganne, if it pleases. Morganne Rouler, initiate of Strife. My teachers didn't want me to leave the Lightfort, but when I heard an avatar of Strife was holding court in Greenhall, I had to come."

"Avatar of Strife," Elsa said with a snort. "Is that what she's calling herself?"

"It's what everyone is calling her. Who do you think she is, if not the blessed of the bright lady?"

"A child, in over her head. She doesn't understand what she's facing, or why."

"And you do?" Morganne asked. "Then maybe that's why everyone is scared of you."

"Maybe." Elsa looked down at where she had been sleeping. There was nothing to take with her. Everything she owned or cared for had been left south of the Tallow, along with Frair Lucas. She wondered where he was, what he was doing. And Martin, as well. Surely they would be all right. When she looked up, Morganne was watching her closely. "You said the vow knights have not welcomed me into their company. Do they have some sort of secret meeting place?"

"Secret? No. But they rest and stand watch at the third flame, always between Sophie and the enemy."

"Take me to them. I will make my own welcome, and see what sort of heresy has settled on their hearts."

"Oh? And if you find them to be heretics, what will you do?" Morganne asked.

"This blade will cut more than gods, child." She rested her hand on the hilt. "Now lead the way."

23

MALCOLM STOOD AT the edge of his camp and watched the last shower of bright color as it drifted slowly to the ground. An army had fallen out of the sky, and was now forming up in opposition to the celestial army. A column of knights was risking the open ground, riding hard and fast toward Malcolm's position. He didn't recognize their banners, but they wore the armor and confidence of vow knights. The celestial army was already adjusting, trying to cut them off.

"Friend or foe?" Jaerdin asked.

"Gods know. But if they're friends, we've just about got an even fight on our hands."

"And if they're foes?"

"Then we are still helplessly overmatched, and doomed to die in glory," Malcolm said cheerfully. He clapped the duke of Redgarden on the shoulder and smiled. "So the more the honor, and the better the tales will be told of our bravery."

"You have a touch of madness, Houndhallow." Jaerdin tugged his cloak closer to his neck, but there was a hint of a smile on his lips. "I'm not even sure which you're hoping for."

The riders reached them. They were led by a young woman, her long hair drawn back in a tangle of braids, her armor as bright as the day it was forged. She waved at them, then drew her riders to a halt.

"Lord Blakley, Lord Jaerdin! It is good to meet you on such a glorious field!"

"That remains to be seen," Malcolm answered. "For whom do you ride, and for what purpose do you greet us?"

"I am Sir Galleux, knight of the winter vow. I ride under the banner of Sophie Halverdt, lord of Greenhall, and true avatar of the Lady Bright. She has taken the winter vow, and sworn to rid the north of the gheists, and finally avenge her father's betrayal at the hands of the heretics of Cinder. And as to my purpose, I was ordered by my lady to seek your alliance, so that we might join our forces, and crush the apostate scum!"

Malcolm turned to Jaerdin, beaming. "See, Redgarden. We might not die gloriously after all. A pity."

Malcolm marched to the head of his lines and surveyed the battlefield. The celestial army had taken on a surreal quality since the arrival of Halverdt's force. A constant mist hung over their ranks, and among the bristling squares of spears and proud banners of knights, other shapes loped and howled. Whatever pretense of holiness the celestial army had previously maintained was gone. They were an army of demons, bound to flesh and sworn to dark forces.

"You see now what we face," Sir Galleux said. She had stayed at Malcolm's side since the alliance with Sophie Halverdt had been signed, acting as Halverdt's representative in the Tenerran army. "Their true selves are revealed. Is any sacrifice too great to counter such a threat?"

"I get nervous when people start asking questions like

that," Malcolm said. Before Galleux could say anything more, he continued. "But it's good to have them out in the open. If Sacombre had worn this face in Halverdt's court, I don't think any of us would be standing here today."

"Sacombre depended on the shadows, and the dark god's mask, else his task would have been incomplete. This type works best in darkness. We will expose them to the light, and see how flame fits their guise!"

"Yes, well. Has Sophie Halverdt made her preparations?"

"See for yourself." Galleux pointed to the south, where Halverdt's glittering forces lay. A steady pulse of light was gathering in their ranks. The celestial ranks were trapped between Halverdt's troops and his own, waiting to be cut in half. "Dawn has come to winter, and Strife's fury with it."

Malcolm didn't answer. Galleux and her companions seemed fond of lofty talk, and it made him uncomfortable. They spoke of summer and Strife as though they were endless, and winter as a pox to be cured. Worse, they never named Cinder anymore, calling him the dark god, or the god of masks, or simply the grave.

Malcolm worried at how far the heresy had come. But he had an inquisitor's blood on his conscience, and perhaps because of that, the questions Catrin DeBray had once asked him came to mind: What was wrong with hating the grave? Why venerate winter? He couldn't remember the answers he had given her.

The faithful celestial in him shivered at these thoughts, but he couldn't deny them. Love of his wife had brought him here, and yet he wasn't sure Sorcha would approve of this company.

"Gods grant that you're right," he said finally. "It makes

me uneasy that they are willing to act so openly, though. There must be some trap in it."

"They only reveal themselves now because they're desperate. Because they know they are up against a true man of faith, and the lady bright. Their time is at an end, and so they draw all their power. They can no longer hide."

"Or because they no longer wish to hide," Malcolm said wearily. "Because they know their strength is enough to crush us utterly. Because the deception is no longer necessary."

"You need to learn to trust in the light of Strife," Galleux said.

"And you need to learn what you're truly up against. You haven't faced these monsters in battle before. I have."

"I am a knight of the winter vow, Reaverbane. I have killed more of these feral gods than you will ever see," Galleux answered confidently. "I know how this battle will go."

"Facing a single gheist, lost and unworshipped, is not the same as meeting a column of mad gods directed by a mortal soul. And before you answer, I will remind you that every gheist you faced, you did so with an inquisitor at your side, to guide and temper you."

"We no longer need the harness of the dark god," Galleux said. "We are free to burn as we must. My knights and I will see to the flank. Be bathed in summer's light, Blakley."

"Burn well, sir. And pray you are not consumed."

"If that is what the goddess requires, then so shall I give," she answered with a laugh. When she was gone, Malcolm turned again to the misty ranks arrayed against them.

"What are you still hiding, you bastards? What lies under that cloak of fog?"

He was still musing when the battle horn sounded.

On the opposite line, the growing light of Halverdt's army turned into a steady glow. Ranks of shields glimmered like small suns, and the knights wheeling on their flank left trails of embers in their wake. Between Malcolm's line and that of Halverdt, the thick mass of the celestial army shifted, ready for battle.

"I suppose we'll find out in the charge," Malcolm muttered. He waved to his squire, and spurred his horse forward. "Form the lines. Prepare for the charge."

A ragged cry went up as Malcolm joined his few remaining knights. Their plan was simple. Advance, hold the celestials in place while Halverdt fell on them with her full strength, then provide the anvil against which Halverdt would crush the celestial line. If they were lucky, they would smash through the celestial line and cut them off from retreat into the Fen. Halverdt and Blakley would form a crescent, pinning the celestial army against Bassion's forces in the Reaveholt. He could only hope that Bassion would fight on their side, once she saw what was unfolding—that her fear of the celestials would overcome her hatred of Tenerrans.

If it didn't work, the celestial army could disappear into the woods, and gods knew where they would go. Malcolm didn't like the idea of tromping through the Fen all winter, looking for mad priests and bound gheists.

"Sir Bourne, Sir Doone, you are with me today," Malcolm said. Most of the mounted knights he was bringing to this battle were actually Bourne's sworn riders. Rather than split them up, Malcolm kept them at the core of the battle line. They were flanked by ranks of spear and axe. "Remember, our job is to threaten, but not fully engage. Leave the killing to Halverdt."

"Best pray she doesn't make it through to our lines," Bourne said grimly. "I can't swear I'll stay my hand if Colm Adair's murderer presents herself."

"Your lord was killed by Tomas Sacombre," Malcolm snapped, "the same man who tricked Lord Halverdt into war and then, by the gods, murdered him. I know your family has generations of grief against Greenhall, but for today, at least, try to keep your mind on the task, and your axe away from the necks of our allies."

"Aren't they calling it Flamehall now, anyway?" Doone asked with a smirk. "We can come up with a whole new series of reasons to hate them once this is all over."

Bourne grunted but gave no other answer. Malcolm signaled to the squire.

"All advance. Slow advance!" he called. The horn went out, and Malcolm's thin line began marching toward the celestial forces.

"I would feel better with support," Doone muttered.

"Aye, but we don't have enough archers to disrupt their lines. Best to keep them in reserve. Godsbless, the celestials don't seem to have archers of their own."

"They do. Just not facing our direction," Bourne said. "They know the true threat. We're not even worth their arrows."

They continued the slow march toward the celestial mass. The line of dark shields was obscured by strands of mist, rising from the ground even though the sun had burned the rest of the valley's gloom away hours ago. Malcolm watched the line and waited. Horns sounded inside the mass. Black shadows rose and fell, pallid skin glimpsed between waves of fog, a jagged mouth wide enough to sunder a horse, bristling with black teeth. Beyond the celestial lines, Halverdt's forces rolled forward, their whole front glimmering with light.

"How you think they do that? The light?" Bourne asked.

"I'm assuming they're on fire," Doone said. "Dipped their heads in pitch and lit the wick. Pretty much what I'd expect from these sorts of zealots."

"Don't say that sort of thing with Galleux around," Malcolm warned. "She has a low threshold for heresy."

"Don't we all, these days?" Doone twisted to watch their own right flank. Galleux and her band of vow knights trotted impatiently toward the celestial line, as neat and prim as if they were on parade in the streets of Heartsbridge. "You think that one takes a pass at us, before this is over?"

"She is the least of our problems, Doone. Eyes forward, please. There is movement in the darkness."

The movement was confusing at first. The mists had closed over the shieldwall, hiding it completely from sight, and now the wall of fog was churning like a waterfall. Unbidden, Malcolm's line faltered and slowed, until they came to a stop. The horns repeated the call for advance, but no one moved.

"We'll be in it soon," Bourne said eagerly. "I will see the pair of you in the quiet, gods willing."

"Gods willing," Malcolm said. Cold fear gripped his heart. Standing a charge of steel and blood was one thing. Waiting for the gods to pour their wrath on you was quite another.

With a snap, the fog receded, leaving only grass behind. The line of shields had disappeared. The banners and columns of knights, only hinted at beneath the mist, were nowhere to be seen. The mist traveled quickly west, toward the Fen.

"They're running!" Bourne shouted. "With me, lads!"

He spurred his mount forward, sending the lumbering brute into a rolling trot, as fast as the beast would go. Malcolm hesitated, trying to figure out what had happened, how the whole celestial line could have just disappeared.

"Unless they were never there," he whispered to himself. "Bourne, hold! Steady, all lines, hold steady!" The horns echoed his call, but there was chaos in his ranks. Some of Bourne's knights followed him, staying even with their leader, while among the blocks of spear and axe, the urge to charge was offset by a lack of targets.

The last of the mist coiled on Malcolm's right flank, churning like a storm. Doone pointed in that direction.

"They must be there! Trying to break through to the Fen! We must charge, my lord!"

"If they got so far afield while our scouts watched, surely they could have gotten away before we advanced," Malcolm said. "Why wait until we're marching closer to disappear? Why?"

"We charge, or they escape! You must signal the charge!"

The squire stood behind Sir Doone, the trumpet tentatively at his lips. Malcolm shook his head.

"It's not right. Hold the line. If they've made the Fen, we'd be fools to rush in after them. We join with Halverdt and combine our strength, then send scouts after. It's the only way."

Bourne was still loping forward, his axe held high as he skirted the front of the Tenerran line. Seeing his approach, Sir Galleux raised her golden sword and howled, then charged the coiling mass of fog that hovered a few hundred feet ahead of her. Her group of vow knights followed, pouring out of the Tenerran line like golden wine from a shattered bowl. They disappeared into the gray clouds of mist.

The sounds of battle rose up from the mist. Steel sang against steel, and brilliant light shot through the fog. Doone turned and looked at Malcolm with irritation.

"It's not right... it's not right," Malcolm muttered. He looked across the field at Halverdt's lines. They, too, had stopped when the mists disappeared, and now seemed at a loss. He shook his head. "Wheel and advance. On the double. Wheel right and advance. Riders, with me!"

A ragged shout went up from the Tenerran line as the flanking blocks of foot turned slowly to their right, shuffling over the uneven ground. Malcolm spurred his riders forward until they were clear of the footmen to their right, then started to wheel them around as well. It was a messy formation, but it was the best he could do.

As they turned, Malcolm looked to his left at the field where the celestial lines had been. The grass was churned up, as though hundreds of feet had marched over it. So they had been there, at one point. But how then did they get so far across the field, and in so short a time?

As soon as his riders were aligned, he called for the gallop, hoping to catch up with Bourne before the big knight and his scattering of followers crashed into the mists unsupported. If he hurried, he might—

Screams rose up to his left. Malcolm turned just in time to see wide piles of grass flip up like shutters. Creatures came out, demons, with skin of stone and root. They pushed through the earth like fish in water, leaving a rut in the ground behind. In their wake, the celestial army rose up, like corpses from massed graves. The nearest of them were practically in Malcolm's flank before he realized what was going on.

"Flank, flank, flank!" he shouted, and the squire struggled

to match his urgency. Malcolm cut across the line of his riders, dragging several along with him as he changed direction suddenly. One knight went down, tangling three more in his wake, and now the center of Malcolm's column of mounted knights was in chaos without a single arrow being loosed.

The demons crashed into the bloc of spearmen behind Malcolm, the flanks of which were trying to turn to meet the charge. Spears broke like twigs against their stony skin, and soon the sound of tearing flesh and screaming, dying men filled the air. Before Malcolm could absorb that thought, a wave of enemy spearmen met his riders.

He wheeled to face them, throwing down his spear and drawing the black feyiron of his blade. Malcolm could hear Sir Bourne ahead of him, howling like a madman, and the panicked screams of his fellow knights as they tried to wheel. The momentum of their charge had already been broken, and now they were set upon by rank after rank of massed spears.

Malcolm had time to scream his fury before the celestials closed, and then there was only the breaking of steel and flesh, and the roaring sound of his heart beating in his head.

24

IAN STUMBLED THROUGH the great hall, drawing concerned stares from his servants. He waved them off. The pain in his chest swelled, branching through his ribs like lightning, until he was sure his heart was going to burst. He reached the stairs to his private quarters, but was waylaid by Sir Clough. The young knight, her eyes narrowed and brow creased, took Ian by the arm and led him into a side chamber.

"What is wrong with you? These people are frightened enough without their lord stumbling drunk through the halls."

"I'm not drunk, it's just..." He knuckled his wound, pressing until the pain subsided. "It's nothing."

"Folam's wound?" Clough said. "I thought it was no longer bothering you."

"It wasn't. But since Gwen left, there have been fits. Nothing I can't push through, but worrying." Ian straightened gingerly. "What I wouldn't do for a priest of Strife. Or even an inquisitor. Someone with godly power."

"Nothing rest won't fix. Come, I will see you to your room."

"No, there's no time. I must speak to the foreman of the doma, and ensure the repairs are on schedule. No one is going to rest well until there is holy ground within the walls of Houndhallow."

"Let the foreman worry about the foreman's work. You must rest." Before Ian could protest, Clough strong-armed him up the stairs and into his chambers. He was still blinking away the pain as she laid him on his bed. "Now, stay here. I won't be a minute."

"Where are you going?"

Clough didn't answer, but went to the door and opened it with a bow. Nessie nodded to her as she stepped inside.

"This was a trap, wasn't it? Getting me away from the repairs so she could..." He gestured at his sister in frustration. "You're in on this together!"

"I had nothing to do with your pain, my lord," Clough said with a smile. "Though I think the gods sometimes work in ways we can't understand." She bowed again to Nessie, whispered a quick, "My lady," and left, closing the door behind her.

Nessie waited a long minute, staring at her brother and listening. When the outer door to Ian's rooms latched shut, she came to his bed.

"You're hurt?" she asked.

"An old wound. It will pass," Ian said stiffly.

"There are healers in the village. Nothing magical in their herbs, of course, but if they can ease your discomfort—"

"Why are you here, sister?" Ian snapped.

Nessie paused, folding her hands together. She was still very young, but Ian could see their mother's steel in her face, in the way she held herself. Nessie went to the end of the bed and folded a blanket over Ian's feet, then sat down.

"You're avoiding me," she said.

"I've been busy. In case you didn't hear, there was a battle inside our walls. We're only alive because I was able to negotiate a peace with Gwen Adair. Even then, our losses were great. The damage to—"

"The damage to this castle is being repaired. By masons, by stonecutters, by carpenters... they don't need your help. They need you to get out of the way. That's most of what leadership is, you know. You never noticed it in Father, because you were too busy with the sword, but he was best when he was elsewhere." She turned awkwardly on the bed, young eyes piercing his. "Why did you kill Tavvish?"

"He rebelled. He disobeyed my orders and took matters into his own hands. He had to be punished." Ian crossed his arms and looked out the window, flushing. "A lesson had to be taught."

"And how is he to learn that lesson if he's dead?" Nessie raised her hand to silence Ian's protest. "Yes, yes, the lesson wasn't for him. Tavvish thought he was doing the right thing, the thing our father would have wanted him to do. You weren't here, at the battle. Master Tavvish stood by my side, descending into the keep only to add his strength to the last lines of defense. He took a terrible wound, trying to protect me. So you can't blame him for mistrusting the pagans, after all that. You can't blame any of us."

"You too? Nessie, the tribes were deceived by Folam, you know—" She motioned him to silence once again, and he swallowed his words. Nessie slid from the bed and paced the room.

"I know your arguments, and I believe them. But you've been so hung up on being right that you couldn't see the trouble you were creating. Perhaps the tribes are truly our allies. But they were never going to find peace here, not so soon after killing so many of our friends. You can't ask a mother to trust the man who killed her son, just because he was deceived. The tribes wanted to believe Folam. Just like your servants wanted to believe Tavvish."

"This is not the sister I remember," Ian said lightly. "Weren't you playing with dolls when I left for the Allfire?"

"Weren't you faithful to the church, last we spoke? Did you swear to guard me from any harm? Promises die, brother. People change."

Nessie leaned against the door, crossing her arms. Where he saw their mother in her before, Ian now saw their father. "What matters now is that the tribes are gone, and the castle is ours. Make it ours, truly. These people need a lord, not an apologist for the pagans. If you wanted to make a case for the tribes, then maybe you should have gone with them."

Before Ian could answer, she opened the door and left. He lay in bed, staring up at the ceiling and wondering if she was right.

It was well after midnight before Ian was able to get to sleep, and even then his dreams were troubled. When he woke up, it was to the unshakable feeling that someone was watching him from the window. He slid from his bed, snatched his sword from the post and crept through the shadows. The air outside was crisp, the winds still, but there was no one to be seen. Ian was about to return to bed when a pulse of agony went through his chest, spreading out from his wound like the roots of an old tree. He rubbed at it, squeezing his eyes shut until the pain passed. When he opened them again, the guards were opening the sally gate in the outer wall. By the light of the guardsman's lamp, Ian saw three riders enter the castle. They were in dark robes, and carried the black staves of Cinder.

"What the hell?" he muttered. Grabbing his robe, Ian hurried out of his chambers, startling the guard at his door. "Find Clough, have her meet me in the courtyard. And then be sure my sister is safe." He hurried off before the man could move, rushing down the stairs and stopped in the passageway outside the great hall. The three newcomers were already inside.

They were priests of Cinder. All three looked haggard, as though they had been on the road for a long time. Their leader was perhaps the tallest man Ian had ever seen, though his gaunt frame gave him a look more like a siege ladder than a giant. His gray beard was neatly trimmed, and when he looked around the hall, the priest's eyes lit up at the sight of the hearth. His companions were unremarkable, each deferring to the giant's presence. Their robes were tattered and their eyes sunk deep in their faces. Servants scurried around them, offering wine and bread, both of which the priests accepted gratefully.

"They came up the southern road, my lord," Henri Volent whispered in his ear. Ian jumped and turned to find him wrapped in the darkness of his cloak, skulking in the shadows. "They were riding like the world was on fire behind them. Clough wanted to ask your permission to grant them entrance, but your sister ordered the gates opened."

"So Clough knows they're here. Where is she now?"

"Hiding Nessie, much to your sister's consternation. Your sister trusts too much. Especially when it comes to the church."

"Well, we just evicted a whole bunch of pagans. I guess we have to trust someone. Do you know these three, from your days in Greenhall?"

"Tall one's Veureux. A scribe at Cinderfell, last I heard. The other two are strangers, though they could be from the winter shrine as well, for all I know. Veureux was good to my master, but so was Sacombre."

"I imagine the church of Cinder is scrambling to cover themselves after Sacombre's heresy. Strange that a scribe would be on the road, though. Ah, they've noticed us." Ian strode from the shadows, still dressed in his robe and carrying the naked blade of his sword like a walking stick. "My frairs," he said, raising his voice. "To what do we owe this late visit?"

"The hour is late, though hopefully not too late," Veureux said. He bowed, introducing himself and his companions, Tession and Macre, all hailing from Cinderfell. "The woods have become almost impassable, with gheists and pagan marauders. We hoped to find friendly patrols on entering Blakley lands, but instead had to fight our way through countless vile spirits before we could win your walls. And even then, we were nearly turned away."

"As you say, the hour is late. We have recently suffered a treacherous ambush within our own walls, and barely survived the attempt. If our patrols have not met your expectations, frair, it is only because most of my warriors are either dead, watching these walls, or south with my father, fighting the heretics."

"Dangerous times, my lord. I pray your father is well. Is your mother here, to see to our hospitality?"

"I am your host, and this is your hospitality," Ian said,

waving to the empty hall and his brandished sword. "Now speak your piece."

"We heard that Houndhallow had fallen, and we felt its doma fall to corruption," Tession said. "We came to bring it a blessing."

"From Cinder? Or from the church?"

"They are the same, my lord," Veureux said stiffly. "Unless you've lost your faith in Heartsbridge?"

"Heartsbridge has nothing to do with this. The seat of the celestriarch is hundreds of miles away, and it might as well be on a different star, for all the good he has done us. The celestial church has done nothing to ease the suffering of the north, other than send more soldiers, half of whom fall to heresy as soon as they cross the border. We find our faith in actions, my frairs. So what is your blessing?"

"We wish only to see Houndhallow restored to its holy glory, Ian," Veureux answered. "Whatever your faith, do not deny that your people deserve some comfort. The comfort the church can provide, even if you will not seek it."

Ian stood stiffly for a long moment, then relented. "It is true, our doma was destroyed in the battle. We have no priests to sanctify it, though the walls and ceiling must be rebuilt before—"

"Nonsense," Veureux said. "This is why we are here. The gods have provided. Show us the doma."

"But the fire… the walls…"

"Fire burns and walls collapse, but the gods remain. If the ground has been desecrated, then we must repair that, before anything else can be done. Despite our long journey, we must do this, before we may rest." Veureux motioned to the doors. "If you please."

"Volent, gather a guard, and show the frairs to the doma," Ian said. "I will be with you in a moment."

"Your presence will be needed, my lord."

"Yes, I'm sure. But I'm not going to witness this in my dressing robe. I won't be long." He grabbed Volent before he left, lowering his voice. "A double guard, and more in the courtyard. I don't trust them."

25

THE TWIN TOWERS of the Fen Gate appeared in the distance, looming out of the fog like broken teeth. The pagans had been skirting the edge of the Fen for a week, following Gwen's lead and the weather, marching through snow and sleet to reach this shelter. Now that they were here, though, Gwen was less sure of herself.

"I never thought I'd be here again," she said. "It feels wrong, somehow. That after everything, I should return to this place."

"Coming home always gives me a sense of impending doom," Bruler said. "Though I don't often ride at the side of a half-gheist madwoman. And this is not my home. Nor is it yours, any longer."

"I don't think I have a home," Gwen said. "This was my family's home, and they're gone. I have no claim on this place. Still, something doesn't feel right. Don't you feel it?"

"Huntress, I have been in the saddle for a week, and half that time has been spent bending my head to sleet so cold it would freeze a witch's—" He glanced at Kesthe. "It's been cold. So I feel nothing, and want more than anything to sit by a hearth and taste beer that hasn't been cut with sawdust."

"Lady Adair is right," Kesthe said, ignoring the Suhdrin

knight. "There is something out of place about the castle." She closed her eyes and muttered an invocation. "More death than I would think. We should send scouts."

"More death?" Bruler said incredulously. "Do you have any idea the battles this place has seen since the Allfire?"

"It is more than that," Kesthe answered. "There is... there is something lurking within the walls. You said the inquisition purged the shrine beneath the crypts. We must be careful. Lady Adair, let me send three rangers and a witch, to bless our path."

"We're too close," Gwen said. "If the Fen Gate is in the enemy's hands, they will have already spotted us. Sending scouts alone would be giving those men over to the grave. We will scout in force."

"Very well." Kesthe turned to the rangers waiting behind them. "Duncan, Kight, Holme, gather three dozen good blades and take them to the castle walls. If you see nothing—"

"I will lead them," Gwen said. She glanced back at the gathered rangers. "If they can keep up! Hyah!"

She spurred her horse forward. Bruler was still swearing when he caught up with her. Two dozen riders galloped close behind.

"My lady, you need to do a better job of assigning tasks and accepting the help of others," Bruler shouted over the wind. "That is the nature of leadership."

"I have assigned tasks. Kesthe is in charge of the main body, because they didn't follow us. And you are here, because it is where you belong," she answered with a smile. "A leader doesn't always need to give orders, Bruler. Good people know what they must do, what their duty is, to gods and thrones, and they will do it."

"It is not that easy," Bruler said, but smiled as he shook

his head. "For most people, it is not that easy."

Gwen laughed and rode faster, disappearing into the trails she had ridden since childhood. The silver and black stream of her cadre, steel and leather, horse and blade, followed close behind.

It thrilled Gwen to be on these trails again. They were thick with memory; the hundreds of hunts she and her father had ridden, the gheists and boar they had ridden down. The secret tracks of deer, the silent hours spent waiting for the flush, time spent alone among the trees, or quietly with her companions.

All of whom were dead. Even her father. Especially her father.

Gwen's heart fell. Why was she here? When she brought the pagan army out of Houndhallow, it was to reclaim her home. But her home was gone. Even these woods, so familiar, were a foreign land to her. It was heartbreaking.

So lost in these things was Gwen that she didn't notice the river until her horse was chest deep and balking. Gwen gripped the reins hard, barely keeping her saddle. Eventually she was able to work her way back to the shore, where Bruler and the others watched in wonder.

"This was not here before," Gwen said. "This path ran straight to the front gates, dry the whole way." She looked up and down the river. It flowed deep and narrow, disappearing into the forest to her right. "There is no river this deep near here that might have been diverted."

"Rivers don't just spring out of nothing," Bruler said.

"They do when gheists are involved. That's what I scented before. Pagan gods, unsettled and roaming." She turned her horse along the bank and started to follow the river toward its source. "Come on."

They followed the river until they came upon a shallow pool with a spring at its middle. Clear, cold water boiled out of the ground.

"There," Bruler said. "Nothing unusual about that. A new spring. Now we can leave off all this talk of gheists and get back to the castle, and that promised beer."

"This is no natural spring," Gwen said. She dismounted and plunged her hands into the pool, drinking deeply. "As clean and fresh as spring. This is god touched."

"The elder of tides is back at Houndhallow," one of the rangers said. "We might be able to scare up one of her witches in the main column. See what she has to say about this."

"No need," Gwen said. "I've seen this before. This is Fianna's work."

"Fianna went south, with that inquisitor," the ranger said.

"Aye, she did. But she left someone behind."

"Sorcha Blakley." Bruler grimaced as he looked around at the surrounding forest, as though he expected the lady of Houndhallow to step out from behind a tree. His brow creased. "I remember now. When Lord Blakley abandoned the castle, there was a bit of a fight out here. There was talk in the camp after, that his wife ended it. Drowned a cadre of knights. I didn't believe it. But maybe I was wrong. Stories of Lady Blakley have spread throughout the north… I wasn't sure what to make of them. But if she did this, someone must have trained her. Maybe the Blakleys are secret pagans after all."

"No," Gwen said. "Fianna changed her." She touched the pool of water again, then shook her hand dry. "If this sort of power still exists outside the castle, gods know what we'll find inside. The inquisition should have purged this pool long ago."

"Unless they're fully engaged cleansing the castle itself," Bruler said. "Those halls were haunted beyond mortal ken."

"That's my home you're talking about," Gwen answered. She swung back into her saddle. "Let's see what we can see of the castle, and make our decision then."

Gwen abandoned the trails and led her cadre through the woods. The going was slow, but stealth was more important than speed. The light crunch of snow and rattle of armor was the only sound as they wound their way through the forest. Gwen was troubled by the lack of birdsong. Even in winter, the forests of the Fen were usually alive with birds and other woodland beasts, but now it was as quiet as a tomb.

The closer they got to the castle, the stranger the world became. The trees seemed to bend toward them, and the sky was obscured by mist and overhanging vines. Gwen's breath hung in puffs of cloud that seemed to linger long after they passed, adding to the grim atmosphere. Near the main road into Fenton, Gwen called a halt.

"There should be traffic. Even if the castle is in enemy hands, the people of the village will have returned to their homes. They can't live in the courtyard of the Fen Gate forever."

"Unless they've fled entirely," Bruler said. "There were few Tenerrans in the village when I was here. Most went to Dunneswerry, or north, fleeing the war."

"Then patrols, at least?" Gwen asked. "Surely your commanders would not abandon the roads completely?"

"We were ranging far in search of Lord Blakley. I was north of Harthal when Sir LaFey and Ian found me and converted me to their cause. But by now, Malcolm's position on the Tallow is well known. How many have joined the Suhdrin forces there, and how many remain at the Fen Gate?" He shrugged. "Who knows?"

"We are going to approach the road. If it is empty, we will continue along it, until we sight the main gate," Gwen said. "I really thought they would have noticed us by now."

"Are we looking for a fight?"

"No. But I thought there would be one. Come on. The godsroad is just up ahead." Gwen took up her reins and led the cadre through a copse of trees and onto the road.

As they rode out, they gasped as one. They had happened upon a small roadside shrine, one of those that maintained the sanctity of the blessings of traveling inquisitors and the faith of their vow knights. But the shrine had been profaned. The symbols of Cinder and Strife were broken, the icons of the church torn down and thrown away. Cracks spiderwebbed across the tiny altar. The ground at its base was freshly charred. When Gwen approached it, she could feel a sharp malevolence emanating from the stone.

"That's troubling," Bruler said.

"Whatever the inquisitor did to the shrine must have spread outward," Gwen answered. "I can think of no reason why a man of the church would have profaned these shrines."

"You are making a lot of assumptions." Bruler looked nervously up and down the road. "We shouldn't be here. This was a fool's errand. The Fen Gate is lost to us. We should head south, and join our strength to Blakley's."

"I do not want to leave my home in such a state. If a darkness has settled there, the least I can do is bring it some light," Gwen answered, and trotted down the road.

Bruler turned to the cadre. "Stay here. If we come around

that corner at a gallop, start running. We'll catch you up."

"No one here is going to abandon Lady Adair," a ranger said.

"I do not doubt your loyalty. But right now I'm not sure the best thing we can do is ride in force against the castle gates. The less dangerous we look, the less likely they are to send a legion nipping at our heels. Stay. We'll be back."

The ranger looked discontented, but didn't follow when Bruler rode away. He caught up with Gwen long before they reached the final corner to the gate.

"What will you do if they hail us?" he asked.

"Answer back. But if they invite us inside, I will gladly decline."

"Thank the gods. I think those men would tear the gates off with their hands if you were captured. And die in the process."

"Would that their elders were half as loyal," Gwen said as they turned the corner. The Fen Gate loomed ahead.

The castle itself was under repair. Scaffolding covered parts of the walls and front gate, while the section of the keep they could see above the walls looked as if it had been recently restored. Judging by the state of the village, many of the materials used in the repairs had been stripped from the homes there; most of the village was gone, replaced by rutty tracks and sawdust. Gwen came to a halt.

"They've done so much, in so little time," she said. "How is that possible?"

"We are in a time of impossible things. I'm glad I joined Ian's party, and never returned to my post here. I am not cut out for mean labor."

"Even if they bent the army to this task, they couldn't

have rebuilt the keep. It was devastated. They would have had to tear it down and start again."

"They have clearly not bent the entire army to repair," Bruler said, pointing. "That's a column of knights making their way through the outskirts of the village. LaGaere's men, by their colors." He glanced over at Gwen. She was dressed in ranger's leathers, a pagan if ever he saw one. "Hide as much of that beneath your hood as you can, and maybe let me do the talking."

"They've seen us already. I don't think we'll be talking," she said. Bruler looked back to the column. As they cleared the village, the knights were ramping up to a canter with their spears lowered.

"They might still be amenable to words. I know many of LaGaere's company. Decent folk, if you can get past the scorn they hold for all other human beings."

Gwen wheeled her horse, tightening her grip on the reins and scowling.

"Look closer!" she yelled, then spurred her horse and shot off down the road, back the way they had come.

Bruler narrowed his eyes. The lead knight rode without her helm, long, black hair streaming behind her head. She seemed loose in the saddle, as though she were barely holding on to her seat, despite the sharp discipline of her lance and shield. Her head lolled forward, then fell spinning from her neck, onto the ground. The rest of the column ran over it.

The dead knight rode on, lowering her lance and spurring her mount into a gallop.

"Not much for talking, no," Bruler muttered, then wheeled his horse and hurried after Gwen. The dead followed close behind, silent and fast.

26

THE CELESTIAL LINE slammed into Malcolm's position with a thunderous crash. The first to fall were Sir Bourne and his cadre, caught out in front of Malcolm and the rest of the Tenerran knights. Malcolm watched as Bourne's companions scattered in the first wave of lances. Of the big knight himself, there was no sign.

Malcolm got enough of his own riders turned in to the celestial charge to survive the initial impact. A lance skipped off his shield, the knight wielding it pitching forward as their mounts collided, the weight of the charge shocking both men. Malcolm brought his sword down, glancing off the heavy steel of his opponent's weapon arm, hacked again and again as the knight tried to disentangle himself from the charge. Finally the man dropped his splintered lance and drew his own sword. As he raised his blade to strike back at Malcolm, Malcolm thrust, driving the point of his sword into the chain of the knight's armpit. The knight flopped back in his saddle and was still.

There was no time to enjoy even this small victory. The dead knight didn't move, pressed in place by the mass of riders behind him, but on Malcolm's other side one of the Tenerrans fell, horse and rider disappearing into the trample.

A celestial wielding a mace in both hands, swinging madly, quickly took his place. It was all Malcolm could do to block the attack, the flanged head of the mace denting his shield over and over again. The man's momentum took him past Malcolm, deeper into the Tenerran formation.

More celestials filled the gap, and Malcolm was quickly isolated from the rest of his knights. Celestials passed him by, each offering a quick sword strike or passing blow before continuing the charge. Malcolm parried feverishly, taking as many of the shots on his shield as he could before the face of the bulwark splintered and fell apart. He threw it aside, taking his feyiron sword in both hands and laying into the nearest celestial.

The celestial knight attempted to dodge Malcolm's attack and continue into the Tenerran formation, but this time Malcolm wouldn't let him pass. He sundered the knight's shield in one blow, knocked it out of the man's hands with the backswing, then brought his sword down on the steel brow of his helm over and over until the metal crumpled. The knight slid free of his saddle and disappeared into the mud below, leaving his wide-eyed horse behind.

"Get out of here," Malcolm shouted at the horse, slapping it on the rump with the flat of his sword. The beast charged back the way it had come, disrupting the knights who followed, knocking one to the ground and turning three more aside.

The fury of his attack left a brief clearing around Malcolm. He stood up in his stirrups and surveyed the field. The two gheists that had apparently dug the trenches to hide the celestial forces were running amuck through Malcolm's columns of foot. The celestials facing those columns were hanging back, apparently afraid of getting caught in the demons' scything claws. In the center, celestial knights had broken through Malcolm's position and were wheeling around for another pass. The churning mist at the end of the valley still hid Sir Galleux and her vow knights. Far behind, Castian Jaerdin held the reserves. There was so much chaos that the man probably didn't know where to commit, but if he didn't throw his knights into the battle soon, there would be no victory to salvage.

Malcolm's view was interrupted by a gheist. The beast had fought its way free of the ranks of spear and was now charging headlong into the Tenerran center. Its rampage caught the celestial knights as well, just as they were wheeling closer to the Tenerrans. It burst through their lines and started hammering toward Malcolm.

The gheist loped forward, thick arms rolling under shoulders as big as barrels, with a mouth that looked like a geode, bright, sharp teeth disappearing into a howling maw. As it drew closer, Malcolm could see shards of loose stone sloughing off its back, leaving a cloud of dust in its wake.

Malcolm dug his knees into the sides of his horse and charged. The black blade of his sword raised high above his head, the destrier galloping below him, the sounds of battle faded from his mind. The world slowed. The Tenerrans and celestials around Malcolm paused in their battle, eyes following the Reaverbane as he shot across the field of battle into the waiting jaws of a mad god.

The gheist struck, one massive paw swinging straight through Malcolm's horse, turning the creature to pulp. Its stony claw clipped Malcolm's leg, and then he was flying through the air, twisting and turning, the sky meeting the ground. He struck the gheist shoulder first, bouncing off stone to roll limply to the ground. Malcolm lay face down in the mud. Pain hummed through his body. Around him, the screams of dying horses and knights continued.

Malcolm slowly pushed himself to his knees. The gheist's leg was within reach, its torso rising up above the battlefield as it swung wildly at the Tenerran knights who were rushing to protect Malcolm. The black splinter of Malcolm's sword wavered near the creature's shoulder, buried deep in its stony flesh. Malcolm stood and stumbled back.

"My lord, take my hand!" It was Sir Bourne, reaching for him, somehow still alive after the initial charge. Malcolm twisted to reach the massive knight, but as their hands got close, Bourne glanced up. He set his jaw and drew back, massive hands wrapping around his axe, raising it high and screaming.

The twin fists of the gheist slammed down on Bourne, leaving only a crater where the valiant knight had just been. The force of the blow knocked Malcolm to his knees. He stared at where Bourne had been. Gone. Just gone. He started screaming.

The gheist began to withdraw. Pieces of Bourne's armor, dripping with blood and bone, clung to the demon's fists. Beside the carnage, Malcolm's sword lay point down in the mud. He ducked under the gheist's arm, grabbed his blade, and whirled to face the beast. The gheist's eyes were swirling points of broken light, nestled deep in sockets of crystal shards, set above that impossibly deep mouth.

"He was a good man!" was all Malcolm could manage. He swung, cutting into the gheist's arms, feyiron burying into stone, sizzling and spitting divine blood onto the grass. The gheist screamed in pain, rolling back onto its haunches, turning a confused eye on Malcolm. Malcolm struck again, this time lunging forward, driving the tip of the blade into the gheist's knee. That mouth, lined with crystals and stretching into eternity, rippled open wider and wider until it looked as if the gheist were trying to swallow the sky.

"Good men need to stop dying for this bullshit!" Malcolm shouted. He swung hard into the gheist's belly, severing the rocky skin, opening it like a tent. His sword dragged through the scree that crumbled off the wound, moving slower and slower until Malcolm, with all the strength in his arms and all the fury in his heart, couldn't move it. The blood that poured out was gritty and black.

The gheist snapped its whole body forward, slamming its chest into Malcolm and knocking him flat. The howl that boomed from its mouth blew like a tornado, tearing up chunks of earth, sending them flying. Knights downwind tumbled from their mounts, and horses reared up and bolted, fleeing the storm of a dying god. Malcolm curled up around his blade, covering his head in an attempt to keep the screaming wind out of his ears. The sound turned his bones into tuning forks, humming through his skin.

When the sound stopped, Malcolm cautiously looked up. The gheist lay still on the battlefield. The light in its eyes was gone. Slowly, cracks formed across its back, cracks that widened into fissures. Dust eroded off its skin, hissing as it streamed onto the ground. Pebbles bounced off it, adding to the growing pile of detritus that surrounded the gheist. Finally, an enormous snap shattered the air, and two final cracks crossed the gheist's body. It crumbled into a low hill of dead boulders and spreading moss.

"The hound!" someone shouted in the distance. That

voice was answered by another, echoing the hound, before a chorus of, "The hallow!"

Malcolm collapsed against the gheist's body, his whole body shaking with exhaustion and sorrow. The stone was cold against his face.

"They will not wait for our lamentation." Sir Doone rode up, leading a dead man's horse. There was blood all over the saddle, and the trappings were celestial. She handed him the reins. "Galleux rode out of that cloud and is handling the second gheist. But that one devastated our southern flank, and the ranks of spear opposite are pressing to engage. The celestial heavy horse is gathering for another charge, as well. Your soldiers need you."

"As the gods will," Malcolm muttered. He pushed himself up and took the horse. "But I've had my fill of this."

"War does not ask when we are done with it," Doone said. She flicked her reins and turned to face the coming celestial charge. "Bourne died well."

"No, he did not. None of us ever do," Malcolm answered. "Squire! Horns to me! Lances form up, and prepare for the countercharge!" He didn't give the horns time to answer, but the surviving Tenerran knights were already at his side, flocking to the banner of the Reaverbane, the god slayer, hero of a thousand battles. Malcolm glanced side to side, grimacing at their eager eyes, their ready smiles. He raised his sword and swept it down toward the celestial line.

"Charge!"

Malcolm fell into a numb cycle of battle, of charge and countercharge, individual melees swirling together into an endless cloud of blades and dying soldiers. The growing ache in his body blotted out any other thought, pain layered upon pain, until there was nothing but the sword in his hands and the enemy dying at his feet.

He lost two more horses, each time replaced by eager squires. Wherever he went, Malcolm was surrounded by knights, anxious to be a part of the legend of the Reaverbane, adding their blood to the endless toll of Malcolm's debt. They rode with him, they died at his side, they were replaced by others. Only Doone remained.

As night fell, Malcolm found himself sitting atop a small hillock, staring at the carnage. Men and women fought like children, arms and legs too tired to lift their blades, armor smeared in mud and the gore of lost comrades or defeated foes. Scattered horses wandered riderless across the plain, cropping at grass and flicking an ever-increasing swarm of flies away with their tails. The two dead gheists formed shallow hills in the middle of the field.

Sir Galleux rode up next to him. Her golden armor was dented, many of the fine runes peeled free of their inlays, the icons of Strife broken or missing. She paused at his side, then sheathed her sword and smiled.

"We will break them, my lord. The gods have granted us that."

"Not tonight," Malcolm said. He raised his eyes and looked at the other end of the battlefield. Sophie's armies were still fully engaged with the bulk of the celestial army. There was no sign of surrender on either side, no sign of imminent victory. "Sound the withdrawal. We will mend our wounds, adjust our plans, mourn our dead, and return to this in the morning."

"Houndhallow, no! Have you lost faith in the bright

lady? Have you forgotten the promise of the winter vow?" Galleux grabbed his arm in a steely grip. "We will bring the sun into winter, summer into night, light into darkness. We can't stop now!"

"That's a grand motto, and a decent way to live your life. But we cannot see at night. The soldiers are exhausted. Hell, I can hardly hold my sword. If we don't fall back, more men will die from falling out of their saddle than to the enemy's blades. Sound the withdrawal."

"I will not!" Galleux said. She held her hands out, palms up, and tilted her head to the sky. For a brief moment, Malcolm was reminded of the earth gheist, just before he had killed it. "I call on the fury of Strife! Goddess of war, bless us; lady of fire, light our way!"

"Galleux, that is enough! We have—"

An eerie flame flickered across Galleux's palms. It licked up her arms, forming a nimbus of pale light across her chest. When it sheathed her face, Malcolm flinched away. Galleux's eyes opened, wide and mad.

"The goddess of war is upon me!" Galleux yelled. Her voice was a hollow bell, pealing across the battlefield. Weary knights turned curious eyes in her direction. "Receive her gift, and victory!"

A wave of thin flame washed out from her. Malcolm felt a brief heat, then a lightness in his chest. The weariness lifted from his limbs. His back straightened, no longer weighed down by his armor. He raised his hand and flexed it. Pale flames covered his fingers, dancing back and forth across his palm like quicksilver. The fog of fatigue that clouded his mind lifted, to be replaced with murderous fury.

All around, the knights of Tener and Suhdra turned

bright with flame. Their flesh did not burn, their armor did not melt, and yet cloaks of flickering fire danced and warped around them. As one, their eyes turned bright and violent.

Malcolm did not need to call the charge. They lusted for war, and poured down the hill in a burning wave, screaming madness as they crashed into the celestial force.

They burned like torches, only to be quenched in blood.

27

GWEN RODE HARD and fast, with the dead on her trail. Bruler was close behind her. As soon as they came around the corner and into sight of their scouts, Gwen started waving her hand frantically. As one, the scouting party started trotting in her direction.

"Go back! Go back!" Gwen yelled. But it was hopeless. Her shouts only drew their concern. The scouts sped up, drawing weapons. "Gods in stone, don't they know how to follow orders?" she muttered.

The dead followed close behind. At first, they could be mistaken for any other war party; riding hard, banners furled, lances couched and shields set for impact. They charged in good order. But closer examination revealed their unnatural form.

The knights following the headless Suhdrin knight were all in a similar state. One rode with his ribcage exposed, another's head was half caved in, while his companion bristled with arrow shafts. Only one knight seemed whole, though his skin was bloated and a stream of dark water flowed from his mouth.

They wore the collected colors of Suhdra: Marchand, LaGaere, Fabron, Halverdt. These were the houses that had ridden against the Fen Gate in the first siege, the remnants of which had been left in charge of the castle when the Orphanshield forced Malcolm out and gave the Sedgewind Throne over to the church. Whether these knights had died in the initial battle, during Malcolm's flight, or during some later tragedy wasn't clear. All that Gwen knew was that they were dead, and they were trying to add her to their ranks.

"We need to decide, my lady," Bruler said at her side. "Whether we are going to fight, or whether we are going to run." He nodded to the scouting party, who were riding at them full tilt, weapons drawn. "Because this lot seems ready to fight."

"Now I wish they would take orders," Gwen said. She reined in and turned to the approaching wraiths. "How does one fight the dead?"

Bruler pulled to a stop next to her and drew his sword. "The way one fights anything. Hit it with something sharp."

The wraiths showed no sign of slowing, but neither did Gwen's scouts. If she and Bruler stayed where they were, one or both of them would be trampled. "Into it, then," she muttered, and spurred into a canter.

As the former huntress of Adair, Gwen had never really trained to the sword. The spear, though, was like an extension of her arm. She pulled a hunting spear from its sheath and rose up in her saddle, using her knees to compensate for the horse's gait. When she let fly, the spear sank halfway down the shaft in the lead wraith's chest. The dead knight kept coming, seemingly oblivious to the injury.

"In retrospect, it seems obvious that killing the dead won't work," Bruler said. "We'll just try cutting them into pieces." He snatched a hatchet from his saddle and tossed it to Gwen. "With my compliments, my lady."

The two sped up, finally meeting the wraiths as they thundered down the road. Gwen ducked beneath a clumsy sword, bringing her axe into the jaw of her attacker with a meaty thunk. Bits of skull and meat flew into the air, but then she was past the first wraith and fending off the sword of the next. Something sharp brushed her knee, and she looked down to see bony frills along the back of the wraith's horse. Whatever grim fate had met the knights, the horses had not escaped.

She was still tangling with the trailing wraith when her scouts met the front of their charge. The crash of steel and flesh echoed through the forest. A handful of her rangers galloped along the side of the road, firing arrows into the wraiths as they passed, flights whistling past Gwen's head to thud loudly into dead flesh. After the charge was past and both sides were circling for a second run, Gwen could see that two of her cadre lay dead in the road. Their enemy's ranks were untouched. Gwen and Bruler shared a look.

"Smaller pieces," Bruler said, then charged forward.

"Kight!" Gwen shouted, straining to remember the ranger's name from earlier. "Return to the main column. Let them know what is happening, and that we will need support."

"It is against my honor to leave the field of battle, my lady."

"The current situation asks for more than honor. Go, and quickly!"

The ranger balked, but at a word from Bruler turned and rode off into the woods.

By now the wraiths had turned and were bearing down

on them. They cantered forward in a wide line, apparently hoping to sweep up the rangers beside the road as they passed. Their headless leader directed them with her blade, urging them forward.

"I have iron in my blood!" Gwen yelled. She stood in her saddle and shook her axe, giving a high, piercing cry. The rangers took it up with enthusiasm, adding trilling shouts to her scream. Gwen charged.

Her enthusiasm was short-lived. The wraiths attacked with purpose this time, pressing the advance rather than striking and passing through. Three of them surrounded Gwen, pushing her to the side of the road. Their blows were slow and purposeful, but when she blocked one with the bit of her axe, the force nearly wrenched her shoulder out of its socket. She was still recovering from that when the headless leader twisted around and laid her sword through the neck of Gwen's horse. The beast went over with a scream, rolling and nearly crushing Gwen.

Gwen hopped back to her feet, but was now at a severe disadvantage. The wraiths towered over her on their mounts. She tried the same strategy, burying the head of her axe in the neck of the leader's horse, but got no reaction. Backing away, Gwen stumbled over her own dead mount, grabbing one of her spears as she flipped past the saddle. She was able to keep the wraiths at bay, pinning them in the shoulder or chest, shoving them back, then turning her attention to the next. It felt like a game of hammerjacks, without the ball.

Bruler crashed into this dance, swinging hard with his sword and ignoring his own well-being. He crushed the arm of one of the wraiths, followed up by shouldering the corpse to the ground, then directing his horse to crush it with a series of quick steps that broke bones and shattered steel. When he was done, the wraith could only twitch helplessly in the mud. Bruler looked down at Gwen.

"Smaller pieces," he said, then charged back into the melee.

The two remaining wraiths stared at their ruined companion for moment, then bolted after Bruler. Gwen knelt by her horse, offered it mercy, then unbuckled her spear sheath and threw it over her shoulder. She marched up to the crushed wraith and plunged a spear into its skull. The creature moaned without mouth or throat, creating a droning howl that shivered Gwen's flesh.

"Bloodwrought steel has no effect on them," she mused. "What sort of monster has the inquisition created? And why is the Orphanshield raising his own dead to fight?" Gwen looked up at the distant towers of the Fen Gate. "That is, if the church still holds the walls, and hasn't succumbed to Sacombre's corruption."

Gwen was shaken from her reverie by the thunder of hooves. Kesthe and Kight turned a distant corner, leading the fastest elements of Gwen's army. She couldn't help but smile.

"Honor might have frowned on Kight's leaving, but it's good to see it hastened him back. Scouts, clear the road! I don't think Kesthe will be able to turn this charge aside!"

Her rangers fell back to the side of the road, dragging Bruler with them, leaving the road to the wraiths. The demons seemed oblivious to their danger, but as Kesthe and the others approached, she slowed down.

"Is this all it takes to frighten you, huntress?" Kesthe shouted. "Loose revenants? See how they answer to their elder's call!"

"Kesthe, wait!" Gwen shouted, but the elder of bones was already acting.

Holding her staff above her head in both hands like a trophy, Kesthe started chanting in an ancient tongue. Something stirred in Gwen, tightening around her lungs and plucking the strands of her muscles. The wraiths, previously inattentive to Kesthe, turned slowly and began to approach her. At the elder's command, they dropped their weapons. Kesthe stopped chanting and swung down from her saddle.

"You see, Gwen? The gods have no need of our fear. The celestials have removed themselves so far from death, tucking it neatly away in the quiet house, that even the simplest ghosts terrify them. These are nothing more than soldiers too stubborn to die. An old trick, and easily sent on to their rest." She stretched out her staff, waving it above them, then slicing down. The wraiths fell like dropped puppets.

"Nothing to it. If you wish to train with me, I could—" Kesthe sucked in her breath, then turned back to the dead.

A web of black energy appeared on the ground around each of the wraiths, like ice suddenly cracking. It extended, racing forward until it touched Kesthe's feet. The elder drew back, but she was not fast enough to outpace death. Her startled yelp became a horrified moan. Kesthe fell to her knees. Gwen knelt beside her.

"Elder? What has happened?" Gwen looked back at the wraiths. They had not stirred, were rather decomposing in front of her eyes. A knight with the bloated features of a drowned man lay with open mouth, the stream of water coming out slowing to a trickle as his lungs were finally emptied of their burden. Gwen looked back at Kesthe. "If you are feeling well, we should press on to the castle.

There's no telling what will be waiting for us."

"Do not trifle with the dead," Kesthe said. She looked up, and Gwen stumbled back. The elder's face was changed, the lines of her eyes as black as ink, her lips curled back in a feral grin. Even her skin was different, as though she had slipped into the pallid flesh of the dead. When she stood, the rangers took a step back in horror. "Leave them in their graves, or be prepared to feed the grave yourself!"

Kesthe, or whatever force had consumed her, threw her arms wide, cackling. Mist crept up from the ground, especially thick in the forest that surrounded them. Gwen backed away until she bumped into Sir Bruler. The Suhdrin knight was watching the elder's performance with sword in hand.

"This has gone dark in a hurry. But I don't think the rangers are going to like it if I just walk over there and put a sword into their elder's belly."

"No, no, I don't think—"

Someone screamed in the forest. Everyone whirled around, just in time to see one of the rangers stumble from the trees, clothes disordered, and eyes white with fear.

"Hands! Hands in the mists! Gods spare us, elder, what have you done?"

Those closest to the forest stepped back, drawing swords and soothing nervous mounts. The mists were dark and thick, winding between the trees, hiding the trunks from view. As the forest disappeared around them, the mist reached into the air, blotting out the sun as well.

"Enough of this!" Bruler said. He marched over the Kesthe and raised his sword. "Leave the grave where it is, witch!"

Bruler was stopped by a tug on his foot. He looked down

and saw a hand emerging from the gravel road, the skin as thin as paper, wasted to the bone. He tried to pull away, but the hand moved quickly, dragging him away from the elder. Bruler fell, screaming as he was pulled toward the forest.

All around the road, people started to scream. Horses bolted, throwing their riders, as hands, claws, and less identifiable appendages grabbed at their legs. Those who fell to the ground quickly fell silent; stone-hard hands crushed their skulls, pressed into their eyes, tore out their bellies with blunt fingers. The mists grew thicker, swallowing their screams.

Gwen threw down her spears and ran at Kesthe. The elder grinned at her approach, gesturing to the ground.

"Do you dance, my lady? Even the dead like to dance."

The hands that grabbed at Gwen were lithe, the soft skin somehow more horrendous than the rough fingers that were digging through the rest of her cadre. They moved with liquid grace, sliding over Gwen's legs, flitting aside when she struck at them with her axe, plucking at her heels, pinching her toes. She stumbled forward, barely keeping her feet, not wanting to fall victim to the dead.

"You have to fight it, Kesthe," Gwen shouted. "If I can do it, surely an elder of your stature is able!"

"Why should I? This seems a fitting end for you, and those foolish enough to follow you. Oh, I'll admit to a certain hesitation, but what is the grave but emptiness? And what is more empty than the void?"

Gwen hesitated, a little shocked at Kesthe's pronouncement. It almost cost Gwen her foot, as one of the thin hands gripped her ankle and twisted, throwing her to the ground. She rolled into a ball, hacking at the hand and severing it at the wrist. Cut off from the ground, the strange hand turned to dust on her blade. As soon as she was free, she jumped at Kesthe, keeping clear of the ground as she flew.

Kesthe saw her coming, and raised her staff. The elder swung, but Gwen wasn't attacking. She only needed a touch, and if she was willing to sacrifice, it was easy enough. Kesthe's staff cracked into her shoulder, but Gwen's hand came down on the elder's face. That moment of contact was enough. Gwen opened the wounds of her soul.

A presence hung on Kesthe like a scarecrow, clinging to her soul, wrapping through the fibers of her being. A bad stitch in the complex tapestry of the human soul. Gwen reached through the elder, grabbed the corrupted strand, and pulled.

Kesthe went rigid, eyes rolling into the back of her head, arms out. She dropped her staff. The corruption resisted, twisted as it was into the elder's bones, at home in a witch so accustomed to the grave. But Gwen was relentless. She drew the darkness into herself, pulling it free of Kesthe like a bad tooth.

Black veins grew around Gwen's eyes. They shot out, creeping down her cheeks, forming a ring around her neck, burrowing into her chest. It hurt, like whiskey poured into a wound, but Gwen held on. It only fought her for a moment, a moment that seemed like an eternity, but then the corruption snapped free of Kesthe's soul and buried itself in Gwen.

The two fell apart like lovers fainting from the effort of their embrace. They landed flat on their backs in the center of the road. Kesthe's face faded back to its former state, young and beautiful, her skin unblemished. The veins on Gwen's flesh receded, but only a little, their darkness lurking beneath the surface, waiting to strike. The two women lay there for a long heartbeat, staring up into the sky.

The hundred grasping hands collapsed into dust. The mists rolled back into the forest, gone as fast and unnaturally as they had arrived. Gwen sat up.

"What happened? What did you do?" Bruler asked, staggering over from the forest's edge.

"The gheist was corrupted. Some remnant of the void spirit, woven into its soul. Whatever is happening here, the void priests are involved. I was able to draw it out like poison, but it has settled into the wounds left by Fomharra." Gwen sat up and winced. "I don't know how often I can do that."

"Nor do I," Kesthe said. "But I thank you. It was like the grave had turned sour… evil. It was a nightmare waking."

"Only thing I know about drinking poison, it'll kill you eventually," Bruler said.

"Yes, it will. Don't be there when that happens," Gwen said. "I don't know what's going to happen when this thing gets out of me."

"Where else would I be at such a moment, but at your side," Bruler said. He sheathed his blade and looked over at Kesthe. "I don't know how we're supposed to treat with the Orphanshield now, huntress. You look more demon than girl."

"I never meant to treat with him. He has taken my castle, his church has taken my gods, and his heretic has taken my family." Gwen stretched out her hand and saw the whorls of shadow squirming under her flesh. "And the void has marked me, for good or ill. We need to move quickly."

"What would you have us do, huntress?" Kesthe asked. There was a hint of humility in the elder's voice.

"This changes nothing. Whether the Orphanshield has surrendered to the void heresy, or whether he has been deceived by one of Sacombre's kin, the man has taken my home, and I mean to take it back." Gwen stood and dusted off her trousers. The surviving rangers stared at her in horror. "Gather these men and lead them to the castle. I want you hammering on the gates in twenty minutes. Thirty, if you want to bury the dead first."

"Where will you be?"

"Going over the opposite wall," Gwen said. "I need to see what's happening in my father's house." She paused. "My house," she said stiffly. "My home."

28

THAT NIGHT, LUCAS dreamt that his heart was torn from his body and replaced with a shard of ice. He woke up, gasping for breath, clawing at his chest. Martin rolled to his feet, sword already in hand, looking around frantically.

"It's nothing, nothing at all," Lucas said. But it was something. When Martin kept staring at him, Lucas waved a hand. "I think the weather will be changing soon. That's all."

True to Lucas's vision, the next morning the weather turned hard into winter. Heavy snow fell from the moment they awoke, quickly piling up and making the road near impassable. They hunched close to their saddles as they rode, the world beyond their hoods disappearing into a veil of heavy snowflakes and dark trees, trusting the horses to keep to the road. The snowfall dampened every sound, until they were left with nothing but their own ragged breath, and the squelching clomp of their mounts.

It wasn't until the patrol surrounded them that Lucas heard their approach. The black-clad riders overtook Martin and Lucas, wheeling to cut off their advance, riding tight beside, until their knees were touching. Lucas threw off his hood, blinking into the snow.

"Whoever you are, we are friends. We mean no harm."

The lead rider laughed, pulling her mount close to Lucas's side. Her shield was covered in burlap, and she wore a heavy cloak over her armor, so Lucas couldn't tell whose banner she claimed. The knight leaned close, peering into Lucas's face.

"How can anyone be a friend to all? Surely you have some loyalties, old man."

"Only to the gods, and the church," Lucas answered. Beneath his robes he laid a hand on his dagger. "It has always been my call to befriend everyone in Cinder's name. Even those who would name me enemy."

"Generous, and often fatal." The woman cocked her head. Her hair was bound in a long plait that looped around her neck like a scarf. "You are Frair Lucas, unless I miss my guess. I saw you at Greenhall, dining with my lady."

"You serve Sophie Halverdt?" Martin asked. The knight glanced at him and snorted.

"I am not that sort of fool. My cadre hails from Galleydeep, though Lady Bassion has led us to this foul clime. How anyone survives in this weather is beyond me, or why they would want to defend it."

"I recognize you, Sir Tasse," Martin said cheerfully. "We crossed spears at the Allfire, two seasons ago." He sketched a bow in his saddle, sending an avalanche of snow tumbling down his forehead. "Sir Martin Roard, of Stormwatch."

"Indeed we did, Sir Roard," the woman said with a crooked smile. "A good tussle was that. The young struggle with such energy, if not much form. The last time I saw the two of you, you were escorting the heretic Sacombre to Heartsbridge. Has his justice been served?"

"Yes and no," Lucas answered. He pulled his hood

close, covering his exposed neck. "And while this meeting is fortunate, the weather is not fit for conversation. Do you have a shelter nearby where we could sit? I will explain it all."

"Shelter? Yes, we do." Tasse wheeled her mount. "A whole bloody fortress of shelter. I trust we can find room for you. And my lady will want to hear your explanation."

"Fortress?" Martin asked.

"Aye!" she answered. "Lady Bassion has taken the Reaveholt! Quickly now, before the sun sets, and winter has its teeth in our bones!"

The great southern gate of the Reaveholt, never before taken by Suhdrin spears, never opened but in peace, stood wide open. The colors of Bassion hung from its walls, the banners sodden with snow. Martin and Lucas clattered across the drawbridge and into the main courtyard. The space was crowded with horses and tents and dozens of campfires. Tasse pulled them up short.

"Stay here for a bit. Lady Bassion is touring the infirmary. She will want to see you directly, I imagine."

After she had ridden off, Lucas leaned in to Martin, whispering. "I never thought I would see this keep fallen. But there is no sign of battle, no broken walls or shattered gates. I wonder what became of Sir Bourne."

"That man would not have given up without a fight. Unless there was treachery involved, he would have given battle."

"Yes. And yet, here we are." Lucas looked around the courtyard, counting banners and tallying houses. "This is the army that Bassion took north, to reinforce the Fen Gate. Seems they never made it."

“Fewer of them. And look, priests of Cinder, and knights of the celestial guard. When did they join the fight?”

“Gods know,” Lucas said. While the priests were free to move around, their tents were surrounded by guards, all keeping an uneasy watch on their every motion. And the celestial guard had their armor, but not their arms. “But they don’t look too happy, or too well trusted.”

They were interrupted by the approach of Lady Bassion. The duchess of Galleydeep strolled out of one of the keeps, surrounded by a dozen guards and two knights of the winter vow. She wore her hood high and tight to her face, and was dressed for battle under her cloak of black and gold.

“Have they been searched?” Bassion asked Tasse as they drew near.

“No, my lady. This is Frair Lucas. You remember him from—”

“Search them,” Bassion snapped, folding her hands at her waist. Lucas couldn’t help but notice that she was shaking. “How dare you bring them into my presence without searching them first!”

Sir Tasse bent to the task, helping Lucas from his saddle and handing the reins of both their horses off to a squire before going through Lucas’s cloak and bag. He surrendered his dagger and the few remaining implements of the naether. Martin offered his sword, but Tasse seemed uninterested in it, or him. When she was done, the knight bowed to Lady Bassion.

“They are clean, my lady. It is safe.”

The vow knights flanking Bassion did not let down their guard, though, and Bassion herself seemed timid as she approached. Finally she threw back her hood, and Lucas understood better.

"My gods, Galleydeep, what happened to you?" he asked, staring at the puckered, blackened scar that covered half her face.

"I was twice betrayed. First, by my faith in Cinder and his servants, and secondly by Lord Blakley." She related the tale of their battles, when the priests had slaughtered their own and raised gheists in the midst of her army, and then the ambush that had eventually led to the capture of the Reaveholt. Lucas suspected she was leaving much out.

"And what of you?" she asked. "What became of Tomas Sacombre?"

"Dead. Though he escaped for a while, it seems his rescuers only had so much use for him. We buried him south of Gallowsport," Lucas said. "And then we followed Halverdt's army north. For a while."

"Was their departure as strange as their arrival outside my walls?"

"They're here? Thank the gods. They have my vow knight."

"Then she is probably lost to you," one of the vow knights said, a tall, thin man with hair as black as night. "A heresy grips Halverdt's force. She has swayed many loyal knights of the winter vow into her fallacy. With Lady Bassion's help, we hope to crush it before it spreads."

A harsh wind blew through the courtyard, causing Lucas to grab his cloak and pull it tight to his throat. The cold stole his breath away. When he looked up again, Bassion and the vow knights were looking to the sky with fear.

"I know you're southern born, my lady, but surely a winter wind is not cause for fear," Lucas said. "We are north of the Tallow, after all."

"It is not the wind that frightens me. It is winter. Terrible things have happened outside these walls," she said. "And more terrible things are to come. The wind is the least of it."

"What have you seen?"

"Come. The words are not enough," she said. "But stay close. There are many here who will not trust a priest of Cinder, no matter whose blessing they have. It would be best if you don't stray from my presence. There's no telling who might seek their revenge."

Lucas furrowed his brow, but Bassion turned sharply and marched back to the keep. It was the northern tower, the same one he and Sacombre had ridden through, months earlier.

As they walked, Lucas kept his eyes open. The clutch of priests of Cinder watched them closely, almost longingly, as they crossed the courtyard. Most of the soldiers ignored them, beyond paying homage to their duchess, but more than a few gripped swords and scowled at Lucas. The back of his head itched, as though hundreds of eyes were boring into it, but every time he turned around, all he saw were knights looking hastily away.

"I don't understand Bassion's story of the battle. Why would priests of Cinder summon gheists and kill their own? It makes no sense," Martin whispered as they passed into the keep. Even here there were no signs of struggle. Lucas wondered what had become of Bourne's servants. He would have to ask, if Bassion ever showed any friendliness.

"It makes sense if they're no longer priests of Cinder. You saw Sir Horne and her companions. Dressed like priests, but calling to the old gods in Gallowsport." He paused as they started climbing the winding stairs up, waiting until the vow knights escorting them had fallen far enough behind to offer some privacy. "I imagine this is the same order, though I have no idea to whom they pray or at which altars they swear allegiance."

"Could they be pagans? Who else but the tribes hold a leash to the gheists?"

"If they are pagans, then they are the worst of the tribes, because they bend most of their power to destroying the old ways. Sacombre hated the tribes."

"And Horne killed him, remember. He may have been fooled this entire time," Martin said. He was about to continue when they came out onto the roof. The view took his breath away.

On the fields below the Reaveholt and stretching nearly to the horizon, three armies were camped. Just north of the gate lay hastily constructed trenchworks, dug through ground that should not have yielded easily to pick or shovel. Banners of the celestial church hung over the trenches, tents spotted the land beyond, and a massive bonfire twisted into the sky. The other two armies camped close together, with only a little space between them, and that patrolled by knights of both forces. The white and black of Houndhallow hung over the smaller camp, while the larger flew Halverdt's new sigil. A great number of vow knights moved throughout that camp.

"Our new heretics," Bassion said quietly. "Sophie Halverdt, and Malcolm Blakley. We are running out of faithful souls in the north."

Lucas heard her words, but did not mark them. His eyes were drawn to the center of the fields, where a great battle had clearly been fought. Weapons and bodies lay strewn across the ground, but that is not what held his attention.

It was there. The emptiness he had sensed in his dreams, slowly collapsing, and drawing the world in with it. Whatever had happened here, the void it left dragged on his soul.

"It is the heart of winter," he muttered. "Drawing in death, and darkness with it. Cinder is falling into this place. Cinder and all his graves."

29

IAN DRESSED QUICKLY and went down to the ruined doma. Volent was waiting in the courtyard, surrounded by about a hundred nervous guardsmen, recently dragged from their sleep to watch three priests say their prayers.

"You don't trust these three, do you?" Volent asked. "Not with all that's happened at the Fen Gate?"

"Who am I supposed to trust? How can I trust you? Our families have more than history, Deadface."

"I am not that man anymore," Volent said. "I have defeated that darkness."

"We are all the person we used to be, for better or worse." Ian surveyed the ranks of tired soldiers. "And where is Clough?"

"She refused to leave your sister's side. Said someone had to protect the future of this household, if you weren't willing to do it yourself." Volent paced by the entrance to the doma. "We shouldn't do this now. Not at night, not in the middle of winter. We should wait."

"What better time to seek Cinder's blessing, Volent? Come on. We can submit to cowardice later."

The two went into the doma. The walls had been scrubbed clean, but the floor was still littered with the wreckage of the fire, and the altar at the far end of the room was a shattered ruin. Veureux and his two assistants stood in the middle, heads bent close together, whispering. On Ian's arrival, they turned as one, pale faces among the shadows.

"We will need light, Sir Blakley."

"Of course. Volent, have the servants bring braziers, from the main hall, if no others can be found spare. And see that they are lit with frairwood."

"Mundane light will do nicely, Ian. Frairwood protects, but it disrupts, as well. We must have clear air to do our business."

Volent hesitated, but at Ian's impatient gesture, the knight marched out of the open door and disappeared. Ian turned to the priests.

"I thought to wait for this until the roof was restored, at least. My people have been working for days to see it done."

"That would explain why you had not yet sent to Cinderfell for a new frair, given Daxter's unfortunate death. If you meant to replace him at all, that is," Veureux said. He crossed his arms, regarding Ian with a cocked eye and smug smile. "What really happened here, Blakley? This room is a riot of gheists and violence. Who killed Frair Daxter?"

"Pagan tribesmen," Ian answered simply, unwilling to say more than was necessary.

"And did these pagans break into Houndhallow, to loot the doma and desecrate it? There are signs enough of battle, but they are months old. The walls are repaired, and the keep refurbished, but the doma stands untended. How do you explain these things?"

"There was a siege. The pagans attacked, but they were tricked into it by a heretic... a man named Folam

Voidfather." He went on to explain how he and Gwen Adair turned Folam's deception to their advantage, ending the siege. "Afterward, the tribes sheltered in our courtyard. But tensions flared, leading to the damage you see now."

"Tensions that led to the death of a priest and the destruction of this temple?" Veureux paced as he talked, slowly drawing closer to Ian. He looked Ian in the eyes, seeming to weigh him with those gray eyes. "And where is Gwen Adair now?"

"Gone. Returned to the Fen Gate, I believe. She could have taken the castle, and killed every one of us. I was able to talk her down."

"You had the huntress in your grasp, and you let her go?" Frair Tession asked sharply. "I have trouble believing that."

"Believe what you will. I am here to defend Houndhallow, and protect it from any force that would bring it down. Regardless of who they swear allegiance to," Ian said. "It was not Gwen's will to destroy us, and I thank her for it."

"A good inquisitor would find cause to question that, Blakley," Veureux said. "But I was never cut out for the inquisition. These things will sort themselves out later, after this—" he waved his hand "—this unpleasantness. We are here to bless your doma. So let us be about that."

The three priests returned to their work. Volent came back with half a dozen servants in tow, each carrying a brazier. They set the iron torches up around the room, then filed out. The bright flames did little to warm the room, though, and it wasn't long before Ian was shivering in the winter night. The priests seemed unaffected by either the cold or the dark conditions, but set about clearing the floor and laying icons of the celestial faith out around the room. Volent watched them nervously.

"Volent, the men must be freezing out there. Let them return to their beds," Ian said, suppressing his own shudder. "There's no need for them."

"They are soldiers, Ian, not scholars. Let them stand in the cold. It will do them some good." He glanced at Ian, smirking through his ruined face. "You are free to return to your bed though, my lord, if this wearies you."

"I'm not tired. It's just this cold. Gods almighty, but the wind cuts." Ian shivered again, a quake that rattled his teeth. His wound felt like a crevice of ice in his chest, sucking warmth out of his blood with each breath. Volent creased his brow. "I'll be fine. Never mind."

"We are nearly ready, my lords," Veureux said. "Though I am afraid we must have privacy for this last part."

"You want us to leave you alone here?" Volent asked.

"I'm sure your column of guards will keep us safe. We won't suffer Daxter's fate, though I am touched by your concern, Sir Volent," Veureux said. "Sir Blakley, your doma will be holy again in no time."

"But—"

"This is not up for discussion, gentlemen. Outside, please." Veureux escorted them to the doorway, pulling a makeshift cloth across the entrance after them. Ian stood staring at it for a long time.

"Okay," he said. "This might have been a mistake."

"Cunning insight," Volent said. "But what do we do? Go charging in with all these swords?" He looked around at the collected hundred, then shrugged. "I actually like that idea."

"Perhaps later. For now, I want to know what they're doing, and why. And why it has to happen now." He looked up at the walls. "Good news is, there are other ways into the doma."

"Like this open door," Volent grumbled, gesturing to the curtained gap. "And we have all these guards with us..."

"Enough," Ian said. "If they suspect we're watching, they might stop, and then we'll never know what they're up to. Come on."

Frair Daxter's rooms were much as he had left them; spare and quiet, the simple furnishings offering little comfort. Ian paused by the small celestial shrine beside the bed, wondering if Daxter had said a final prayer before he went to do his treachery. The icons of Cinder and Strife were laid across the altar's calendar, marking the day of the priest's death.

"He was a good man," Ian whispered. "Good men sometimes do terrible things."

"We don't have time for this," Volent answered. "If the priests look for us, and we're not waiting outside, they'll know something's up."

Ian nodded, leaving the shrine as it was, hurrying through the antechamber that led to the doma. The lock and barricade slid smoothly from their seats. With Volent crowding him from behind, Ian opened the way and peered into the candlelit doma.

The three priests were gathered around the broken remnants of the old altar. A burning flame rose out of the altar's shattered face, held in place by an iron brazier unlike any Ian had ever seen. The spokes of the brazier rose like twisted roots into the air, tangling together around the pan of coals to contain the flame. The flame itself burned blue, lashing over the iron spokes and sending trails of cinders across the iron arms, until flame and brazier joined. The arms of the braziers seemed to writhe under the flame's heat.

The light that played across Veureux's face did not move as light should, but rather as water, spilling through the planes of his skull, pooling on his forehead, swirling in his eyes, cascading across his cheeks. He led a chant, echoed in the voices of the other two priests, hardly more than a whisper, though Ian could hear it clearly. His wound hummed at the sound of it, like a tuning fork picking up the pitch of a distant bell.

"Where did that brazier come from?" Volent whispered. "It's not one of ours, and they weren't carrying anything that large. And that sound..."

"I know. It sets my teeth on edge. I think we've seen enough. There's nothing of Cinder in this," Ian said. Volent grabbed his arm.

"This is not your fight, Houndhallow. Go back and find the others. I will take care of this."

"But surely—"

"These are the men who led my master astray. These are Sacombre's ilk, and his brethren. I never got my pound of flesh from the high inquisitor, but I will be happy to take it from these three." Volent's ruined face twitched, something that might almost have been a sob, then he turned away. "Your men need you, Blakley. No one will miss me, if this goes poorly."

Volent stepped into the light just behind one of the chanting priests. The three men stood in rapt attention, their will focused on the flickering torch of the altar, ignorant of Volent's approach. He raised his sword and put the forte of the blade hard into the nearest priest's skull. The back of the man's head crumpled like a clay pot, and he pitched forward, cracking the front of his head against the iron cage of the ever-burning flame.

Volent stepped over the twitching body. His features were twisted into a cruel scowl, the jigsaw remnants of his face crushed together in hatred. The other two priests stumbled back from their ritual, eyes wide with shock, the strange light pooling on their faces shimmering and wild. Veureux stared down at the corpse slumped at the base of the altar.

"That was a mistake," he said, quite simply. He looked up at Volent as though he had spoken out of turn during a service. "What are you doing, dear Henri? Don't you see what we can offer you? Don't you see the gift we promise?"

Volent didn't answer. Instead, he lunged at the tall priest. Veureux drew a tangle of shadows out of the air and threw them in Volent's path. The strands of darkness hissed against Volent's flesh, searing through his clothes and sparkling on the surface of his chain mail. Volent pushed through them, swinging efficiently at the priest, two quick chops that caught the man's upturned arms. The tip of Volent's blade sank into bone. Veureux spun away, screaming.

"Enough!" Tession shouted. He raised his hand, and a spike of black light sprouted from his palm. He threw it at Volent, but the spear skittered off Volent's shoulder before spinning off into the night.

"Your tricks won't work on me, priest," Volent growled. "I have been into the depths of your hell, and purged the demons of your realm. The naether holds nothing for me!"

He rushed forward, swinging wildly at Tession. The priest flickered out of existence, each strike passing through a shadow of the priest, steel dragging through black ribbons, failing to land a blow. Volent howled in frustration. Tession fell back, drawing Volent farther and farther away from the altar.

The air grew cold around them. The naether leaked into the mortal world, turning the ground to ice, frosting the iron of the half-dozen sconces that lit the room. A hazy fog grew around the pair as they receded deeper into the night.

Ian stepped out of the shadows as Tession and Volent disappeared into the misty darkness. Veureux groaned helplessly at the edge of the firelight, dragging himself away, leaving a streak of blood on the stone floor. Ian walked over to him and turned him over with his boot. The priest cried out, covering his face with badly slashed arms. Ian kicked the man in the ribs, then pinned him in place with a heavy boot in the chest.

"You are the last mistake I make, Veureux! I will see this heresy burned from Cinder's faithful, even if it takes my last breath!"

"I have already... already done that," Veureux said. He was gasping through the pain, his voice soft with shock. "There are few left to purge."

"Because you have turned them?"

"Because I have killed those fools still faithful to Cinder. Cinderfell stands empty, and Hollyhaute, and beyond. Soon there will be none of the... vow... to stop us."

Veureux's flesh began to glow, like the coals in the twisted brazier on the altar. Veins of orange light stretched across the dying man's flesh. Rays of coruscating light sprang up from the veins, spinning in brilliant fans of jeweled color.

"And now my emptiness comes," Veureux said placidly. "The true quiet. The void. Farewell, Blakley. Your failure will be the stuff of legend."

The priest was wracked by one last spasm, then a spear of light pierced his chest. It burned up into the sky, slicing clean through the stone roof of the doma, turning night into day. Ian shielded his eyes from the dazzling line. Heat washed over him, and he was forced to stumble back.

A ripple of power went through the ground, rolling out from the spear and over Ian. When it hit him, Ian's chest turned to fire, and his bones to ice. He fell to one knee. The wound in his chest throbbed like a hot coal. Dropping his sword, Ian grasped his chest, digging into the flesh, trying to pluck the pain out of the scar.

The light faded. Ian took a few painful breaths and struggled to his feet. In the darkness, something stirred, tapping against the stone floor, scenting the air. Ian backed away.

"You should not fear me." The voice came from the darkness, sliding silkily through Ian's mind. He realized numbly that the ever-burning flame on the altar had gone out. A few torches still flickered in their sconces behind him, but they gave only pale light, too weak to make more of the speaker than shadows. "They made me, after all. Long ago. Though this is not the place of my birth. A new birth, then. A new living."

The tapping grew closer. Ian set his feet and raised his sword.

"Whatever you are, I will not run," Ian said. "I stood at the Fen Gate with the god descended, and in Greenhall when the hunter gheist reaved without mercy. I have faced darkness and exile and fear. If this is the day of my death, I will face it."

"Good for you," the darkness whispered, then resolved into an old man with a cane. His skin was flaked with ash, and his eyes were the pure white of the moon. "For I am the quiet, the silence that waits beyond death, the empty grave and the forgotten mercy.

"But you may call me Cinder. Kneel before your god."

Ian ran.

30

THE FORESTS AROUND the Fen Gate were unnatural. Shadows crept through the trees, and mists clung to mossy stones. These no longer felt like the forests of her youth, any more than Gwen felt like the child who had wandered them. She crept warily along, spear in hand, twitching every time a twig snapped or a leaf rustled.

From the outside, the Fen Gate looked unchanged. Knowing the destruction that had befallen it, though, she couldn't help but wonder what forces had bent to its recreation, and what other changes had occurred inside. When she reached the edge of the former village, Gwen couldn't help but sit and stare.

What was this place? Was this where she had woken up on the Allfire to find dresses laid out for her by Mab the Younger? Were these the streets she had walked in celebration of Lady Strife? Was that the tower where she had caught… what was his name? It escaped her. She was forgetting so much, and not six months had passed. How could this be?

Gwen stayed in the woods, circling around to the rear walls. Once there, she settled in and waited for her rangers to make their assault on the front gates.

From her perch high in a tree overlooking the rear

approaches of the Fen Gate, Gwen was able to see down into the courtyard, and the front gates beyond. She knew from Sir Bruler that Malcolm had fought a battle within those walls, eventually forced out by celestial proclamation. Of those battles she could see no evidence, but since the repairs, there was no reason to think she would. The soldiers manning the towers and patrolling the walls were dressed in nondescript black, and looked very much alive. She could only wonder what had happened to the Suhdrin garrison, and to whom these soldiers were loyal. She barely understood her enemy.

While she watched, there was a commotion around the gate towers. A low horn sounded, and the rattling chain that lowered the gates began its cacophonous descent. The guards went on high alert, but their attention migrated to the front of the castle. That was the best she could ask for. Gwen shimmied down the tree and started toward the rear wall.

When she was a child, Gwen had climbed up and down this wall a hundred times, usually to hunt rabbits in the woods after dinner, when she was supposed to be studying her calendar. She was glad to see the repairs hadn't ruined the handholds that littered the wall, allowing her to crawl slowly up its surface. Every moment she spent on the wall was another opportunity for one of the guards to notice her and send up the alarm. She held her breath with each handhold and foothold.

Despite a dozen missteps and a few close calls, Gwen reached the ramparts, and slid soundlessly over the wall without being seen. She scurried down a pole ladder, dropped into an alleyway near the stables, and hurried behind a pile of barrels in the lee of the Hunter's Tower. From there she peeked out into the courtyard.

Much was changed. From here, she could see that the internal setup of the castle was very different. The courtyard and many of the surrounding buildings had been torn down and replaced. What she had thought from a distance were the kennels appeared to be some kind of prison, comprised of iron cages stacked one on top of the other, three levels surrounded by catwalks and chains. The stables were gone as well, turned into a stronghouse, surrounded by black-clad guards. Only the keep and Hunter's Tower remained, though what they looked like inside, Gwen could only guess.

The kennel-prison was filled with figures, but none of them were moving very much. Occasionally one would stir their chains, or moan, but other than that the wall of cages was eerily silent. The guards watching it stared numbly toward the front gates. If they stayed distracted for a moment longer, Gwen would be able to make a break for the Hunter's Tower, and her former rooms.

She was just about to move when the door to the stronghouse opened. A puff of incense rolled out, followed by two priests. One was the inquisitor Frair Gilliam, known as the Orphanshield. Gilliam strode purposefully out, hands resting on the twin hilts of his swords, wearing the full regalia of the inquisition. The other priest was younger, though he seemed bent with age or concentration. He shadowed Gilliam's every move, and carried an iron box in his hands.

"It seems the deeper we get into this, the further we get from the truth," Gilliam said. He gestured in frustration toward the cages. "I would not have thought LaGaere capable of such heresy. But your methods have proven very effective, Frair Morrow."

"It is your wisdom that guides us," Morrow said. "My

methods are mere tools in your capable hands."

"Still, it troubles me we did not root out this corruption earlier. What horrors could we have prevented? How many deaths?"

"You mustn't let that weigh on you, frair," Morrow answered. "The things that could have been are not. We can only do as the gods ask us."

"It will weigh on me, no matter what you say." For the first time, Gilliam noticed the activity at the gates. "What business is this? Another gheist? You there, what is happening?"

The soldier Gilliam addressed stopped trotting toward the gates, saluting as he pulled up short. "A column of riders at the gates, pagan rangers, harassing the outriders. We have seen no siege equipment, and they are staying just out of bowshot."

"More of Blakley's rebels," Morrow whispered. "You were wise to expel him. A pity there was not a more permanent solution to that problem."

"I should have executed him when I had the chance," Gilliam muttered. "But there was just no evidence of heresy. We must stay within Cinder's will."

"We must, we must. And yet, the deaths we could have prevented, if unfettered from the need for reason..."

"Yes... yes..." Gilliam answered quietly, as though in a daze. "Another regret."

"Your justice will be served soon enough, my lord," Morrow said. Gwen could barely see him from her hiding place, but his voice was as smooth as silk. "Once we have brought enough of the penitent into our ranks, we can ride to Houndhallow and burn the Blakleys from this land once and for all."

"We can't go anywhere until we've purged these walls,"

Gilliam said, and Gwen detected something of the dreamlike in his voice, as though he was repeating something he had heard in his sleep. "The corruption runs deep. Never where you expect. Not even the faithful are safe from its taint."

"Yes, my frair," Morrow purred, and stroked the iron box in his hand. "But soon. Soon you will be done with it."

"Soon," Gilliam answered, though there was no emotion in his voice. He turned to the soldier, who was still waiting. "Have the penitent take care of this nuisance. We must not be disturbed. Not until the shrine is cleansed."

"They have already defeated a column of the penitent. We cannot—"

"Do as you are told," Gilliam snapped. He whirled away from the soldier, and Gwen caught a brief glimpse of his face. The priest's eyes were red-rimmed and wide, and his features slack. He looked like he was wasting away. For a moment, Gwen thought he was looking directly at her. She ducked behind the barrels and started praying, but no alarm sounded, no footsteps approached. When she heard them again, their voices were farther away, and muffled. She glanced up.

Morrow was leading Gilliam into the tower keep, guiding him by the hand, almost supporting him as he walked. Gilliam was now carrying the iron box, but its weight seemed to drag him down. As they were about to disappear into the keep, Gilliam paused and turned around, peering in the direction of the cages.

"I swear I saw something back there. A spirit among the dying. I should—"

"You are mistaken, frair. Your place is in the shrine. Doing Cinder's work."

"Yes, but..." Gilliam's voice trailed off. He took a step forward, directly toward Gwen. She gripped her spear, preparing to defend herself from whatever horror the frair summoned.

Morrow gestured with his hand, and the shadows of the courtyard deepened. The dozen prisoners in the cages moaned as one, and then the shadows lurched forward, darting across the courtyard and into Frair Gilliam. He shuddered with each impact, though there was no sound or fury to their charge. One slithered through Gwen on its way to the frair, and she caught a breath of cold stones and the grave. It reminded her of the witches' hallow, the quiet tomb of Fomharra, where all of this had begun. The shadows passed, and Gilliam shook his head.

"In the shrine," he said weakly. "Doing Cinder's work."

The two priests disappeared into the keep. Outside the walls, horns sounded, and the song of steel and hammering hooves. Battle had been joined, though Gwen hadn't seen anyone go out the sally, or over the wall. But that didn't matter now.

The Fen Gate was in the hands of Frair Gilliam. And Frair Gilliam was in the hands of a demon.

The keep was much as she remembered, only empty of life. The last time she was here, the halls were crowded with the dead and dying. Her father among them. Gwen was momentarily stilled by this thought. She hadn't been here when they died. Well, not all of her. Trapped in a gheist, rampaging against the outside of the castle. Gwen had few memories of that day. Still, she knew they were dead. Knew it from the god of death, who she had tried to lock into the hallow, and failed.

"Get a hold of yourself, Gwendolyn," she muttered. "Mourn them later."

There was no sign of the two frairs, but Gwen knew where they would be. Morrow mentioned the shrine, and purging the corruption from the castle walls. With the doma destroyed, there was only one shrine in the Fen Gate; the pagan altar, hidden deep in the catacombs, the heart of the Adair heresy. She hurried toward it.

They didn't rebuild the doma, Gwen thought as she snuck through the abandoned corridors of her former home. *I wonder why not?*

It was a question that would have to remain unanswered, for now. Through the catacombs and to the stairs leading down into the shrine, Gwen's attention sharpened, and her pulse increased. It was strange that no soldiers walked these corridors. At the very least there should be priests, guarding against pagan manifestations. Hadn't Bruler claimed they bricked over the stairway? Why would the Orphanshield reopen that barrier? Why was he in the shrine at all?

Gwen had her answer when she reached the top of the stairs. A steady cloud of incense blossomed up from the depths, but it wasn't frairwood. It smelled like hot metal and blood. Chanting drifted through the incense, words in a language Gwen didn't recognize. She started down, spear in hand, heart in her throat.

The way was lit with torches, and the walls were plastered in bloody handprints, long dried. Deep gouges scored the stone. The stairs themselves were soft with moss, and the sound of splashing water carried up. She smelled dry leaves and mildew. The chanting settled into two voices. Morrow, in the unknown language, followed by Gilliam, in high celestial.

At the bottom of the stairs, Gwen peered around the corridor and into the chamber. It was larger than she remembered. The walls were rough-hewn, the runes and sacred niches of the pagan shrine obliterated by the excavation. At the center of the room was a new altar, made of driftwood and lashed together with chains. A second look revealed that the driftwood used to make the altar was taken from the Sedgewind throne; the holy icons still dangled from their cords. Why would they use the ancestral seat of House Adair to make an altar? And why here, in the shrine to Fomharra, the pagan god of autumn?

Gilliam and Morrow stood on opposite sides of the altar, with the iron box between them. They were just beginning their ritual. With each iteration of chants, one of them would place his hands on the box, drawing power into the container. It was no surprise to Gwen that while Gilliam was channeling naether, the natural power of Cinder and the inquisition, Frair Morrow was drawing on the everealm. The everealm was home to the pagan gheists, the source of their power and their life.

How is the Orphanshield not seeing this? How is he so easily deceived? Gwen wondered.

Morrow finished his invocation, and Gilliam began his. But as the Orphanshield spoke, Gwen realized that Morrow's mouth was moving, whispering the words Gilliam breathed. Something was badly wrong here. Gwen wasn't sure what to do. The inquisition was no friend to her, but she was bent on stopping Sacombre's void priests wherever she found them. Was Morrow one of them, or did he belong to the pagans, another hidden priest of the old ways, like Gwen? She hesitated.

As Gwen watched, the iron box folded open, a complicated matter that looked more like a flower blossoming than a lid, much too organic for iron. The twin voices of the frairs rose, and lines of power erupted from the walls. The bloody handprints warped and shifted, peeling away from the stone and drifting toward the box. As they fell, they turned into autumn leaves, brilliant in the reds and oranges and yellows of that dying season, glowing with inner light. They fell into the box. Gwen straightened, trying to get a look inside.

Inside the box was a heart, made of leaves. It was enormous, and growing with each leaf that fell into the box. Veins of growing roots spread out from the heart, snaking rapidly across the face of the altar, to twine themselves into the driftwood. The heart beat with a slow rhythm. A familiar rhythm.

The heartbeat matched Gwen's own, speeding up as she realized what she was seeing. This was the heart of autumn, the soul of Fomharra, the goddess of autumn, linked inextricably to Gwen's soul. When she tore her gaze away from the box, her eyes locked with Frair Morrow.

"We have been waiting for you, huntress. What is a heart without blood, after all?"

31

ELSA FOUND THE cadre of vow knights sitting in meditation around their bonfire, ritually sharpening their swords and reciting the liturgies of the bright lady. Most of them were unknown to her, too young to have been in the field for long. Some looked like they were barely out of their initiate's robes. But one old face warmed her heart.

"Sir Voight," Elsa said as she approached the circle. "Of all the zealots I thought to find in Sophie Halverdt's mad army, you are the last."

"But still a zealot," he said. Tomas Voight was older, not quite Malcolm Blakley's age, but his copper hair was shot through with white, and his neatly trimmed beard was gray. He had been one of Elsa's mentors at the Lightfort. In her memory, his hair shone like fire, and his bladework was the finest she had ever seen. "Elsa LaFey. Gods be good, but when they told me you had joined our crusade on the outskirts of Greenhall, I could scarcely believe it."

He set aside his blade and stood, no sign of age or fatigue in his limbs. Elsa shook his hand, smiling. "I would not say that I have joined you, Tomas. Some of your number captured me, just before the whole—" she gestured in the direction of the plain of dead flowers that was slowly wilting to the south "—whatever you want to call that. Ritual of burning. I'm not here of my own free will."

"Lady Halverdt is arming her prisoners, then? These must be desperate times." He held up his hands at Elsa's protestations. "No, no, I know the story of your capture. I'm the one who gave the order. Be at peace, Elsa. I'm glad to see you didn't bolt when you had the chance."

"I haven't settled on that, yet," she said. "That's why I'm here. You lead this cadre?"

"By the grace of Strife and the will of my brethren, yes. I was on my way back to the Lightfort when word reached me of the tragedy at Greenhall. I came north to seek revenge on the pagans who attacked Halverdt's throne, only to find them already fled. But I found a better purpose. A higher calling."

"What higher calling is there than protecting the faithful from the gheist?"

"Ending the gheist, once and for all," Voight answered. "Ending the need for the winter vow, and the inquisition."

"That's what Sophie Halverdt told me. You know she's calling herself an avatar of Strife. You know that's heresy."

"It's heresy to claim that falsely, but she hasn't made the claim at all. Others have made it in her name." Voight shifted on his feet, looking over his shoulder at the rest of the vow knights. Most of them were watching the conversation with curious eyes. He took Elsa by the shoulder and turned her away from the bonfire. "What else would you call her? You have seen what she can do."

"I have seen nothing. Or worse, I've seen nothing that could not be accomplished by a witch." Elsa's words stopped Voight in his tracks. "I'm serious. You've spent more years in the field than I have, but we both know the pagans hold real power."

"Sophie Halverdt was raised in the church. She spent her youth in a convent, studying the rites of Strife, under the tutelage of the holiest souls from the Lightfort. And you accuse her of heresy?"

"Who was Tomas Sacombre, but a holy man? And look what became of him."

"Sacombre was an inquisitor of Cinder. The high inquisitor, at that," Voight said. "Why should I be surprised he fell into darkness?"

"You are missing the point! Cinder and Strife stand together. We always have, and, gods ordain, we always will. If Sacombre was a heretic, there is nothing to say that the high elector, or the celestriarch, or Mistress LeViere, or any of us can't also be deceived."

"Is that an accusation, or a confession?"

"Neither, and both," Elsa stepped back. "What are you doing here, Tomas? How can you follow this girl, when gheists are still rising throughout Tenumbra, and the whole of the north is at war?"

"I am fighting the battle at hand," Voight said. "You saw the army we face. Sophie Halverdt led us here to destroy that army, and burn the corruption it represents out of the church. Only then will Tenumbra be safe."

"What's that supposed to mean? Are we fighting demons, or fighting the church? I look around and see a lot of banners of Strife, but where are the inquisitors? And how do you claim to stand for the church when none of Cinder's faithful dare join us?"

"You know what I mean."

"Tomas? Where is your inquisitor? Francis Thieppe, that was his name."

Voight's expression grew sour, and his hands curled into fists. "We separated. There was an argument, a gheist that he would not tame, and I left him on the road to Gallowsport."

"But he lives, as far as you know."

"What sort of monster do you think I am? Of course he lives. I have fought and bled and prayed at that man's side for decades. I wouldn't cut his throat as he slept." Voight drew himself up straight, glaring at Elsa. "This is a war, not a cull."

"And when it comes to that? When Sophie Halverdt finishes whatever she's doing here, and marches this army to Cinderfell, and starts stringing up every priest and saint of Cinder that she comes across, what will you do then?" Elsa narrowed her eyes, hand casually on her sword. "Because that's where this ends, Tomas. That's where this is going."

"Who are you to make accusations? Show me your flame, draw summer into your blade, and then we can talk about who is walking on Strife's path, and who has gone astray." He waited a long moment, finally smiling cruelly when Elsa didn't move. "No, you can't do those things. Because the bright lady has abandoned you. I suggest you think long and hard about that, Elsa."

"Sophie has gone mad, Tomas. You must see that."

"Perhaps. But sometimes madness is of the gods. I may not trust Sophie Halverdt, Elsa. But I certainly trust the goddess who is working through her. It's not my fault you've lost faith." Voight was about to turn away, but he paused. "One last word. Even the tamped flame can be rekindled. Do not throw away Sophie's help, just because you don't trust the child. Our enemy is great. But we are greater."

With that, he turned on his heel and marched back to the bonfire. One of the young vow knights asked him a question, but Voight's answer was lost. Whatever he said, the young knight looked back at Elsa with shock and fear on his face.

Elsa stumbled through the camp, ignoring young Morganne's protests and the stares of the people she passed. Tears stung her eyes, but she refused to acknowledge them. She skirted the edge of the wilting plain of flowers and walked into the forest. She could see the Reaveholt to the south, and the rocky bluffs of the Tallow at its feet.

Everything had gone upside down for her at some point. When Elsa tried to think back to when that had begun, she couldn't quite fix it in her mind. When she had come out of the Lightfort, it was to a life that she understood. Hunting gheists, protecting the faithful celestials throughout Tenumbra, tracking down pagans and keeping them from endangering their neighbors with heresy, or worse. Straightforward.

Even when her assignment took her north, Elsa was glad. She preferred the thick forests of Tener to the perfumed courts of Suhdra, and if the risk of gheists was greater, so was the need for holy protectors. That was where she had met Frair Lucas, in the quiet halls of Cinderfell, itching to be on his way.

At first, Elsa didn't understand Lucas. Most of the inquisitors that she had known were zealous to a fault, committed to the dangerous balancing act of worshipping a god of death and judgment. Lucas was different. His worship of Cinder was earnest, but his judgment was more lenient.

He was more likely to understand why people did things, rather than simply condemning them for what they did, or how. While many in the north feared the inquisition, Lucas was loved in certain parts of Tener, and if their hunts didn't always lead to pagan henges, it often brought her face to face with gheists in need of putting down.

The business with Gwen Adair still bothered her. Elsa had never been convinced of the girl's innocence, or the necessity of her hidden god. Lucas had a theory about the gheists, that their endless slaughter and seasonal rebirth was what was driving them mad, and could even be destroying the land as well. So when he learned of Adair's heresy, Lucas wanted to observe, rather than arrest. They had followed Gwen all the way to the witches' hallow, and watched as the child summoned and bound one of the great old gods of the pagan faith.

Perhaps that was where she had gone wrong. It was not the vow knight's mission to stand idly by while pagan gods roamed the earth, and yet that was what Elsa had done. Even after the heresy of the Adairs was revealed, as well as that of Tomas Sacombre, Elsa had not struck. She had let Gwen escape, and the god with her.

That was why Elsa had let Lucas go his own way. By duty, she should have accompanied him to Heartsbridge, but she couldn't do it. Her vow, her mission, was to Gwen Adair. To find her, to hunt her, to bring her to justice. She still remembered breaking the news to Lucas. He had not taken it well. Neither of them had.

Despite all that, even as Elsa hunted, this time with Ian Blakley in tow, she was unsure what she would do when she found Gwen. Judgment was an inquisitor's business.

Vengeance belonged to Strife, but Elsa held no anger in her heart toward the huntress. If anything, she felt bad for the girl. And when they did find Gwen, it was to fight at her side at Houndhallow against this new heresy, these void priests. Elsa wasn't sure what to think of them.

All she truly knew was that the goddess who had been so close to her since she was a child, the light that had burned in her heart and fanned the flames of her joy for decades, was gone. Had vanished in the final reckoning against the voidfather. Gone from her heart, from her blood, from her mind. Something Elsa had done must have offended the bright lady, and Strife had withdrawn her blessing.

Withdrawn it and given it to a mad child. Sophie Halverdt, who had done nothing to earn the favor of Strife, was suddenly the gifted avatar of flames. Surely there was something wrong about that. Surely that wasn't just.

No, Elsa thought. *But it certainly was vengeful.*

Alone in the woods, she unbuckled her sword and pulled the leather band from her hair. It had been so long since she had drawn on the power of Strife that Elsa's hair had begun to grow back. Her usual charred locks were giving way to cascades of soft hair. It tickled her face and drove her mad. It wasn't a vow knight's hair. It didn't feel right, but she couldn't bring herself to cut it or burn it away. Somehow that would feel like cheating. Like pretending to be something that she wasn't. That she would never be again.

The thought of never drawing Strife's flame again sparked both fear and rage in Elsa's heart. She sat on the ground, crossing her legs and laying her blade across her knees. This is how she had sat when she'd sought Strife's blessing in the past, on the rare occasions when the mistress of summer had seemed far away. Elsa had tried this a dozen times since Houndhallow. One more time wouldn't hurt.

She started by concentrating on the beat of her heart. Strife's power stirred in the blood of the faithful, echoing through the bloodwrought runes of the vow knight's blade and armor, drawing the flame into existence. As she meditated, though, she could feel nothing. The blade was cold, her heart silent, the song of her blood muted. The doors that led to Strife's realm were closed, as if they had never been there at all.

Elsa breathed through the dozens of exercises she had learned at the Lightfort, reciting liturgies and invoking promises given her by the priests. They echoed through her head, falling on deaf ears. The promises were broken.

It wasn't me. I didn't break my promises, not to Strife, not to the church, or Lucas, or my parents, Elsa thought. *I've been true! I've been faithful, and holy, and just. This isn't my fault. I'm not the one who broke this deal. It was you! It was Strife! I'm the one who's been abandoned. I'm the one!*

Anger kindled in her heart, and she fed it. If Strife was the goddess of flame and joy, well, she was also the goddess of hate. She was petty, she was vindictive, and Elsa was done with her. If this was how she was going to treat her faithful, abandoning them without warning and without instruction on how to return, then Elsa wanted nothing to do with her. There were better gods. There was a better hope, even if Elsa had to forge it herself.

Something stirred. Deep in her heart, nestled against that anger, nothingness became flame. Elsa's eyes shot open. She leapt to her feet, snatching the sword as it tumbled from her knees, and gave a shout of joy. Stoking the flame, she drew it into her blood, and thrilled at the sudden heat that filled her. Winter be damned!

Elsa drew the blade and pushed fire into the runes. They sparked to life, then blinding fire coruscated across the steel. She howled with joy, holding the sword aloft and feeding more and more power into it. The sword became a bonfire. She could feel, just at the edge of her attention, young Morganne watching her from the clearing. Elsa turned and laughed, and the child disappeared into the trees.

The flames grew and grew, and Elsa filled them with her anger.

32

IN THE COURTYARD of Houndhallow, shouts of panic and horror filled the air. Ian stumbled out of the doma, fear numbing his legs. Waves of freezing mist clung to his face. The columns of guards had scattered, running from the malevolence leaking out of the doma. Considering the things the people of Houndhallow had seen and the evils they had faced, Ian couldn't blame them. He found Volent kneeling just outside the entrance to the sanctuary.

"Henri, can you walk? We have to muster the guard."

"Tession got away. Did something to my heart, and got away," Volent said quietly. When Ian laid a hand on Volent's shoulder, he flinched. "Leave me, Ian. I am no good to you."

"There was a time when that was true," Ian said. "But not now. Whatever has crossed us in the past, we have gotten through it. Together." Ian hooked an arm under Volent's and heaved him to his feet. "Now get moving."

Volent looked at him curiously. His face was blank, without fear or anger, but the scars that crisscrossed his features had turned black.

"Whatever has frightened you, Ian, there is no point to it. We will die here, or we won't. What does it matter?"

"Well, there's the dying part. I thought I was okay with

that for a while, but it turns out I'm not, so, please." He tugged on Volent's arm. "I'm not going to leave you here to face him alone."

"Face whom?" Volent asked, looking over Ian's shoulder. "Ah, yes. I see."

Ian looked back. Cinder was a bare outline in the mists, drawing them into himself, his eyes shining like twin moons behind the clouds.

"You don't know what he is, Volent. Trust me..."

"Oblivion. That is death enough for me." Volent shook Ian off and faced the approaching god. "Leave it to me. Emptiness will always find a home."

Ian hesitated, but Volent shoved him away and turned back to the shrine. After a heartbeat of uncertainty, Ian turned and ran into the courtyard.

"Banners of Houndhallow! Brave swords of the north, hear me! We have been betrayed. Gather your courage, and stand with me once again into the night!"

"They will not hear you, Ian Blakley, Ian of Hounds, coward son of the Reaverbane," Tession said. The priest had been lurking in the shadows of the courtyard. He was dressed still in the vestments of the celestial church, but carried a black staff of twisted metal. "I have plucked what courage they might have had from their mortal hearts, and turned it to my will. You must stand alone, and die alone."

"I don't fear your threats, void priest. Folam underestimated the strength of the Blakleys, as did Sacombre. We overcame them both. And now I will defeat you, as well."

"Your father bested the heretic Sacombre," Tession said. He drew the staff across his chest, then snapped it straight, pointing at Ian. "But you are not your father."

A hideous energy poured from the staff. It struck Ian in the chest. His wound answered. The shards of Folam's pendant squirmed beneath his skin. Light danced across his chest, tearing away his robes, splintering the chain of his shirt like frayed rope. Ian stumbled back, trying to remain upright even as the pain pressed him down. Finally he fell, first to his knees, then his hands and face were pressed to the filthy ground. Snow filled his mouth, snow laced with blood. He could hear screaming; his own, the fleeing guards, the air itself. He pushed himself up on one hand and grabbed at his chest.

The wound was no longer empty. The black roots of a tree grew from his flesh, sharp and sticky with his blood. As Ian watched, the tree stretched spindly fingers toward the ground. He could feel its roots burrowing through his ribs, filling him, feeding on him. His fingers scrambled at its tiny branches, but the wood was as hard as iron, as sharp as steel.

"These things have been forgotten," Tession hissed. "I will remind the world!"

Black roots stretched out from Ian's chest, feeling their way toward the hard-packed soil of the courtyard. He wrapped his hands around the trunk rising from his chest, trying to pull it free, but it was as much a part of him as his bones. He screamed out, but only Frair Tession's tepid laughter answered.

"We hoped to do this at Cinderfell, you understand. To draw the darkness down where it had first been lifted up. But Houndhallow is more than a worthy home for our new god. Don't you think?"

"Fuck you!" Ian shouted, but the pain of the blossoming wound turned his voice to a whimper. Tession bent closer to Ian.

"This is what we were looking for. That rebel spark! When you charged that gheist outside of Greenhall, we knew we had our man. A pity it took so long to harvest you. But I'm not sure I've seen a finer vessel."

Ian tried to answer, but the tree growing out of his chest was becoming difficult to manage. He fell forward, and the trunk slammed into the ground. Branches twisted through his lungs, and a whole web of roots unfolded from the base of the trunk, spreading across the hard earth. They melted into the ground, burrowing like worms. Ian gasped in pain, and then the tree started to grow.

It lifted him off the ground by his bones. The agony of its birth became unimaginable. Ian screamed and screamed, his throat growing raw, until a tangle of branches crawled up out of his mouth and silenced him.

He hung quietly over the courtyard, staring down at Frair Tession. Some part of his mind wondered what had become of Volent, where Nessie might be. Whether his father was alive, or dead, or still fighting. Tears streamed down his cheeks. Ian tried to move, but the tree held him in place. It was still growing, taller and taller, wider and wider. At first he thought it would tear him open, bursting through his flesh, but soon realized the tree was lapping over him like water. He sank into it.

The last thing he saw was Frair Tession, smiling sharply and shaking his head. Then the bark closed over his face, and there was only darkness and the sound of branches scraping across the stones.

He was there forever. Ian could feel the roots clawing through winter-ravaged earth, feel the trunk push aside cobblestones as it grew wider, taste the wind in the branches. Like flowers turning to the sun, the tree reached and reached toward the darkness growing inside the doma. And the darkness reached back. Deep in the shadows, the spirit of Cinder sang to the tree, of homecoming and remembrance. Of heartbreak. Of longing.

Eventually the growth stopped. Time passed, time that couldn't be measured. There was no passage of days or nights, no meals; time passed without sleep. There was only the deep vibration of the earth, pulsing between the tree and the shadow. It was a song that passed through stones and shivered the earth, though Ian was sure that if he were outside the tree he wouldn't be able to hear it at all. Ian's heart stopped, but the rhythm of the earth continued. He melted into it.

In time, there was another presence. Hands on his bark, a voice traveling through his branches. Cold hands. Cold words. They didn't mean anything to him, but the presence in the doma took notice. It struggled, trying to run from the voice without abandoning the tree. There was pain, of a reunion long anticipated and suddenly interrupted. Fear of abandoning something sought after, yearned for, and finally found. But fear also of the voice, and what it could do. What it was already doing. Ian watched this exchange from afar.

Suddenly, he was drawn into it. The voice changed, and Ian fell through the tree, into the song between root and shadow. He became aware of the tree, seeing it from the outside for the first time. It was black and tall, with gnarled limbs barren of leaves, reaching up into the sky. Its bark was ash. Among its branches hung pagan icons, tied with leather and swinging in the breeze. Frair Tession knelt beside the base of the tree, whispering into its roots. How much time had passed? Where was Volent, or Clough? Where were his people?

No time, he realized. *No time has passed. And there is no one to save me.*

The gaunt frame of Cinder, summoned from the shrine by Ian so long ago (or yesterday? Or just now?) stood at the door of the profane doma. It watched the tree with unabashed longing.

Another sound filled the air. Horns, and shouting. Ian tried to turn his attention to the world beyond the courtyard, but found himself unable to look that way, as though he were in a dream that contained nothing more than the tree, the courtyard, and the song. Even the walls of Houndhallow seemed a distant horizon, lost in the fog.

The tree wavered, but the song continued. He descended into the branches, sliding through bark until he was facing Frair Tession. The priest's whisper hissed across his mind, promising chains and threatening freedom. Ian glanced behind him and saw Cinder reaching out, thin hands stretching thinner to cross the space between shrine and branches. He turned back to Tession.

"You can't do this! I won't let you!" Ian yelled. He wasn't sure where his voice was coming from, or who could hear it, but Tession continued his whispers. Ian hauled back and punched Tession in the throat, watching as his hand, ghost-limned and bright, passed through the priest's skull without resistance. Frustrated, he punched again. This time Tession opened an eye, scowling in Ian's direction.

"Be gone, spirit. You have no place here," Tession said. Ian felt a tug at his heart, as if he were caught on a fish hook. "The god of graves answers to me now."

"Not yet, he doesn't!" Ian answered. He threw himself at Tession, but before his ghostly form could reach the priest, Tession raised a hand and whispered. Ian flew back against the tree, hanging against its bark like a leaf caught in the wind. He couldn't move.

"This will be over soon, young hound," Tession said. "We are almost done with you."

Ian tried to scream, but there was no air in his lungs, and no shape to his mouth. He twisted against the tree like a man on the gallows, waiting to be cut down. Tession knelt again and began to whisper. On the platform above, Cinder drew closer.

Something about the gaunt man on the stairs was familiar. The frame, the cracked lips, the tentative way it stretched out its hand toward the tree. It was all very familiar, like a dream Ian had once. Or like a dream he had been captured inside. He looked back to Cinder, then down at the tree.

Elsa and I were trapped in that dream, Ian thought. *She couldn't do anything because she was... she was trapped in the trees. But the old man, Night himself, he only let us go when I drew Death's attention to his little deception. But what does that have to do with this? What is this tree, and why is Cinder drawn to it?* Cinder was closer now, and Tession's whispers were coming faster, more urgent. *And who do you draw to scare away the god of winter?*

Summer, of course. But how...

Ian looked down at his hands. His veins were black, their ends sprouting from his flesh in thin branches that dripped poison, and his fingers were tipped in gnarled, hungry roots. Whatever seed the voidfather's wound had planted in Ian, it had taken to his flesh, and was growing through him. The tree might have sprouted, but the corruption that twisted it was still in Ian's blood.

Ian was the poison Tession hoped to use against the winter spirit. The tree was only the bait, though it had grown from him. If the tree was harmless without Ian's presence, then the only choice was to remove himself from the tree. But how?

He thought back to the dream. If he couldn't call on another power to force Cinder's hand, he would have to draw Cinder's attention elsewhere. He cast about the courtyard, unnatural eyes roaming through the doma, scanning the walls, feeling out the spiritual weight of Houndhallow. His mind brushed against his sister, and Sir Clough, standing together facing the door to their room, waiting to die. He sensed the fear of his people, watching from windows, still in their nightclothes, as their lord was turned into a pagan god. Ian felt terror beyond knowing, and then he felt emptiness. Emptiness.

Volent?

Huddled beneath the shattered altar in the doma, a man made of nothing but wounds and emptiness. In a blink, Ian hovered over him, his form weak so far from the roots of the tree. He reached down and drew the man's attention.

"Volent," he whispered, and his voice sounded like the scratching of wind-stirred branches. "I need you."

Henri Volent lay still and cold. His eyes were open, staring blankly toward the shadow-wrapped form of Cinder. The hems of his clothes were singed. At first Ian worried that the man was dead, but as he watched, Volent's chest rose and fell with shallow breath. Ian tried again.

"Sir Volent, you have to get up. I need you to do something for me."

Volent blinked and turned toward Ian's hovering form. He took a long moment to focus, then smiled.

"Sir Blakley. I see that he's gotten a hold of you, as well. I thought I was done with him, but all the handles were still there. He wields me like a sword, Ian. Like a glove. Sacombre knew me well enough."

"Sacombre is long gone, Henri. You need to get up. There's something you must do, or all is lost."

"All is long lost, Ian. Finding it is just the first step in losing everything. Why search? Why get up at all? Best to be born in the grave."

"This is not the man I knew. The Henri Volent I knew—"

"You never knew Henri Volent. Henri Volent died a child, and has been walking around ever since, waiting for the gods to let him go. And they have. They finally have." Volent laid his head back down, nestling harder against the altar. "I don't want to get up anymore."

"Then fuck Henri Volent," Ian snapped. "Give me the Deadface."

"You were never his friend, Ian. Neither of us was. Leave me in peace."

"I will not," Ian said. He reached down and brushed the hungry veins of his hand against Volent's shoulder. "You are needed, Volent. Come when you are called."

The black roots latched onto Volent's shoulder, squirming across the armor toward his neck. Volent's eyes snapped open. He thrashed against the stone, trying to batter the black lines before they reached his flesh. But the darkness was drawn to Volent like metal shavings to a lodestone. They poured into his scars, running between the cracks in his face, quenching his tears. Volent screamed, but slowly his face grew still. The jigsaw ruin of his flesh flowed together, leaving only dark veins under the skin. He stood and turned to Ian's hovering image.

"You do not know what you have done, Ian Blakley," Volent said.

"I have done what was necessary. And now it is your turn. Go, disrupt the ritual, and bring this tree down."

"You misunderstand our relationship, Ian." Volent looked around the platform, finally spying his sword, and retrieved it. "You have given me the corruption meant for the god of winter. Do you think that makes me indebted to you? Worse, do you think it makes me subservient?" Volent's dead voice had returned, as soft as a whisper and as sharp as knives. He stalked toward the courtyard, testing the weight of his blade. "I don't think so."

"What are you doing?" Ian asked. He followed Volent, hovering just beyond his shoulder. The courtyard came into view, and Cinder's gaunt form, long fingers tangled with the black tree below.

"What I want. And I've wanted to do this for a long time." Volent came up next to Cinder and looked him over. "Hello, old friend. What do you think they'll make of this?"

Cinder only glanced at Volent before turning his attention back to the tree. Volent shrugged, drew back his sword, and cut Cinder in half at the jaw. The blade sliced cleanly through the gheist's pallid skull, leaving chin and jowls but severing the rest of his head. Cinder's hands shot up in shock, snapping back to their normal size, rustling the tree in their hasty retreat.

"No!" Tession screamed. The frair fell back from the tree, shielding his face, howling. "We were so close!"

"And you will never be closer," Volent said. He turned back to Ian. "As for you..."

The blade came so fast that Ian didn't even have time to be surprised. He felt it in his gut, then there was darkness and a pressing weight all around him, as though he were drowning. Ian tried to scream, but it came out in a creaking groan that never left his lips. He dropped, and when he opened his eyes, Ian saw that he was hanging from the black tree, tangled in the straps of leather and pagan icons. The bindings cut into his flesh, squeezing him black and blue. He swung there painfully, unable to move. Frair Tession cowered at the base of the tree, iron staff twisting in his hands, staring at the shadowed entrance of the doma. The Deadface still stood in the doorway of the doma, but of Cinder there was no sign.

"I expected more," Volent said, almost casually. "Kill the god of winter and gray lord of the quiet house... you'd think there would be more to it than that. Poof, and he's gone. No cataclysmic tide of spirits, no flames, no cracks in the earth. Just silence. But maybe that's all we can expect of the grave. Anyway—" he hefted his sword and started walking toward Ian "—who will be next? Which of you will be the first to find out what death is like, now that Cinder is no more?"

Frair Tession turned and ran for the keep. Volent shrugged and turned to Ian.

"Looks like it's you, Ian. A fitting end for a troublesome child, don't you think?"

33

THE ARMOR FELT right. It wasn't her armor, her blood wasn't forged into the steel, and there were no runes across the chest or pauldrons to focus her holy fire, but it still felt right. In fact, Elsa no longer needed runes to draw Strife's flames into her blade, or to wrap herself in summer's protective light. The flames came at a thought, almost as though they were eager to consume.

Elsa drew her sword and shifted her mind to the fire lurking in the blade, waiting to be summoned. It called to her, and she answered. Flames sizzled across the steel, throwing sharp shadows and heat through the tent.

"Godsbless!" Morganne yelped. The squire jumped aside, covering her face as the flames grew. Elsa chuckled, then tamped the sword and sheathed it. Morganne blinked in the sudden darkness. "Is that really necessary?"

"If you knew the joy of it, you would not ask that question," Elsa said. "To have lost this power for so long, and to have it back." She laughed and flexed her hand. Fingers of flame danced across the gauntlet. "It is like a lame man being able to walk once again. No, not walk! To fly!"

"I would be content with walking," Morganne said. She turned back to folding up Elsa's new robes, gifted by Lady

Halverdt from her personal wardrobe. "LeViere would not train me. She said I lacked the discipline."

The tent flap opened and Sophie Halverdt came in. She was beaming as she looked around Elsa's humble quarters.

"Discipline is for joyless Cinder. Strife's gift is joy, abundant and full," she said. "Sir LaFey, where are the ornaments I gave you? This place is nearly as drab as an inquisitor's festival!"

"I prefer a simple room, though I thank you for your generosity. What is the enemy's disposition this morning? Has Malcolm Blakley answered your summons?"

"The lord of Houndhallow does not simply answer my every call. But we have come to an understanding. Our forces will join together this glorious day, with the heretics dying between us! Malcolm Blakley and I will sign our alliance in the blood of evil men."

"My place is with the vow knights. If there are gheists among the heretic's host, we will need to cut them down before they can engage the rank and file."

"Actually, your place is at my side. Sir Voight is anxious for you to join them, but it is my will... it is Strife's will, as well, that you remain with me."

"My lady, you do not keep an arrow at your side and throw a knife across the room. Use each weapon as it needs to be used. The power Strife has gifted to me should not be left in the sheath!"

"Your zeal is admirable, sir. Have no fear, it will be rewarded. Sir Voight and his men have been distributed throughout the battle line, in anticipation of widespread heresy. We will see many gheists, many opportunities for glory."

"Then why am I being wasted in the back lines, rather

than meeting the gheists on the field of battle?"

"You are being held in reserve. Voight can handle whatever small demons the heretics are willing to throw into the fray early on. Summoning and controlling these creatures costs them much. They will not draw on their greater powers until they must. It is Voight's job to ensure they are forced to make that choice. And when they do, when they show their true power—" Sophie stepped close, tapping Elsa in the chest "—it is your job, your destiny, to destroy them. Completely."

Elsa tilted her head and smiled. "I will answer that call, my lady. I was born to destroy the gheist."

"Forged," Sophie said. "By Strife herself."

As night fell, Elsa was growing impatient. The churning wall of mist that concealed the far side of the battlefield had receded to a narrow column, leaving the forces of the celestial heretics exposed to Strife's burning light. The celestials were formed up in a narrow V shape, with the point grounded in that column of mist, and the two arms spread down the valley. The shorter arm faced Malcolm's army on the ridgeline opposite, while the longer, thicker arm lined up against Sophie and her radiant hordes. Elsa couldn't see much of the far battle; Malcolm's banners would occasionally sway and swirl, but for the most part the duke of Houndhallow seemed to have recovered from the initial ambush in his flank. Elsa was strangely relieved.

As for the armies of Halverdt, Elsa wasn't sure what to think. Sophie was fighting with disengaged calm, allowing her forces to grind individually against the celestials, with little real advantage. Knights charged and fell back, ranks of spears and halberds surged forward, held ground, were flanked and eventually surrendered their positions. Every once in a while a gheist would erupt from the celestial lines, and Sir Voight and his knights of the winter vow would throw themselves into the melee. Every time that happened, Elsa's blood stirred. She wanted to be down there, reaping glory and sowing discord in the enemy ranks. That was her place. Not here.

"My lady, night is falling. If we are to end this battle with Strife's glory, we must move decisively, and soon," she said. Sophie sat placidly by, watching the fight, not answering. Elsa rode closer. "We cannot let night drive us from the field of battle. Our strength is in the sun."

"Tell me about your vows, Sir LaFey," Sophie said.

"My vows? What are you talking about?"

"The winter vow. To carry the light of Strife into Cinder's realm, to remind people that even in the darkness, there is hope in the dawn. That vow."

Elsa looked helplessly down at the battle, then back to her strangely complacent commander. "There's not much more than that. Protect the church, aid the weak, stand firmly by…" She paused, because she had sworn to stand firmly by Cinder, and her inquisitor. Where was Frair Lucas? Hopefully safe on the other side of the Tallow. Surely Martin could see to him. "Mostly we swear to shine brightly in the darkness, to bring summer into winter's hearth."

"Then why does nightfall frighten you? Look up. All the stars, sir, and none of them beholden to Cinder's pale light. Have you ever wondered whose host they are, if not his?" Sophie raised a hand to the sky, motioning to the few pinpricks of light that pierced the dusk. "Might they not be children of Strife, holding her light in the darkness?"

"This is... Why are we discussing theology, my lady? The heretics are before us. We have the strength to crush them, but you hesitate. Why?"

"Sometimes darkness must grow, so that light's full glory may be shown." Sophie peered across the battlefield, intent on Blakley's distant banners. "Not long now."

Elsa fidgeted uncomfortably. The fire of Strife burned inside her, itching to get out. She wasn't sure how much more patience she could manage. Lucas had always been the patient one, lending a few calm words whenever Elsa's temper was up, listening while she vented her anger, her fury. Without him around, Elsa was pretty sure she would start chewing iron and spitting flame pretty soon. She hoped he was—

A sharp light pierced Elsa's mind. She threw her head back, flame coursing from skull to spine, light clouding her vision. She could feel the fire being drawn from her, like sparks fuming from a forge. The heat grew and grew, until it was a glorious pain that stretched through her entire body. Even in her shock, Elsa could hear herself whimpering.

Finally it stopped. She slumped forward in her saddle. Sweat drenched her brow and the long curls of her hair. She sat there, shoulders heaving, eyes swimming in the sudden darkness.

"And so we begin," Sophie whispered.

"What was that?" Elsa whispered. "I felt it entering the world... a terrible light... an anger..."

"Anger is Strife's gift, sir. And through you, it has been given to my army. Their sacrifice will be worthy of the bright lady."

A distant light grew on the horizon. Elsa looked up

and saw pillars of light shooting into the sky from the field opposite. Three became a dozen, became a solid wall of sharp flame where Malcolm's army must be. Elsa sat up.

"What is happening?" she asked frantically. "What have you done?"

"Have faith," Sophie said. "This is not of them, but of us. Of you." She turned to Elsa, smiling. Her eyes swirled with amber sparks that drifted down her cheeks, tangling in the golden strands of her hair. "We are bringing true faith to the north."

A great cry went up over the battlefield, like a thousand men screaming their last defiant breath. In the ranks of the celestial army, banners swirled and horns sounded. They pulled away from Sophie's lines, realigning themselves to Malcolm's forces.

"Have reinforcements come to Malcolm's line? Did you know this was going to happen?"

"His line has been strengthened. Given the gift of Strife. You asked what I was waiting for." Sophie stood up in her stirrups and signaled to the herald nearby. "Close the ranks and seal the ends of the valley. None of our enemy can be allowed to escape, no matter what happens." As the horn sounded, she turned back to Elsa. "I was waiting for the will of the goddess."

"We're not going to advance?"

"We will not have to," Sophie said. "Our enemy will come to us. With me, sir."

Sophie led her small escort forward, gathering stray knights and bannermen as she went. Elsa stayed at her side. As they approached the front lines, Elsa saw that there was increasing chaos in the celestial ranks. Points of light appeared among them. The wall of flame was gone, but bright lights filled the battlefield, throwing strange and frantic shadows into the forest, and across Sophie's lines. It looked almost like a lightning storm was chewing through the celestial army, flashing and sparking and disappearing once again, only to burst into new light somewhere else. The ranks of Sophie's army were absolutely silent, watching the light show in rapt attention.

"Steady, everyone," Sophie called out. "Steady and they will come."

On the far flank, near the twisting pillar of mist, a skirmish broke out among the columns of celestial spearmen. A tangle of soldiers spilled into the open ground between celestial and Halverdt lines, some men running in panic, others wheeling around to face whatever disturbance had broken their ranks. A single figure burst into the open, a man made of light and fury. He wielded two swords, one in each hand, and was hacking madly into the celestials, wheeling and spinning, cutting through shields and chain as if they were made of cloth.

The celestials turned on him, holding him at bay with spears and calling for their friends to help. Anyone foolish enough to engage him was cut down. Finally they fell on him as one, hacking and stabbing, driving spears through his belly, pinning him to the ground. And still he fought, breaking spear shafts and stumbling forward, still swinging those flaming swords.

Finally he stumbled. A celestial knight lunged forward and struck him in the back of the head with an axe, getting a sword in the knee for his trouble, but soon after, the soldier of light dropped flat to the ground and died.

A cloud of sparks wafted up from his body, dancing in the fresh night, until they disappeared up among the stars.

"What manner of spirit was that?" Elsa asked. She looked over at Sophie. The duchess of Greenhall sat attentively, leaning toward the battle. The girl had an impish grin on her face. "What have you done?"

"Brought the light of Strife into the night," she said. "That her glory may be revealed for all to see."

There were a dozen burning figures among the ranks of the celestials. No, a hundred. They tore through the dark-clad ranks of the heretics with mad abandon, attacking recklessly, dying gloriously. Most were on foot, though they wore the shining armor of mounted knights, as though their abandoned horses could not keep up with their zeal. The cloud of embers was joined by another, and another, until the air over the battlefield was thick with dying sparks. But for every cloud, there were dozens of celestial dead.

The long, steady wall of the celestial army finally broke, tumbling across the empty ground like water spilling over an eroded dam. They threw down their weapons, shields, and banners, breaking toward Sophie's lines in desperation.

"Cut them down," Sophie said. "And be careful of the radiant ones. They will not be easy to stop." Then she turned and rode away.

Elsa stayed and watched the slaughter.

34

THE ONLY GLORY was bloodshed. The only need was destruction. The only light was the fire burning from Malcolm's heart, and the only fear was in the eyes of his foes. Malcolm Reaverbane cut a swathe through his adversaries, singing as he killed.

The enemy collapsed around him. Malcolm remembered riding a horse, a dim memory that seemed unnatural to him now. Why ride when he could run? Why run when he could fly! The speed of his blade propelled him through the crowded battlefield. Wherever his foot touched the earth, it left ash and boiling stone.

"Come to me, blade-prey! Come to me, corpses-walking! Come to me, you who have not yet seen the light of Strife, that I may deliver you from your wretched lives!" Malcolm spied a banner and its attendant shieldguard, and sped toward it. "Offer me your steel, and I will take your blood!"

The shieldwall turned in his direction. Beyond the scared faces of the men-at-arms, huddled behind their shields, Malcolm saw one of the priests—Cinder's priests, or heretics like Sacombre; he didn't care. They were opposed to the light, and he was light's greatest champion, its brightest flame. He trotted in their direction, howling.

Malcolm struck the shieldwall like a comet, jumping in the air and landing with both feet on iron-bound faces. One man's shield crumpled, knocking him flat, and then his two companions were pressing their shields against Malcolm, trying to drive him back. He set his feet and shoved, putting his shoulder into one man while striking with his sword at the other. The flame-chased edges of his blade cut through steel and wood and flesh, leaving an edge of smoldering pitch. On the other side, his shoulder blow knocked the man flat. Malcolm sliced through the fallen soldier's belly, then turned back and drove his sword straight through the first soldier.

By now the rest of the shieldwall was in a panic. They split apart, leaving their fallen companions to die in the open. The priest stood alone, staring at Malcolm with a look of annoyance.

"There is more to this fight than blades," the priest spat.

"The sword serves me well," Malcolm roared. "It will do for your death."

The priest laughed and drew a vertical line with his staff, slamming the head into the ground. The air split in its wake, opening up into darkness. A pallid fist reached through, feeling out the earth before being joined by another arm, a third, and then a whole gheist crawled through the rift. It looked like a hound, but with human arms instead of legs, and hands as long and spindly as giant spiders. Its fur was thin and wispy, the pale flesh beneath riddled with scabs and pus.

"Another hound for your hallow, Blakley."

"Another body for the grave," Malcolm spat. He kicked a fallen spear into his other hand, then charged forward.

The hound snapped at him, following the spear with

swollen jaws, finally catching the barbed tip between its teeth. Malcolm leaned into it, pushing the gheist's head back, and brought his sword down on the creature's neck. Thick muscle parted, but the gheist thrashed its head, shattering the spear and catching Malcolm on the knee. He went down, but rolled to his feet just as the gheist pounced. Strong hands gripped his shoulder and arm, the beast's chest plowing against Malcolm, forcing him down. Teeth snapped just above Malcolm's head. He shoved the forte of his blade into the creature's mouth, driving the sword back until it was in the crook of the demon's jaw. The gheist continued to try to bite down, cutting itself deeply in the process.

The air that rolled out of the gheist's mouth was thick and fetid, washing over Malcolm in a miasma of death and decay. Bile filled Malcolm's throat, but he held on. The hands on his shoulder tightened, straining steel and pinching chain. With his left arm pinned against his chest, and his right straining to keep the gheist's jaws away, Malcolm was nearly helpless.

"It is good that your lady has learned to use her gifts," the priest purred, not ten feet away. "Not like you, Blakley. Such a waste."

The sound of the man's voice infuriated Malcolm. His eyes swam with rage, his blood boiling. He screamed his anger, and pushed up with the sword. The blade started to pull free of the gheist's jaws, and the creature bit harder, twisting the steel in Malcolm's hand. But at the same time the gheist's head tilted up, exposing its throat. Malcolm stopped screaming and clenched his jaw, then drove his helm into the gheist's soft throat.

Flesh collapsed, the gheist pulled back, but Malcolm had

lost none of his frenzy. He butted his head into the gheist's throat again and again, grinding the metal of his helm against soft skin, blood spattering into his eyes, his mouth. The gheist yelped, then choked and screamed at the same time. Something snapped under Malcolm's brow. The gheist released him and rolled away, head lolling back and forth as it struggled to breathe.

Malcolm got to his feet. The blood splattered across his chest began to sizzle and cook away. He took his blade in both hands and drove it into the struggling gheist's chest. It snagged against a ribcage, punctured a lung, slid through muscle. Still the gheist fought. Malcolm leaned his chest into the hilt, putting his full weight on the sword. Suddenly, it punched through, piercing heart and back, burying itself in the dirt beyond.

The priest stared down at the dead gheist, disbelief in his eyes. Finally, his jaw set, he looked up at Malcolm.

"You will need better gods than this," Malcolm raged.

"And you will need another sword!" the priest yelled, drawing a blade from his belt. It was long and narrow, a Suhdrin dueling foil, but more than sharp enough to pierce chain and slither its way into Malcolm's flesh. The man stabbed forward, driving Malcolm back, struck again and again as Malcolm stumbled away.

But Malcolm was gifted of Strife, and had no reason to fear this foolish man and his gentleman's sword. The next time the priest struck, Malcolm caught the blade in his hands. The razor-sharp edge sliced through the chain of Malcolm's gauntlets, but he barely felt it. He snapped the blade in half, then lunged forward and grabbed the priest by the neck, lifting him up so that his feet dangled in the air, kicking at Malcolm's shins. The priest slashed at Malcolm with the fractured haft of his sword, scoring Malcolm's arms and face.

"A better god!" Malcolm roared. Strife's fury filled him, turning the sparkling light that shone from him into flame. The fires coursed up Malcolm's arms, consuming the priest, turning his robes into a banner of living flame, rushing down his throat and cooking the meat of his lungs. Malcolm held him aloft until the crackling fire died down, then threw him aside and bellowed his rage.

The celestials threw down their weapons and ran.

Malcolm came to himself hours later. The flame passed from his sword, the heat from his flesh. He fell to his knees and began to shiver. There were bodies everywhere. Many were those of his own soldiers. He looked down at his hands. Deep cuts scored his palms, the wounds now clogged with dirt, until the blood that seeped into his chain gauntlets was black.

"What has happened to me? What have I been?"

There was no one to answer him. Slowly, Malcolm got to his feet with the aid of his sword and limped back toward his own lines. He dragged the sword behind him, trailing the tip through the mud. Mists rose from the ground, turning the first light of morning into spun gold, obscuring his view. Horses passed just at the edge of his vision, knights dressed in gold and crimson, flying the flame and saltire of House Halverdt. They thundered through the fog like lightning in distant clouds. One of them noticed Malcolm and wheeled in his direction.

"Pagan or celestial?" the knight shouted. When Malcolm

didn't answer right away, he circled and lowered his spear. "Answer me, vagrant! Are you one of Cinder's heretics, or a blessed celestial of Strife?"

"I stand with the gods, to be judged," Malcolm said. He raised his head and threw his helm aside. The bloody knots of his hair hung like rope around his face. "You have no right to weigh me. Neither you nor any mortal born."

"With ink like that, you didn't ride here in Halverdt's train. That makes you either a pagan of Cinder's heresy, or one of Blakley's tame northern curs." He poked at Malcolm with his spear, drawing a grunt. "So which is it?"

"Neither answer satisfies my blood," Malcolm said. "Which are you? A true knight of the winter vow, or one of Halverdt's murderous zealots?"

"Pagan it is," the knight spat, then drew back his spear to pin Malcolm to the ground. "The gods have mercy on your soul."

"Hold, friend," Castian Jaerdin called. The duke of Redgarden rode through the fog, his armor clean and his silks spotted with sweat. He glanced down at Malcolm before addressing himself to the vow knight. "This man is Malcolm Blakley. Your lady signed an alliance with him. I trust you are not going back on that arrangement?"

The knight froze in place, looking unhappily down on Malcolm. For a moment, Malcolm thought the man might strike anyway, and alliances be damned. But finally, slowly, reluctantly, the knight stood down.

"My apologies, Houndhallow. We did not think to find the lord commander of our Tenerran allies in the thick of battle, and without escort."

"We lead differently in the north," Malcolm spat. He

lowered his sword, but did not sheathe it. "Thank you for your consideration. Good day."

The vow knight hesitated, looking from Malcolm to Jaerdin, then jerked his reins and wheeled away. Jaerdin laughed as the man disappeared into the mists.

"Not satisfied with killing half the celestial army, Malcolm? Thought you'd wet your blade with Halverdt's blood, as well?"

"Castian?"

"Yes, my friend?"

"I lost my horse. And I cannot let go of my sword," Malcolm said. Then he collapsed to the ground.

Soft light drifted in through the canvas. At first Malcolm thought it was a layer of fog blocking out the sun, but then a stiff breeze shifted the tent, and the sky fluttered overhead, and he understood where he was.

More than that, Malcolm understood what he was. He was freezing to death. He sat up in his cot. Furs slid from his shoulders, sending him into deeper shivers. His hands and feet were numb, even under the furs, and his breath puffed into fog. Malcolm looked down and saw that he was naked, his body the same tangle of scars and patchy gray hair it always was, though his skin felt thinner, and his muscles older. Even his bones were cold.

Gathering the furs that had fallen away, Malcolm sat up and looked around. There were two cots and a table, along with a small stove that sat on a bed of stones, its chimney slipping through the canvas in a leather cuff. The coals were dead. Even the rug that covered the floor was stiff with frost. He shook his head and stood up. There were voices outside.

Castian Jaerdin and a handful of knights huddled close to a fire, warming their hands and talking, while a thin stew boiled in the pot. A thick blanket of snow covered everything else. Dozens of low humps stretched out into the fog; other tents, and other campfires. Even the lanes between the tents were clogged with snow.

"Houndhallow!" Castian called, and the rest of the knights looked up, then stood. "We assumed you were dead, but the nurses kept insisting you would live."

"You both may be right." Malcolm shuffled through the snow and settled onto the bench, accepting a mug of mulled wine. Even as he drew it toward his mouth, frost formed a skin on the surface of the liquid. Malcolm wasn't sure he had ever been so cold. "What has happened during my slumber? How long have I been out?"

"Three weeks," Jaerdin said. "And winter, in all its glory."

"The celestials?"

"Those you and your fellow madmen failed to kill have retreated north of the Reaveholt. They are backed against the Fen, though something keeps them from going any further. We think they are in negotiations with Lady Bassion."

"Negotiations?" Malcolm asked. Jaerdin only shrugged.

"Messengers have been seen going between the two. We can only guess at this point. Godsbless Sir Bourne never saw this day; he would kill every Suhdrin soul in camp, out of spite."

Malcolm didn't say anything, just stared into his mug and tried to breathe. Memories floated through his head, memories of killing, of murder, of death. Worse, the memory of his fury, and the thrill he felt when each life snuffed out at his hand.

"What did she do, Redgarden? What did Galleux do to my men?"

"Ahem, well. We were hoping you could tell us. We were still in reserve, and apparently too far away for—" Jaerdin's voice trailed off, and he looked nervously among his companions "—for whatever happened. By the time we reached the lines, you and the rest of the Tenerran army were gone. Busy butchering celestials, and getting butchered in turn."

"How many of my men are left?"

"A hundred, at best. But none of them are worth a piss. Most are lying in Halverdt's ward, moaning and chattering their teeth and talking about the dead. We had to pry you out of her hands, and then only with the promise we'd let her know as soon as you woke up." Jaerdin took a long drink. "I don't think she's done with you yet."

"I'm well done with her. Whatever that was, whatever demon she gave us over to, it was not of the church." Malcolm drew his furs closer, gripping them so tight he thought he might break his fingers. "I am not a priest, or a prophet, but I know my gods. And that was no spirit I wish to bend the knee before, ever again."

One of the knights beside Jaerdin gave a deep sigh of relief, and bent to whisper to his friend. They exchanged looks with Jaerdin, who nodded. Both men stood and left without another word.

"They were worried it still had you. Not a few of the survivors have risen from their beds only to kill, with teeth or hands or whatever else they could get hold of. It is good to see you have control of it."

"I do not. Did not. It was a spirit of pure rage, pure

murder, and I was the sword and the flame it wielded. I am only myself because it has passed me by." A deep shiver shook Malcolm's core, and he dropped the cup of wine. It hissed into the snow, turning it red. "Gods, if I'm myself at all. I've never been so cold."

"That's not just you. Winter rolled a heavy hand against us the morning after the battle. Almost like all that flame and heat offended it. The storm has raged all these three weeks. I've never seen anything like it." Jaerdin was quiet for a long minute, watching his friend closely. Finally, he leaned in and lowered his voice. "Malcolm, what are we going to do? Which is the greater evil: Sophie Halverdt, or the celestials? How are we to do good, with allies like this?"

"Gods know," Malcolm said. "But I will not be Halverdt's sword any longer."

"She outnumbers us, has her agents throughout the camp, and has your few remaining men locked in fever in her tents. If you were to raise a hand against her, they would be the first to die." Jaerdin poured the dregs of his wine into the fire, watching as it hissed and spat on the logs. "And we would follow soon after. We don't have the men to destroy her."

"No," Malcolm said. "We don't. But I know who does. The celestial heretics. And Bassion, if she'll lend a hand."

35

GWEN THREW HER spear at the void priest, then ran back up the stairs, away from the shrine. Metal struck stone. She must have missed. No time to worry about that now, though, as she took the steps two at a time.

"There's nowhere to run, huntress!" Morrow shouted. His voice changed pitch, screeching words in a tongue she had never heard. A flash of light traveled up the staircase, following the bloody handprints like trace lightning, shooting past Gwen in a bolt of crimson and black. The air changed, and the stones of the walls started to come loose. One by one they slipped free and tumbled onto the stairs. The passageway cinched shut in front of Gwen, closing off her escape.

Gwen skidded to a halt. The staircase simply disappeared into a rough stone wall, pebbles still tumbling free to bounce down the steps.

"We have wrested the tribe of stone from the tribes." Morrow's voice came from all around her, echoing through the rocks. "Even if Cahl were still alive, he would not be able to stop us. What hope do you have?"

Before Gwen could answer, stony hands sprouted from the walls, grabbing for Gwen, one of them snagging her cloak and tearing it free. She screamed and struck at them with the last of her bloodwrought spears. The hand shattered, but another replaced it. She was about to strike again when she felt movement under her feet.

The stairs were eroding in front of her eyes. The smooth stone steps, cut in the years before the crusade, formed by the oldest of tribes and protected by ancient spells of deception, fractured and split. Stone turned to sand and began to slither down the passageway, back toward the shrine. Gwen tried to keep her footing, but then one of the stone hands bashed her in the shoulder. She fell, and kept falling, sliding head first down the corkscrewing passageway.

Frair Morrow was waiting for her at the bottom of the stairs. He stood with his arms spread and a hooked knife in each hand. Sand piled up around his feet, and his arms were too widely spread to protect his belly.

This man is a priest, Gwen thought. *Not a fighter.*

Digging her foot into the sand, Gwen slowed her descent enough to get her left hand under her. Sliding down in a controlled fall, she directed herself right at Morrow's feet. The priest laughed in anticipation of the kill, even threw his head back. Gwen jumped, stabbing forward with her spear, putting the full weight of her body behind the strike.

She was lucky enough to surprise him, lucky enough to get on her feet and into the air without falling, or losing her handle on her weapon, or simply banging against the wall. Unfortunately, sliding down a hill of sand is a difficult place to attack from, and Gwen's luck didn't hold. She got into the air, but her attack fell short, and she wobbled on her feet as she landed.

Morrow's joy turned to surprise, then rage. He batted her speartip away, then swung with his other blade, trying to take Gwen's head off. She spun the blocked spear and struck him in the temple with the butt, then they slammed into each other and both went tumbling into the chamber. Gwen landed with a thud against the Sedgewind altar, rocking the iron box. As she struggled to her feet, Gwen saw that Gilliam hadn't moved. The Orphanshield was staring sightlessly ahead, his hands at his side, fingers slightly curled.

"At least there's only the one of you," she spat. She snatched a sacrificial knife off the altar, its barbs and hooks fitting strangely in her hand, and turned to face Morrow.

The void priest had fallen at the base of the stairs, his feet buried in sand, and now his legs were slowly getting covered. Gwen wondered for a moment if the avalanche of sand would eventually fill the chamber, but then realized she had more pressing concerns. She rushed forward, knife in hand.

Morrow saw her just in time to throw his arm up, taking the blow to his wrist. He screamed in pain, but when Gwen pulled the knife back its complicated barbs hooked into Morrow's flesh, and came out of her hand. The void priest sat up, staring at his bloody arm.

"Damned witch! I'm going to tear you to pieces for this!"

"Not before you bleed to death," Gwen snapped, then punched him hard in the jaw with her left hand.

"You know, for a heretic, you've done a terrible job," she said, straddling the blubbering priest. "You kept the inquisitor here alive, and you know that's not going to go well, not when Heartsbridge gets its hooks into you." She bent down, twisting the blade out of Morrow's arm, drawing more blood and more frantic screams. "It doesn't take more than a passing glance to see that something's not right here. You've got to learn to hide a little better. At least, until you're stronger."

Something slammed into the back of Gwen's head, knocking her into the hissing avalanche of sand. Grit filled her mouth and eyes, choking her, blinding her, joining with the numb shock that was spreading through her head. Gwen could feel the sand covering her, but she couldn't summon the strength to move. Slowly, she rolled onto her back.

Frair Gilliam stood over her, hands still clenched into fists, but hanging limp at his sides. His eyes were unfocused and staring at nothing. Even his breathing was shallow. Frair Morrow grunted as he stood, cradling his bloody arm in his other hand. There was blood all over his face, and tears running down his cheeks.

"You will pay! You will pay! All of you, your families, your damned lords and their stupid little..." He choked on his sobs, face twisted into a rictus of misery. "You will pay for everything you've done!"

Morrow reached into the sand and grabbed Gwen's foot, then started dragging her. For only having one hand, Morrow was much stronger than Gwen expected. She slipped beneath the sand briefly, then slid out, her head banging on the stone floor, rattling her teeth. Her vision swam with black pools. She was about to pass out when sharp pain in her shin pulled her awake. Gwen screamed and tried to pull her foot free, but the catatonic Orphanshield was holding her ankle firmly in both his hands, while Morrow peeled away her legging, taking a good bit of skin with the leather.

"This has been too long in coming. All you old families, thinking you'd dodged the god's revenge, when you've forgotten even the least of the true legends. Saying your secret prayers while taking the church's bread, living the southerner's life, as if you deserved it. As if any of you deserved this!" Morrow struggled to keep the knife still, wincing each time he tried to use his injured arm. He wiped sweat from his face, then slid the box under Gwen's foot. "Well, this is what you fucking deserve!"

He plunged the blade into Gwen's leg. Her screams cut through the air, barely human, as the knife slipped through meat and muscle. Blood poured into the box. Morrow threw the knife away, his eyes glassy and bright, his hands shaking.

"What you deserve! Soon the whole of the north will understand what they've forgotten!"

Gwen was still trying to get her foot away, but Gilliam was unmoved. The inquisitor just stood there, staring straight ahead while Gwen bled out in front of him. She could hear the autumnal heart beating, drinking in her blood, gasping for more. Vines crawled out of the box, fixing into the altar, spreading to the walls and into the stones. They twined around Gilliam's chest, his neck, began to squeeze tight. The Orphanshield's face started to turn blue, and still he didn't flinch.

Gwen tried to push away from the altar, but already the vines were crawling across her legs, looping over her shoulders. Golden leaves unfurled from the creepers, turning the floor into a shimmering carpet of shivering light. Gwen tangled her fingers in the vines and pulled. Maybe if she got enough of them, she could trip Gilliam, knock him free of that iron-vise grip.

Frair Morrow stomped on her hand, grinding it painfully into the stone. She gasped, the pain a bare echo of the misery in her leg, but it was enough to shock her. He didn't say anything, just grimaced down at her, his face twisted in tears and hatred. There was no escape.

Gwen let her mind go. If her body was trapped, at least

her spirit could struggle. The whole castle was choked with strange spirits, turning the walls and forest and very stones of her house into a foreign land. She recognized that now that her body was breaking. It wasn't time or memory that made Gwen feel like an exile in the Fen Gate. Something was here. Something malevolent.

She reached out and felt the boundaries of the room. The heart was familiar, but in a broken way, like a favorite bowl that had been shattered. Fomharra. Gwen had no idea what had become of the autumn spirit after it abandoned her in the witches' hallow, but if this bound heart was a part of it, she feared for the Fen God. But there was more, behind Fomharra, a pulsing darkness that crept into every living and dead soul in the castle. Gwen stretched toward it, letting her soul come loose from her body. A shade of it passed through her.

A moment of terrible cold, more than cold, an emptiness that reached through her, squeezing her heart numb. Gwen's soul fluttered away, blown on winds as sharp and strong as steel, spinning away from her body like a rag. She tried to breathe, but the air around her was stone, the cold stone of the grave. She fell.

Back into her body. The impact arched her back, thrashing her limbs, turning her body as taut as a bowstring. Her hand slithered out from under Morrow's foot but, though it was a struggle for him, Frair Gilliam held on to her legs. Morrow jumped back, snarling.

"You have given me what I need, huntress. I was sure we would spend months draining this place of your essence, of the spiritual dregs of your family's heresy, before we could revive the autumn spirit. I would say that sometimes the gods provide. But we both know better than that!"

He reached across the altar and plucked a knife from Frair Gilliam's belt. For a second, Gwen thought he would plunge it into Gilliam's chest, but instead Morrow laid it over his own palm and sliced the skin. Even though his hand and arm were already covered in blood, the new wound opened and started to bleed profusely. The blood that came out wasn't red, or thin, or human. It was black and bubbled like pitch as it dripped down Morrow's fingers. He held his arm over the iron box, mixing his own blood and the foul ichor with the heart of leaves.

As soon as the blood touched the heart, Fomharra arrived. The hundred bloody handprints burned orange, becoming autumn leaves, shuffling onto the floor to stir in a mad wind that blew from the heart. Morrow covered his face and backed away, sheltering against the wall. The Orphanshield didn't move, though his face was swollen and nearly black. Gwen began to rise from the ground, carried aloft by Fomharra's spirit. Light wove through the air, strands of clean power, the familiar bindings of the Fen God, summoned into the heart of the Fen Gate.

As soon as Fomharra arrived, the black strands of Morrow's blood started to corrupt it. Gwen saw this, knew this, felt this through her bones. It was the same as the dark god that now lurked beneath the castle. The joyous storm of autumn's power turned sour. The winds grew cold, the leaves gained a razor's edge, the warm light that glowed through the air turned bilious and foul. The stink of rot filled the room.

For a brief moment, Gwen had Fomharra's power, just as she had when she rose from the witches' hallow. Her hold on it slipped immediately, as Morrow's corruption warped the god's power, bent it to destruction. She could feel it slipping away from her. But it was still enough.

Gwen reached out for the void spirit, the dark spirit that was turning the Fen Gate into a nightmare. Its cold arms wrapped around her soul, but she shrugged it off, sifting through the hundreds of tendrils that had worked their way through the castle, looking for a specific corruption. And here it was, wrapped around one soul, paralyzing it. She grabbed the tendril and poured Fomharra's power into it. The darkness strained, it stretched, and finally it snapped.

Frair Gilliam stumbled back, letting go of Gwen's leg, his eyes wide in sudden suffocation. His hands scrabbled at his neck, pulling on the vine that was choking him, finally grabbing his sword and cutting the vine loose from the heart. The vine turned to dust, its leaves flaking and falling to the ground. The Orphanshield stood goggle-eyed, staring in shock at the room, at Gwen hovering in front of him, at the crawling heart of autumn and Frair Morrow, who was already charging toward him with knife in hand.

"For the love of the gods, inquisitor!" Gwen shouted. "Damn something!"

Morrow jumped over the altar and stabbed at Gilliam, but the old inquisitor still had fight in him. He brushed aside the knife, holding Morrow by the collar and staring at him in wonder. Morrow tried again, punching the knife toward Gilliam's gut, but the blade turned off Gilliam's sheath, barely scratching his wide belly. Gilliam grabbed Morrow's wrist, punched him once in the face, then dropped his limp body to the ground. He stood there, taking deep, gasping breaths, clearly in shock.

"You have to break it before it gets out, Gilliam. You have to destroy it!"

"But I don't... what is happening? Lady Adair? Where

have you been? The inquisition has some questions—"

"Damn it!" Gwen snapped, half command, half frustration. She grabbed what little control she still had of Fomharra's power and threw it at Gilliam. A torrent of leaves, sharp and sick, blasted into the old man. He stumbled back, falling to the ground, immediately becoming tangled in the growing roots of the heart. They grabbed at his ankles, wrapping around his arm, trying to pull him into the ground.

Gilliam pushed himself to his feet, then drew the shorter of his swords and started slashing. Leaves and roots flew through the air, bleeding light and corruption. He stood upright and summoned a veil of shadows, pulling Cinder's power into a shield to protect him from the gheist. The torrent of leaves sloughed off the naether, turning to embers as they fell. Gilliam straightened to his full height and locked eyes with Gwen.

"By Cinder's power, be condemned!" he shouted.

Darts of twisting naether shot out from the inquisitor's blade, slicing through the wind and piercing Gwen to the heart. Fomharra's power snapped free from her soul, twisting and howling as Gilliam cut it down. She could feel it dwindling. Gilliam fought his way forward, shrugging off the howling wind and cutting leaves, severing the web of light that tried to hold him in place. He drew his other sword, long and silvered, the runes of Cinder chasing up and down its blade in purple light. Gilliam whispered an invocation, then drove the sword into the autumn heart.

The iron box shattered. Gwen caught a glimpse of burning leaves, and then she was thrown against the wall. Her head smacked against stone.

In the cold heart of her soul, Fomharra fled, leaving her once again.

36

HENRI VOLENT EMERGED from the shadows like a death sentence. Ian could only watch as the man once known as the Deadface marched ominously toward him. The leather straps holding Ian in place creaked and he swung slowly from the black tree.

"I have to admit, I don't understand what's going on, Ian," Volent said. "I just watched you drop from that tree like a newborn foal's balls, but gods damn me if it makes any sense. And that guy over there." He nodded over his shoulder at the place Cinder had fallen. "I could have sworn to you that was Cinder himself. Bloody damned lord of winter, and he fell to my blade as quick as fog to sun. And now here you are, tied up and delivered like a present."

"You don't have to do this, Volent. We rode together at Houndhallow, and a dozen battles since. You don't have to kill me."

"People are always telling me what I do and do not have to do. What I must do, for honor or duty or family. First it was Lord Halverdt, but it turns out he was mad, and under the influence of Tomas Sacombre, who was himself possessed by the god of death. Then it was you, for a while, convincing me that I could be a better person, if I just chose." Volent reached the bottom of the stairs, but instead of coming directly to Ian, he strolled around the black tree, talking to the close walls of the doma. "If I just chose! As if the things we do in life are choice, and not destiny. But I think I know better, Ian. I think I've seen behind this little game of yours."

"I'm not playing any game, Volent. We fought together against Folam Voidfather, as my father fought side by side with Lord Halverdt to destroy the Reavers." Ian shifted in his bindings, but they only pulled tighter. He could see movement in the far reaches of the doma out of the corner of his eye, but couldn't tell what it was. "We stopped Tession. I don't understand why you've... you've..."

"I am what I am, Ian," Volent snapped. He came around the tree, and back into Ian's field of vision. Ian struggled against his bonds, but couldn't move. "But you knew that. Knew it when you poured that corruption into me. Just another lord, using me as a tool for his own darkness."

"There was no other way! I had to—"

"There is nothing you have to do, Ian. You just said that yourself." Volent crossed the distance between them and stood in front of Ian. "We rode together at Houndhallow. We were never going to be friends, but we were becoming allies. And like everyone else, when you needed me for your own purposes, you used me and threw me away."

"I didn't know what would happen, Volent. I swear to you, I just needed to get the poison out of this tree, to do whatever I could to foil Tession's plan."

"And now you have, and look what it has cost me." Volent gestured to his face, eerily beautiful and yet utterly broken. "I would rather be a monster than this. Do you know what I had to do to free myself from this face? To free the world from who I was? Do you have any idea?"

"Volent, please—"

"The Deadface, Ian. I forgot who I was, but now am reminded. It's best you know as well." Volent stood in front of Ian and raised his sword. "Know the name that will end you."

"I am not yours to kill," Ian said. Volent paused, his dead eyes curious. "I have enemies enough, Volent. Among the pagans, in the houses of Suhdra, even in my own family. But I am not your enemy, and you are not mine, just as I am not your lord, nor you my servant."

"And yet you think to command me. To stay my blade."

"I'm not commanding you. I am reminding you of our bond, and of the enemies that we have faced. Sacombre used you, and Halverdt, and Cinder himself. But I have not. I will not."

"Then why did this happen? Didn't you ask me to end this ritual; and to do that, didn't you poison me with this darkness?"

"We both know who you are. What you are. I didn't make you anything worse than you already were. You can blame your face for your actions, or the demon that rode you all those years, or the poison you carry now. But we are what we do."

"Easy for a duke's son to say," Volent answered with a sneer.

"No easier than it is for a monster to think he's something else. Kill me if you must. But know that it is Henri Volent who holds the blade and spills the blood. No one else."

Volent stared at him for three long breaths, the anger and hate boiling in his eyes, though there was no emotion on his still, dead face. Finally, his shoulders slumped.

"I am that man," he said. "And I always will be."

"I'm glad to hear you say that," Ian said, relaxing slightly.

Volent drew back and struck, a quick swing that came at Ian in a blur. Ian screamed, then fell to the ground. His bonds were cut, though the blade had nicked his face. Volent stared down at the blood.

"You could use a scar," he said, then wiped his blade and looked away.

Ian scrambled frantically free of his bonds, wiping the blood from his face. His chest was seeping as well. He pulled open his shirt. The wound Folam Voidfather had given him was bleeding ash, but he felt no pain. He looked over at Volent.

"Thanks for not killing me."

"I'll thank you to forget it. And me." Volent turned and marched toward the door. The guards were filtering back into the doma, staring in horror at the tree, and the bodies of the dead priests. But those who saw Volent's face, and what he had become, showed the most fear of all.

"Where are you going?" Ian called after him.

"Away. Where lords cannot command, and gods cannot judge."

"But you can't—"

"My lord, riders at the gate!"

Ian rushed outside. Guards were rushing to the gates, and the sound of distant horns and shuffling hooves reached Ian.

He called up to the guardhouse, "What banner do they fly?"

"The hound, my lord. It's your sainted mother!"

A smile broke across Ian's face. "Volent, find my sister! She'll want to—"

But when he looked back, Volent was gone.

They searched the castle, but there was no sign of either Henri Volent or Frair Tession. Sorcha did not believe her son's promise that Volent was redeemed, but neither did she trust her own eyes when she saw the tree growing in the courtyard. Ian's explanations sounded like nonsense, even to him.

"It's been months since I was last in Houndhallow, and look what you've done to it. I did not want to come home to a ruin. And what about you? Last I heard of you, dear son, you were looking for Gwendolyn Adair. And you found her, yes?" Sorcha asked. They sat in the empty great hall, Ian warming his hands by the fire, his mother sitting casually in a light dress, as though it were the height of summer.

"In a manner of speaking," Ian said. Again, he tried to explain what had happened at Houndhallow after his return with Elsa: how the pagans were tricked into attacking by the voidfather, and how the void priests betrayed them all. His wound, Master Tavvish's ambush, the slaughter. Her eyes narrowed at the news of Tavvish's death, but she said nothing. Ian was just finishing when the door banged open and Nessie came in, with Sir Clough close at hand.

"Mother!" Nessie shouted. She ran across the room and threw herself into Sorcha's arms, unfazed by her mother's strange appearance. Sorcha buried her face in Nessie's hair, breathing deep. After a few moments, Nessie pulled back and looked into her mother's eyes. "I've not had a letter from you since you left to pull Father's backside out of the fire."

"And you won't get a letter from me, talking like that," Sorcha said. "We're at war, darling. That doesn't mean we can talk like barbarians."

"I'm just repeating your words," Nessie answered, unabashed. "And besides, I think I've grown enough to swear, if the situation warrants."

"All right, all right. A matter for another time. I'm glad to see you, darling."

"I'm glad to see you, too. Now if only Father were here."

"He will be, soon enough," Sorcha said. Though she was hugging Nessie, she locked eyes with Ian. "If we have to drag him home kicking and screaming."

"Is that why you've come, Mother?" asked Ian. "To draw me back into Father's war?"

"You can stay here, if you prefer. Stay behind safe walls and wait for the war to come to you. But it will, Ian. It will. Make no mistake."

"I have never run from it," Ian said. "But there is just as much a war here as anywhere else. You saw the tree—"

"I was going to ask about that," Sir Clough said sharply.

"You have seen the tree in the courtyard," Ian finished. "The void priests struck this very morning. If I hadn't been here, it might have gone badly."

Clough looked put out at that. She turned to Sorcha. "What is the situation in the field? Are the forces of Houndhallow in need of our help?"

"They are mostly dead," Sorcha answered. She still had Ian pinned in her gaze. "And those who live are under the sway of a dark spirit. Understand what I'm asking. If we march south, it is to save your father. But if his will has failed, we may also need to save him from himself."

"I have only the garrison here," Ian said, "and a few knights who have joined me along the way. Not enough strength to make a difference."

"Where do you think our strength lies? In swords? In horses? You must bring your blood south, Ian, and your name. The son of Malcolm Blakley rides to save his father. Tener will answer that call."

"Tener will not," Ian said.

"Tener already has," Sorcha answered. "Abandon the castle—"

"I have only just won it!"

"Abandon Houndhallow, and save your father. Our full strength, and nothing less." Sorcha rose and looked around the room. "We don't have time to debate this. Hesitate, and we are lost."

Ian sat back in his chair, staring into the flames. He wanted to stay there forever, and never seek glory again. But, of course, he didn't.

One week became two, and heavy snows blanketed the roads until they were moving at a crawl. By the time the forests thinned and the hills leveled into the rolling plains that dominated the approaches to the Reaveholt, a third week was quickly slipping away. Ian ordered the army into shelter, taking advantage of the last heavy forest to break the wind and give a little protection from the snow. Their train wound through the forest for miles. Everyone came south, every cook, every soldier, every servant. Houndhallow was empty. The strength of the hound marched through the snow.

"This is as close as I want to get with the full force," Ian said. "At least, until we know the disposition of the forces arrayed against us, and where our allies stand."

"If they still remain," Sorcha said. "When I left your father's side, he was desperate enough to be making deals with Sophie Halverdt. If she hasn't betrayed him yet, the celestials might have broken them both."

"Might have, could have, but we won't know until we see for ourselves."

"I will organize a scouting party," Clough said.

"I will be leading the scouts," Ian said. "If there is advantage to be gained in the geography, I would rather see it myself. And if the armies have already fallen, well, I would see that for myself as well."

"It's foolish to send the commander to scout the lines," Sorcha said. "Let one of your sergeants do it."

"Let's not pretend this is my army to command, Mother," Ian said with a smile. "Once we know Father's disposition, I will report it to you, and you will decide how he must be saved." He kissed her on the forehead, shivering at the touch of her strange skin. He could tell by the look in her eyes that his reaction bothered her, so he bent again, and didn't flinch this time. "Be safe, Mother. And watch my sister."

"I have risked the loss of husband and son to this war. Don't think I will let her fall, as well."

Ian squeezed her shoulders one last time, then left the council tent. The snow was falling heavily, and the air was as cold as Ian had ever felt. He wrapped his arms around himself, squinting into the wind. He barely noticed Nessie sitting by the entrance to the tent, until she hopped up and started to follow him.

"You're going?" she asked.

"I am. Anything's better than freezing to death in this

cold. It's always warmer in the saddle."

"That's a lie," she said simply. "Be careful, brother. This winter isn't natural."

"It's just weather, Ness. You're right, it's very cold, but no worse than any other year." He glanced down and could see she saw through him. "Maybe we've grown soft in Houndhallow, huddling by the hearth, sleeping under furs and drinking mulled wine. This is how our ancestors lived."

"Our ancestors are dead. Just be careful." Nessie turned abruptly and disappeared into the driving snow. Ian shook his head.

"Everyone's scared of a little snow. After everything we've seen, it's winter that shakes their hearts," he muttered. Still, he pulled his collar tight to his neck, and hunched lower into the wind. The shiver that ran through his heart had little to do with the cold.

37

LADY BASSION GAVE them a room in the western tower, with a small window that overlooked the rapids of the Tallow. The rest of the tower was given over to soldiers of Galleydeep, and the few vow knights who rode with them. It was no coincidence, Lucas thought, that their room was more secure than most prison cells. For all her kind words, Helenne Bassion still did not trust any member of the house of Cinder. But especially Lucas.

Several days after their arrival, once the pattern of captive life was established and Lucas felt he could push boundaries, the frair returned to the courtyard to speak to the other priests of Cinder he had seen on his way in. He left Martin in their room to guard their things, but also because Lucas wanted to have a conversation that Martin would be better off not hearing.

The guards circling the encampment of priests watched Lucas with mistrustful eyes, but made no move to stop him from approaching the other priests. It might have helped that Lucas no longer wore his vestments; he was dressed more like a scholar than a priest, and walked with the help of a traveler's staff instead of the silver and black crook of winter.

The priests knew him, though. Lucas had served with

several of them in Heartsbridge, taken vows with them in Cinderfell, even argued theology with them when he was a younger man and interested in such things. They watched his approach like beaten dogs, anxious for attention but wary of the stick.

"Brothers," Lucas said when he was close enough. Several stirred from their places around the fire, but most only turned their heads in his direction, faces slack. They were malnourished, and the thin robes of their vestments were hardly proof against the cutting wind that whipped through the courtyard. The sight of their suffering sent a chill through his bones. One of the priests stood.

"Frair Lucas, you seem well," he said. Lucas had to squint into the man's face to recognize him, so wasted were his features. "Yes, I am Cassius Vermette, humbled at long last. We no longer need to argue about Cinder's task of endless sacrifice as reflected in our daily suffering." He pulled his thin robes closer and smiled a joyless smile. "I have suffered enough in this life. I am ready for the quiet, or the coming of summer."

"No priest of Cinder should ache for summer's arrival, friend. It's bad theology." Lucas clapped the man on the shoulder and was shocked by the knobbly bones and wasted muscle. "The years have been hard on you."

"No more than on any other," Vermette said. "Lady Bassion, on the other hand—"

"Keep your tongue, Vermette," another priest said. He was facing away from them, huddled by the fire. "You don't know where this man's loyalties lie, nor his purpose in coming to us."

"François, you know Frair Lucas. You supped with him."

"Yes, I know the frair. I remember him in different clothes, though." The priest twisted around, looking at Lucas with distaste. Half of his face was covered in mottled bruises. "Have you given up on Cinder, Lucas, now that it is dangerous to call his name?"

"I am as faithful to Cinder as I have ever been."

"The faithful are here, Lucas, around this fire. Suffering. And yet you have rooms in the tower, and a lordling of Suhdra as your escort. And you appear before us in a layman's clothes, as though the vows of Cinder mean nothing to you!"

"These are dangerous times. I have seen priests murdered on the open road, and monasteries burned without remorse. There are many claiming to be faithful celestials who have thrown Cinder aside, and cling now only to Strife. A mob, led by knights of the winter vow, chased us out of Greenhall," Lucas said. "If I didn't travel in disguise, I would not be here at all."

"Cinder asks difficult things of us, sometimes," François said bitterly. Frair Vermette took Lucas by the elbow and turned him away.

"Do not judge him for his anger," Vermette said. "François lost many friends to Bassion's fury. But anger is Strife's realm, and we are of Cinder. He will come around. Why are you here, brother? There is nothing but trouble here."

"Everywhere is touched by this present conflict," Lucas said. "I was tasked with bringing the heretic Sacombre to Heartsbridge for judgment, but met trouble along the way." He summarized his journey from Houndhallow to Greenhall, after Sacombre had revealed his heresy; and LaGaere's betrayal of his trust, his flight with Sacombre, and eventual death at the hands of the man he was trying to help. Finally, he spoke of Sir Horne's heresy.

Vermette nodded sagely. "We have seen reversals, too. We thought we were rallying to Bassion's aid, to put down Blakley's rebellion and return the church's guiding hand to Tener, but we were betrayed. Not by Bassion, as some would like to believe, but by our own brothers. But Bassion and her people hold us in contempt because they saw priests of Cinder summoning gheists and murdering their friends."

"Why does Bassion let you walk free at all, then? Why not lock you in the cells?"

"Because the host of Cinder lost as many souls to those heretics as did Lady Bassion. The heretics murdered priests, celestes, vow knights... any who got in their way." Vermette sighed. "There was a time I understood the things of this church, but I have no idea what is happening to us, even now."

"I have seen the heretics at work. They understand us because they are us; inquisitors, vow knights, priests of winter and summer. Sir Horne was a faithful knight of Suhdra, and yet she summoned gheists as though she was born to the tribes. I don't know how they got to be so widespread, or what they're after, but they have turned the church against itself, and Suhdra and Tener have followed suit." Lucas glanced over at the other priests. "These men and women suffer not for their faith, but for their fear. We need to band together with the truly faithful of Strife, and root this corruption out."

"Then you had best start with Lady Bassion. The duchess will not kill us, but she won't let us live, either." Vermette glanced up at the north tower, where Bassion held court.

"They take us away to their secret chambers, one at a time, and we don't come back. Frair Villar went last night. I felt his death in my dreams. It is only a matter of time before it is my turn in Lady Bassion's little room."

"I will do what I can, brother. Trust me."

"Thank you, frair." Vermette shook his hand, thin fingers disappearing into Lucas's palm. "And thank the gods you have come. If she will listen to you, we may be saved."

"I work not to save you, but the church," Lucas said. "And all Tenumbra with it."

Lucas returned to his rooms to find Martin standing nervously by the door. The boy had washed and changed, and was once again wearing the red and yellow of House Roard. Lucas raised his brows.

"Have you carried that outfit all the way from Greenhall?" he asked.

"Lady Bassion provided it, though where she got the material... never mind. She sent something for you, as well." Martin nodded to the narrow bed in the corner of the room.

Two robes lay spread across the blankets. One was black, chased in silver, the robes of an inquisitor. They were slightly too large for Lucas, and were thin at knee and elbow. Lucas wondered what had become of the previous owner. The other robes were pale cream and fresh. Penitent robes. Lucas ran his fingers over the fabric.

"She is not subtle, our Lady Bassion," Lucas said. "I take it we have an audience with her?"

"In an hour. Which will you wear?"

"Both, and neither. I have nothing to repent, and nothing to hide." He turned sharply to the door. "Come on."

"Where are we going?"

"To our audience. Lady Bassion may rule this castle, but the church holds dominion over everything under the sky. Helenne has forgotten her place in the world."

Out in the courtyard, the soldiers and priests lounging around watched the pair very closely. They processed from their tower to Bassion's, Lucas in the lead, Martin only a step behind, neither man looking left or right as they marched. No one got in their way. No one, that is, until they reached the door to the northern tower.

The guards refused to budge. As Lucas approached, both men crossed their halberds, barring the way. Lucas scuffed to a halt.

"I am Frair Gillem Lucas, inquisitor of Cinder, and the gods' faithful representative on earth. If you have any respect for the celestial church, or the gods above, you will let me pass."

"Your audience isn't for another hour. In the meantime, Lady Bassion has ordered there are to be no priests of Cinder in the north tower," one of the guards said. "My apologies to the gods."

"It is not to the gods you must apologize, but to me. For generations, Heartsbridge has been the center of Suhdra, and all Tenumbra as well. The Circle of Lords meets there, not because it is their will to do so, but because it is the will of the celestriarch. And you think to defy me now?"

"Our loyalty is to Galleydeep, not you. If you want—"

"We both know the lie in that. If the celestriarch orders House Bassion stripped of its lands and titles, and its lord exiled, it would happen. At his word alone."

"Then go to Heartsbridge and win his word," the guard

answered. “Until then, no priest of Cinder enters this hall.”

Lucas paused, drumming his fingers on his staff. Finally he leaned in, until his nose was only an inch away from the guard’s face.

“Let me ask you a question. If I truly wanted to get past, and I was a danger to Lady Bassion, do you think you could stop me?”

“These are my orders, my—”

“Have you tangled with the naether? Have you fought a demon carved from your own nightmares, given shape, set against you by the will of an inquisitor? Does your armor stop the shadow’s blade?” Lucas split his face in a maniac’s grin. “When you go to sleep tonight, do you think that sword will do you any good in my realm?”

“You are not making your case, Lucas,” Martin said tightly.

The two guards looked properly terrified, but Lucas’s rant had drawn the attention of the rest of the courtyard. Two dozen armed knights lounged attentively nearby, hands resting on swords, ready to spring into action. Lucas looked around, then patted the guard’s chest. The man flinched back.

“My apologies. You are only doing your job, and that is all any of us can do. Just remember that, while you answer to Lady Bassion, she is only mortal. I answer to the gray lord, Cinder, god of graves and winter. And I will do my duty to him, no matter the cost.”

Lucas turned on his heel and was about to walk away when a voice came from inside the keep. “Let them pass.”

The guards looked around in confusion, then slowly pulled their halberds back. A knight of the winter vow walked past, slight and beautiful, wearing a veil of cream lace across the face of her helm. She stopped in front of Lucas.

"You are Frair Lucas, inquisitor to Sir Elsa LaFey, the same who escorted Ian Blakley through the wilds, and followed Gwen Adair to the witches' hallow."

"I am," Lucas said, turning slightly toward her.

"Go through," she said, and stepped aside.

Lucas paused, glancing at Martin, then addressed the vow knight. "Sir, have we met before?"

"No. But I have stood with Malcolm Blakley, and with Sophie Halverdt, and now I am here. Your words make sense to me. Whatever has come before this, the church must stand together."

"Thank you. I will remember this."

"If you must. We will have much to forget, when this is through. Much to forgive." She bent her head and walked away, disappearing into the crowd of hulking knights that surrounded them. But the guards did not move to block Lucas's entry. He and Martin hurried through.

"That was strange," Martin said. "Who do you think she was?"

"I'm not sure. But for now, let's take advantage, before those guards return to their senses."

The tower was built around the northern gate, and protected it from invaders. The main passage was riddled with murder holes and archer eyes, and the floor was crossed with multiple runnels, each crossed by a small bridge. Martin looked down at the channels with curiosity.

"For blood," Lucas said sharply. Martin nodded and hurried on.

They found Lady Bassion holding court at the end of the hall, between the chains that held the massive outer gate in place. She was sitting on a throne, legs primly crossed, hands resting on a naked sword. A strange cup rested beside her, steam coming off its surface. Two vow knights stood rigidly at her side. When Lucas entered, the two knights drew their blades.

"Has it come to this, Galleydeep? Lord Halverdt kept priests at his side, whispering fears into his mind, warping his soul with terror. Look what became of him. Do you wish to follow his path?"

"Gabriel Halverdt kept priests of Cinder at his side. These are vow knights," Bassion said, gesturing to her companions. "Brighter hope, from a brighter god."

"Whereas you keep your priests of Cinder penned up outside like dogs, starving to death. Do you think the gods will judge you less harshly because you've chosen a different heresy than his?"

"You have not suffered under Cinder's gaze as I have." Bassion folded her hands in her lap, but the stiff anger in her voice carried through the room. "I let those priests live. That is more than they deserve."

"The celestial church is Cinder and Strife, bound together, standing against the ravages of the gheists and the dangers of moral decay. It is not one or the other, depending on your mood, or your experiences in life. I am sorry that Sacombre's heretics tricked you. I am sorry so many have died at the hands of men and women pretending to be faithful priests of Cinder. But it is that deception that must be remembered, not the betrayal. These void priests want to split the church, set Strife against Cinder, and Tener against Suhdra."

"Then they seem to have succeeded. Outside these walls, Sophie Halverdt has clearly thrown her lot in fully with Lady

Strife, and these... these void priests, as you name them, most wear the black and silver of Cinder. As for Suhdra and Tener..." Bassion threw her hands up in frustration. She snatched the chalice from the table beside her and drank a hurried draught, wiping her mouth with the back of her sleeve. She grimaced at the cold slither of chain across her lips. "What do those names even mean anymore? Every house must stand for itself, or fall by itself. Every ally has betrayed me. Every friend has turned their back on me. My power is in these walls, and this sword, and nothing more."

"Then we are lost. All of Tenumbra is lost," Lucas shouted. He turned away, marching angrily out of the room. Martin followed. As they reached the door, Lady Bassion's voice overtook them.

"Be careful what you say, Lucas! You are only in this castle because of my good will, and your comfort is fragile. Displease me, and I will throw you to the wolves at my gates. Or worse!"

Lucas drew up short, turning angrily back to the throne.

"If this is what you think of as good will, then I will gladly take the wolves. At least they only bite once before the kill."

Before Bassion could answer, Lucas stormed out.

38

THEY WORKED IN silence, three figures against the snowy backdrop of the courtyard. The wreckage of the Fen Gate was silent, a broken crag that surrounded them like an unholy henge, finally robbed of its power. Gwen tried to keep her thoughts on the task in front of them, to not look around at the broken walls, the shattered windows, the empty rooms. There were too many memories there. Too many regrets.

Frair Gilliam rose from the intricate circle and dusted off his hands. They had cleared a place in the snow and filled it with the instruments of their varied faiths. From Gilliam, the silver and iron symbols of the celestial church, icons wrought in the blood of holy men and women, crafted to dispel the feral gods of Tenumbra. He placed them in divine order, muttering and checking his placement against the stars and the calendar.

Elder Kesthe offered a wilder magic. She filled the circle with totems of the tribe of bones, bound in leather and crafted from stone, echoes of the very gods Gilliam sought to dispel. She let her hands be guided by the spirits, chanting and whispering as her fingers nudged the totems into ley lines that her eyes couldn't see. They snapped into place like lodestones. Smoke from the dozen fires that surrounded them began to swirl in strange patterns, answering to the swelling power of the ritual. Gwen could feel a change in the air, in her soul.

From Gwen Adair, they had power, and the corruption to stain it. Both priests watched her nervously as she stepped forward. Gwen did not belong to either of their sects. There was a time when that would have bothered her, this sense of not belonging, of outsideness. But Gwen was adjusting. This was her life. This was her gift to the world.

"Are you ready?" Gwen asked.

"As ready as I can be," Gilliam answered. He nervously ran his palms over the hilts of his twin swords, before clasping his hands together in prayer. "Though I'd feel a measure better with a troop of guards at my back."

"You saw what this thing did to Marchand's men," Kesthe said. "We can't risk it. If it corrupted our rangers, we'd just be wandering the forests alone."

"The gods are with us," Gwen answered. "We are never alone."

"Hardly comforting," Gilliam said. "Just be about it, witch."

Gwen smiled and closed her eyes, then stepped into the circle. Her feet brushed the consecrated ground, and a spark went through her skin. It was there, waiting to pounce, slavering in the darkness.

"Prepare—" And then her breath was taken from her.

The thing growing beneath the Fen Gate was larger than even Gwen could have imagined, and she had already brushed its mind during her struggle in the shrine. It spread throughout the castle like a cancer, eating through the walls and burrowing into the very spirit of the Fen Gate. For a moment, Gwen wondered if this was some remnant of the corruption the inquisition had always feared, a splinter of the dark spirit that led to the fall of the castle and Sacombre's heresy. But no, there was nothing of Fomharra in this demon. There was nothing but destruction.

Gwen stood in the circle consecrated by the Orphanshield and Elder Kesthe, staring in horror at the gheist that twisted through her home. It was a pervading darkness, tentacles latched on to fragments of memory, shadow images of Gwen playing with her brother, Grieg, in their childhood. Of her parents, and then their parents and grandparents, generations going back to the foundation of the castle, and House Adair. Back to the tribe of iron. Back to the days of the gods.

All that history swirled together, presenting Gwen with lightning-quick flashes of memory, scenes half-sketched in shadow, shot through with the corrupting darkness that now held the Fen Gate in its thrall. Each memory came and went, leaving Gwen with only a breath of the time that had been, the times that were lost, the secrets that they held. They fled from her mind, until only the corruption remained. Then it was past. Then she was alone.

The gheist surrounded her. It filled the castle, towering into the air on limbs as smooth and liquid as oil, twisting like smoke, as hard as stone. Lithe arms reached for her from the walls, snaked out of the ground, rose from broken stone and shattered doors, beckoning, longing. They wanted to take her home. Home as it was, a place of memories, without the regrets. Without the mistakes. Without the heresy and the lies and the deaths. Home.

"No," Gwen spat. Tears streamed from her eyes. "No.

That place is gone. You offer nothing but a lie. A lie made worse by its promise." She rubbed her face. Kesthe and Gilliam were outside the circle, frozen in place. When Gwen smeared the tears across her cheeks, they came away in icy splinters. She turned to look at the Hunter's Tower, her home for years and years. "No!" she shouted.

The gheist collapsed on her, crashing like a wave on the thin shield of the holy circle. Black smoke skittered across the invisible shell of the circle's protection, a storm against glass, beating down on it. The air rang like a bell. The demon's howling fury drove Gwen to her knees. She covered her ears with her hands, screaming back, begging for it to stop, to end, to die.

The circle shattered. The image of the gheist froze and splintered, spinning away in shards of terrifying darkness. The real world rushed in, filling Gwen's mind with silence. She knelt among the instruments of the circle, knees scuffed by the rough stone of the courtyard.

"What happened?" Kesthe asked. "Did you see it? Is it still here?"

"It is," Gwen said.

The shadows of the courtyard came alive. Cracks in the wall turned to dark arms, as thin and fast as lightning. The shattered windows that looked down on the courtyard moaned; broken stone turned to teeth, shattered glass glinting with dark malevolence. The ground shook and fissured. Smoke rose into the air.

Gilliam's swords were out in a flash. He drew naether from the air and the season, robing himself in Cinder's cold power. Gwen had a flash of Frair Lucas, a memory of the inquisitor facing off against the hunter gheist in the wilds of the Fen, his form turning to shadow and violence.

"In Cinder's name, I condemn you! By winter's power, I will destroy your heart!" he bellowed. Bands of naether wrapped around his body, an orbit of purple runes that spun slowly in the air, binding his flesh to the god of winter. "Flee, or know the true power of the inquisition!"

"Gods don't listen to speeches, frair," Kesthe snapped. She raised her staff of carved bone and breathed an invocation into it, then slammed the butt onto the ground. A circle of rumbling earth spread out from the impact, growing until it enveloped the three of them. The shadowed arms of the gheist tried to reach across the boundary, but dove into the ground, disappearing as they crossed the circle. "The grave consumes all," Kesthe growled.

"Not memory," Gwen said. She stood, drawing two short spears from her quiver and holding them crossed in front of her. "Not even the grave can hold that."

True to Gwen's word, the tentacles of shadow that Kesthe's circle had consumed burst suddenly from the ground, scattering the icons and throwing the elder to the ground. Kesthe screamed in frustration, rolling away from the attack and spinning her staff like a hammer. A surge of inky darkness washed across the ground toward them, its surface bubbling with tiny mouths, each one whispering a different story. Gilliam countered it with a scythe of purple light, cast out from his blades, empowered by the inquisitor's gravelly voice. The two waves met, the air boiling at their contact, until the darkness subsided.

The gheist flooded the courtyard. For every whipping tendril that Gilliam severed, or gibbering wave that Kesthe shattered with her staff, three more rose from the broken stones of the Fen Gate. The gheist was a god of memory, and this place was thick with it, memories that went back to a time before mortal breath stirred the air of Tenumbra. There was no way two priests, even as powerful as this witch and this inquisitor, would be able to defeat it.

Gwen fought as her training taught her. Her spears were effective against the shadowy limbs that grasped at her from the ground, the flickering shades that rose from behind windows or reached out of the walls to lunge at her heart. Most dissipated at a touch, but a few fell screaming under the bloodwrought steel of her weapons, and those were memories she recognized. Her mother's disapproving face, her father's jovial laughter, the sound of Grieg playing in the hallway while she prayed, all memories given teeth and anger and the will to cut her to the bone. But memories can't be fought. They can't be defeated. As corrupt as this gheist was, it was true to its nature.

"It's no use!" Kesthe shouted. "We need to fall back. This will take all the elders, and a bit of luck besides! We have to leave this place!"

"Godsbless, but you're right," Gilliam said, panting. "I will hold it here. Get to the gates!"

"You'll die!"

"In the service of my god," Gilliam said. "Yes, I will die."

"There has been enough dying," Gwen said. "Leave it to me."

She spun her spears one final time, clearing a space in the grasping darkness, then buried both weapons point down into the courtyard. Holding the shafts like the edges of a window, Gwen closed her eyes, and opened her heart to the darkness, and to regret.

The last time Gwen saw her parents, they were already

dead. The gheist brought them back to taunt her, animating their voices, piecing their torn bodies back together, lifting them from the grave long enough to drive her mad. It hadn't worked. The loss was too sharp in Gwen's mind to fall for a puppeteer's tricks.

But this was different. Here were her parents as she remembered them, as she loved them. Her father on the Allfire, chastising Gwen for drinking too much wine in front of her brother. Her mother, watching from the tower as Gwen rode off for her first hunt, the secret of their heresy shared in a look, the lie that they had to tell to keep the Fen God safe. And Grieg. Young Grieg, not yet drawn into that lie, marching through hallways and singing nonsense songs, praying earnestly in the doma, mouthing the words of the invocation at each evensong. A faithful boy. Still a child.

Dead, because of her lies. All of them. Her mother and father both had made their choices, long before Gwen was born, and their parents before them. But Grieg made no choice. He just died.

Memories of her brother flooded Gwen's mind, each one tinged with sadness, each one limned in shadows. The gheist pressed against her, whispering her failure in her ears, promising release from this guilt. Gwen let the promises drift through her mind, let herself pretend she could release her pain so easily.

Without the pain of loss, the memory meant nothing. That was the gheist's corruption, this promise that couldn't be fulfilled. Gwen knew. But she let herself believe, if only for a moment. Then she opened herself more fully, not to the memories and their pain, but to the corruption that the void priests had infected the gheist with. Thinking its victory was at hand, the gheist rushed forward, filling Gwen's heart, clawing at the inside of her soul. Only when it was trapped in the complicated weave of Gwen's spirit did the gheist see its error. Only then did it understand.

The spirit of memory fell through Gwen as if she were a sieve, straining out the corruption, filling her mind with everything that she had lost. What she had lost, yes, but what she had gained, as well. The memories of her family could not be tarnished by their loss. They were made sharper, more precious, filled with light. She would cherish them, despite the pain that they brought.

As for the corruption, Gwen absorbed it. She purified the gheist, skimming the darkness from its surface like spoiled milk, leaving only the spirit of memory behind. No longer tethered to the Fen Gate by the corrupting influence of the void priests, the gheist dissipated. Gwen fell to the earth.

A glimmering light drifted out of the ground. It looked like a cloud, mingled with a thousand faces, each appearing and disappearing so quickly that their features blurred together. Vast expanses opened in the sky, a field of green so bright it could have been gemstone. Mountains as sharp and high as the sun itself, dusted with snow. A hearth, warm and inviting, and the family that huddled around it. Battlegrounds, birthing chambers, the soft scent of wool, a treasured toy. All these things and more pulled softly away from the castle, shimmering as they rose into the sky, to mix with the clouds and eventually disappear.

"What was that?" Frair Gilliam muttered. The old inquisitor looked around the silent courtyard, his voice muted and soft. "I saw… I saw my mother. My wife. Our…" his voice broke. "Our children."

"The god of memory," Kesthe said. "No wonder I couldn't hold it. The void priests corrupted it, used it."

"They were trying to sift Fomharra from the memory of my family, stripping our history for its spirit," Gwen said. She got to her feet slowly, head still spinning. "They nearly succeeded."

"But they did not," Kesthe said. "And now the god of memory can go free."

"We can't let that thing roam the world," Gilliam said in shock. "Drinking the memories of its victims! Haunting the dreams of the innocent." He reached for his staff, to bind the gheist.

Kesthe took his hand. "It is not our enemy, inquisitor. The gheist is free, and must be left to do its business. Without it, we would forget our families, our failures. Our hope."

"Some things should be forgotten," Gilliam said shakily.

"No." Gwen turned to face the inquisitor, one hand casually on her knife. "The old gods are not our enemy, Orphanshield. It's the void priests and their corruption that we must fight against."

"But... but..." Gilliam's eyes grew distant. He cast about the courtyard, seeking the gheist among the shadows. When it didn't rise, his shoulders slumped. "I have been fighting that war for so long..."

"We all have," Kesthe said. She put a hand on his shoulder. "And now we must let it go. A greater threat has arisen, and it will not be defeated in small wars and petty vengeances."

Gilliam turned to her slowly. His face was old, wrinkled, filled with sadness. But he nodded, and Gwen thought she saw a spark of hope in his eyes.

"So be it. I never would have believed it, if I hadn't seen... But you saved my life, huntress. You saved me, when you shouldn't have."

"We have to stand together. There's no one else to stand with, and if we don't, the void priests will destroy our gods," Kesthe said. She glanced at Gwen. "We can't do it alone."

"No, we can't," Gilliam agreed. "So what now?"

"We find Malcolm Blakley. He's the last strong voice in the north, and perhaps our last hope for an ally among the Tenerrans. We will tell him what we know, and what can be done about it," Gwen said. "Do you have any idea where he went?"

"South," Gilliam said. "To the Reaveholt."

"To the Reaveholt, then." Gwen pulled her spears out of the ground, giving her home a final look. It was but ruins now. Ruins and memory. She turned to the gate. "And may the gods guide our steps."

"All the gods," Kesthe answered.

"Wherever they lead us," Gilliam said.

39

IAN LED FIVE riders down from the forest heights, keeping to the scrub as they approached the plains around the Reaveholt. Their progress was slow, both because of the snow and also the need to keep to whatever cover they could find, winding through defiles and hopping from grove to grove. The same weather that impeded them also kept other armies' scouts out of the woods, and let them make their way to the plains without being spotted.

When they finally breached the treeline, Ian was shocked by what they found. Not one, but three armies camped around the Reaveholt, with Bassion's colors still flying from the citadel's walls. A host of celestial guards had set up fortifications just north of the Reaveholt, while two armies lay further west, well away from Ian's own position. Of those two, the largest and closest flew banners of red and white, graced with flame. Their tents stood between Ian and the smaller encampment of House Blakley. They were cut off from his father.

"What are we to make of this, then?" Ian mused out loud. "Mother said that Malcolm had allied with Sophie Halverdt, but that encampment looks more like a prison yard than a meeting of equals. And the celestials seem focused on the

Reaveholt. Why, when an army sits in the field before them? They shouldn't be pinning themselves against the walls of the castle, not when they could be taking to the open field."

"There has already been a battle, my lord," one of the scouts said. A sharp-eyed man pressed into service for his eyes, if not his skill with the sword, he was peering into the distance. "Hard to see with the snow, but clear signs of heavy movement near that ridgeline."

The ridgeline in question was little more than a fold in the plains, but it was enough to offer some strategic advantage. The field south of it looked strange, as though a city's worth of colorful trash had been dropped in the snow. Ian pointed at it. "What do you make of that?"

The man stared for a long time. "Flowers, my lord?" he said uncertainly. "And not as much snow. I can see grass."

"Flowers. No less likely than anything else," Ian said with a sigh. He sighted the bonfire in the center of the Halverdt camp. "At least they're staying warm."

"There is... That's strange." The scout's voice was still tinged with uncertainty, even a certain amount of wonder. "There is a tree in that fire."

"That is what fires are made of. Burning trees."

"No, no, not that at all. The tree isn't burning, it's..." He scrunched up his face, trying to make sense of what he was looking at. "It's a tree made of fire. Flame instead of leaves."

Ian stared down at the camp. Sure enough, he could see a black trunk in the middle of the bonfire, and branches stretching out. The flames dangled from those branches like leaves, weaving through the air.

Just like the tree in Houndhallow. The corrupted spirit of Strife was here, as well.

"We have to get a closer look," Ian said.

"Won't be easy."

"We didn't come all this way to do easy things," Ian said. "Follow me."

As they left the trees behind, the snowfall grew heavier, and their view of the plains impossible. By the time they started toward Halverdt's camp, Ian could see no farther than ten feet, and that only when he lifted his head from his cloak. From his place at the head of the line, Ian couldn't see more than a couple of his own riders. If they got lost or wandered away, there would be no finding them.

This place brought strange memories to Ian. He had already nearly died on these plains, when the witch Fianna rescued him after the battle of White Lake. Cold had nearly killed him then, and that was in the height of summer. It would be ironic if he returned to this place in a different season, only to die in flames.

A snowball struck Ian squarely in the back of the head. He swore and turned around. The sharp-eyed scout behind him sat casually in his saddle, staring hard at Ian.

"What the hells was that for?" Ian asked. The man only nodded to his right, without looking away. Ian looked in that direction.

Four riders emerged from the blizzard, white shields crossed by the red saltire and three tongues of flame. All four were watching Ian and his fellows curiously. Ian turned back to the front, unsure what he should do.

"Hail, patrol! Any sight of the heretics of Cinder?"

"Nothing but snow and bloody… snow," Ian answered back. "For you?"

"Our swords are still clean, and our vengeance unfulfilled." The leader spurred his horse, drawing closer. Ian grimaced.

"A simple 'no' would have sufficed," he muttered to himself. He twisted back again, catching the sharp-eyed man's panicked look. "Right, nothing for it."

Ian kicked his horse and peeled away, riding hard and blind through the snow. His scouts followed, leaving the other patrol behind. Wind and snow battered Ian's face, the speed of his passage throwing his hood back, scooping wet slush down onto his neck. He rode quickly through the blizzard, but the faster he went, the less he could see. It was only a few seconds before Ian was separated from the rest of his group. The sound of a horse thundering through the snow followed him, but he had no idea if it came from his own men, or those of the Suhdrin patrol.

A line of thin lights spread out before him. A picket line, most likely belonging to the Halverdt camp. While he hoped to learn more about the bonfire at the center of this camp, screaming in at a full gallop was not a method for success. He veered away, drawing the attention of the guards standing at the picket. A few shouts followed him, but he was gone and back into the blizzard before anyone could follow.

Whatever hope he'd had of sneaking into Halverdt's camp was blown. His only hope now was to get his men away safely. Ian slowed and turned around in his saddle, squinting against the wind. The horse that was following him grew closer, but wasn't slowing down.

"The hound!" Ian shouted, waiting for an answer.

A blossom of light shot through the blizzard, framing the outline of a knight on horseback. Even the man's eyes burned with flames. He was riding low to the saddle, shield up and sword drawn. The flames dancing over his head turned the snowfall into a blanket of mist, further obscuring him.

"Against the night of winter!" the man yelled, charging forward.

Ian barely got his sword out before the man was on him. The flaming blade crashed against Ian's guard, spitting pitch onto Ian's cloak and startling his horse. Small flames pitted his clothes and saddle, but the knight seemed unharmed. He wheeled, swung, shoved his shield against Ian's riposte, and then hammered his horse into the side of Ian's mount. In the snow and panic, Ian was nearly unseated, only staying in his saddle by dropping his guard and holding on for dear life. Ian's horse shimmied to the side. The knight pressed forward.

Strike and strike again. The flame from the knight's sword was heating up Ian's blade. His fingers blistered on the hilt; the skin of his wrist scorched. Ian started to sweat, not from effort, but simply from the waves of heat washing off the knight. The man's horse was flecked with foam. The blizzard swirled around them in a torrent of mist, flakes melting, dripping, turning to ice on the side of Ian facing away from the knight, hissing into steam against the man's chain.

"Like all pagans, you will die!" the knight shouted. "Like all heretics, you will burn for your sins. The true light of Strife has been shown! The shadows of Cinder must be eradicated from all Tenumbra!"

"I'm not a heretic!" Ian shouted back, because he couldn't think of anything clever to say. "You're a heretic! Heretic!"

"Silence!" Swing and counter-swing, Ian's blade dancing off the man's shield, their swords coming together in a shimmer of flame. Ian punched the knight in his exposed throat, backing away as he gagged. It was only a brief respite. When he wheeled around, the knight threw away his shield and grabbed his sword in both hands. The flames that traveled along the blade grew brighter, larger, scything through the air with each swing.

Ian was on fire. What started as a few pits of flame had spread, and now his cloak, his tunic, and his saddle all crackled with flame, while bright embers dropped into his horse's mane. The creature was in a panic, kicking out whenever the knight drew close, forcing Ian to focus more on staying in his saddle than his swordplay. The knight took advantage, swinging wild and hard.

Finally, Ian fell. One of the knight's blows took him across the shoulders, searing his flesh with hot chain and throwing him from the saddle. He tumbled into a snow bank, which started to melt the second he hit it. The sound of his horse galloping off into the blizzard was soon drowned out by the burning knight's laughter.

"Do I kill you here, and let the bright lady's flames burn a confession from your bones? Or do I take you to Lady Halverdt, and let her decide your fate?" The knight came closer, his flames tamping down, until only the fire in his eyes and the inferno of his blade remained. "What do you have to confess, pagan? Are your sins worthy of the avatar's attention?"

"I am Ian Blakley, son of Malcolm, heir to Houndhallow," Ian said, standing up. Ian held his sword to the side, hoping to win the man without further violence. "My father has made an alliance with your lady. Take me to them, and let her explain."

"Ian Blakley, son of Malcolm," the knight said cheerfully. "That makes this so much simpler. Death here, then!"

Ian rolled to avoid the knight's downward blow. The flaming steel buried itself in the snow and packed earth beneath. While the vow knight struggled to release his sword, Ian came to his feet.

The vow knight was a living torch. Flames wicked off his back, curling into the air in crimson waves that turned the air into mist. His clothes burned, turning to ash, mingling with the snow. The steel of his chain mail shimmered in the darkness.

"You are no knight of the winter vow," Ian said. "I have known Elsa LaFey, and others. They burn with glory. You simply burn."

"You know nothing of glory, pagan." The knight gave up on his sword, leaving it in the snow. As he stepped away, a final blaze of flame traveled up the steel then snuffed out like a torch. The blackened blade pinged and cracked in the sudden cold. He drew a knife, spreading his arms to Ian in greeting. "The days of vows, and meditation, and reason are at an end. These are the days of fury."

"You really are a heretic." Ian shifted on his feet, bracing for the knight's attack. It came quickly, a stab at Ian's neck, another at his chest. When Ian blocked them both smoothly, the knight scored his dagger across Ian's wrist, drawing a trickle of blood.

"There is no escape. There is no hope, not for you or your ilk. We will burn you from the earth, one pagan at a time." The flames traveled up his arm, circling the dagger in a corona, sizzling as it touched the steel. "Strife's avatar on earth will end your pagan night!"

Ian ignored the knight's words, focused entirely on the dagger and the flame. The knight was now crying tears of pitch, black liquid bubbling down his cheeks as he fought. But unlike Elsa, the man's skin was not entirely immune to the heat he was producing. His flesh boiled beneath his tears, and black char gathered at the corners of his eyes. A seam of fire cracked open on the knight's fighting arm, traveling from biceps to wrist. His chain mail strained over the burning fissure, but the links cracked and ripped apart, sending molten steel across the snow.

The knight screamed and threw himself forward. Ian blocked the man's flurry of blows, dodging to one side as the flames grew. He punched the pommel of his sword into the knight's chest, cracking ribs, sending a shower of sparks out, like a collapsing bonfire. Flecks of burning embers sprayed across Ian's face, forcing him to stumble back.

Streamers of hot fire twisted around the knight's armor, hissing as the metal cracked, searing the knight's image on Ian's brain. Ian turned, shielding his face, as the conflagration consumed the whole knight. His screams disappeared into the squeal of flame and rapid crackle of popping chain links.

The second the flames died down, winter returned in all its fury. Sweat and mist froze on Ian's clothes, sending shivers down his back, all the way to his bones.

"That is not a glory I would wish on any man," Ian muttered. He got closer to the dead knight. His armor was plain, unadorned with bloodwrought runes or the symbols of Strife that every vow knight wore. "I'm not sure what he was, but there's nothing holy about it."

The knight's skin was cooked and peeling away in wide chips of ash and ember. As his skin flaked away, Ian caught sight of something that made him uncomfortable. He bent down.

A deep rune was gouged into the man's skull. On closer examination, there were dozens of smaller inscriptions across the bone of his brow, and down his cheeks. They swirled with ember light, like the last cinders of a bonfire dying away.

"Nothing sacred. Nothing holy," Ian whispered. The man's sword lay next to his body. Ian picked it up and sheathed it. He snagged the fallen knight's horse and swung into the saddle, then turned and started ambling toward his father's camp. "I must find my father. I must warn him."

40

"THIS DOESN'T FEEL terribly wise," Castian Jaerdin said to Malcolm. The two men were on the edge of their camp, with no company but their horses and the snow. They watched nervously as the picket line around Halverdt's camp peeled open to admit Malcolm. Soldiers from both factions patrolled the small strip of land between their camps, but Sophie Halverdt had established an additional picket line between them. Malcolm hadn't been inside that camp since Jaerdin smuggled him out, when he was unconscious and wracked with fever, but now a summons had arrived and he was riding in alone.

"Sometimes courage is needed more than wisdom," he told Jaerdin. "Sophie Halverdt will not release my people from her damned infirmary unless they are needed for battle, and I'm certain they won't be truly well until they are out of her burning grasp." He grimaced at the memory of his murderous and joyful rage during the previous battle. Malcolm no longer believed that the spirit that had possessed him was that of Strife, but he couldn't prove it. "I will press for battle when I talk to Halverdt. All you have to do is get through to Lady Bassion."

"Our messages have fallen on deaf ears, if they have reached her at all. But I will continue trying. I have heard word of an army gathering in the Fen, as well, wearing pagan garb and skulking among the trees."

"One war at a time, Redgarden. If Halverdt refuses to release me once I am back in her camp, the army falls to you. I trust you will do what is right."

"I will do whatever right the gods reveal to me, and probably die in the effort." Jaerdin sighed. "At least the snow has stopped."

Malcolm nodded, then rode forward. The twenty yards between camps felt like the longest, slowest charge he'd ever taken. When he was inside the picket, the guards pulled the barrier back into place behind him, and disappeared into their tents. Even with the iron braziers that filled Sophie Halverdt's camp, the wind was bitter.

Once he was inside the camp, Malcolm kept his eyes open and his fingers crossed. For all he knew, his soldiers were still incapacitated. Halverdt surely wouldn't agree to battle if a third of their allied forces were sick in bed. Malcolm had recovered, but only because Jaerdin had snuck him out of Halverdt's camp.

Malcolm's worries disappeared as he rounded the corner. Sir Doone stood at loose attention by the side of the road, her back to what must be the infirmary tent. Malcolm nodded in her direction.

"Come to fetch us, my lord?"

"I am here to discuss the matter with Lady Halverdt. She insists you must still be watched closely, and that you are all happy in your accommodations," Malcolm answered. "You're looking well, at least."

"Tell Sophie it's too damn warm," Doone said. "That tree is giving me fever dreams."

"Gods pray we will be free of it soon enough," Malcolm said, then hurried on. If Doone and the others were of sound mind, that was one burden off his mind. Now to lift the other.

The lane opened into the camp's central courtyard, and the burning tree. The light and heat of the strange tree were felt throughout both camps, but with the intervening picket and pavilions, Malcolm had never gotten a good look at it. Up close, it was as strange as he believed, and as terrifying as he feared.

The tree might have been an oak, but its leaves were flames, and its trunk glistened black and slick under the fire without being consumed. Waves of heat washed off it, pushing against Malcolm as he rode by. After a few seconds he was sweating through his linens. A few seconds more and he was riding faster, just to get away from the black and burning tree.

He wasn't able to get far. Sophie's pavilion was at the head of the clearing, tent flaps thrown wide to the tree's glory. A rank of vow knights stood outside the pavilion, their armor glowing in the reflected light of the burning boughs, apparently completely comfortable despite the heat. Malcolm dismounted and strode into the tent, throwing off his gloves and cloak and loosening the collar of his doublet.

"Gods, woman, how can you stand that heat?"

"Pure heat is good for the soul. I would ask how you tolerate the dark and cold of Tener, but you are born to the night, so it's no wonder you are comfortable in its embrace." Sophie sat on a pile of silk cushions at the head of a table laden with food and wine. She was still in her fine chain armor despite the gentleness of her surroundings. A handful of advisors sat around the table, including at least two vow knights. Malcolm walked to the chair furthest from the tree, turned it so his back was to the flames, and sat down.

"I glory well enough in summer, but that doesn't mean I sleep on a bed of coals, or light my evening reading with a bonfire." Malcolm looked around the room, happy to see at least a few of the advisors looked as uncomfortable as he felt. When he saw the face of the vow knight seated next to him, however, he had to suppress his shock. "Sir LaFey?"

"Lord Blakley," Elsa said. She didn't look herself. The angry scars across her cheeks were starting to heal, and her hair was longer and softer than he remembered. "It is good to see you well. I feared you were dead."

"Last we spoke, you were accompanying my son from the Fen Gate, in search of Gwen Adair. What became of that mission?"

Elsa glanced to the head of the table, with just enough worry in her eye to put Malcolm on edge.

"Perhaps we should speak of that later. Your son was well last I spoke to him, but much has happened since then."

"Sir LaFey does have an interesting history, doesn't she?" Sophie purred. "So many important things and important people have passed through her care. And here she is, with us, at the end. Right where she belongs."

"If I could know this was the end, I would be glad," Malcolm said. "My bones are tired, and the battle has been long."

"I promise you, Houndhallow, your struggle is nearly complete."

"Enough of this," Malcolm said, standing. "I came to a council of war. So let us make our plans. Lady Halverdt, it is necessary for me to have my knights at my side. I appreciate all that you have done for them, but I have healers and priests in my camp, as well."

"This is not mere sickness. They have been touched by the glory of Strife, as were you. They cannot be healed by bedrest and earnest prayers."

"If they should be healed at all," a heavy-browed man said. "Why would you want to heal away the blessing of the goddess?"

"Whatever happened to us, blessing or curse, it was brought on by one of your adherents, Halverdt. Sir Galleux kindled the spark that turned my people into fire."

"And in so doing, Galleux gave her life. Gladly, I might add. But it was not Galleux who brought this into the world," Sophie said. She motioned to Elsa. "It was your friend, Sir LaFey."

Malcolm turned to Elsa and raised his brows. She nodded.

"I felt it, drawing from the flames and traveling through me. It would seem I am a conduit for this... blessing."

"If you don't trust me, Houndhallow, perhaps you can trust Sir LaFey. You trusted her with your son, after all."

"That was not my choice," Malcolm said quietly. "And neither is this, apparently."

"As for the battle," went on Sophie, "the celestials have set themselves up in a strong position. We don't know Lady Bassion's intentions. She has received messengers from the celestial camp, and so may have given herself to heresy; and there is the matter of her attack upon her own side when she took the Reaveholt. I never trusted her, not really." Sophie sat back on her cushions. "She was supposed to win Sacombre's head for me, and lost that, probably on purpose. Too taken with herself to truly serve the gods. We must assume she and the celestials have come to some sort of agreement."

"We can assume no such thing. That army killed hundreds of her knights, and broke her army in half as they were massing." Malcolm pushed food around the table, uncovering the map that was supposed to be the center of their conversation. "She has lost as much to the celestials as any of us. Until she strikes her banners and opens her gates to their army, I will assume she is with us."

"Really? Even after she betrayed you by taking the Reaveholt?" Sophie asked. "Bassion stands for Bassion, and no one else."

"There is a difference between self-preservation and joining the enemy."

"How do you explain the messengers that have gone between them, then? Our position is already precarious enough. We have to assume an alliance between them."

"I agree," the heavy-browed advisor said. "Best to hold our lines and wait for reinforcement. Surely some house in Tener, or additional forces from Heartsbridge, will break this stalemate."

"Remember who cut down Bassion's army in the field, and then ambushed her while we were negotiating an alliance," Malcolm said. "The heretics of Cinder. Keep in mind the murder of Lord Halverdt, also at Sacombre's hand. Yes, Bassion took the Reaveholt, if only to save herself. We can squabble about past wrongs and crossed borders once this is over." He slammed his fist down on the table. "My friends, darkness itself is before us. We must join together, with any banner that would have us as allies, and bring that darkness into the light."

There was a flurry of conversation around the table as potential allies were named, and possible strategies discussed. The heavy-browed advisor even suggested abandoning the field and marching on Cinderfell, to "restore the light of Strife in the darkest of holds." Malcolm listened for a while, growing increasingly uncomfortable in the heat. Elsa was bent in prayer or concentration. She looked ill. When he looked up at Sophie, the duchess's eyes were firmly on his. He cleared his throat and spoke up.

"Is this how the blessed of Strife wage war?" His voice cut through the chatter, silencing the room. For a moment, the only sound was the crackle of flames from the tree outside. He looked around. They had to be reminded of their faith in Strife. He might not like Sophie's zealotry, but it was better than Cinder's darkness. "Is this how the bright lady asks us to do battle?"

"What do you mean?" Sophie asked.

"Plans and alliances and weighing the wisdom of striking down the heretic." He pushed his chair back and started walking around the tent. "Does the vow knight hesitate when facing the gheist? Does summer tremble when night falls, or does she burn hot throughout the darkness? We have the enemy before us. We have already broken him once. Why do we relent?"

"There is the matter of strength, Houndhallow. We can't just—"

"You say that I was blessed by Strife. Maybe I was, and maybe her light still lingers in my eyes. Because I look at these forces, at these maps, and I don't see an enemy to be pondered and maneuvered around." He stabbed his finger at the map, thumping down heavily on the celestial camp. "I see a darkness that must be lifted! I see winter, and swear to you that I have the flame to melt it!"

Sophie was already on her feet, eyes bright as she scanned the map.

"Lord Blakley, I have always known you as a careful general. What has changed your disposition?"

"The heretic is before us," Malcolm said. He drew his sword and laid it on the table. "Give me my reins, and I will trample him into dust. With Strife as my light, and her flames as my armor, nothing can keep us from victory."

Sophie smiled, a wicked smile that reached all the way into her zealot's heart. She looked around the room and nodded.

"To battle, then. And may Strife light our way."

Malcolm returned to camp, reported his success to Castian Jaerdin and the other lords of their host, then left them alone to plan the coming disaster. He went back to his tent and lay down. The weight of Halverdt's burning tree pressed down on him, even at this distance. It was all he could do to not gather his furs and crawl out into the snowstorm, praying for relief and winter's touch, even if it meant his life.

He had to wonder at that tree. It wasn't natural, of course, but nor was it the sort of display the celestial church or Lady Strife were given to. That its heat should reach him all the way across the camp was disturbing.

Worse, he knew that it wasn't heat or light that reached him, but something more. Something deeper, pressing not against his skin, but against the spirit that moved through him. He felt it lingering at the edge of his temper, sparking anger and mistrust, drawing him back to that glorious fury.

Even though he walked around like everyone else, Malcolm could tell that the fire Galleux had kindled in him was not gone. It was only waiting for something to stoke it back to life, and then he would be lost to it. And this time, Malcolm was sure he wouldn't survive.

Did the rest of his soldiers contain the same forge in their hearts, tamped down for now, waiting to blaze out of control? By demanding battle and their freedom, had he provided the spark that would return them to madness? How could he know until it was too late? How could anyone?

Malcolm lay in bed, worrying deep into the night. He was nearly asleep when a sound disturbed him. Very quiet, a tearing of cloth, like linen parting under a very sharp knife. He came awake to the touch of a blade on his throat.

"Hello, Father," Ian whispered. "I hear you've gone mad."

41

IAN'S FATHER LOOKED old. His hair was more white than gray, and the wrinkles that bunched up around his eyes and in the folds of his mouth spread like spider webs over his face. The hair across his chest was as white and fine as cotton silk, and the hatchwork of scars that Ian had known and admired since childhood now stood raw and puckered across an old man's skin.

How had this happened? Six months, and his father had aged a lifetime.

Malcolm lifted a finger and brushed it against the sword at his neck. When Ian didn't immediately pull the blade away, Malcolm raised his brows.

"Have we come this far, son?"

"There are people in this camp saying you burned with the light of the sun, led a charge against ten times your number, and came out on the other side alive and well. They say you are touched by Strife, you and all your host. Lady Strife and I aren't on the best terms, Father."

"That shouldn't come between us," Malcolm said. "And as for the rest, let's just say that I have my doubts."

"War has made a heretic of you?"

"No. But it has not made me a zealot, either. Now get this

sword out of my face before I break it across your backside, boy."

Anger flared through Ian, and then laughter. He sheathed the blade and stepped back, ready to run if his father called for the guards.

"How did you get in here?" Malcolm asked. "There are supposed to be measures against such things as swords at my throat as I sleep."

"It's fairly easy for me to pass as a soldier in the army of Houndhallow," Ian said. "Harder to walk the camp without being recognized, to be honest. Redgarden nearly bowled me over at one point."

"Be glad it wasn't Sir Doone," Malcolm said with a smile. "She would recognize you at a hundred yards."

"Is she...? Has she...?"

"Doone is alive, though confined to the infirmary in Sophie Halverdt's camp. And since you haven't bothered to ask, your mother lives, as well, though I haven't seen her since I joined up with this lot."

"I traveled here with Mother," Ian said. "She continues to be well."

"That is probably my fault. Getting too close to the sun, and driving her into the wilds. I'm glad that she came to you, rather than striking out on her own." Malcolm's face clouded. "Does she speak of me?"

"Why do you think I'm here, Father? She has uprooted every servant, soldier, and soul in Houndhallow to wrest you from this infernal pact."

Malcolm nodded thoughtfully. He swung his legs down to the floor and gathered his furs around him. He seemed about to ask a question when Ian blundered on.

"What is happening here? I find you in the company of Sophie Halverdt, who has clearly gone mad, waging a war against the celestial guard, treating with the very houses that chased us out of Greenhall and killed our friends at White Lake. I have heard stories of burning pillars, gheists made of flowers, whole armies disappearing into a lake of flames..." Ian gestured helplessly. "It's all too much to believe, much less understand."

Malcolm rolled his shoulders, the joints crackling noisily in the silent tent. When he locked eyes with his son, Ian could see the father he remembered from his childhood, buried under all the scars.

"I have come a lot further than I expected, Ian, and by a different path than I thought I would walk. We have all made mistakes. I am still learning to live with mine." Malcolm stretched, then stood up and went to the table to stare down at the map. "I have avoided this war with all my energy, but it cannot be avoided. There will be no peace without this fight. I see that now."

"Victory at any cost? Even an alliance with Sophie Halverdt?"

"I like to tell myself that I had no choice, but there are always choices." Malcolm nudged some pieces around the map, finally turning to face his son. "It is the choice I made. Another mistake, perhaps, but it can't be undone. You cannot imagine the threat we face in the celestial guard. The things I've seen, Ian. The things I've done."

"You don't hold all the blame, Father. I wasted months following Gwen Adair, when I should have been at your side."

"I did not allow you to be at my side," Malcolm said.

"And I stand by that. You would have been wasted in this battle. And my sins would now be on you, as well. Perhaps this way you can preserve the Blakley name."

"I'm not sure the church will recognize me as your heir, even if I do survive."

"I stood by and watched an inquisitor killed in cold blood," Malcolm said sharply. "So neither of us is in Heartsbridge's graces, I suspect." He smiled weakly at Ian's shock, then turned back to the table, busying himself with things that didn't matter. "He threatened your mother. It's no excuse, but it's mine. I stood by a hundred times as inquisitors tracked down and executed suspected witches in my lands, but when he raised his hand against Sorcha..." Malcolm's voice trailed off. "When he threatened her, I could not step aside."

"I'm glad," Ian said. "Glad that you finally see that. Have you forgiven Fianna for what she did to Mother yet?"

"If I could. After this is over, maybe I'll travel to Heartsbridge and speak on the witch's behalf. If I'm not taken there in chains, that is. If she still lives."

"You are not the only heretic, Father. I killed a vow knight, just now, outside the picket of this camp. Or what I thought was a vow knight," Ian said. He explained about the runes in the man's bones, his lack of control of the flames, the inferno that consumed him when he died. "Whatever gift Sophie Halverdt has given them, they do not know how to contain it. It burns them from within."

"I am familiar with that fire," Malcolm said. Ian creased his brow, but Malcolm waved his questions away. "We don't even know who our enemies are anymore. Be they saints or heretics."

Ian came to the table with his father. They were quiet for a long while. Finally, Malcolm cleared his throat and spoke.

"You are my heir, Ian. You are my son. Whatever the church decides."

"I know. I know."

Malcolm nodded quietly, then set the marker he had been fiddling with down on the map and let out a long, pent-up breath.

"So. What of this battle, Ian? Surely you didn't come all this way to seek my forgiveness, or my apology. You say Sorcha has brought an army from Houndhallow?"

"Of scullery maids and pagans. There is some strength in it, and if this battle were fought with heart instead of steel, we would win it a thousand times. The glory I imagined as a child, the battles I dreamed of fighting..." Ian's voice was very fast now, very nervous. "Anyway. Whatever path you've followed, mine has been just as strange. I came here to speak with you at Mother's bidding, and by her will. Without her you would have to stand this fight alone. So what are your plans?"

"Betrayal," Malcolm said. "I have seen it enough. Now I must employ it. Sophie Halverdt cannot be allowed to grow in power." He lowered his voice, leaning in to his son. "I have been in secret communication with Helenne Bassion. I am not the only one. The celestials offer her peace, if she promises to hold fast in the Reaveholt, and not join our fight."

"They have already betrayed her once. Mother told me about your battle, how the inquisitors summoned gheists and destroyed Bassion's lines. Why would she believe them now?"

"She has already agreed to their terms," Malcolm said.

"In exchange for their mercy, and my death."

"Gods, that woman. How can she be so cruel?"

"She does so at my request," Malcolm said. He started arranging pieces on the map, lining up the celestials, placing golden tokens for Halverdt's lines, a blue banner for House Bassion in the Reaveholt. "Listen carefully. Tomorrow I will take the lead of Halverdt's forces. I have convinced her to throw caution to the wind and attack with all her might, to crush the celestials under Strife's glory."

"That will never work. The celestial guard is dug in north of the Reaveholt. Even if it were a fair fight, it would take more than Strife's glory to shift them," Ian said. "And it's not a fair fight. The void priests have the gheists at their sides."

"Void priests?"

"Heretics of Cinder, or maybe they're pagans," Ian said. "It's hard to say, anymore. The witch Fianna was among their number, and Sacombre as well. They have betrayed pagan elders, murdered Suhdrin lords, and led the houses of Tener astray. The true enemy, though all they seem to want is chaos."

"Chaos is the birthplace of power. If they mean to seize Tenumbra, getting us to kill each other is a fine way to go about it." Malcolm rubbed his face. "You should believe more of the stories you hear about Sophie Halverdt. It will be a good fight, but in the end, we will fail. The celestials will break us, and I will sound the retreat. Even if we're winning."

"That sounds... foolish?"

"Yes. Because I have seen Halverdt's madness. The celestials are one enemy, but not our only foe. Neither the void priests nor Sophie Halverdt can win this fight. Both must be destroyed if we're to restore order to Tenumbra."

Ian looked over the map. "I don't see any other forces on the board, Father. Especially now that Bassion has sworn to stay out of it."

"She has, but that was a lie." Malcolm scooped the golden tokens of the army of Halverdt back, pushing them with the black tokens of the celestial guard. "As we fall back, the celestials will pursue, exposing their southern flank to the Reaveholt. Thinking themselves safe, you see."

"But Bassion will attack? You have her word?"

"I do. She will pour out of the Reaveholt as we pass, slamming into the celestial flank. Hopefully, we will have done enough damage to the celestials that their lines will break. I will rally Halverdt, those who remain, and press the attack." He pushed the pieces together on the map, smiling. "All sides will be devastated, and an end to the war assured."

"A dangerous gambit. If Halverdt fails to retreat, they will see your duplicity, and come for your neck. And if the celestials complete their rout, Bassion will not have the strength to defeat them."

"Wars are won with dangerous gambits, son. And this is a war we must win."

"What's to keep the celestials from simply retreating? Disappearing into the Fen, or north toward Cinderfell?"

"Because the gods have provided," Malcolm said, smiling. "Where are your forces?"

Ian picked up an unmarked token and placed it on the board. Malcolm grabbed it and scooted it south. "There. You will cut off their retreat, and overrun any who think to flee."

"I lead kitchen maids," Ian said. "Not the best allies in this fight."

"I will take any mob led by my son," Malcolm said. He clapped Ian on the shoulder. "With you at their head, they will not fail."

Ian shook his head. "Does Redgarden know?"

"It was Castian's plan. He leads the northern flank of Halverdt's army. Originally he was supposed to cut off the retreat, but now that you're here, that will not be necessary."

"I will need to move quickly. The celestials will undoubtedly have outriders here and here." Ian pointed to the map. "I will attack the night before, to cut them off from the main body, and prevent them from warning their masters of my presence."

Malcolm paused for a long moment, then nodded. "Very good. But keep your mother out of this."

"Do you honestly think that is possible?" Ian asked with a laugh. "She will ride beside me, or before me if I am not going fast enough." Both men stood smiling down at the table in wonder at Sorcha's strength. Ian laid his hand on his father's shoulder. "Come back to the Houndhallow camp with me. Just you. I got in; I can get you out. Speak with Mother."

"I... I can't do that. If I see her again, I won't be able to go through with this. I can't say goodbye twice." Malcolm set his face, strengthened his voice, and still sounded feeble. "I can't put her through that farewell, knowing what is to come."

Ian's hand dropped, but finally he nodded. "I will give her your love."

"There's no need," Malcolm said. "She has always had it."

* * *

When he left, Ian shook his father's hand, then embraced him, then didn't want to let go. It was Malcolm who finally took him by the shoulders and pushed him back out the way he had come.

"Go with the gods," he said. "Whoever they may be."

Getting out of the camp was simple. Ian kept his hood high and his shoulders down. When he got to the stables, he unhobbled his horse, then waited for the far patrol to pass. When they disappeared, he mounted and rode into the night.

"Did you think you passed unmarked, Ian Blakley?"

He turned sharply, drawing his sword. Castian Jaerdin stood just beyond the stables, covered in shadows. The duke of Redgarden chuckled.

"You and your father have been laughing and talking and arguing about gods know what in that tent. It's good. I haven't heard him laugh for months, not truly." Jaerdin stepped into the light. "Are your plans settled?"

"They are," Ian said. "Are yours?"

"Of course. Did you see Sir LaFey?"

"Elsa's here? I wondered where she had gone," Ian said. He squinted into the camp, as though Elsa might rise up out of the shadows. "I think I assumed she had simply wandered into the woods to die heroically against some gheist. It seemed fitting."

"She is Sophie Halverdt's mascot now. It seems she has a peculiar ability to draw the powers of Strife."

"Ah. But you don't think—"

"It doesn't matter what I think. Your father didn't tell you, but I thought you should know who you'll be facing in this battle. Friends and allies, families and heretics... those who are closest to us make the most difficult enemies."

"She is only deceived. Once we reveal who Sophie is, and what she is doing, Elsa will surely turn from her."

"She may. Or she may not. But you need to be prepared, either way." Jaerdin turned back to the shadows. "The patrol is returning. You had best be going."

Ian was about to say more, but the jingling of chain mail reinforced Jaerdin's warning. When he looked back, Redgarden was gone. Ian grimaced, then rode off at a gallop.

42

THE ORPHANSHIELD WAS uncomfortable with their method of travel. Kesthe and the other shamans seeded their path with spirits, weaving gods of wind and road into the forest trails, speeding their way. The Orphanshield rode at their fore with a hand on his blade and Cinder's name on his lips. "In case the demons turn on us," he said.

"The trained hound does not bite the master," Kesthe reassured him. "We are only drawing the attention of the spirits. They barely notice our passing."

"Some things cannot be tamed. The sea, the wind. Death." Gilliam licked his lips, staring into the blur of road and forest that welled up before them. "I will stand my guard."

"You must learn to trust our new allies, frair," Sir Bruler said. The Suhdrin knight had been instrumental in persuading Gilliam to join their cause, and had served as the Orphanshield's personal attendant since their departure from the Fen Gate. "We want the same things. The church justified, and the heresy of the void priests ended."

"Well, I wouldn't say that," Kesthe answered with her quirky smile. "But the heresy, at least. That we can agree on."

They made good time eastward, bending the forest to

their will and their horses to the road. At night they slept under Frair Gilliam's care, their minds shielded by his prayers and supplications. Each morning the witches woke up unsettled. "I have never slept so soundly and yet woken so restless," Kesthe said one morning. "My dreams are a part of me, huntress. The priest steals them."

"You understand the danger we're in, elder," Gwen answered. "And so does the Orphanshield. He is only trying to protect us from the things stalking the night."

"Always afraid of the pagan night, these churchmen."

"With reason. Or have you slept through the last six months?"

One morning Gwen woke to find Frair Gilliam gone from camp. Bruler led her to where the frair knelt in a secluded grove, his robes undone and his bare chest turning blue in the cold. Gwen thought the madness of their travel had finally gripped him, but as she approached, she heard a familiar song on his lips. She waited respectfully at the edge of the clearing until he was done.

"Is it already Frostnight?" she asked. Gilliam rose slowly, slipping his robe back over his shoulders, rubbing the warmth back into his skin. He shook his head.

"Nearly. I lost track of the months, obviously. My days in the Fen Gate are a blur, and this strange road—" he gestured helplessly back to the camp, to Kesthe and her witches "—made celestial observations difficult. But in my prayers last night I found it. Cinder's face is turning toward us. We are approaching the longest night of the year."

"Six months," Gwen said with wonder. "Six months since this began."

"What begins in fire always ends in cold," Gilliam said.

"That is the way of the church." He tottered over to her. "Given our travels, I suspect this will be the last time I am able to perform the rites. Will you accept the blessing?"

"I shouldn't..." Gwen took an uncertain step away. "I mean, it's not like I can claim much faith in the church, frair. If I draw Cinder's eye now, in my heresy..."

"You knelt each Frostnight at the altar of Cinder and received the blessing of judgment your whole life, Gwen. Do you think the judge of all didn't know what was in your heart? And he didn't condemn you then, so who am I to condemn you now?" He raised his hand, steady as stone. "Cinder's blessing is for all, no matter their corruption. No matter their place on this earth."

Gwen closed her eyes and stepped forward. Gilliam's hand cupped her forehead. His skin was cold and rough, and he smelled like old sweat and incense. It was comforting somehow.

She didn't hear his words, so familiar as to be rote, but when it was over her heart felt lighter. Her burden was no less, but at least she had passed beneath the judge's eye and walked away. That was something.

Kesthe had barely started to weave their path into the forest spirits when the road opened before them and the field of battle unfolded. An abandoned camp spread out before them, with a burning tree at its center, and row after row of tents stirring gently in the breeze. The air was unseasonably warm. Frair Gilliam glared down at the burning tree.

The army of the tree was marching away from them, already arranged in their battle lines. They faced a much larger force, flying the celestial flag, though mists wove through their ranks and darker shapes lurked in the fog. The Reaveholt anchored the southern end of the battlefield.

"Is that Bassion's flag flying from the castle?" Gwen asked. Gilliam didn't budge, but Kesthe trained her eyes in that direction.

"A golden boat on yellow and blue?" Kesthe asked.

"Yes, that's Galleydeep. What is Lady Bassion doing this far north? And how did she gain the Reaveholt?" Gwen surveyed the field. "And who leads this army of light? It looks like Halverdt's banner, but with flames. And the tree—"

"We must destroy it," Gilliam said sternly. "It is an abomination. I have never seen such power."

"Trees do not burn in Heartsbridge?" Gwen asked lightly. Gilliam turned toward her. His eyes were glassy and bright.

"Tonight is Cinder's holiest night, of frost and winter. That is a totem of spring. Not of summer, nor of Strife. How could Halverdt have been so blinded?"

"There are vow knights in Halverdt's ranks," Kesthe noted. "Are you so sure of yourself, priest?"

"He is," Gwen said, drawing closer to the tree. She could feel the familiar hum of its song. "As am I. This god is known to me."

"But how could it..." Kesthe's voice trailed off. "The god of flowers? From Greenhall?"

"The same. It has consumed the ranks of Halverdt." Gwen closed her eyes, but the impression of burning leaves, each one a flower of flame, was seared into her mind. "Sophie Halverdt is not deceived, frair. She is possessed."

"By one of the most dangerous gods of the tribes,"

Kesthe said. "We condemned it generations ago, when its madness nearly destroyed us all. The vernal god was the twin of Fomharra, who was hidden in the Fen. Without one, the other cannot be opposed."

"We must oppose it," Gilliam said. His voice was full of confidence and anger. "If it is the last thing I do, that tree must be quenched."

"Then we strike now. While it is unguarded," Gwen said. She turned to the leader of the rangers, a large woman named Deidra. "Form ranks and prepare to march. We attack the camp!"

"The camp is empty. And that is Malcolm Blakley down there. Shouldn't we be joining our strength to his, against—" she pointed at the celestial host and the gheists in their midst "—against those demons?"

"I fear the tree's protectors will become apparent soon enough. Steel your men, and bind them to blessings of the gods. We will need all the help we can get."

The spears were still lining up when Gwen saw movement among the tents. Only a handful of figures, but enough to let her know they were being watched. She could feel their power swelling, even at this distance. She drew Gilliam's attention to them.

"Fallen knights of the winter vow," he spat. "We will be hard pressed to overcome them without divine help."

"The gods will answer," Kesthe said confidently. Her witches were preparing themselves, flanked by shamans and bolstered by a loose mob of pagan rangers. "We should strike before they are ready."

"But the spears and riders—"

"Will join us when they are ready, or in the grave.

Whichever comes first," Gwen snapped. "Deidra, follow when you can. Frair Gilliam?"

The Orphanshield drew his twin blades, kissed the symbol of Cinder on each hilt, and nodded.

"Lead on, witch. And may Cinder guide us true."

43

FRAIR LUCAS WOKE to the sound of drums. He rolled out of bed to see Martin peeking into the hallway through the cracked door, holding his sword behind his back. The heir of Stormwatch looked nervous.

"What's going on?" Lucas asked.

"Troop movements inside the castle. They've pulled the guards down to a skeleton crew. Sounds like they're massing in the courtyard."

"Are the celestials attacking?"

"Gods know. But this isn't a training exercise."

Lucas got up and started to dress. He left his traveler's clothes beside the bed, instead unfolding and pulling on the priest's vestments that he'd been avoiding. Martin watched uneasily.

"They're still imprisoning people in those colors," Martin said.

"They may well lock me up no matter what I wear," Lucas answered. "If I'm to face my god, I would rather do it in the gray and black." He slid the icon of Cinder over his head, then unwrapped the staff he had been hiding on their trip north and laid it on the bed.

"You're no good to anyone dead," Martin said. "Either

way, I'm not going out there without my chain mail."

Lucas waited patiently while Martin strapped on what little armor Bassion had left him. She didn't want either of them fully prepared to fight, in case it became necessary to arrest one or both. Still, she could not deny a lordling of Suhdra his sword, and the chain and doublet that went with his title. It wasn't plate-and-half, but it would turn a blade or two.

Once out of their room, Lucas and Martin were quickly overwhelmed by the changes to the castle. There was still a light cordon around their rooms, but most of the remaining troops of House Bassion were in the courtyard. The priests of Cinder were no longer in the courtyard, and had been replaced with column after column of tightly packed halberdiers, archers, axemen, and knights on foot. Rank after rank of mounted knights pressed against the northern gate, their mounts jittery, the riders talking quietly among themselves.

They found Lady Bassion on the walls overlooking the battlefield. She rested in the shade of a pavilion, though there was little sun to justify its use. Bassion was swaddled head to toe in furs, and was sipping mulled wine that was being warmed in a nearby brazier. Two knights of the winter vow stood guard, the same two who had attended her during Lucas's last audience. They watched the inquisitor approach with sneers on their faces.

"Frair Lucas. I was worried you wouldn't join us for today's festivities," Bassion said. She waved to a pair of benches near the parapet. "It promises to be memorable."

"Lady Bassion. I take it there's to be a battle?"

"Yes. Lord Blakley has convinced that firebrand Sophie

Halverdt to plunge forward, as foolish as that sounds." Bassion drank from her cup and sighed deeply. "He has a plan, you see."

"A plan?"

"Yes. A whole conniving feast of betrayal and misdirection. We're to play a part, you and I. At least, that's what he's promised. And I hate it when promises aren't kept." Bassion squinted and waved to Martin. "What do you think, young Stormwatch? Will Malcolm and Sophie be able to carry the day?"

Martin surveyed the battlefield. The golden lines of Halverdt were heavily outnumbered, but he had seen them fight the week before. Anything seemed possible.

"They don't have the numbers, but if Malcolm Blakley thinks it wise to attack, then I'm sure they'll find victory. Houndhallow does not play his hand if he's unsure of the outcome."

"No, he does not," Bassion said, a wicked smile on her face.

"What of your forces, my lady?" Lucas asked. "You are mobilizing at last?"

"In accordance with Malcolm's clever plan," she answered. "He believes he can drive them against my walls. I get to swing the heroic final blow. Isn't that lovely?"

"So you've put your differences aside? You will come to Malcolm's aid?"

"When the time is right, yes," Bassion said.

"You said I had a part to play in this?" Lucas asked.

"You and your fellow priests of Cinder," she said, casting a sly glance in his direction. "I have given them their freedom. They are preparing now. Someone will have to stand against the gheists the celestial forces are sure to unleash on our ranks. I'm glad to see you've decided to wear your vestments again."

"And what of your oath to never trust the church of Cinder again?"

"I don't have to trust you. I just have to use you, against our common enemy, of course. Trueau!" she called over his shoulder. "Is everything ready?" Lucas turned to see Sir Trueau, the vow knight he had seen outside Bassion's tower, as she reached the parapet.

"I have said the prayers I know," Trueau answered. She glanced at her fellow vow knights. "What of the two of you?"

"They know their role," Bassion said, then leaned back in her couch. "Do sit, Lucas, Martin. You are blocking my view."

They sat uncomfortably, perched against the side of the wall. The lines below began to stir and march. Lucas lowered his voice, so only Martin could hear.

"There is more going on here," he whispered. "Be ready."

"Always," Martin said.

Below them, the battle started.

44

MALCOLM'S ARMOR WEIGHED more than it should. The false dawn of Halverdt's burning tree flickered across the linen of his tent, filling the space with heat, sapping his strength. He felt like a lamp burned clean of its oil, a flame going only on fumes. Dawn was still hours away when he stepped out of his tent and into the crowded lanes of the camp. Castian Jaerdin was waiting for him by the campfire.

"You look worse than death, Houndhallow," he said. Jaerdin drew a mug through the wine mulling over the flames and handed it to Malcolm. "This won't help, but at least it will be a warm death."

"I'm already sweating through my chains," Malcolm said. "Truthfully, I want nothing more than to reach the field of battle, and be away from that damnable tree."

"The gods are listening, Malcolm." Jaerdin glanced at a cadre of vow knights who were walking nearby. "Be sure they like what they hear."

"I no longer care who hears what. I will fight for them, and die at their side if I must. If they don't find me pious enough to give my life for their cause, that's their problem. Not mine."

"I worry more about the kind of death they might ask of you, and your family," Jaerdin said. The vow knights continued on, never looking back at the two dukes of Tenumbra. "They march around like kings appointed."

"Their goddess walks the earth, in Halverdt's form and will. Can you blame them?" Malcolm drank some of the bitter wine, forcing it down despite the sweat already beading on his brow. "It will be settled today, Redgarden. Whatever is to happen, it happens on this day."

"Gods willing," Jaerdin said. He tossed his dregs into the fire and stretched. "I will be glad to return south. You have a fine land, Malcolm, and a proud people. But the weather is shit."

Malcolm laughed, shaking his head. "It's not my fault you were raised weak, Redgarden. Perhaps a season in the ice has done you some good."

"The company has been good. The conditions..." Jaerdin shrugged. "I will be celebrating Frostnight at home for a while, I think." He nodded to a group of Suhdrin knights riding past, on their way to the lines. The motley colors of their tabards, crests, shields, and heralds stood in stark contrast to the dark morning. "Are your people prepared, Malcolm?"

"They know what they are to do. I haven't had more than a moment alone with them since the last fight, Halverdt's hawks watch them so close. Doone nearly dropped her jaw when I told her the plan." Malcolm threw his mug in the snow, then collected his cloak and signaled for his horse. "But they are Tenerran born. They will be ready."

They stood in silence for a while as the squires collected their mounts. Finally, Jaerdin turned to Malcolm and lowered his voice. "Your visitor the other night. He is well?"

"I wasn't aware his visit was widely known," Malcolm said.

"Do you honestly think the heir of Houndhallow could walk into my camp and not be recognized? I had to set a guard around your tent to keep the curious away, and even then, the lanes were unusually busy for the middle of the night." Jaerdin paused, staring off into the distance. "To be honest, I wasn't sure if I was going to be carrying one or the both of you out of that tent on your shields."

"He did put a sword to my throat," Malcolm said with a laugh. "But we had a good talk. I may be more of a heretic than he is, when the scales are weighed. The middle of war is no time to solve a father's sins against his son. We will settle things more clearly once we're all back in Houndhallow."

"Once you've settled the peace here, persuaded Sophie Halverdt to give up her new heresy, and determined the claim on the Fen Gate, and restored the church—"

"Enough," Malcolm said grumpily. "Let an old man dream of better days. Let him hope a little, will you? It's not like you're getting back to your sun-drenched vineyards until these same things are resolved."

"Eh, yes. Well," Jaerdin answered, collapsing a little. "Fine. This battle first, and tomorrow for tomorrow. I must see to my ranks, Houndhallow. Gods keep you."

"And you, Redgarden." Malcolm clasped the man's hand, then drew him into a close embrace. "You have been a good ally, Castian, and a better friend. There have been few enough of both these days."

"Who would I be, if I didn't return the love you and your family have shown me, Malcolm? Be safe."

The men parted, going to their separate forces. There was much to be done before the battle was joined, and little time.

Sophie Halverdt was waiting for Malcolm at the head of his column. He winced when he saw her, but forced cheer into his voice.

"Greenhall! We ride to Strife's victory, and her honor!"

"We do, Houndhallow. I'm glad you accepted this burden. It stirs the souls of my troops to be led into battle by the Reaverbane himself."

"Not long ago their blades were turned against me," Malcolm said. "But no matter. We are united in Strife's will. Let's show these heretics what becomes of those who oppose the light of summer!"

"You have caught the zealot's rhythm, if not his heart," Sophie said. "No matter. Fight like you believe, and Strife will grant you victory." Malcolm was about to protest, but Sophie only laughed. "Fly my banner, Houndhallow, and the troops will follow."

"And where will you be, my lady?"

"To your right, in the shadow of the Reaveholt. A pity Helenne Bassion never responded to my overtures, but hardly surprising. That woman was always a coward." Sophie rode away, waving to Malcolm as she went. "Go with Strife!"

Malcolm didn't answer. Sir Doone rode up to report.

"The corps from Houndhallow can't number more than a hundred. The rest of this lot belong in stocks, or a madhouse. Not counting the vow knights, of course."

"I would take a dozen from Houndhallow over the rest combined. A hundred is more than enough," Malcolm said. He eyed the steady ranks of Tenerran knights in his service, wearing the black hound of his house, many watching his every move reverently. He was risking their lives, as well as his own, on a very dangerous plan. All he had to do was keep them alive during the rout, then turn them against Sophie in the confusion. He nodded. “Very well. Prepare the lines. We advance on my command.”

3

THE LONGEST NIGHT

45

THE LAST MILES were the slowest. Ian rode at the head of his little army, with Sorcha on one side and Sir Clough on the other. He kept thinking he saw Henri Volent in their company, skulking among the infantry or riding just beyond the outriders, but each time he went to check, the man wasn't there. Ian couldn't decide if they were visions or just his imagination playing tricks on him. Worse, he didn't know which he preferred.

Their force was a motley collection of Suhdrin knights who had joined his force following the siege of Houndhallow, Tenerran soldiers from the garrison, and the few refugees from Houndhallow who were capable and willing to carry a spear. More willing than capable, most of them. A good number of pagan rangers had joined them on their trip south, drawn to the young hound's banner, and the shining light of Sorcha Blakley. They told him their people had sent them to enforce the Blakleys' place as the unifier of Tenumbra. It was something even Ian didn't fully believe, but it drew banners to his side, and earned him vows of loyalty from those who marched behind him. Looking back at the gaudy colors of the Suhdrin knights, the grim plate of the knights of Houndhallow, the varied arms and armor of the volunteer foot, and the dark leather of the pagan outriders, Ian was amazed that all these people were following him. If only he knew what fate he was leading them to, he might be able to sleep at night.

They marched in narrow column through the forest, angling toward the northern flank of the celestial forces. Ian was alert for outriders or scouts, though his own rangers reported there was nothing ahead of them, not until they reached the main force of the celestial guard. Still, Ian was careful. He didn't want to spoil his father's plans, or tip his own too quickly.

"You look thoughtful," Sorcha said. Ian shook his head, but she persisted. "Your father looks that way, when his heart is heavy."

"It is not my heart that is heavy, Mother," Ian said. He glanced over at her. Even in the grinding cold, Sorcha refused to change from her formal silks, or wear more than a light cloak. She insisted that she didn't feel the weather. Still, it made Ian feel like he wasn't caring for her properly. Though if his mother had proven anything this last year, it was that she could look after herself.

"I finally march to battle," he said, "to join my father's side, and restore the name of Blakley in the north."

"Then what is bothering you, son?"

"I wonder at the world this battle will leave behind. What does victory even look like? Can the church be restored, when it has lost so much faith among the people? I will no longer stand by while the inquisition hunts the gods to extinction; my time among the tribes has taught me that much. But I'm not sure all the houses of Tener will follow suit. And if they don't? Is that another war we have to fight?"

Sorcha laughed, a strangely human sound from her inhuman throat. It reminded Ian of his childhood, the moments of joy sprinkled throughout his youth. Sometimes he found it hard to see his mother in this spirit riding beside him, with her glowing veins and the mad tangle of living hair. But Sorcha Blakley was still in there.

"These are the things your father would worry about, as well. The things he's probably worried about right now, even as he rides to battle." She leaned back her head and closed her eyes, as though lost in memory. "His burden has never been light. I fear that not even the grave will give that man the rest he deserves."

"Let's leave talk of graves for some other time," Ian said. "Not while we're riding to battle."

"There is no more fit topic," Sorcha said. "Sailors sing of the sea, farmers of the soil, and the warrior's song is for the grave." She paused for a long moment, her eyes narrowing as she scanned the forest. "I had a young priest with me for a while. Catrin DeBray. She believed the time had come for the church of Strife to shun the house of Cinder, to reform the celestial church into the church of summer, and the sun. 'Why worship a god of darkness and death?' she would ask. But I know. Life always leads to death. Without the grave, the cradle is nothing but a promise unfulfilled. We live to lay down the burden of life, so that someone else may pick it up. Summer is joyful, as is birth. But winter..." She pulled her mount to a stop. Ian slowed, watching her. "Ian, we have been seen."

"By whom?" he asked, looking around. Gray trees stretched in all directions, and there was no noise out of place in the early-morning forest. "I see no one."

"Neither do I. But I feel them, searching my waking dreams. Form the ranks and prepare to advance."

"Now? We're miles from the battlefield. If we rank up now it will be hours before we reach the celestial flank. The battle will have already been decided, and likely lost."

"It may already be," Sorcha said. "Ranks, Ian. It is not the celestial flank that we will be meeting."

"Who are we fighting, then?" Ian asked.

The forest creaked around them. To the south, along a gully that wound its way through the snowy underbrush, a handful of figures appeared. Ian strained his eyes. Priests, for certain, but he couldn't see what they were doing. Even as he watched, they raised their arms, chanting to the sky. The trees shifted and came alive. There was almost no change, but immediately a wall of gray trunks and shifting boughs began marching toward them in a steady line.

Faces peeled open in their bark, and gnarled branches curled into arms. Trunks split, widening into skirts of twisted roots still damp with mud, oscillating like a wave as they swept across the snow. The forest came alive.

"We fight the gods," Sorcha said quietly.

"Signal the ranks," Ian shouted over his shoulder. "Sir Greau, Sir Hollard, swing west and anchor our line. Do not charge! We don't know how wide this attack is, nor how quickly we will be flanked. Dugan, try to form a shieldwall among this bracken." The horn beside him sounded, answered by confused signalmen up and down the line. The column slowly split, filtering into the trees, tired soldiers fumbling spears into a wall. He looked back at the approaching trees. "They are coming too fast. We don't have time to hold a line."

"Our only way out is through," Sorcha snapped. "They weren't expecting us. We have to punch through."

"I like her way of thinking," Sir Hollard said. He and Greau hadn't moved yet, were staring glumly at the advancing enemy. "I am no good at holding lines. I was born for the charge."

"But the foot, the archers," Ian protested. But even he saw the impossibility of the situation. "How do we know how many there are? How far we'll have to pierce before we're through them?"

"Look around, Ian. We are in a forest. That's how many of them there are."

Ian grimaced, then set his jaw. He nodded.

"Knights with me, Suhdra and Tener. Mother, organize the foot brigades. We will punch a hole; you'll have to drill through it. A fighting march is the best we can do." He turned to the squire. "Signal it."

"I don't have a signal for that, my lord," the boy said nervously.

"March, march on the double." Ian grabbed the hound banner from the squire's saddle and quickly unfurled it. "Follow the colors!"

The horn started, and the confused ranks of marching soldiers behind them milled about for a long moment. Outriders from the tribes were collapsing to the main column to see what was going on. Sorcha spun her horse and hammered back to the column of foot, screaming and filling the air with her light. There was no time for better plans.

"May the gods see you through," he said to the knights of Suhdra and Drownhal who had gathered around him. "Otherwise I will see you in the quiet. Advance!"

The knights cheered, spurring their horses. As they surged forward, lances lowered, dodging between trees and over shrubs, they shouted out the individual oaths of their various houses. "Light in darkness!" "Against the night!" "In iron, truth!" "This mountain stands!" "The tides always rise!" "Neither peace nor war!" Ian gripped the banner in his left hand, drew his sword, and charged.

"The hound!" he screamed. "The hallow!"

46

THE BATTLE STARTED in a short exchange of bowfire between Halverdt's left flank and the celestial right. Ranks of archers emerged from the celestial lines, huddling behind huge wheeled barricades to launch flight after flight into Halverdt's line. Castian Jaerdin commanded that flank, at least in theory. Malcolm could see the duke of Redgarden ordering a counter charge with light horse that scattered the archers, but exposed them to a brief sally of pikemen, supported on both sides by heavy horse. It was a short fight, with both sides leaving behind their dead.

"Jaerdin knows better than that," Malcolm grumbled. "He should have held his line and waited for return fire to clear them out."

"Castian Jaerdin is trying to lose this battle," Sir Doone answered. "As are you, my lord."

"Right, right. Hard to keep that in mind." With a shudder, the entire Halverdt line began to advance at the pace of their slowest troops, the ranks of long spears that held the center left and right, on either side of Malcolm's column of knights. Arrows sowed the ground in front of them, like feathered grass springing up from the snow.

"We'll need to split our force, to keep them from

annihilating us all in the initial charge," Malcolm said. Looking across the field, a block of celestial guard on foot, nearly as wide as the entire army of Halverdt, held the center. It was flanked by mounted knights, and further supported by smaller blocks of halberdiers. Archers waited behind the central block, sending arcing fire high into the air. It was inaccurate, but reminded Malcolm and his allies to keep their heads up. "Signal Greenhall to pin those mounted knights. We'll have to trust our spear to deny the charge, and see what we can do about those guards in the center."

The horns sounded, signals passed back and forth, and Sophie started her slow, rolling charge at the celestial line. The black-clad knights across the field answered the challenge, and left their lines. It was better than Malcolm expected.

Light glimmered through Sophie's cadre of knights as they charged across the field. Malcolm couldn't help but feel a thrill at the flames sparking from her horse's hooves, the flowing ash trailing from her cloak, the bright arcs of lightning dancing around her blade. Halverdt may have taken her father's mantle of zealotry, but she was doing it in grand style. She crashed into the celestial knights with a shout. The two columns came together like lances, splintering apart, crashing steel on steel, horses toppling into the snow, only to wheel around and pass again. The sound of it was incredible.

Other columns of knights streamed out of Halverdt's lines to follow suit. They charged whatever opponent they faced, slamming into spear lines, blocks of pikes, other knights. One cadre even dodged between the abandoned barricades to attack the archers as they fled. The celestial line wavered.

"Gods help us, we may win this damned thing," Malcolm said. He held his own riders back in reserve. On either side, the blocks of supporting spear murmured nervously, itching to get into the fight. For now it was only a cavalry charge, lances shattering shields, horses crushing any who fell before them, whether they were friend or foe. The wide block of celestial spear loomed closer. Along the edge, individual shields turned to face the nearer threat—Sophie Halverdt and her zealot knights of the winter vow. The line bubbled and flexed, then a column of foot broke free and wheeled to slam into Sophie's flank.

"That's our signal," Malcolm said. "Advance! Knights at the trot, foot at the double! Advance!"

"Against the night of winter!" The call was taken up along the Halverdt line, and soon the whole ragged block of zealots was shambling forward. It was all Malcolm could do to keep them from running, and then only because his own mounts were in the way. Slowly they closed with the celestials. "Remember, Doone: enough damage to ensure their collapse, but we want to pull away intact. Stay alive! Let Halverdt's rabble take the brunt."

"Easy enough," she barked, raising her sword. "Charge! Charge! Spears to the front! Charge!"

A ragged scream broke loose from the foot troops. They broke into a run, their shieldwall foundering, spears getting tangled and quickly abandoned as the ranks mixed. Those in front lowered their weapons, but tips quickly dragged against the ground, shattering under the inertia of the charge, or slipping from frenzied hands. Spears were discarded for swords, shields thrown aside. Light flashed through their ranks. Flames licked up from screaming mouths. Their armor started to glow, each ring in their mail shimmering with inner light.

Malcolm fell back, reining in his remaining knights of Houndhallow. The mob lapped around them, smashing madly forward, heedless of the danger. The light grew. The flames reached toward the sky.

As they crashed into the celestial shieldwall, a wave of flame washed over them. The heat was startling. Shields cracked, spears leapt into flame, sweat-soaked leather caught fire, terrified screams joined by the exultations of the zealots.

Malcolm felt it in his bones. The cinders of his own madness glowed to life, bloodlust etched into skin, the very screams like music in his ears. Without thinking about it, he spurred his horse forward. Doone took his shoulder.

"My lord? What are you doing?"

He turned on her, eyes wild, face twisted into a rictus of fury. "Release me!"

"If we just throw ourselves—"

"Release me!" he screamed, then charged, howling, into the fray.

The flames crackled around his head like a crown of fury. Malcolm grinned, riding the madness into the enemy lines, and scattering them with his sword.

In madness they fought, grinding through the celestial ranks like a millstone. The joy of war seized Malcolm. He galloped across the churned snow of the battlefield, sword held high, trailing flames like a banner. The flickering forms of the rest of his cadre loped beside him, knight and horse sheathed in light, their screams lost in the din of war. The enemy came at him like a cliff face, and Malcolm the tide. A black wall of shields rose up before him, spears bristling, tiny helms filled with terrified eyes. It was all so clear, so close. He struck.

The sound of impact deafened him. Malcolm broke through the first line of spears, only to stumble on the second, and was up on the third. The shattering spears of the celestials caught immediate flame, bursting into bright sparks that hung over the charge like constellations. Malcolm kept his saddle, but around him several of his companions tumbled to the ground, some rolling to their feet, some staying in the mud, their flames guttering in the snow.

Malcolm laid into the spearmen pressed against his shins. Their formation was too tight, compacted by the crush of Malcolm's charge. Malcolm's sword became a constant arcing whirlwind of flame and black feyiron, the strange blade passing through steel and bone like loose burlap. Smoke rose from burning corpses, hanging like a banner over Malcolm's head.

It was glorious. This murder was everything he lived for, everything he would die for, the only true purpose in life. Malcolm lost himself in the slaughter. His heart sang, even as it burned too brightly, too fast, each breath taking years off Malcolm's already fragile life. He could feel his skin sizzling against the hot steel of his armor. The thick linens turned to ash, but it didn't matter. The flame would keep him.

Suddenly he was alone on the field. A ring of dead bodies surrounded him, their broken bodies trampled into the mud. Several dozen of his knights remained, flame-maddened horses wheeling back and forth, chomping at the bit. Malcolm cast about, looking for something to kill. The need, the hunger, chewed at his bones. Finally he saw the enemy, black banners waving over their ranks. A flight of arrows arced out from behind them, falling on Malcolm and his cadre. One of the arrows buried itself in Malcolm's shoulder.

There was a moment of bright pain, then he tore it out, trailing ember-filled blood. The shaft of the arrow caught fire in his hands. He threw it aside and roared his fury.

Wind grabbed him by the heart and pulled. Malcolm strained against it, but it had him by the bones, the flame, the blood. He urged his horse forward, but the beast was frozen in place. Strands of light twisted up out of his flesh, spinning through the air, joining a hundred other skeins, each one being drawn out of his other knights and tangling together, like wool knitting together.

At the heart of this tapestry of burning light was Sir Elsa LaFey.

Elsa stood in the middle of the coursing web of light, her chest heaving, eyes closed, hands stretched out before her. The light burrowed into her, digging channels in her armor, dancing through her hair, turning her skin into beaten bronze. The snow at her feet vaporized into mist, the mud beneath baking under her boots, cracking in the heat. A flash of light swallowed the sky, and the wind stopped. Malcolm lurched in his saddle. Peace settled over him. Madness drained from his blood.

"What happened?" Malcolm muttered. He looked around. Those few dozen of his remaining knights teetered in their saddles, eyes wide in shock. He put a trembling hand to his shoulder, feeling the edge of his wound. The flesh was cauterized, the scar as hard as stone. He looked up at Elsa.

"The flame has found a different home," she said through gritted teeth. When she opened her eyes, lightning flashed across her cheeks, tracing the lines of her old scars. Her eyes glowed like forge-stoked coal, warm and bright. She took a precarious step forward, then another, slowly gathering her strength. "It was drawn through me. I simply closed the tap."

"How long can you hold that?" he asked.

"Until I die," she answered. "We have come too far, Houndhallow, for you to throw yourself away so easily."

Malcolm looked around the battlefield. Sophie's column was in splinters to his right, and the remnants of the blocks of spear milled between them. The celestial line was shattered, but they held more in reserve than Malcolm could offer. Smoke obscured the battlefield to his left.

"Where is Jaerdin? Where is my son? Have they taken the flank?" The pain in his shoulder flared. When he looked down, he was shocked to see burned blood across his chest, leaking into the rings of his mail. His arm was stiff and cold. "Can we fall back without being routed?"

"We may not have a choice." Sir Doone rode up, flames still tracing paths through her armor, blackened ash smeared across her eyes. "They are coming,"

"The celestials?" Malcolm asked. She pointed.

Out of a swirling fogbank, shapes loomed up, gaining speed as they approached. Malcolm turned his horse to face them, then thought better of it. Nightmare eyes glowed in the darkness, traced in lines of silver fire.

"The gods," Doone answered. "We make our stand, or we die!"

47

THE WIND RIPPED through Gwen's hair. The closer she got to the Suhdrin camp, the warmer the air became, until her skin prickled uncomfortably, and sweat beaded on her brow. Gwen was reminded of another desperate charge, that time into the little village of Tallownere, with Sir Merret and Frair Lucas at her side. So many of that company were lost at the Fen Gate, the rest fled with Blakley's army, or returned to their homes to hide their loyalty to the heretic Adair. She wondered if her father's men blamed her for their shame, or their ghosts for their misery. She wouldn't blame them if they did.

These thoughts were driven from her mind as they reached the camp. The flames from the burning tree at the camp's center turned the ranks of tents into brightly drawn waves, their shadows stark, the glow from their canvas sides as warm as firelight. Gwen was trying to pick out the figures she had seen earlier when one of them stepped out of a tent along the perimeter and drew his sword. Gwen swerved to intercept him. Bruler and Gilliam fell in behind her.

The figure was in full plate, and wore a tattered red tabard. Rather than a helm, his head was surrounded by a glowing aurora of fire, the flames mingling with his orange hair, spitting curls of smoke into the air. He carried a double-handed sword. The blade was etched in golden runes, and glowing lines of power ran along the forte, flickering like lightning in his hands. The ground under his feet smoldered. His eyes were pits of burning coal. He raised his sword in their direction, then fell into an easy guard.

Gwen bore down on him. She drew a spear and threw it, drawing another before the shaft found its mark. The thrown spear turned to splinters as it arced down toward the man, its ash shaft flaring into cinders. The bloodwrought spearhead tumbled on, striking the man's armor before evaporating in a shower of sparks. The vow knight laughed. His voice sounded like the roaring of a forge.

Gwen rose in her stirrups and drew her spear back to throw again. Her time with the pagans had taught her much about spirits and the forces that governed them, but she had no gheist to call on. What Gwen did have was the corruption she had siphoned off Kesthe and the god of memory, a darkness that now twined through her bones like cancer. She laced the tip of her spear with the corruption. A black ribbon of energy fluttered around the spear like a lady's favor. She threw.

The spear arced through the air, streaming lines of night sky as it fell on the vow knight. The shaft began to smoke, but the destruction of the physical bolt did nothing to the darkness that trailed it. Speartip and shadow twisted together. The vow knight noticed the change only at the last moment, swinging his flaming sword to block it. Steel met bloodwrought iron, and the tip burst into a blossom of flaming light. The shadows wrapped around the knight, clinging to him like tar. His armor sizzled at their touch, and soon he was swinging madly, cutting tendrils of deep night sky and shaking them loose. His wild face was twisted in concentration as Gwen drew near.

She drew her sword, spinning it in her hand and then striking as she passed. Her blade glanced off the knight's pauldron, skidded across the steel before slapping against his cheek. The flames in his hair scalded Gwen's fingers, and she almost lost her grip. She thundered past, and turned her horse to attack again.

Bruler and Gilliam bore down on the knight. Bruler rode high in his saddle, spear tipped forward, as perfect a form as you would see at the Allfire tournament. Beside him, the Orphanshield was wrapped in a nimbus of naetheric power. A veil of purple light wrapped around his shoulders, and his swords crackled with black light. The vow knight whirled to face them.

A wave of flame curled up out of the ground in front of the knight, rushing toward the charging Suhdrins. It widened, so that the nearby tents caught fire, growing taller as it roared forward, until it towered over Bruler's head. Gwen lost sight of the pair of riders, and was desperately pulling another spear from her quiver when a line of shadow pierced the center of the wave. The curtain of flame split open, curling back just far enough to let Bruler dash through, then Gilliam. The vow knight gestured, and the flames dissipated like morning fog.

Bruler reached the vow knight first. His spear shattered against the man's chest, pitching the knight back, staggering him. In a normal man the blow would have pierced his heart and sent the corpse flying, but the vow knight kept his feet, swinging his massive sword as Bruler passed. Bruler blocked the attack with his shield, but the steel face hissed and bubbled, raising a cloud of black smoke into the air. Bruler yelped and threw the shield away.

It was the Orphanshield whose blow struck true. The

frair threw a scattering of darts from his swords, tiny shards of naetheric power that hammered into the vow knight, driving him back. The knight's hysterical laughter echoed over the field. As Gilliam got closer, the knight spun his sword once and set it to strike, both hands gripping the hilt like a banner. The nearby flames from the burning tents, the tongues of light dancing around Bruler's discarded shield, even the glowing leaves of the black tree at the camp's center, hissed and drew toward the vow knight's sword. The air roared as infernal light boiled around the blade, glowing into a tower of swirling flame. Gilliam rose in his stirrups, swords held high to strike, the veil of his naetheric armor peeling away before the vow knight's aura.

They came together, both swinging hard, the bright line of the vow knight's sword cutting through the air like a lighthouse beam, the bulwark of Gilliam's shadows clenching tight as the fire dashed against it. Blinding flames and guttering darkness filled the air, and then Gilliam was past and still riding.

The vow knight reeled. The left half of his body had turned black, and the flame of his sword guttered along the blade, flickering out. He spun to face Gilliam, but when he planted his left foot, the leg shattered into ash. Cracks ran along the dark half of his body, the baked shell of his armor crumbling as he turned. He came apart in long splinters. When he struck the ground, the knight's body was briefly limned in blinding light, lines of flame that disappeared a second later. A final flame crawled along his sword, reaching toward the black tree. Then it, too, died.

Gilliam's horse slowed to a trot. The inquisitor slumped forward in his saddle, chest heaving, eyes glazed. Gwen hurried to his side, afraid that the old man would fall to the ground. He was only winded, though. When she touched him, his skin was as cold as ice, and twice as hard.

"Frostnight," he said with a huff, still trying to catch his breath. "It has been decades since I drew that much power from the naether. And I barely tapped Cinder's well. A dozen inquisitors could end this fight on a day like this."

"We don't have a dozen. We have you," Gwen said. "Can you continue?"

"I must," Gilliam said. Bruler rode up, concern etched across his face. His cheek was scalded on the left side, where he had been holding his shield, and he held his arm gingerly. "We must hurry. There are more of those damnable knights in this camp. They are only now becoming aware of our presence. To the tree!"

They wheeled and started galloping toward the burning tree. Its black branches towered over the camp, the flaming leaves that surrounded it as bright and hot as forge coals. Their heat pressed down on the trio, a physical wall that they had to push through. Sweat soaked Gwen's armor. Figures darted among the tents, most on foot, rushing to catch up with them.

"Almost there," Gwen promised, though it felt like the tree receded with each step, like a mirage.

The roar of the tree was so loud that Gwen didn't hear the other sound until it was too late. The first thing she noticed was a quiver among the distant tents on the far side of the tree. Howls and shouts finally reached her ears, then she noticed a wave of soldiers rushing toward them. At first she thought they were being charged. Then she understood, by their frantic screams, the way they trampled their own tents, their lack of weapons.

"It's a rout," she shouted, pulling up short. Looking over the heads of Halverdt's retreating army, she saw a line of black mist, and then faces, twisted and misshapen, their eyes burning silver: the celestial army in pursuit.

The first of Halverdt's broken army reached them. Men and women in light chain, their faces bloodied, eyes wild, ran screaming past. They ignored Gwen and her companions. A few became a dozen, became hundreds. They were pressed back. Gwen wheeled her horse, shouting over the panic.

"Retreat to our line! We have to prepare for the celestials. We have to hold our own ranks together."

Bruler nodded, galloping back, but Gilliam lingered. He was staring at the tree.

"We are so close…"

"Not close enough. We'll be trampled if we stay here, and those gheists will not wait for us to destroy that tree. If we can even do it alone in these conditions. We have to run!" Gwen shouted. Gilliam's face fell, and he turned.

Gwen gave the black tree, now burning even brighter than before, a final look. It was surrounded by fleeing soldiers and panicked horses. The dark line of the celestial forces was getting closer, their progress slowed only by the trampled bodies of their enemy. Malcolm was somewhere in all of this. She was sure of it.

Finally, Gwen turned and galloped off, with the Orphanshield at her side. A hundred yards beyond the camp's perimeter, she watched Sir Bruler reach the ranks, rallying them into a hard line of steel shields and long spears. These hundreds, versus the celestial gheists, and whatever troops supported them.

They had to hold.

48

MISTS CLUNG TO the celestial ranks, rising from iron braziers among the lines and tangling with the spears like woolen floss. Where the two armies met, traces of light shone through the mists, giving the whole battle the look of a distant thunderhead, flickering with heat lightning.

Lucas and Martin watched from the ramparts, their attention divided between the battle and Helenne Bassion, who had not moved from her grand pavilion, which was draped in silks the colors of House Bassion, with the crest of Galleydeep wrought in gold on the side. The doors of the litter opened wide, giving the duchess a full view of the fields below. She sat like a queen on her throne, swaddled in fine furs, still sipping her wine. Lucas could see Martin's attention was on the cadre of knights of House Bassion who were nearby, their armor as bright as sunlight, their heraldry as sharp and precise as if they'd been on parade, rather than watching a battle unfold.

"So," Lucas said finally, to Martin. "Is this going well, or poorly?"

"I can't decide. I've seen nothing of the other priests, and those vow knights look a damn sight too comfortable with our condition. Still, we have our swords—"

"No, no, the battle," Lucas said. "I could never follow the movement of troops. It all looks like churned mud and screaming horses to me."

"Oh. Yes, well, it's not that much different down there. Malcolm has broken deep into the enemy ranks, to my surprise. That charge should have failed an hour ago, but it keeps rolling on. Their horses must be nearly dead. Only thing keeping them from breaking the celestial line is the sheer numbers in opposition." Martin narrowed his eyes, trying to see the far end of the battlefield. "There's something happening over there. Too hard to see, though."

"When will they show themselves?" Lucas muttered. "When will their priests strike?"

"You believe they will? I honestly think that the only thing keeping Bassion inside these walls is the simple fact that they're fighting with conventional forces," Martin said in a whisper. "If they show their true nature once again, she couldn't possibly hold back."

"You would be surprised what sort of cowardice a lord of the realm can justify, when behind sturdy walls, surrounded by strong guards." Lucas darted a look at the vow knights. "Though how those three remain silent is beyond me."

"Is the battle not keeping you entertained?" Bassion asked, her voice lilting. "Must I bring a bard to distract you, frair?"

"I just wonder how long you will stay out of this fight, my lady. It seems that if you lent your strength to Lady Halverdt now, the day might be won."

"Or lost forever," she answered. "They push too far. Blakley, especially, is overcommitted."

"We have both fought at Malcolm Blakley's side,

Galleydeep," Martin said. "He does not overcommit. If he has won so much ground, it is only because he sees the advantage of it, which we cannot judge from here. I urge you—"

"The time for this conversation has passed, gentlemen. My plans are laid." Bassion took a drink. "But the urgency has passed. As you can see, the battle is going quite well. Whatever dream of heroism has been haunting you, it can pass into forgetfulness. The day may well already be won."

"And if you are wrong? If the battle is lost because you held back?" Lucas asked. He stood and strode forward, earning nervous stares from the vow knights. "What will you do then?"

"I will still hold the Reaveholt," Bassion purred. "As you know, this castle has never fallen to siege."

"You may want to ask Sir Bourne about that," Lucas snapped.

A chill passed through the audience. Helenne sipped her wine and studiously ignored Lucas. The three vow knights edged closer. Lucas held up his hands.

"I am not a man of battle. All I know is that the threat below us calls for no quarter, and will offer none in return. If we do not stop it here, holding the Reaveholt, or the Tallow, or any other damned barrier you wish to name, will not matter. None of it will."

"Your advice has been noted, inquisitor. If I need it again, I will ask," Bassion said. "Now take a seat, please. You're making me nervous."

Lucas sighed and turned back to the battlefield. Something had changed.

"What is happening?" he asked. Martin followed his gaze, then stood and leaned against the parapet.

"Halverdt's forces are dividing. Sophie's banners are drawing close... no, they're falling back. Malcolm's lines are overwhelmed. He's falling back. The whole line is falling back!"

Lucas whirled on Bassion. "Now is your moment, my lady! Surely if you mean to have a say in this battle, you must do it now!"

"Malcolm's forces are attacked from behind!" Martin said. All heads turned to follow his arm. Among the tents of Halverdt's camp, a battle was breaking out. It was much too far away to see any details, but a line of troops moved along the ridge, and fights consumed the neat rows of tents. "If Malcolm retreats now, it will be directly into the teeth of that assault."

"Lady Bassion, the time for games is past. Open the gates of this castle and let your allies inside."

"I do not take orders from a priest," Bassion snarled. "Especially a priest of winter. And I won't risk this castle to save Blakley's pagan hide."

"Then you have failed them. You've failed them all." Lucas gathered his robes and motioned to Martin. "Come on, Martin. I will not stand by and do nothing while the Blakley banner falls."

"Sit down, priest. Or face my wrath."

"Your wrath? Ha! What will you do, execute me? Throw me in prison? There's nothing you can do that can frighten me, my lady."

"You may be surprised," she said with a smile.

"What do you mean by that?" Sir Trueau asked. She had removed the lace veil that usually covered her face, and was not dressed for battle. Curiously, Lucas noticed that all three vow knights were wearing silks and leather, rather than chain and steel. Before he could ask, the vow knight repeated her question. "I was privy to your discussions, Lady Bassion. I delivered the missives to Malcolm's hand. You promised him aid. Do you now mean to leave him hanging?"

"I am tired of this," Bassion said. "Be silent, and watch the battle unfold. For all your words, victory is far from lost. Lady Halverdt has powers you would not imagine. I have seen them. I fear them, even, and if her loss means those powers disappear as well, I will not complain."

"At what cost?" Lucas said. "If Halverdt falls but the celestial heretics remain, we will have put down one madwoman and replaced her with a whole pantheon of mad gods. If you don't—"

"I said enough!" Helenne Bassion rose from her throne and walked down the short steps. She set her wine glass on the parapet. "You are ruining a perfectly good battle. This audience is over! Return to your rooms, and I will call for you when the matter is decided. Until then..." She swept her arm wide, as though she could scatter all of them like bowling pins. Her hand clipped the wine glass, knocking it onto the stone. "Be gone!"

The glass shattered, spraying fragments across the narrow floor. What spattered from the cup, though, was not wine. It seeped black and thick into the cracks of the walls. Blood, and something darker. The largest vow knight stared at the stain as it spread.

"My lady?" he whispered. "What is the meaning of this?"

"She is one of them!" Martin shouted. "That is why she hesitates!"

"Damnation," Bassion muttered. She turned to Lucas. "You are endless trouble, Gillem Lucas. I should have let Horne finish you the first time."

Trueau was the first to move. All she carried was a mercy knife, but she drew it and leapt toward the duchess of Galleydeep. The other two vow knights were still staring in wonder, and the circle of guards was too far away to act. Trueau closed the distance in a heartbeat.

Bassion was faster. She flashed a palm at Trueau, muttering twisted words, the veins of her ruined face growing dark as she spoke. A wave of light shot out from her hand, passing through Trueau. It threw the vow knight back, knocking the knife from her hand and leaving her curled in a ball on the ground. As the light passed through Trueau, it took something with it, a heavier brightness that leaked from Trueau's bones and eyes, spilling into the air and dissipating like mist.

Trueau's screams cut through the larger vow knight's shock. He drew his knife and took a step forward. The web of light echoing from the duchess washed over him, and when he fell it was against the parapet, and then over the wall. His tumbling body dashed against the ground far below. The other vow knight slowly raised his hands, dropping his knife.

"Guards," Bassion said, turning her attention to Lucas and Martin, "seize these four and restrain them. They are no longer a threat. And it would be a pity for the frair to not see this game played out to the end."

49

BRANCHES WHIPPED AGAINST Ian's face, and a tangled mist pulled at his hair, chilling his skin. At first he thought it was just the trees, that the enemy was still far ahead, but then a tree leapt out at him, forcing him to swerve to the side. A twisted face peered out of the bark, eyes as black as stones, acorn teeth and a mouth that spewed rot. A dozen branches descended on Ian, crashing against his armor.

He raised his sword and started chopping. The gheist shattered like an empty shell, bark scattering into dust, wood splintering, the withered leaves rustling against his skin as gnarled fingers scrambled for Ian's throat. He jerked back, punched the whimsical-mad face with the pommel of his sword, and reeled away when the visage burst and a hive of flying ants poured out of the wound. They swarmed over Ian, biting, hissing, stinging, crunching loudly in the joints of his armor whenever he moved. When Ian screamed, they poured into his mouth. They tasted like sour honey. Bile raced up his throat, down his chin, across his chest.

"Push through!" Sir Clough shouted as she raced past. A sprite of tangled vines clung to the back of her saddle, sinking nettle-thin stingers into her mount's thick flesh. She disappeared among the trees. Ian followed, spurring his horse and leaving the hissing cloud of ants behind.

The trees closed in. Ian wheeled past a tangled wall of grasping vines, smashed his mount into an elm that crumbled at the impact, then swung his sword into the rotten trunk of an oak that had been dead for years before the gheist had claimed it. The sharp steel of Ian's sword bit into the soft wood, but the rotten flesh closed around the blade. The hilt jerked out of Ian's hand. He tried to turn back, but the oak rumbled on, and another tree crashed into his face. Ian grabbed the iron haft of his banner in both hands, fought off the assault, and pushed through. The underbrush clung to his boots, and his horse screamed as sharp spines picked at its legs. A tendril of thornwood whipped around Ian's hand, biting through the chain gauntlet before he could pull free.

So surprised was Ian to run into a human on foot that he did not at first realize what he had found. A man stood in a clear space, hands spread wide, eyes closed in concentration. He was dressed like a farmer, but his beard was carefully trimmed, and his hands had never seen a day of labor. Ian glimpsed a flash of iron at his chest, an icon dangling at the end of a leather cord. Ian's horse screamed again, and the man opened his eyes.

The second he saw Ian, the man clapped his hands together and punched in Ian's direction. A sound like a swarm of hornets buzzed past Ian's ear, shredding the air like rent cloth, but when Ian flinched away he saw a cloud of tiny teeth disappearing into the sky. The man drew his hand back to his chest and whispered into his palms. He was watching Ian with tight, angry eyes.

Ian jumped from his horse, planting one foot on the

saddle and leaping across the space between them. His opponent's eyes went wide, and he threw his hands forward again, but whatever incantation he had been forming was incomplete. A thin mist of black shapes, amorphous and sobbing, hung between them. Ian fell through it and brought the hound banner down hard on the other man's skull. It cracked open like an egg.

The trees closest to Ian collapsed, keeling over with startled roots in the air, arms and cruel faces frozen in place. They cracked as they fell. Branches tore open, trunks split, shaggy jaws turning to splinters. Horses screamed at the sudden obstacles, balking and throwing their riders, or stomping in place as they wheeled, trying to find a safe passage.

The rest of the forest was closing in on them. Trees crawled over the shattered husks of their brethren, reaching for Ian, moaning as they came. Ian swung back into his saddle, raised the blood-speckled ruin of his banner, and shouted at the top of his lungs.

"Find the priests! They have to stay close, and their death destroys the enchantment!"

The nearest knights wheeled away, diving into the underbrush, chopping through the tight-knit arms of the forest. A cloud of angry teeth shot up from nearby, then another, and then that section of the forest fell apart. Ian started hacking at the closing circle of living trees, hewing limbs and crushing trunks. Something about the enchantment ate the heart out of the trees, leaving them thin and brittle. He was quickly covered in sawdust. The iron haft of the banner was bent, his fingers ringing from the constant, humming impact of iron into bark, but he was able to keep the gheists at bay.

There was a shout, and Sorcha appeared, surrounded by frightened halberdiers. They flowed through the fallen forest like a river of steel, chopping and cutting, clearing a path for the rest of the army. Sorcha saw Ian and waved. Ian answered with the banner, then turned and plunged deeper into the melee.

Except there was nothing deeper. The trees thinned, the ground pockmarked with gaping holes where the gheists had ripped themselves out of the earth, trailing roots and clods of dirt. Only a few narrow saplings remained, dormant for winter. Beyond the clearing the ground descended before opening onto the field of battle. They had been fighting in the woods for hours, and the sun had climbed well into the sky, giving Ian a good view of the battle on the plain below.

What he saw terrified him. The delay in the forest had kept him from delivering his forces into the celestial flank during the planned collapse of Halverdt's line. It was much too late for that. The celestials had pushed Halverdt's army, and Malcolm Blakley along with it, all the way to their own camp. The burning tree at the camp's center was surrounded by a mad melee. Gheists lurched among the collapsed tents, and the ground around the camp was littered with bodies.

Beyond the camp, another line of troops stood at the edge of the forest, preparing to receive the charge. Ian couldn't make out their banners, but they certainly weren't of Greenhall, or Galleydeep.

"Friend or foe, do you think?" Ian asked his mother as she reached him, pointing in that direction.

"We will find out when we cross blades with them, if it comes to that," Sorcha said. "For now, our concern lies elsewhere."

She drew Ian's attention to the center of the field. While the near flank of Halverdt's army had completely collapsed, there were still elements in the middle that held. The celestials washed around them, breaking against their shields like waves against the cliffs of Stormwatch.

"There, look! Your father!" Clough said. Sure enough, the ducal banner of House Blakley flew at the center of the formation, near that of House Halverdt, the new red and white flaming banner of Sophie's zealots. Ian's heart jumped to see his father was still fighting, that his forces hadn't joined the rout. He was in a dire place, though, his position surrounded and Sophie Halverdt at his side.

Farther away, the gates of the Reaveholt were just opening.

"Bassion is late to the fight as well, I see," Ian said. "So there is still hope."

"No," Sorcha said. "Not for Bassion, at least."

Ian wrinkled his forehead in confusion. His mother's sight was recently beyond mortal ken, another effect of her transformation, but he saw nothing to worry him. Blocks of knights rumbled out of the castle, unfurling the blue and yellow banner of Galleydeep. They started toward the center of Halverdt's remaining line, speeding up until they were in a full charge.

"That will break the celestial hold," Ian said happily. "All we'll need to do is clean up the stragglers, and..." His voice trailed off as the celestial formations split open, letting the knights of Galleydeep pass unhindered. Bassion's forces did not stray from their path, picking up speed. Ian could hear the rumble of their charge from where he stood. "What the hell is she doing?"

"Breaking her enemy," Sorcha said. Her words were just dying in Ian's ears when the charge smashed into the Halverdt shieldwall. The forces buckled and broke, scattering under the weight of Bassion's heavy horse. The celestial guard pounced. A thick melee ensued, engulfing the ordered ranks in a mad battle. The banners of Blakley and Halverdt wavered and then fell.

"We have to save him," Ian said. He grabbed a horse and swung up into the saddle, snatching a spear that was lodged in the ground. "Clough, gather the ranks."

"That is not our mission, Ian. Bassion has betrayed us. We can't just ride down there and—"

"To hell with Bassion, and to hell with you." Sorcha urged her horse down the hill, followed by a handful of eager knights.

"You heard my mother!" Ian surged forward, not looking back to see if the rest of his column was following. The thunder in his ears told him they were.

Ahead of him, Malcolm's forces disappeared under a wave of mist. Ian bent close to his mount, whispering in his ear, urging him on, faster and faster. The mists closed, and Ian lost sight of where his father had fallen.

50

THE CIRCLE OF Bassion's guards drew their blades, stepping forward. Martin grabbed Lucas and pushed the frair behind him, drawing his own sword as he did.

"There's no reason to die, Martin," Lucas whispered. "She's not interested in you."

"I can always find a reason to die," Martin said. "Now be quiet. This isn't going to be easy."

The guards edged forward, five of them, still wary in their approach. That was disappointing. Martin had hoped they would underestimate him, rush in confidently. Now he would have to pick them apart one by one. He stole a glance at Lucas. The frair looked utterly drained. Whatever Bassion had done to the vow knights, it had hit Lucas as well.

"I have always admired your spirit, Roard. Your father made a good ally in the Circle, and your house has a long history of serving Suhdra well," Bassion said. She walked casually to Sir Trueau, pressing a forefinger into the vow knight's forehead and pushing her over. Trueau flopped to the ground, eyes wide in shock, gasping for breath. Bassion laughed, her voice lilting through the air. "Do not make a foolish decision now that could ruin your fine heritage."

"How could you do this? How could you betray your

fellow Suhdrins? The void priests killed half your men!" Martin asked. He danced toward the circling knights, driving them back, but his attention was on Helenne Bassion.

"The void priests killed the troublesome half. The ones too honest to their gods, or too sentimental for their own good," Helenne said. "I had to round a few up myself, and even then, my purge is not quite complete. But I have to thank you. I've been looking for an opportunity to rid my company of these troublesome priests. You and your friend have finally given me the will necessary."

"I don't understand! Sacombre, Folam, the whole lot... they're pagans! They're heretics!"

"Visionaries. Prophets. What does it matter what you call them?" Bassion carefully placed a foot on Trueau's throat and began to crush the life out of the helpless knight. "They are a convenient path. The right blades for necessary murder."

Martin edged toward Trueau, but the guards intercepted him. In his distraction, Martin had let them surround him, and now he was hard pressed to keep his head attached to his shoulders. The five guards attacked in unison, forcing Martin to fall back, bullying his way past one guard while frantically blocking and riposting the other four. He grabbed Lucas and shoved the priest toward the stairs, but a quick glance into the courtyard told Martin there was no escape in that direction. A block of spearmen stood formed up in the mouth of the gates, and several dozen more knights and men-at-arms gathered around. There was frantic discussion going on among the soldiers of Bassion. Apparently their lady's betrayal was not universally known.

"Well done, Martin. But you have struggled enough. Surrender, and I will make you my champion," Helenne purred. "I can offer you more than skill with a blade. More than glory and wealth. I can offer you power. Such power as you've never seen, and never imagined."

"What will you do when Heartsbridge comes for you, Helenne? Galleydeep lies at the foot of its power. They will grind your walls to dust, and turn your halls into catacombs!"

"Why don't you ask Sir Trueau what she thinks I'll do?" Helenne answered. She smiled down at the vow knight, whose face was turning blue. Trueau pawed at the ground, her movements growing weak. Martin's heart raged, but he couldn't get past the guards. Helenne looked up at him. "The church is easy enough to deal with, if you hold the right knife to the right back. Trust me. The pagans don't understand half of what they've forgotten of the old gods. They don't even know their own history!"

Beneath them, the gate boomed open. A thrill of victory went through Helenne's face.

"The charge has begun, Martin. Even now Halverdt runs back to her camp, her precious tree, and her false god," Helenne spat. "And now you must choose, Roard. You will be amazed at the power of the void, Martin. Power that could be yours, if you are willing to swear the vow to my throne."

"I want nothing to do with your demons, witch," Martin spat. "My house has fought for the church, and we will stand by it still."

"The power of the gheists is interesting, yes, but I am offering you so much more than that. Aren't you tired of the Circle of Lords? The fracture between Suhdra and Tener? This land should be united, don't you think?"

"It is united! By the church!"

"Does this look like unity to you? Gabriel Halverdt did

little good with his life, but he was right in one thing: the pagan north cannot be trusted. It must be held by the head, like a snake, lest it bite. It's a pity Suhdra has never had the will to crush that snake." Helenne offered her hand to Martin. "I will unite Suhdra, and Tener, and all Tenumbra. This island will bow before its queen."

"Do you really think the void priests will hand the island to you? The tribes? You have no idea what you're talking about."

"When this is over, I don't think they'll have a choice." Helenne's face fell a little, disappointment creasing both the beautiful half of her face and the ruined. "A pity. You would have made a fine champion." She motioned to her guards. "Be done with—"

Helenne threw her head back and screamed in pain. Trueau, still at her feet, had driven her mercy knife into Helenne's calf. Burning veins of fire spread from the wound, wrapping around the duchess' leg. Helenne stumbled back.

"You have no power here!" she howled. "Die, and your damned goddess with you!"

"Strife's might never truly sets," Martin said. The guards were distracted by their lady's distress. Martin rushed forward, helping Trueau to her feet. She was struggling to breathe, but the fury in her eyes would keep her moving, Martin was sure. He glanced over at the other vow knight, the man who even now cowered beside Helenne. "Get to your feet, man! Your god needs you!"

Helenne turned toward them, then grabbed the vow knight by the neck and pulled him close. He hung from her grip like a rag.

"This one serves me now," Helenne said. She pulled Trueau's knife from her leg and drew it across the vow knight's neck. Hot blood spluttered down his chest, running down Helenne's arm and soaking into the fine silk of her dress. "As will all Tenumbra!"

The vow knight fell to his hands and knees, staring down at the growing pool of blood beneath him. He sputtered, trying to breathe through the cascade. As he died, he reached toward Martin, crying.

"To hell with this," Martin said. He shoved Trueau into Lucas's arms, then pushed both priests down the stairs. "You will get the judgment you deserve, Bassion, even if I have to deliver it myself!"

"But not today, apparently," Bassion crooned. "Run, little knight. Run into the arms of your falling gods!"

Martin ran down the stairs after the priests. Helenne's laughter followed him.

Fights had broken out across the courtyard below, Bassion killing Bassion, knight slaughtering peasant, farmers overwhelming men-at-arms with clubs and sheer numbers. The cobbles were slick with blood. Martin ran as far as the upper chamber of the gatehouse, kicking in the door and rushing inside.

It was already a bloodbath. Soldiers of Bassion lay dead around the room. One was dragging himself away from the door, leaving a long smear of red blood on the floor. On the other side of the room, a knight stood, staring out of the archer's eye at the battle below. At the sound of the door crashing open, she whirled around. It was Sir Travailler, commander of Bassion's vast navy. Her eyes were pinpricks of anger.

"Roard! Are you part of this damned betrayal?" she barked.

"Only on the 'getting betrayed' end of things," he said.

"Do you follow Bassion's new heresy?"

"No. I guess I'm going to need to find a new lord to swear my vows to," she said. As Lucas and the badly injured Sir Trueau tumbled after Martin into the room, Travailler marched across the room and slammed the door behind them. "Find something to shove against this, will you?"

They dragged a bunk from the guardhouse in front of the door. No sooner had they secured it than someone outside started hammering against the door. Travailler returned to the narrow window. "What the hell is going on out there?" she muttered.

"Lady Bassion has thrown her lot in with the celestials. A long time ago, it seems." Lucas held up a hand to stop Travailler's protest. "I know, they killed her own people. All part of her plan, apparently. But she has shown her hand."

"There goes Halverdt's last stand, and Blakley with it," Travailler said. "It's just a matter of mopping them up now."

Martin ran to the windows and stared as Blakley's banner collapsed into the whirling melee. He couldn't believe his eyes. He turned and ran to the chains that held the portcullis in place. He took the hammer that lay there for this purpose, gripped it in both hands and knocked the block clear of the windlass. The chain screamed past, links chattering as they scraped over the stone. The portcullis fell, trapping the rest of Bassion's forces inside the castle.

"That's the best we can do," he said. "Now we just have to pray that Malcolm can hold out until reinforcements arrive."

"Pray to who?" Trueau muttered. "Who is left that will answer our prayers?"

No one responded. The hammering on the door filled their heads.

51

THE LIGHT WAS dying. As the corrupted gods of the north rumbled toward Malcolm's line, a wave of mist billowed over them, blotting out the sun. The air, temporarily warmed by the army of the light, grew chill. Malcolm's breath hung in front of his face in icy clouds. His heart hammered in his chest, but he felt no fear. They were coming. He was ready.

The gheists that lumbered toward him were twisted and broken. Black vines crawled across their bodies, digging into divine flesh, leaving puckered scars behind. Their skin was pale and spotted with disease. Whatever deities they had once been to the tribes, these gods no longer answered to their ancient rites. They were bent only to destruction.

"Sophie Halverdt is not breaking, my lord!" Doone shouted over the thunderous charge. "She is rallying her forces on the right!"

Malcolm looked in that direction. Though the left of Halverdt's force was completely routed (and gods pray Castian Jaerdin was safe in that tumult), the right held steady. Sophie could be seen towering over the ranks, standing on the broken remnant of that damnable cart, the one driven by the half-child with white hair. She was waving her sword and shouting, drawing courage from her troops and throwing them back into the fight.

"We cannot fall back until we know her madness is ended," Malcolm said. "Form the lines! Lock shields! We stand with Halverdt!"

His troops gave a hearty cry and surged. Steel shields clattered together, and spears, broken, splintered, stolen, and whole, bristled along the line. They were down to only a few horses, not enough to form up a proper charge, but not enough to run, either. Malcolm straightened out the line, barking orders, correcting formations, letting the men and women under his banner know that he was there. That he stood with them.

He spared a moment to look at the rout on the left. It was absolute. Panicked horses were dragging their riders through the abandoned camp, the first waves of foot soldiers just reaching the picket line. Maybe they would rally around their damned black tree. Maybe not. Either way, they were out of this fight.

The walls of the Reaveholt stood silent to his right. Bassion would keep her promise. She had to. Hopefully before his own lines broke.

"Steady now!" Malcolm shouted. The gheists were nearly to them. Celestial handlers trailed just behind, surrounded by halberdiers in black and gray. The broader celestial line followed at a distance, marching in step across the snow-churned field the gheists had just covered. First the gods, then the heretics. Malcolm picked his spot on the line, near the center, not far from the banners. Best to be seen. He raised the black blade of his feyiron sword and shouted. "The hound! The hallow!"

"The hallow!" some answered back, and then the gods were on them.

Directly in front of Malcolm, a gheist the size of a small house reared up on its stubby legs, roaring as it smashed down with fists as big as barrels. A dozen spears punched into its leathery chest, piercing skin and drawing divine blood, shafts bowing and splintering as it pushed forward. It screamed in pain and swept an arm across the forest of spears, snapping them in half. Still bristling with the broken hafts, it picked up a soldier and crushed her head in its hand. Her twitching legs kicked against its face as she died.

Malcolm leapt forward, his mount jumping the wavered shieldwall to land at the feet of the ravaging gheist. It chest was shot through with dark veins just beneath the skin, pulsing with purple light. Malcolm's horse reared back and hammered steel-shod hooves into the beast's throat. Malcolm slashed at the gheist's arm. It dropped the corpse of the dead soldier and howled in pain.

Malcolm wheeled and struck, a rapid series of blows that cut across the gheist's arm, shoulder, chest, and neck. Each strike severed flesh, the feyiron cutting easily through its thick skin. Whenever he struck one of the black vines that curled across the creature's body, the feyiron would hum, as though it had struck stone. The gheist stumbled back.

Behind him, the Blakley troops roared in victory, surging into the gap left in their lines and bolstering the shieldwall. With the line reinforced, Malcolm spun around and urged his horse over the shields of his compatriots.

The gheist rallied. The black vines stretched across its body, filling in the wounds and burrowing into the flesh. The veins of purple light under its skin grew darker, its skin paler.

It roared and lashed out at Malcolm. Just as he was about to jump back to safety, the gheist backhanded his mount, crushing its legs and chest. Malcolm tumbled to the ground, briefly hidden by the screaming horse, hooves crashing into the ground next to him, kicking up frozen clods of dirt. Malcolm rolled, briefly covering his face, and the horse spilled away, crashing down the line to topple the next gheist. Both went down in a heap. Malcolm struggled to his feet.

The gheist towered over him, howling in pain, shaking enormous fists in the air. It brought them down, cratering the ground in front of Malcolm, then drew back to strike.

Behind him, the shieldwall broke forward, washing over Malcolm in a tide of screaming soldiers. They slammed into the gheist, hacking into its thick hide with axes and swords, using shields to hammer at joints. The gheist stepped back, scattering the troops as its talon-tipped foot rose into the air, stumbling as it tried to retreat. It slid on blood-churned mud, fell to one knee, then crashed its arm into the horde of armored gnats that swarmed over it. The blow went wide and it lost its balance. As it pitched forward, the soldiers of House Blakley streamed over it, covering it in a blanket of chain mail and hacking steel.

The soldiers to the right and left of Malcolm's position weren't so fortunate, however. The gheists there punched through the shieldwall, crushing skulls and shattering steel as they went. The ravaging gheists wrapped around Malcolm's small force. The shieldwall closed around him, circling into a ring as the first lines of celestial guards reached them.

"Closer, closer, don't let them through," Malcolm shouted, dragging soldiers back into line. "Don't lose heart, soldiers of the hound! We will answer steel with steel, and blood for blood! We have nothing to fear, not even death! Stand tall and be counted in the ranks of the brave!"

A rain of arrows clattered off their shields, downing a precious few soldiers, but the ranks closed and the wounded were dragged to the center. The celestial guard approached cautiously, lapping around the circle of Tenerran steel, closing off their retreat. Sir Doone stumbled out of the chaos. Her left arm hung limp, but her face was twisted in determination.

"Halverdt is encircled, but her banner still flies, my lord!"

"As does ours! The day is not lost, Doone, not while I still breathe! We must fight to her side. Shieldwall, at the half-step, advance toward Greenhall's banner!"

Malcolm's troops began a slow, shuffling march, the two lines of shields facing back and forward holding their position while soldiers in the center dragged the injured along. The right flank, closest to Halverdt, advanced in her direction, filling the gap left behind with troops from the middle of the formation. The left flank fell back, cycling their numbers into the center to help with the injured, then taking their place in the gaps left by the right flank. Slowly the formation crawled toward Halverdt like a giant snail, leaving a trail of their dead, or those too badly hurt to be moved. Malcolm stood at the center, coordinating the whole movement.

As they approached the Halverdt position, Sophie saw what they were doing and started giving orders. The near flank of her line burst open, covering the distance between the two in a series of rapid advances. The two formations merged, like drops of water running together. Malcolm pushed through the chaos to Sophie's side.

"Lady Halverdt! You weathered the storm, I see."

"Houndhallow. Well done taking down that gheist. We'll make a vow knight of you yet." Sophie's eyes burned with infernal light, and her voice echoed in Malcolm's bones, but she was smiling, mad and free. Her banner flickered with half-seen flames, as though a dream of it burned overhead, almost reaching the mortal realm of the waking. "The true faith is finally blossoming," she shouted, waving her sword. "Come, you heretics of shadow, come and be burned by the light!"

A roar went up from the tight knot of soldiers, but it was drowned out by an answering shout from the celestial lines. Malcolm scrambled onto Halverdt's broken wagon to see what was happening. A smile crossed his face.

"Bassion answers our call!" he shouted. Glancing around, he saw that Sophie's guards were looking elsewhere. Bassion would clear the celestial line. Halverdt's madness no longer had to be tolerated. It was time to strike. He measured her neck for the strike, drawing his sword back. "Justice can now be done."

"Something's wrong," Doone snapped. From the ground below, she grabbed Malcolm's leg. "Hold your blade!"

Her shout drew Sophie's attention. The lady of Greenhall glanced at Doone in confusion, then up at Malcolm. Her eyes lingered on Malcolm's sword, drawn back to strike. She was the only possible target. "What are you doing, Houndhallow?"

His answer never came. The thunder of steel-shod hooves filled the air, and then the shieldwall shattered, blowing apart like autumn leaves to the first wind of winter. They both spun around to watch as a wedge of knights tore through their lines. Malcolm's jaw dropped.

Their attackers wore the yellow and blue of House Bassion. As he watched, they broke Halverdt's shieldwall, and then his. The wagon he was on shattered into pieces, driven apart by the rout. He slid to the ground, landing hard on his shoulder. Doone's voice filled his ears, but all he could see was a blur of steel and mud as she dragged him into the lee of the wagon's wreckage. Bassion's knights lapped around him, driving the remnants of his force into the ground.

The black-and-white banner of House Blakley fluttered overhead, catching in the wind created by the charging knights. It twisted and then fell, to be trampled underfoot by the fleeing mobs that had moments before been ordered troops.

They were broken and betrayed. The celestials had won the day.

Not exactly to plan. He had no hope of breaking them, even with Ian's help. Jaerdin was gone, and Bassion turned. The balance had been so narrow, and now it was upended. He had failed.

"I will do it myself, then," Malcolm muttered. He stood from behind the broken wagon and faced the celestial charge. "They will know me. They will remember."

52

THE CELESTIAL FORCES were an unending tide against the steel of Gwen's shieldwall. They wrapped around the burning tree and came at her position in wave after wave of black-clad axemen. Routed soldiers of Halverdt mingled in, as desperate to reach the safety of the woods as the celestials were to run them down. Gwen stood behind the line of Deidra's spearmen, watching the slaughter.

"What do we do with Halverdt's troops?" the big ranger asked. Her rangers were not made for this sort of fight, and the press was wearing on them. "I thought we were here to fight the void priests."

"Cut them down. The god Halverdt serves should have been destroyed ages ago. We can't let its influence spread."

"I am happy to kill Halverdt's zealots, but... Malcolm Blakley is allied with her. If soldiers of the hound approach?"

"Save the ones you can. Any who will join with our side must be spared," Frair Gilliam said sharply. He shot Gwen a hard look. "I am learning to forgive what I can."

Gwen turned away, angry and abashed. She nodded to Deidra. "Do as the frair says. We need all the spears we can muster."

"I don't understand why Bassion has betrayed

Houndhallow," Deidra mumbled. "As it is—"

"As it is, we have no choice. This is what the gods ask of us," Gwen said. She cast a glance in Gilliam's direction. "All the gods."

"And what of these?" Deidra asked. "Are we to cut them down as well?"

A thin column of mounted knights approached the line. It wove back and forth, charging and then wheeling, each arc bringing them closer to Gwen's position. They wore the colors of Redgarden, and fought with a furious desperation. A cloud of celestial knights pursued them, trying to cut them off.

"Redgarden stood with my family at the Fen Gate," Gwen said. "Give me a horse and your mounted reserve. They will never make it to safety on their own."

"We can't risk our strength—" Kesthe started, but Gwen jumped on an unsecured mount and rallied the anxious column of pagan riders.

"Riders of the tribes, loyal rangers of the gods! Our allies require our steel! Fight at my side, and for the safety of all Tenumbra!" Gwen forced her mount past the spear line and into the celestial ranks. Her horse trampled the nearest foes, dancing in a narrow circle, driving steel-shod hooves into the enemy line. The shieldwall split open to release the pent-up rage of the reserve riders. They poured through.

Gwen turned and led them toward Jaerdin's weaving retreat. The celestial host was shocked by this sudden assault, and fell away from Gwen's advance. Halfway across the expanse, Jaerdin noticed their approach, and turned his column in their direction. The pursuing celestials doubled their pace. The trailing elements of Jaerdin's column were swallowed by their closing flanks.

They came together in a thunderous crash. Gwen's forces passed through Jaerdin's, his ranks opening to let them pass through unopposed. The spirit-mad riders of the tribes, as much shaman as knight, followed Gwen to slam into the celestial knights. Free from their pursuit, Jaerdin wheeled his knights around and charged into the melee, fighting by Gwen's side. The celestials broke quickly, their fragile will smashed by the ferocity of Gwen's attack. She turned to the duke of Redgarden.

"Lord Jaerdin. It's good to fight at your side again," she said.

"No time for pleasantries, child. Do you have support? More troops? Pagan rangers?"

"These several hundred spearmen are all I hold, with half that many rangers again. We should be able to hold this position against—"

"We must advance, while the celestials are still surprised. Malcolm Blakley's position is overwhelmed. If he falls, this entire battle will be lost." He turned his mount and started back into the fray. "I will explain on the way."

"But if we advance, we will be crushed in the rout!"

"The gods will guide us. They must. There is too much at risk. Follow, for the sake of all Tenumbra!"

Jaerdin charged forward, followed quickly by his own men. Gwen paused for a brief second, then turned and signaled the advance to Deidra. The ranger gave her a confused look, but then Gwen charged forward, the horns sounded, and the ranks surged in her wake.

The hammering on the guardroom door settled into a steady drumbeat. Sir Travailler stood nervously by the wall, waiting for Bassion's soldiers to break through the barrier and kill them all. The vow knight, Sir Trueau, lay on the floor, while Martin attended to her.

"They must have gotten to her before Adair's heresy was revealed. Meaning she's been waiting all this time to strike, but why? What good does Bassion get from revealing herself now, just as Halverdt's army is routing her new allies?"

"What the hell are you going on about?" Travailler snapped. "They're trying to kill us, you know!"

"Oh, I would be disappointed if they weren't. Not to mention a great deal more confused than I already am. Are you sure Lady Bassion has not taken on any new advisors in the last year? Someone from the church, or perhaps a scholar from Tener?"

"She would never tolerate a pagan in her court," Travailler said. "What does this have to do with anything? Why aren't you using the naether to get us out of here? Cut a hole in the wall, or something?"

"A better question is why Bassion is not using her newfound powers to destroy us. She dealt with those vow knights easily enough, and believe me, a knight of the winter vow is no easy opponent. And yet she struck three down without a thought. So why are we still here?"

"Whatever she did, it's left no wounds," Martin said. He looked up from the limp form of Sir Trueau. "I can find nothing wrong with her."

"Strife is... she is gone from me," Trueau gasped. "I cannot feel her light at all."

"Elsa spoke of this as well. She was a victim of the void priests. So has Lady Bassion sworn to the tribe of the void? Hardly seems likely for a duchess of Suhdra to take up the old religion with such enthusiasm." Lucas sighed. "Though Sacombre did the same. I shouldn't be surprised that Bassion has fallen to the same heresy."

The door splintered, and an axe-head shone through. It creaked back and forth, then withdrew. The next blow opened a wide hole in the door. Travailler dashed forward and thrust her sword through the gap, dancing back with blood on her blade, leaving screams behind.

"I do not want to die listening to you philosophize about heretics and history!" she snapped. "Stormwatch, help me secure this door! We're going to have to go out the way we came in!"

"We can't let them take this room. If the portcullis opens, Halverdt's position will be lost." Martin answered.

"The sooner the better. Lady Halverdt is a madwoman. We need to start thinking about our own lives!" A commotion outside the door interrupted her. Steel rang against steel, and then the door burst open like shattered glass. Travailler screamed and rushed forward. Her swing met steel, and she was brushed aside.

Elsa LaFey strode into the room. Her eyes went straight to Sir Travailler, giving Martin and Lucas only a glance. When she was sure Travailler wasn't going to attack her again, she walked to the center of the room and pulled Martin to his feet.

"I'm getting tired of saving the two of you. Is she going to live?"

"Trueau?" Martin stuttered, looking from Elsa's glowing form to the limp vow knight on the floor. "I think so, but there's something wrong with her."

"There's something wrong with all of us. Help her up,

someone. We will need every vow knight we can muster. Even the maimed souls."

Lucas hoisted Trueau up, and after a moment Travailler lent him a hand.

"Frair Lucas," Elsa said, "we are needed outside. Bassion's forces are tearing each other apart, and the lady of the castle has made herself scarce. We need to find her and bring her to Cinder's justice."

"How did you get in here?" Sir Travailler asked. "The portcullis is closed, and there are hundreds of Bassion's knights in the courtyard."

"I killed a lot of people," Elsa answered as she turned toward the door. "Stop wasting time in wonder. We have a castle to save."

53

THE BATTLEFIELD WAS chaos. Soldiers swarmed around Malcolm, fighting for their lives, stumbling past in a daze or locked in battle. Shattered spears became bludgeons, swords gave way to knives, shields were discarded for chokeholds. The ground under Malcolm's feet was slick with blood and melted snow. He fought his way forward, pummeling step by step toward the place he had last seen Sophie Halverdt.

Overhead, the light was dying. Hours had passed and Malcolm hadn't noticed. His entire life was consumed with taking one bloody footstep after another, shrugging aside attackers, killing any who raised their sword in his direction, walking over the dead and dying.

He gathered followers. Doone was with him, had always been with him, even though the memory of Bassion's charge was nearly forgotten in the hours-long fight. The melee pressed all around them. Survivors joined in his wake, wearing the colors of Houndhallow or Greenhall, some from distant houses whose place in this fight was forgotten and their loyalty uncertain. Malcolm fought his way forward, and true soldiers knew to follow that kind of drive.

Slowly, the number of celestials Malcolm had to batter his way through decreased. He met more and more soldiers of Halverdt, wild-eyed and fanatical, their faces smeared with blood and mud. They held no lines, carried no shields, swung madly at their enemies with total disregard for their safety. Tears streamed down their faces, shot through with sparks and leaving trails of ash. Most let Malcolm pass. A few opposed him, so consumed with the fury of their burning god that they recognized neither friend nor foe. Malcolm ended their struggles, gave them peace. It didn't matter to him anymore. Nothing would stop him. No one would oppose him.

Sophie Halverdt stood on a pile of bodies. She surveyed the battle with furious eyes, sword in hand, shouting encouragement to the churning mob of her faithful who fought and died at her feet. The bloodshed was catastrophic. Her followers gave heed to neither safety nor form, hacking wildly at the celestial guard who kept coming at them, wave after wave of black-clad knights and soldiers and clerics, each one fighting and dying under Sophie's flame-swept gaze.

As Malcolm approached, the ring of zealots surged toward him. He knocked down the first, a child wielding a dagger in both hands, then blocked an attack from the second. The man's sword clattered off Malcolm's shoulder, but the zealot put too much energy into the attack and pitched forward. Malcolm slammed his knee into the struggling man's face, then shoved him to the ground and stepped over. Zealots to his left and right jumped at him, forcing Malcolm to fend off a series of frenzied blows that left his arms numb and his head ringing.

"Hold! Let him pass!" Sophie shouted from on high. The zealots backed away, falling onto the swords of the celestial guard that were still pressing down on Malcolm. He slipped through their cordon, leaving his motley guard to deal with both the celestials and any errant attacks from the zealots.

He clambered up the pile of bodies. Sophie watched him with unfettered glee.

"Have you ever seen such glory, Houndhallow? The heretics fall before us, and the true light of Strife consumes them, body and soul!"

"Glory, yes, but madness more," Malcolm answered. Reaching the top of the pile, he straightened and stared Sophie hard in the eyes. "What has become of you, Greenhall? What have you done?"

"What have I done? Only what the goddess does through me! I am bringing the light of Strife to this desolate plain. The very fire of the one true flame will spread out from this place, until it fills the world with its glory!" She spread her arms, the sword dangling loosely in her palm. "We are witnessing the birth of a new world, Houndhallow."

"Flames consume, but only to destroy, and they leave only ash behind. Your people are being slaughtered, Greenhall! You have to pull them back!"

"It is the goddess that drives them forward. Who am I to countermand her direction?"

"You are their lord, their commander, and the warden of their souls!" Malcolm barked. "You have lost sight of your throne, just like your father."

"My father was murdered by these people. What cost is too great, to avenge his death?"

"This cost," Malcolm said, throwing his arm wide. "These dead! You are not seeking victory, or vengeance, or even justice. You seek only destruction!"

"The road to glory is lined with the grateful dead. I don't ask anything of them that they're not willing to give," Sophie answered. She straightened up, holding her sword comfortably at her waist, tip down. "Am I to understand that you have lost faith in this crusade, Houndhallow?"

"Faith? Why do we speak of faith, when our armies are broken, and your madness still runs through their veins?" He pointed to the piles of dead beneath them. "More of these belong to your banner than that of our enemies, Greenhall."

"My madness, as you call it, is a gift from the goddess. And it is the only thing that is keeping these soldiers from fleeing. I should have known you would turn as soon as things got difficult, Houndhallow. You let my father down, you let Tener down, and now you are going to let your followers down." Sophie laid her hand flat against her sword, drawing the blade across her palm like a strop. Where steel touched flesh, the metal changed. It crackled with broken fire, scars opening in the weapon, pulsing with infernal light. "You will be my last warning to the north, Malcolm Blakley. The light of Strife is coming for the Tenerran heretics. Submit, and prosper. Defy me—" she pointed the sword at Malcolm, dropping into a formal dueling stance "—and you defy the goddess herself!"

"You're starting to think a bit much of yourself." Malcolm swung his blade, cutting through the air with the black feyiron. Steel clashed, and sparks flew. Sophie fell back, darting out with her blade, touching Malcolm at shoulder, biceps, belly with a series of quick jabs. Everywhere her sword touched, his armor yielded, bubbling with heat. Malcolm felt the tip of her sword brush his flesh. Pain seared his skin.

"Your time is past, Reaverbane." She slithered forward, unleashing a flurry of jabs that Malcolm batted away, his sword ringing with the impact. He stumbled on a corpse and nearly fell. Sophie laughed as she danced away. "Reaverbane. Such a joke. Will they still be calling you that when you're a dotard, rotting away in your bed, muttering children's rhymes to yourself? If you even live that long. If I let you live that long!"

"My life is not in your hands, child," Malcolm said. He steeled himself for the onslaught. When it did not come immediately, he leapt forward, swinging his blade in a wide, sweeping arc. Sophie's laughter chimed through the air as she sidestepped, riposting his backswing, jabbing his toe as he flowed into the next attack. He limped back.

"That remains to be seen," Sophie said. "But I feel good about my chances. I always wondered about you, you know. Were you as great as people said? I only ever knew you as an old man, bristling at my father's every word, playing the church's mule and the Circle's tame barbarian. Don't you get tired of that?"

"More than you will ever know," Malcolm said. He feinted, and Sophie's counter swept through empty air. As she recovered, he stepped forward and punched her in the throat. "Suhdrins always talk too much."

Sophie rolled away from Malcolm, grabbing her throat. Malcolm followed, swinging down with his sword, barely missing as she slipped down the pile of bodies. His next swing took her in her outstretched arm, cracking steel and bone. She finally retrieved her sword and stood, left arm dangling.

"And Tenerrans never learn to smile," she croaked. "But you will. You will!"

Sophie's face was breaking. The raw wound of her throat, skin torn where Malcolm's gauntlet had crushed her windpipe, was peeling open. Cracks formed in her face, and the jigsaw pieces of her face slowly fell out of place. Like a stained-glass window whose panes are out of alignment, Sophie's face took on a nightmare cast. Malcolm saw that she was weeping flower petals, and the glassy irises of her eyes were changing into sunflowers. Her mouth gaped open, and another mouth appeared behind the slack skin of her lips. Narrow jaws, slick bone, teeth as thin and jagged as broken glass, pushed out of her mouth like a child being born.

"An unlovely smile, if ever I saw one," Malcolm muttered.

The gheist wearing Sophie Halverdt struck, swinging her sword with a disjointed arm, the blow as quick and fluid as rainfall. Malcolm barely caught the point of her blade on the forte of his sword, turning it aside. She battered him with the shattered bone-whip of her maimed arm, lurching forward to snap at his neck with nightmare jaws, clawing at his eyes, his throat. Malcolm shoved her back, but she landed bonelessly, rolled as awkwardly as a corpse cut from the noose, and stood back up. Her smile was growing, until it filled the broken ruin of her face.

"They will not remember you when I am done, Houndhallow. I will consume even the memory of you, until there is nothing left but hollow regret and flame!"

Sophie leapt forward, rag-doll arms flailing, jaws cracking together, the sword just a forgotten tool at the end of a broken arm. Malcolm met the charge with his blade, feyiron sizzling through flesh, tearing Sophie's armor and driving her back. The bodies shifted beneath him, and he stumbled, the only thing saving him from her wild attack. Wounds tore open across her skin, but each one glimmered with inner fire. Sparks lined the edges of her eyes. Each time Malcolm cut her, a jet of flame flashed out, and soon her entire body was smoldering. Her sword clattered to the ground, her fingers melted into its steel, flesh and bone tearing loose from her hand. She was burning alive, burning dead, burning out of this mortal world.

"The armies of Suhdra and Tener will bow before me! The church will fall, and the tribes, and all the faithful of the gods old and new. I will carve a kingdom from their flesh, sanctified in flame, burned into the stone of the earth." Sophie started coming apart. Spears of flame shot out of her body, and her voice rang like a dropped bell. Mad flares of burning metal dripped from what remained of her armor. Of her flesh, there was nothing but cracked scar and seared bone.

She charged at Malcolm, howling like a banshee. Malcolm set his feet and slammed down with the pommel of his blade, crushing the howling projectile of her skull. Though it seared his skin, he planted the tip of his sword in the gaping jaws of her throat and shoved, driving the blade down her spine. Sophie came apart around the feyiron sword, splintering like a tree struck by lightning. There was a moment of unimaginable light and heat and flame, then her dry husk rattled against his chest and came apart.

Sophie's remnants took halting steps in a dozen different directions, leg and hips this way, other leg that way, an arm spinning through the air spurting flames like a firework, ribs peeling back and shuffling to the ground. Finally the last wisp of her snuffed out, consumed by its own flame, leaving nothing but drifting ash and a memory of cinders.

Malcolm stood in the center of a blackened circle of ash, eyes wide, face smeared with soot and oily blood. Tiny flames crawled across his cloak, digging into the iron gray of his hair, burrowing through his chain mail like maggots. He let out a ragged breath and collapsed to his knees.

"Sometimes, all you have to do is endure," he whispered. "Endure, and pray it will be enough."

This time, it was.

54

IAN COULD SEE his father was fighting for his life. The glowing figure that had been Sophie Halverdt battered against him. There was a flash, and the world changed. From his place on the battlefield, Ian felt rather than saw the burning tree behind him explode. A wave of flame rolled through the air, the shockwave jostling his bones and turning his teeth into cymbals. He could see nothing in the column of smoke at the center of the celestial army.

"Father!" he screamed, and spurred his horse forward. Tears stung his eyes, but he kept his focus on the smoke and the flame. The horse maneuvered its way through the crashing bodies and blistering swords that surrounded him. Ian choked back tears and screamed again. "Forward! Forward! Into the fray!"

His men didn't need any urging. The celestial army was descending on them. Ian's initial charge had shocked the enemy, scattering them as they pursued the fleeing left flank of Halverdt's army. Now they were re-forming, ranking up and closing on the irritating splinter of Ian's column of knights in the side of their force. If Ian slowed, they would reach him. As long as he kept bounding forward, he would stay ahead of their blades.

Suddenly a flame shot out of the column of smoke that Ian had been riding toward. It caressed the edges of smoke before rolling outward in a wave of barely-seen flame. It washed over the ranks of Halverdt's army. There was a moment of frenzied violence, driving the celestial ranks back. And then… silence.

Ian rode faster and faster, until the wind whipping past his head was roaring. The dark sky stretched out overhead. They burst through the last line of celestial forces and stumbled into the disorganized, milling mass of Halverdt's center, the only part of her army that was still standing. There was a ragged storm of combat, raw and vicious, but beyond that Halverdt's troops stood around dumbfounded. They looked like children waking up from a dream, half-nightmare, half-ecstasy, their weapons and jaws loose. The rest of Ian's column drew up around him, frantic horses wheeling, knights sawing on the reins, trying to slow them down. Sir Clough looked around and laughed.

"This is the army of Strife's fire? They look more like drunkards!"

"Something has changed. A moment ago these men were killing, maiming…" Sorcha brought her horse to a stop, then slid from the saddle. She knelt and touched the ground. "The flame is guttering. Its heart has gone out."

"Something to do with the tree?" Ian asked. Back in that direction, he could make out a fight in the Suhdrin camp, and a column of knights wending their way forward, but the tree itself was as dark as a hole in the world. "Another trick of the void priests?"

"No. Something closer." Sorcha put a hand to her heart. "Your father needs you, Ian. Hurry."

Ian guided his horse through the dumbstruck masses. He reached a small hill of dead bodies, surrounded by stunned soldiers. There was a small contingent of knights of Houndhallow at the base. He caught Sir Doone's eye and saluted, but she turned away. Ian dropped from his horse and ran, skidding, up the hill. His father was waiting.

Malcolm Blakley was slumped on his knees, both arms thrown over the crossguard of his sword. The tip of the feyiron blade was buried in the bodies of the dead. Malcolm's head lolled forward. His chest heaved, and each deep breath rattled loudly in his chest. Ian slid to a halt beside his father.

"Father, are you all right? What's wrong?"

"I have endured," Malcolm said. His voice was thin and reedy. "I have lasted… as long… as I can." He looked up, and Ian's heart flipped in his chest. Malcolm's face was cracked and raw, his lips lined with fissures, his eyes as red as blood. "Another must carry it from here."

"Don't be foolish," Ian said. He threw Malcolm's arm over his shoulder, wincing as the hot metal of his armor burned his neck. "We'll get you out of here. Back to Houndhallow. Back home, and then—"

"And then nothing. And then everything." Malcolm collapsed against him, bowling them both over.

Ian knelt beside him, listening to the rasping draw of his breath.

"Where is my wife?"

"Here, here. I am here." Sorcha glided up the hill, her feet barely touching the ground. She took Malcolm's hand. "You know what comes next?"

"We say things we always meant to say, and then goodbye?"

"Such a stubborn man," Sorcha said, shaking her head. "You were always so stubborn. Be still."

She placed a hand across his face, and closed his eyes. He relaxed back against the bodies of the dead, his own hand coming to rest on a bloodied skull.

"This is no place to die," he muttered.

"Then you should not have come here," Sorcha answered.

Ian grabbed her shoulder. "Mother, you can't... what are you doing?"

"Saving him from himself. It'll be all right, Ian. Everything will be fine. Go win your war."

"But—"

"I said go," she snapped. "Leave me with my husband."

Ian slowly backed away. When he turned, Sir Doone was standing at the bottom of the hill with his horse.

"Halverdt's legions are regaining their heads, and the celestials are gathering their courage. Something must be done."

"My father, he's... he's not..."

"Your father is not yet dead, and you are not released from the responsibility of being his son," Doone said sternly. "If he cannot lead us, you must."

Ian stumbled down the hill in a state of shock, then threw his foot into his stirrup and mounted. There was a gentle rustle through the silent ranks that surrounded him. He glanced over at where his father lay, but Malcolm's face was obscured by Sorcha's body. Sweet light played out from Sorcha's hands, and water ran from her fingers in cold streams. Ian croaked out a laugh.

"He's not going to like that," he muttered. Cold steel brushed his fingers. He looked down to see Malcolm's feyiron sword being pushed into his hands. Doone was watching him very closely.

"They have lost their goddess, and the madness that she brought. But this fight is not yet over. Do something."

"What? I don't know what," Ian said.

"Anything." Rolling thunder boomed over them, the sound of spear striking shield. The celestials were on the march once again. "Anything is better than nothing. Better than slaughter."

Ian looked around at the mob of expectant faces watching him. What would his father do? What would he say? He had no idea.

The truth. The one that he knew, at least.

"Sophie Halverdt is dead, and her madness with her!" he shouted. "You can die at her side, or live at mine!"

"Hardly… inspiring," Doone muttered. "Say something about her heresy. Something about the demon that possessed her!"

"I have had enough of heresies," Ian answered. He stood in his stirrups and raised his voice, until it boomed across the rolling plains of blood. "This war started with a lie, but it will end with a truth! The gods do not stand with us, or against us, or with our enemies! These divisions have separated us for too long, pagan and celestial, heretic and saint, god and gheist! They must end, and the wars they cause with them. Suhdra and Tener only fall because we stand as Suhdrin, and Tenerran, rather than as brothers and sisters of this land! Look, here rides Castian Jaerdin. He stood with my father from the beginning, and now he rides beside Gwen Adair, the arch-heretic." Ian pointed to where Jaerdin and Gwen now approached, looking fretfully at the crowds surrounding Ian.

"And I will fight at their side against those who would divide us. This is not a battle for the gods, but for mortal flesh and blood. This is not a battle between church and pagan, but between madness and peace. Between those who destroy, and those who build.

"I am here to build, to create a new land, to build bonds of peace between Suhdra and Tener. There is nothing I have not lost, but there is nothing I cannot gain." The celestial army loomed closer, their ranks shot through with mist and the hulking bodies of the gheists at their service. "There is this one task remaining. We must come together and kill every last one of these bastards!"

"Why should we die for you, Ian Blakley?" someone in the crowd shouted. "Why should any of us fight at your side, when even your father drove you from his home, and from his banner?"

"You should not die for me, or Malcolm Blakley, or Sophie Halverdt, or any other mortal name. You should live. But if you must die, you should die for those you love, and those who deserve your love." He glanced back at where his mother knelt. His father still wasn't moving. "Even if neither of you know it. Before it's too late."

A murmur passed through the crowd. The celestial army was nearly on them. The clash of steel signaled the start of fighting, and still most of those who remained were milling about. A few threw down their weapons and ran, threading their way through the crowd, to be joined by others in their flight. Ian watched them go and grimaced.

"Fuck it," he said. "Lead by doing, right?"

He raised his father's sword and spurred his horse, then bulled through the milling crowds. The soldiers of Halverdt got out of his way as he picked up speed, hooves hammering against the hard-packed ground. He charged, alone and screaming, at the celestial line.

"The hound! The hallow!" Ian shouted. His voice was ragged, and the juddering image of black-clad celestial troops blurred in his vision, as tears filled his eyes. He couldn't get the image of his father out of his head, lying there, so still. "The hound! The hallow!"

He crashed into the celestial line. The first rank crumbled under his charge, but a spear snagged his mount and pitched him to the ground. The horse screamed, flailing on the earth, hooves narrowly missing Ian as he rolled away. The celestial host closed on him, axes drawn, dark helms silent as they attacked. He fought them off. His father's sword cut through steel like paper, but for every mute warrior he killed, two more rose up. They clambered over the dead body of his horse, pressing him away from his own lines, coming at him in carefully coordinated pairs.

An axe struck his shoulder, and he spun. Steel went into his gut. His legs turned to water. Ian fell to the ground. His father's sword slipped from his hand, and then the sky was filled with twisting mist and the roaring sound of feral gods. Ian punched the nearest face. His fist flattened against steel, knuckles cracking, a jolt of pain going up his arm, leaving the limb numb. Someone's hand grabbed his throat and dragged him to the ground. Ian struggled, but he could feel cold steel at his neck.

"Move and you die," the voice whispered. Ian screamed, and the blade yanked across his throat. He felt warm blood running down his chest. He grabbed at the wound, but the cut was thin and shallow. He looked up to see the knife's bearer tumble away. A spear protruded from the man's throat, glistening with blood. His body jerked away, carried by the spear, and the horseman who bore it.

Knights dressed in gold, knights in red, knights wearing nothing but the dull steel of their armor and the blood of their enemies, flowed over Ian like a morning mist. They poured into the celestial lines like molten iron, burning away the ranks of spear and axe that threatened Ian. In seconds, Ian knelt alone among the dead and dying, his hands still clutched around the cut in his throat. Sir Doone rode up and tossed him a shield. It bore the colors of House Bassion.

"You're just enough of a damned fool to make your father proud, and your mother furious," she called. "Now get off your knees and fight. There are gods to free, and others to free ourselves from."

Ian strapped on the shield, then fished through the detritus of battle until he found his father's sword. He sheathed it, took another from the ground, and charged screaming into battle.

55

THERE WAS A moment of unbearable light, and then the tree exploded. Shards of burning wood arced out over the battlefield, and a shockwave staggered those closest to the smoldering trunk. As silence once again descended on the abandoned Suhdrin camp, Gwen sat in her saddle and turned around to stare at the shattered tree. She was glad to have led her forces away from the camp before that happened.

"Is that good, or is it bad?" she asked. Frair Gilliam rubbed his forehead, wincing in pain.

"Whatever was binding the gheist to the tree has broken. We will not be able to destroy it now, or contain it. But it seems Halverdt has lost her command of the spirit. So both good and bad," he said. "We must make of it what we can."

"Very well," Gwen said. She turned back to the battle ahead, putting the tree out of her mind. "Stay close. There's no telling who here is friend and who is foe. Try to stay out of it as much as you can. Advance!"

The battle in front of them was a churning pit of chaos. On the left flank the celestial and Halverdt forces were intermingled, and the melee was a desperate affair, fought with fists and knives and bludgeons. Small groups of

Halverdt's soldiers churned through the melee like swarms of god-touched bees, killing anything in their path, and dying in droves. As for the celestials, the black-clad soldiers of the heretics tried to maintain order, but commands were lost in the fray, and columns of spear and shield quickly turned into shouting mobs trying desperately to stay together even as their formations were pulled apart.

In the wake of the tree's destruction, there was a brief moment of true violence. A frenzy went through the Suhdrin mobs, short-lived and murderous, like a powder keg going up; any celestial troops unable to reach their own lines were butchered where they stood. Gwen felt a tremendous fury go through her blood, and before she knew it, her fingers were wrapped so tightly around the hilt of her sword that her knuckles were bleeding. Frair Gilliam watched her nervously.

"The corruption calls to you," he said. "You must be careful. It will be very easy for you to lose control of the darkness you have absorbed."

"If that happens, you know what to do," Gwen said.

"Yes. I'm just not sure I'm capable."

The ranks of Halverdt's army, waking from their fury, stood in stunned silence. They let Gwen and her cadre pass unharassed. The celestials had withdrawn, shocked by the sudden violence of the Suhdrin zealots, and unsettled by the trailing silence.

Jaerdin rode up next to Gwen. "Ian and Sorcha Blakley have apparently joined the company," he whispered. "I'm not sure how your priest friend will respond to Sorcha's... way of being."

"The Orphanshield rides next to me," Gwen answered. "Do you think he will balk at her appearance, when the very heretic who started this war counts him an ally?"

"You will have to tell me how that came about," Jaerdin said. "It would have avoided a lot of heartache if he could have been converted to our cause earlier."

"I had to suffer first," Gilliam said, hearing them. "Suffer, and lose all that mattered to me. So yes, it would have prevented much pain, but sometimes pain is necessary for there to be change." He smiled at Jaerdin, his face strained and weary. "This war has shown that, again and again."

"And what will change, frair? What will Tenumbra be when this is all finished?" Jaerdin asked.

"Whatever we make it," Gilliam said. "Whatever we can salvage."

Gwen recognized Ian Blakley at a considerable distance, motioning to them and shouting something to the crowd. She couldn't hear him, and the silent crowd seemed more confused than anything else. Suddenly, Ian hopped onto a horse and charged wildly through the ranks, straight into the re-forming celestial line.

"What the hell is he doing?" she asked.

"It would seem the tree's madness has not completely passed," Gilliam said.

"Or he's still just a fool," Jaerdin answered. He signaled to his men, then charged forward. The Suhdrin ranks parted for them, and soon he was crashing into the celestial line, dragging Halverdt's army along with him. The pagan riders drew their gheists from the air, sparking with everic power as they charged forward in Jaerdin's wake. Gwen stayed put. Only Frair Gilliam remained at her side.

The pair rode up to a strange hill of dead bodies. Sorcha Blakley knelt at its peak, her knees soaking in several inches of bloody water that formed a pool. There was a single body in the middle of the pool.

"Malcolm Blakley?" Gwen asked. The lord of Houndhallow didn't stir. His face was pale, the ink of his tattoos stark against the skin. Wrinkles of worry and age smoothed flat under Sorcha's hands. A dozen wounds seeped blood into the pool. The air over his body glowed with warm, gentle light.

"What happened?" Gilliam asked. He dismounted and went to the edge of the pool, though he seemed unwilling to enter it. "Will he live?"

"He has already gone," Sorcha said quietly. "He endured as long as he could, but this war tore him apart. Help me bring him to his rest, frair."

The Orphanshield knelt in the water and started the long, quiet chant of passing. Water turned to frost at his touch, but Malcolm lay silent. Gwen turned her face away. Tears stung her eyes, but not for Malcolm. For her own father, unmourned and unburied, his body stolen away by the god of death at the Fen Gate. She had not known Malcolm well enough to feel his death as Sorcha must, and Ian. But she knew what it meant to lose a father.

"Ian goes to avenge his father's death," Gwen whispered. "No wonder he seems so mad."

"No. I kept it from him, while I could. Let him be his father's son, for this one day," Sorcha said quietly. She passed a hand over Malcolm's forehead, smiling warmly. "Let him fight with the hope of restoring his father's faith in him. Ian has lost enough today. Let him lose his father tomorrow, with the taste of victory to cut the pain."

"It is done," Gilliam said. Sorcha nodded.

"Look at him. Still the boy, still the poet. Still the man I fell in love with," she said. "Leave me here with him. Let me be his wife for these moments, alone, before I must lift the burden of widowhood."

Gilliam took Gwen by the shoulder and pulled her away. They led their horses some distance before mounting as quietly as they could.

When Gwen looked back, Sorcha was still kneeling beside her husband's body. She was talking to him quietly, smiling and laughing and crying, all of it too much to bear.

Gwen turned her horse and rode away.

The courtyard of the Reaveholt was a seething mass of humanity. Bassion's insurrection had not gone off without a hitch, and now those of her soldiers who were loyal to the church were locked in combat with their heretical brethren. It seemed the core of her most fanatical followers had been closest to the gates when they opened, and charged out into battle, to do whatever misdeed Lady Bassion had given them. That left a scant few trying to hold the keep against a large number of soldiers, vow knights, and angry camp followers who knew nothing of her planned betrayal. The result was chaos.

Elsa strode out of the gatehouse and marched down the walkway that followed the wall. The way was already strewn with dead soldiers, their wounds cauterized, their eyes nothing but empty, smoldering sockets. Martin followed close behind, looking nervously from the corpses to the vow knight, wondering what had become of the Sir LaFey he had known. She seemed much changed.

"Bassion has withdrawn to the tower, and her most loyal

knights with her. Something has happened beyond the walls that has her doubting the wisdom of her choice, but the die is thrown. There's no backing out now." Elsa walked with authority. Martin noticed her footsteps scorched the stone of the walkway, and when she gazed out at the courtyard, sparks swirled in the depths of her eyes. He glanced back at Frair Lucas. The inquisitor was watching his former vow knight with hooded eyes. "We need to secure this castle, in case the loyalists need somewhere to retreat. Are you capable of that?"

"We're not, clearly," Lucas said. "But you may be."

Elsa turned sharply, then smiled. "Yes, I may. I think I may. In fact."

A jolt of heat went through the air, and the distant sound of wood cracking. Elsa's eyes widened, then she stumbled to a halt. She stood at the edge of the walkway, teetering precariously. Martin grabbed her arm, then whipped his hand back. His fingers were blistering from heat that his brain was only now registering. Martin's eyes, too, went wide.

"You're burning up! I've touched coals that were colder. What the hell is wrong with you?"

Elsa didn't move, just stood still, gritting her teeth. It looked like she was putting all her energy into merely staying upright. There was a second wave, this one visible as strands of light that twisted through the air overhead. Martin's heart beat faster, but Elsa felt it harder. She drew her sword and stood there, blade resting gently on Martin's chest. Her hand was shaking. Lucas handed Sir Trueau into Travailler's care and stepped forward.

"Elsa? Dear girl, do you have control of it? Do you need me—?"

"I don't need anything," she hissed through gritted teeth. "I have it. I... have it!"

Whatever supernatural urge gripped her, in a moment Elsa relaxed, withdrawing the sword and staring at them with wide, blinking eyes. Finally her gaze rested on Lucas.

"She's gone again. I thought she was back, that I had reclaimed her... but no. I knew that wasn't right. Whatever Sophie brought, it was not the will of Strife."

"I'm glad you finally see that, though I shudder to think what it must have cost you to learn." Lucas went to her side and put an arm around her. "Elsa, we have to face Helenne Bassion. Can you? Even without Strife?"

"Yes. Yes, I can. If Strife will not answer, then I will do without her strength," Elsa said. A tear rolled down her soot-stained face. "I will face Bassion alone, if I must."

"You don't have to do that. We are here. All of us," Lucas said. He motioned to Martin, Sir Trueau, Sir Travailler, and finally himself. "We will stand with you."

"Then let us go, and end this woman's betrayal."

56

THE LINE COLLAPSED in on him, celestial shields pressed against his chest, restricting Ian's movement. He slashed down at them, sword banging off helms, rough voices shouting insults. Ian fell, and the guards swarmed on him.

"Stop! He belongs to me!"

The guards fell back, leaving Ian on the ground. The battle had been going so well, but he had once again pushed too far forward, and been surrounded. He looked around at the silent ring of black steel. He got up onto his feet, wincing in pain. The celestial line parted, and a pagan ranger walked out.

He wore dark leathers and a cloak that looked like it was made of winter leaves, each one trimmed in frost. His face was covered in a complicated tattoo of oak leaves. He carried two wicked knives, each one shot through with black scars along the runnel, as though the metal had been burned. The man's crooked smile did not fit on his grim face.

"Who are you?" Ian asked. The man smiled and spread his arms.

"I am Aedan Spearson, elder of the tribe of hunters, and chosen by the voidfather to carry on his legacy. I have been following you since the Fen Gate, sometimes closely, sometimes at a great distance, through servants and slaves. Your fame is growing, Ian Blakley. Tession underestimated you. But I will not."

"It is strange to see a pagan elder at the head of an army of the celestial guard. What lies have you told to enslave these fools to your monsters?"

"They are your monsters as well. Where do you think they come from, these misguided fools? I served in your father's army in the Reaver War, before I returned to the old ways. To the true ways. These priests are holy men and women of the church, who found the celestriarch's will a burden, and the inquisition's methods insufficient. The tribes condemn us, but these are their gods we wield." Aedan kicked at one of the bodies at his feet. "We have simply traded their zeal for a more reasonable solution."

"If you served my father, you know he will never give up until he defeats this heresy."

"I know your father well enough, Ian, to not be afraid of him. He will go far, but not far enough. Not as far as I have."

"Is that why you left the celestials? Why you rejoined the pagan tribes?"

"No, child. I am just a man who got fed up with the church, and tired of kneeling to men and women who thought me their betters. I saw power, and I took it. You can call pagans heretics all day, but they gave me a freedom you will never understand." The battle that raged around them shifted, their moment of peace rapidly fleeing. Aedan shook blood off his knives and dropped into a loose guard, crossing his blades in a salute, or an insult. "And now you never will. Either it dies with me, or you will be in the grave yourself, and incapable of learning."

Before Ian could say anything more, Aedan dashed forward, bringing his blades over his head and dropping them, one then the other, on Ian's shield. The strength of the blows drove Ian to one knee. Ian jabbed forward, but mistimed the strike, blade skating wide of the pagan's chest. Aedan hooked Ian's forearm in the cruel barb of one knife, then hacked down with the other. Ian was forced to jab his shield into the man's striking arm, upsetting the swing just enough to spare him. He twisted free, coming to his feet just as the pagan's backswing whistled into his helm. Ian fell flat on his back, dazed.

"Lords always die like this," Aedan said. "On their backside in the mud, wondering where they went wrong. I'll tell you, Ian bloody Blakley, your mistake was being born smart enough to rebel, but too weak to carry through."

At the last word, he held his knives together, blade to blade, and thrust down at Ian's throat. Ian barely got his shield in the way, but the sword pierced the steel and punched into Ian's forehead, tearing his helm apart. Ian rolled away, shaking off the cracked remnants of his helm, stumbling up off balance. Aedan laughed.

"You look drunk, Ian Blakley. Like a child drinking his first cider! Ah, what a pity your father isn't here to see you die. No matter. Once I'm done with you, I'm going to hunt down the Reaverbane and send him in your wake." Aedan trampled forward, kicking Ian's helm away, then laying into him with a series of sharp swings that had Ian backing away. Without his shield, Ian was barely able to keep his opponent at bay, and each blow stung his hand and wrenched the sword in his grip. Finally, a strong downward stroke tore the sword from Ian's hands. He watched helplessly as it pinwheeled away.

"You see, Ian? Hopeless, and helpless. And now you've lost your sword. So, do you want to die standing, or would you rather be on your knees, like a good celestial?"

"I will stand," Ian said. He drew his father's sword. Aedan's eyes lit up.

"There it is! The famous feyiron blade. You know, I've always wondered where your father got it. Not a common weapon for a holy man, you know. Touched by the gods, those blades had to be, and carried only by their closest disciples." Aedan grinned, falling once again into the fluid-smooth twin-knife guard stance that looked so much like dancing. "Will it even answer to a heathen like you?"

Ian shouted, swinging hard. He was still unbalanced from the blow to his head, but the sword flew true, crashing into Aedan's guard and driving him back. The pagan slid away, skirting sideways as Ian drove forward. At first, Aedan was able to block Ian's attacks easily, but the harder he pressed, the further he went, Aedan's expression changed. Glee became respect, respect became concentration, and concentration became fear. Ian's face twisted into a sharp grin.

Malcolm's sword sang in Ian's hands. The feyiron bit chips off Aedan's knives, the black steel humming through the air, as light as wood, as strong as old hatred. Aedan tried to counterattack, but Ian slipped aside and sliced into the pagan's shin. The ranger growled, limping back. Ian pulled up short.

"Where are your promises now, elder of hunters? Where is your victory?" He jumped forward, slashing at Aedan, drawing sparks from the pagan's knives. One of the barbed blades cracked down the center, sending steel splinters into Aedan's hands. Blood laced its way down Aedan's fingers.

Ian smiled. “You have already had your chance to bow. I don’t think I’ll give you another.”

Ian lunged, blade dancing off Aedan’s knife, then swung back and caught the ranger on the iron of his bracer. The man tried to jab but Ian blocked it easily. The ring of watching celestial guards shifted uneasily. Ian started to think about how he would fight his way out of this, should he manage to kill the pagan.

He shouldn’t have worried.

“Enough of this!” Aedan snapped. He backed away, then threw his knife into the ground, where it stuck into the frozen mud. “I am through playing with you, boy!”

Aedan’s arm turned into an expanding cloud of dust, as though he were a statue disintegrating before Ian’s eyes. Black tentacles flickered through the cloud, as fast and indistinct as lightning. Aedan’s chest opened, and then he was rising off the ground, spurting new clouds that were quickly replaced with slithering appendages and talon-tipped wings. His legs burst into a forest of thin spears, held together by membranous webbing, as thin as smoke, and dripping with black ichor. Aedan was nearly twenty feet tall, and growing with each heartbeat. His body was gone, swallowed by shifting chitin and sharp, clawed scythes. Ian took a step back.

“I fear no gods, of this world, or the last,” Ian said. He held his father’s blade in both hands. “This sword has destroyed you once before, when you wore Sacombre’s skin. It will do so again.”

“No, Ian, it will not.” Aedan’s voice rumbled over the battlefield like thunder. “Tomas Sacombre was a priest. I am a hunter.”

A whip-thin tentacle shot out from Aedan’s chest. It

struck Ian in the chest, drawing tiny barbs through his chain mail and into his flesh, and knocking him to the ground. His sword went flying, and his breath along with it. Ian lay there, gasping for breath and hope.

"You made two mistakes, Aedan. The first was not killing me the day we met." Gwen Adair leapt out of the crowd to stand at Ian's side. Her skin was a whorling madness of black lines, twisting and turning just beneath her flesh, and her left eye was a pit as black as coal. "And the second was coming here, when you could have run and run and kept running."

She drew a spear from her quiver, the last spear wrought in her blood, and held it across her chest. Gwen's shadow squirmed with sightless mouths. Ian rolled over and started crawling slowly away. Gwen didn't give him a second look.

"You know that you face the god of death and the void, don't you?" Aedan rumbled. "The very god who destroyed your parents?"

"You are corruption. A disease on the gods of this world, and nothing more," Gwen said. She rested the spear on her shoulder, merely a wrist-flick away from throwing it. "And I mean to free the gods from your foul touch."

She leapt into the air, spear poised for the kill.

Aedan rose to meet her, just as the longest night finally fell.

57

IT TOOK A long hour, spent in bloodshed and hard melee, but they had the courtyard. The betrayers of House Bassion retreated to the northern tower, leaving Elsa, Lucas, and their companions to hold the main gate. An unsteady rain of arrows fell on them from the northern tower, but for the most part, the Reaveholt was secure.

"We have the walls. We need to rejoin the battle," Sir Travailler said. "The Blakleys are getting slaughtered out there."

"Not until Bassion is dead," Lucas answered. "No heretic must be left."

"You are letting your offended honor guide you," Elsa said. "You are an inquisitor, yet you never suspected this woman. You must be reasonable."

"I have had enough of being a reasonable man," Lucas said. "Reason has won me nothing but grief. It's time for a dose of vengeance."

They marched through the twisting corridors of the northern walls, closing in on the tower. This whole area was littered with bodies, mostly wearing the blue and yellow of House Bassion, though a few priests of Cinder lay among them. Lucas paused at each holy corpse and said a prayer.

"How could I not have seen this?" Travailler muttered as they walked. "She has been a good duchess since I was a child. How could she betray her sworn blades? Her own people?"

"Those are questions we won't have answers for if we kill Helenne Bassion," Elsa said. "Vengeance doesn't suit you, Lucas. Leave that to the priests of Strife."

"Don't preach to me, LaFey," Lucas snapped. "We have tolerated enough. Forgiven enough. Sometimes knives are necessary."

"And when the Circle of Lords questions her death at an inquisitor's hands?" Elsa asked.

"Let them come. Let every silk-laced courtesan of Heartsbridge don his well-wrought armor and ride north. I will crush them in the jaws of winter. I will send them home to their lovers in caskets, or pieces, or both!"

"That's enough!" Elsa snapped. She grabbed the inquisitor by the elbow and spun him around. "Don't let Sophie's madness reach you. Don't fall victim to a god of vengeance and selfish pride."

"This is my heart speaking, sir. Not some corrupted gheist speaking through me, not the echo of a mad god whispering through my bones. I am tired of blaming gods for my mistakes, and different gods for my enemies. For once I will take the burden myself. Helenne Bassion betrayed me. Tomas Sacombre betrayed me. The church is better than these people. If I must restore its name in blood, then so be it." Lucas paused, twisting his face in anger, breathing deeply until he had control of his heart once again. "We have fought greater gods than this." He jerked his arm out of Elsa's iron grip. "Now either join me, or oppose me, or get the hell out of my way."

Elsa reared back and punched Lucas in the face. The inquisitor sat down heavily, blinking away the tears that suddenly filled his eyes. She squatted in front of him, lifting his chin to look at the damage.

"You will be fine. But not if you act like this. Yes, the church has failed in this, as it has failed in so many other ways. Our lives, dedicated to destroying the northern gheists, might have been a sham. Worse, we might have been destroying the land we love. But tearing everything down is not the way."

"I know no other," Lucas said quietly. "What will be left, after this? Who will have faith in us?"

"The faithful," Elsa said. She dabbed at the blood dribbling down Lucas's forehead with a bit of cloth, then helped him to his feet. "Now, put away that talk of murder. We must deliver justice to Helenne Bassion, but we must also deliver peace. To her, and to the rest of Tenumbra. Come on."

They went down the hallway and through a door, inquisitor and vow knight once again. No matter that Elsa could barely feel Strife's power, and Lucas wanted a turn at vengeance, they were together again, finally, as they must be.

A patrol of loyal Bassion men-at-arms confronted them, standing in front of a barricaded door. When they spotted Lucas and Elsa, they fell into a shieldwall, bristling with spears. Elsa waved her sword at them.

"Do you stand with or against Helenne Bassion?" she asked

"Our loyalty is with Galleydeep!"

"That doesn't answer… listen. Lady Bassion has betrayed the church. She's betrayed you. I thought her an ally, and now I'm fighting my way through this castle trying to bring her to justice, which is not how I planned on spending today. So if your loyalty is with the duchess, then gods damn you, and I will pray for your souls." Elsa gripped her sword in both hands and marched forward. "Though the only priest of Cinder I know might not be willing to do the rites anymore."

The barricaded door swung open before Elsa reached the shieldwall, and Helenne appeared in the doorway. The blackened ruin of the right side of her face was spreading, as though the corruption in her heart was eating her flesh from the inside. She waved in their direction.

"Still on this crusade, priests? I thought you would have learned the error of that by now. Oh, well. Never mind."

"My lady, return to your chambers. These are—"

"I know who they are, dear child," Helenne said. She raised her chalice in both hands, smiling. "I assure you, I am perfectly safe."

Mist bubbled out of the cup, and lines of red light burst from the guards protecting Bassion. They screamed, higher and higher, flesh withering as their blood drained into Bassion's cup. With a final gasp they fell to the ground. Shields and spears clattered to the stone and were still, mingled with the flayed dust of the soldiers. Helenne saluted Elsa with the cup, then drank.

"What have they made of you, Helenne?" Lucas whispered. "What price have you paid?"

"I'm not sure which I want to answer first. The price? Everything. I have given them everything. And in return?" She drank again, but when she pulled the chalice away from her lips, a long, knotty strand of dark liquid trailed from cup to lip, glistening in the half-light of the hallway. "In return I have gained so much more."

"We don't mean to kill you, Bassion. But we will, if we must," Elsa said, marching forward. She kicked the huddled remnants of the guards aside, causing them to burst into husky clouds of gray ash. "Surrender to us, or try to kill us. Make your choice."

"Oh, I've never wanted to kill you, you fools. You're too useful. Without inquisitors to scare the pagans, and vow knights to be horrified at Sacombre's betrayal, and loyal Suhdrins to accuse Tener of heresy… where would we be?"

"Well, I'm still pretty committed to it," Elsa said.

She swung at Bassion, chopping down with the flame-cracked steel of her bloodwrought blade. The tip bit into the stone transom of the door, sending sparks flying, doing little to slow the blade. But Helenne was far from helpless. She drew a mercy dagger, its barbed hilt made to break blades, and blocked Elsa's swing. With a twist, she jerked the blade away, forcing Elsa forward into the room. She didn't lose her sword, but she did stumble past the duchess. Bassion's blade slipped along Elsa's ribs as she passed.

The room was a mess. Once a solarium, it was scattered with dead bodies wrapped in silk, young hands and soft faces twisted in the final moments of their death. Tall windows looked out onto a balcony, one of the few viewing platforms other than the tower heights. Beyond the windows, the battle raged.

Elsa pivoted to face the door, but Bassion had already fled to one of the windows, chalice in one hand, knife in the other. Lucas rushed in and looked around with wide eyes.

"What have you done?" Lucas whispered.

"We are uniting the ways, inquisitor. Ending the church's terrible reign, and with it the cowardice of the tribes. They were always afraid to claim the powers of the gods, both of them. But we have found a better path. An older path." Bassion picked her way through the corpse-filled room. Elsa kept her sword on the duchess. Bassion laughed.

"Fight me, if you must. But it doesn't matter now. We already have our victory."

Elsa gritted her teeth and struck. Helenne blocked easily enough, her hand too strong, the speed with which she riposted too fast. The tip of her dagger tickled Elsa's neck, then withdrew. Elsa touched the wound, and her fingers came away bloody. Helenne was watching her through cloudy eyes.

"Just a girl with a sword now, aren't you, Sir LaFey? Hardly a match for the likes of me."

"If I may interrupt," Lucas said. He drew a strong bolt of naether out of the shadows, holding it in the air between his two hands while it grew. "I am not so limited. And you—"

Helenne said nothing, just motioned with her hand. The bolt of naether shattered, and Lucas screamed. He tumbled back on the ground, hands going to his face. Black veins popped out on his skin, then skeins of shadow twisted out of him, drawing into Helenne's chalice. She drew it out like a fisherman playing the line. When she was done, Lucas lay on the ground, gasping for breath.

"You are no less vulnerable than dear little Trueau, or any of the others. Your god isn't special, Lucas. Just another demon, waiting to be tamed."

Elsa screamed and charged forward. Bassion twisted away, and the two women came together with a crash that seemed to shake the castle. The duchess stumbled back, falling hard against the wall. The foul liquid in her chalice splashed out, turning the stone into a tapestry of ropy blood and oily darkness.

"You will pay for that. First with your life, and then with your soul," Bassion growled. "I will not be stopped by a couple of priests too damned foolish to see the enemy right in front of their face!"

"You were never a good celestial, Bassion. Your mistake shows that," Lucas growled. He got unsteadily to his feet, hands shaking with rage and fatigue, one bony finger pointing at the duchess of Galleydeep. "You have forgotten the date."

"The date? How in hells could that matter?"

"It is Frostnight, child. Stand before your judge!"

The air turned brittle with cold. Waves of purple energy rose up from the floor, filling Lucas's hands, twisting around his fingers in rings of runic light. His eyes deepened in his skull, leaving nothing but pits of swirling darkness, an emptiness that fell through for eternity.

Bassion laughed. "Have I not proven the worthlessness of your power, Lucas? Do you need another demonstration of my—"

"The cup!" Lucas howled. Bassion's forehead creased, then she snatched the chalice closer to her body, just as Elsa struck.

Elsa's steel fist came down on the duchess' delicate wrist, snapping bones and sending the chalice flying. It fell, shattering on the stone. As it broke, an incredible light filled Elsa's soul. Her bonds were cut, the gates between her and Strife torn open, like a dam breaking under the deluge.

"My lady," she whispered, speaking to Strife. In her heart, Elsa felt the goddess of summer smile, and her power filled Elsa's veins.

Throwing aside the corrupted steel of her sword, Elsa grabbed Bassion by the throat. Fire surged around her hands, fed by Elsa's fury and Strife's blessing. Flames rose up around Bassion's face like a crown of rubies. The duchess screamed for a brief second, before the heat cooked her windpipe and turned her hair to dust. She continued kicking as Elsa lifted her off the ground. Elsa poured more and more fire into her hands, drawing on Strife's blessing, turning months of frustration into a jet of purifying flame. Eventually, Bassion was still. Elsa dropped her.

Helenne Bassion's head was a gleaming white skull, burned and baked in Elsa's fury. When she hit the stone floor, a crack formed around her left eye, and black liquid leaked out. Lucas stood and rushed to the dead woman's side.

"The same, the same," he said. "It's the corruption I saw, oh so long ago, in the spirit bear, and the hunter gheist. In every feral god we've faced since the Allfire!" Lucas passed his hand over the darkness, binding it in naether. "This was the source of her power, the thing that cut us off from our gods, and with which she and the void priests have enslaved the gheists. But what is it?"

Elsa glanced out the window, then backed away.

"I'm not sure," she said. "But I think we're about to find out."

58

SHADOWS STREAMED BEHIND Gwen as she flew through the air, streamers of black moths that fluttered in her wake. Night fell like a banner dropped, turning the dusk into midnight in the beating of a heart. The air, already cold, froze in the lungs of every man and woman watching. Breath turned to frost, blood turned to iron, skin became as chill as snow. But not Gwen. Gwen was burning alive.

Aedan towered over the battlefield. His cloak of leaves transformed into a mantle of skulls, his arms were shot through with seams of black light, sprouting from his flesh into tendrils that whipped through the air, striking and killing friend and foe alike. His head split and split and then split again, a puzzle box of gaping jaws and leering eyes, teeth cracked from top to bottom and filled with swarms of screaming mouths. He was nightmare, and the world couldn't wake up.

Gwen arced out of the sky, her spear aimed straight at Aedan's heart. The air rippled around the course of her descent, drawing luminescent lines against the stars. A swarm of tentacles shot out at her, writhing liquid and black, blotting out the moon. She dodged through them, landing lightly on the largest, sweeping her spear through the veiny mass of its grip, dancing away as the severed limb tumbled from the sky. A dozen more chased her, but she skirted around the attack, slashing through those she couldn't avoid, leaving a shivering forest of black stumps in her wake.

Aedan bellowed in pain. The forest of his scream whipped Gwen's hair and stole her breath. It was nearly enough to knock her from the sky, but the everic power woven into her spear, laced through her blood and bolstered by the stolen energy of the corruption she had taken on, kept her moving. She landed at his bulbous feet. The ground cratered under her boots.

"No one defies death, huntress!" Aedan shouted. "All submit to the grave!"

"You lie to yourself, and to your followers. You are no scion of death. I have seen you, in the iron, in the hound, and in the vow." Gwen danced aside as Aedan slashed out at her, coming down in a squat on the ruin of a wagon. "You are nothing more than corruption, a sickness that must be purged. Tenumbra will be free of you, at my hand, and by my spear!"

"You are nothing, huntress, and will become nothing more," Aedan spat. His voice boomed over the fields like a collapsing tower, felt in the bones and the earth, leaving devastation behind. Those closest to him fell to the ground. "I am the god of the grave and forgetting. There will be no memory of you, now or ever!"

"I kill gods," Gwen shouted, then leapt once again into the air.

Aedan twisted to follow her ascent, crushing frozen bodies under his lumbering legs, his multitude of black eyes flickering as he watched her arc away. Her spear was only a splinter of light against the sky when she threw it. So focused on the huntress was Aedan that he never saw her weapon as it flashed through the air. The bloodwrought tip buried itself in his massive shoulder. It stung, but the true pain was to follow.

Still dancing through the air, Gwen drew the spear back to her hand. Long streamers of corruption grew out of the spear, blossoming like vines and slithering through the air to Gwen's hand. Once they were taut, she pulled the spear free and reeled it in like a harpoon. The wound it left in Aedan's flesh bled corruption, hooked on the spear's barbed head, drawn in by the blood woven into its steel. The black, viscous oil followed the spear to Gwen, lashing around her arm like a scarf before sinking into her skin.

The dark whorls on Gwen's face and neck grew, burrowing deeper into her body, spreading like frost on a window. The black pit of her eye deepened. Distant stars glimmered in its depths.

As the corruption slopped out of Aedan's wound, the massive body of the god shuddered. Pustules burst across his shoulder, spewing webs of darker fluid into the air, strands of darkness that dissolved into fluttering bats, flapping membranous wings into the night. Aedan howled, grabbing at the wound and spitting fury at Gwen.

"Do you think such trickery can save you, Gwen Adair? No spear formed by mortal hands can break the heart of a true god of Tenumbra!"

"I have no interest in saving myself," Gwen said. She clenched her fist, a fist now consumed by the dark corruption of the gheists. She was losing control, and could feel it. *Best finish this fast,* she thought. *Before it finishes me.*

The corruption gheist wearing Aedan's body gripped the ichor pouring from its body and wove it together, creating a net of ropy blackness. He threw it at Gwen, creating a wave of dark liquid that rushed across the battlefield. The ranks of celestial warriors, those few who had not fled at the sight of Aedan's ascension, were enveloped by the rising tide and transformed. Their skin pulsed with streaks of purple light, and their eyes disappeared into their skulls, sockets filling with a slithering mist. They screamed, and then fell.

"It is already changing you, huntress. I can feel it. I can taste it. Soon, you will fall to my power," Aedan purred. The rumbling tide of shadow rolled toward her. Gwen cowered, wanting to leap away, but rooted in place by the magnetic force of the corruption boiling through her bones. She braced herself for impact.

Not ten yards in front of her, the tide suddenly parted, slicing in half like a sail torn by the wind. The black flood crashed to either side of her, peeling back, revealing faces and grasping hands in its depths. She stared in wonder, then turned to look at the place where the tide had broken.

Ian Blakley stood in the gap, both hands wrapped around his father's blade, leaning into the dark current. His face was splattered with spider-thin seams of corruption, the flesh hissing, eyes clenched tight against the pain. When the flood passed, he dropped to one knee, arm thrown over the hilt of the blade, gasping for breath. He glanced back at her.

"Get to killing gods, will you? Or that one, at least."

"Find the priest," Gwen growled. "Bring him. He follows in my wake."

"Which—?" But Gwen was already gone, arcing again into the night sky. Ian turned back to the battlefield, squinting at the dimly lit ranks of soldiers that were still fighting, the flickering light of burning wagons and Cinder's pale face the only light in the sudden darkness. He shivered. "Very well. The priest. He must be somewhere."

Gwen was breaking apart. The corruption was growing through her skin, leaving scar-like ridges on her arms and face, black seams that formed strange and disturbing patterns. The haft of her spear was crooked, the wood given new life by the endless stream of corruption that it had absorbed, the once straight shaft now squirming beneath her fingers like a snake, barely contained. And there was something living in her shadow, seen out of the corner of her eye whenever she landed close enough to a burning wagon or toppled brazier to cast a shadow at all. Gwen tried to not look at it, afraid that attention would give it voice.

But if she suffered, then Aedan was in agony. The towering gheist was slowly toppling. Dead tentacles dragged in its wake, and the massive arms and legs that supported his engorged body had splintered into smaller and smaller forms, leaving shells behind. Aedan's attacks were sluggish, his defenses more and more stubborn and frustrated. He refused to yield, was maybe incapable of giving up the fight that had consumed him, but he was failing. Gwen danced around him in a dizzying pattern of spear strikes and barbed jabs, bleeding the corruption from his swollen, stunted body.

I must do this, before I lose control. I must, Gwen thought. *There is no one else who can face this creature and live. Not even Aedan could survive his own ascension.*

But the corruption was quickly overtaking her ability to absorb it. It was now or never.

Planting her feet, Gwen drew all the energy of the corruption, laced through with the everic powers that still lingered in her bones, and prepared to charge. The earth cracked under her feet, the air fell into the vacuum of her lungs, the stars themselves seemed to lean closer to the earth. Shouting, she dashed across the battlefield, straight at Aedan.

The sound of her passing was like a thunderclap. Aedan's sluggish response was to draw elephantine arms across his face, shielding the gruesome fissure of his jaws from Gwen's charge. She led with the spear, slicing through air and shadow and flesh, until it struck bone and shattered. The splintered shaft broke apart in Gwen's hands, bursting with the light of a thousand stars, disintegrating into a cloud of sparks that rolled across the frozen ground of the field like a tidal wave. They lay in the snow, hissing and steaming, an angry mirror of the starlit sky above, before fading slowly out.

Gwen and Aedan lay still in the center, nearly touching, flat on their backs. As the mists cleared, Aedan got stiffly to his feet, drawing new daggers from his ribcage. He was nearly himself again. Only the wicked bone of the daggers, leaking blood from their new birth, marked him as fey. He stood over Gwen and smiled.

"Is that all, huntress? You have given everything, and still I stand. Do you have nothing else in you?" He squatted over her, crossing the knives at her neck, pressing them against her throat. "Or are you finished at last?"

Gwen's body was a ruin. The corruption covered her skin, leaking out in a thin mist that had a mind of its own, shadows of dark limbs caressing the ground, battering helplessly against Aedan's wrists. She stared up at the sky and was silent.

"Very well," Aedan said. "Good night, huntress. And well fought."

"There is no god of corruption," she whispered. "No spirit of the debased gheist. You are a lie, Aedan Spearson." She lifted her head, one eye as black as the ocean depths, the other bloodshot and crying. "A lie we tell ourselves."

"The gods are the lie, huntress. We are merely the liars."

"No." She shook her head, and the movement opened her skin under Aedan's blades. Blood flowed freely down her throat, to soak into the snow under her head. "I have seen the power of the gods. I have felt their fire and their fury. You're a fool to try to bend them to your will. It will end in nothing but misery."

"My end may be misery, but your end is now," Aedan snapped. He drew the blades together, sweeping them through Gwen's neck, the tips clacking against her spine as they passed. He grinned down at her as her lifeblood bubbled up.

"You're missing something, elder," Gwen said. Her voice was quiet, as though shouted from a great distance. "Your god. Your death. It is mine now."

Aedan frowned, spun the blades together and buried them in Gwen's chest. Her laugh was hollow. The light in her blackened eye was a red spark, bright in the night. She grabbed him by the chest and pushed, sending him flying.

Gwen stood, breaking the daggers off in her chest, leaving the blades to grind against her ribs, throwing the shattered tangs aside. Black webs formed above her shoulders, a mantle of diaphanous wings that shivered in the breeze. Aedan lay on his back, staring at her with horror. He scrambled to his feet as Gwen stalked closer.

"The god of death you accepted, the one Sacombre bound to his flesh and corrupted with the void priests' rites... it is mine, now. So thoroughly interwoven with the corruption, it could not help but leech out with the darkness. My darkness. My corruption." Gwen held her hand out, palm up. A shimmering fog clung to her fingers. "You cannot kill the grave spirit. No more than you can drown fire. And now it answers to my will."

Aedan clasped his hands together, drawing on the everam of his tribe, the elder of hunters sending one last prayer to the old gods. But nothing answered him. He was too far gone for the gheists to pay him heed. He spat and produced two new daggers, spurs drawn from his forearms that twisted in his hands to form blades.

"You must be careful with that, elder. You're going to run out of bones," Gwen said. She gestured, and Aedan's breath caught. His skin grew tight, like leather at first, pulling his bones, then harder. Leather to sun-caked mud, mud to stone, stone into steel. He couldn't move. He couldn't breathe. Aedan stood there, eyes wide with terror, as Gwen drew near. "Know this, Aedan Spearson. Death does not like to be tamed. It will always slip the leash, and when it does—" she placed a hand against his forehead like a benediction "—Death's bite is harsh."

She crushed his skull, a fracture that traveled through his body, collapsing bones into dust and flesh into splinters. Aedan cracked down the spine, chest bursting, arms twisted, legs and lungs wrung out until his screams were freed into the air. He fell like a bundle of sticks cut loose, a hundred pieces, each broken and brittle.

Gwen brushed off her hands, chuckling to herself. She breathed in the bloody air. The field was an open grave, and death stirred all around her. She lifted her face to the heavens and slowly, slowly, rose off the ground. The armies of Tenumbra had brought her a mighty feast, and the spirit of death in her was starved. She opened her jaws and felt something tickle its way up her throat, a damnation slithering into the world. She yearned to give the world the death it deserved. And she would. For their betrayal, for her family, for the suffering these people had caused and the destruction they deserved for it. Gwen would burn all of it down. She was the grave.

Naetheric bands twisted across her chest. She glanced down at this inconvenience, and laughed. Turning, Gwen saw Ian Blakley staring at her, and Frair Gilliam at his side. The priest was struggling to contain her. The sweat beading on his forehead turned to blood as she casually shrugged against the bonds.

"It will take more than the powers of Cinder to contain me, fool," she growled. She focused on the Orphanshield, thrilling at the fear in his blood, the failure leaking from his flesh. "You will fail at this, as you failed your children. Your wife. Those who depended on you most." Gwen grabbed the band of naetheric energy tying her to the frair and gave it a tug, pulling Gilliam to his knees. "Failure is all you know. Cinder is not enough."

"Which is why Strife and Cinder travel together." Elsa drew her sunlit blade, bathing the field in holy light. "I am sorry, Gwen Adair. I counted you a friend."

"Vow knights have no friends. Only people who pretend to not be horrified in their presence," Gwen spat. She lifted a clawed hand… her body was changing, even beyond her awareness. No matter. "I could have killed you at any time. I will not hesitate now."

Elsa swung, and the blade met Gwen's gnarled talons, striking sparks. Gwen held the coruscating blade in stone-hard hands. It cut slowly into her flesh, black blood hissing as fire claimed it, the sword edging forward a tiny bit at a time.

"You cannot save him, Elsa. The god you wield is just another corruption, another tool of the void. Halverdt has deceived you. The flame will answer to my call!" Gwen reached out with her will, grasping at the spirit in Elsa's blade. The flames guttered, but her will slipped off the fire's gheist. Gwen frowned, but Elsa beamed.

"I have found my way back," she said through gritted teeth. "And now you must do the same. I don't want to kill you!"

"You will not have a choice," Gwen snapped. Her mind raced, the corruption in her bones mingling thought and fury. She could taste the death in the air. All she had to do was reach out and grasp it.

But she didn't. Gwen held back. The gheist raged against her, but she held on. She endured.

The two priests were faltering, though. The blade burning through Gwen's talons was scorching Elsa's hands. Streaks of charred flesh twisted down the vow knight's arms, and Frair Gilliam's eyes were closed and his face smeared with blood. Despite her will, Gwen drew on the spirits of the freshly dead that swirled through the air. They filled her with power, power enough to break these two without thinking.

Gwen pushed Elsa aside. The vow knight spun to the ground, dropping her sword. The Orphanshield rolled back, like an old man falling out of his chair, but the second he hit the ground he was up again, reweaving the naetheric bonds Gwen had just broken. She turned on him, grinning, wings flapping. She lifted off the ground.

"My children are dead, and my wife, and my wards. I have no one else to disappoint. I cannot fail, because there is nowhere lower for me to go," he spat. Resetting the bonds,

Gilliam hurled them at Gwen. They closed across her chest, her legs, anchoring her to the earth. She hissed in frustration, but deep in her tumultuous heart, she felt a surge of relief. Not long. Not long now.

"This can't be the end of your journey, Gwendolyn." Lucas finally appeared, his shadowform twisting up out of the ground to hover in front of Gwen's twisting face. "I can feel you inside this demon, fighting. Don't surrender."

"That you live is all the fight I can promise, frair," she said. "And I can't promise it for long. The corruption has me. End it."

"But I can't—"

"End it!" Gwen howled. Her fury blew Lucas's shadowform into pieces. Frair Gilliam fell again, his hands curling into spasming fists as his eyes rolled back in his head. The bonds shattered over Gwen's ridged chest. Elsa charged her, but Gwen swept her aside, both of them screaming in pain and frustration.

Ian's blade pierced Gwen's back between the shoulder blades. Her wings, full of biting mouths and screaming souls, battered his head, but he held on, driving the black feyiron deeper and deeper. She twisted around, knocking him off his feet, but he held on to the sword as it slipped free of the wound. Gwen scrambled at Ian, but he rolled into a guard, dashing aside her talons with his father's sword, fighting feverishly to keep her claws away.

Shadows formed around her, wisps at first, then hands. Frair Lucas appeared, an enormous, shadowy figure made of ribbons the color of night. He wrapped naether around Gwen, pinning her arms. She struggled, but her face relaxed. She locked eyes with Ian.

"I have held it as long as I can. Death has me, but it is the corruption that drives me. Destroy me, and the corruption ends. Let death slip back to its home, but I can keep the corruption with my flesh. End it."

Ian didn't blink. He lunged forward, burying his sword in her belly. It passed through and into Frair Lucas's shadowform. The priest gasped, but the flimsy image of his face screwed tight with concentration. "Elsa! Your sword!"

"Frair, the naether cannot bear—"

"I know what I am asking," he snapped. "For your vow, and the sun rising in winter. You must!"

Ian flinched aside as Elsa's burning sword punched through Gwen and Lucas both. The flaming edge singed Ian's cheek, but he bore down on his blade, holding it in Gwen's writhing body.

Gwen screamed, threw her eyes to the heavens, and died.

A wave of black energy gathered in the air, not around Gwen, but at the edges of the horizon. It rolled toward them, snatching shadows from the ground as it passed, roaring louder and louder until it reached Gwen's dying soul. The moon blinked out for an instant, replaced by a gaping void that held the whole world in its emptiness, and then was gone. Cinder's pale face returned, brighter than ever.

Morning broke, unnaturally early, in the east. Frostnight had passed.

Lucas's shadowform evaporated, drifting in flakes of ash to mingle with the snow. Elsa stared down at Gwen's still form, then threw her sword to the ground and ran back toward the Reaveholt. Ian knelt. He took Gwen's cold hand in his own, pressed it to his chest, and waited.

The battle raged on around them, but it was a battle of flesh and blood. The war was over. It was finished.

EPILOGUE

THEY BURIED GWEN where she fell, a woman without a tribe, a house without a name. She had given herself in the last moments that Tenumbra might be freed of the void corruption, which had been claiming the gods, pagan and celestial, for some time. By binding the corruption to her flesh, she had drawn the poison out of the world. Scraps remained, but only a few, sheathed in the bones of distant adherents to the void heresy.

Malcolm Blakley received a hero's funeral beneath the walls of Houndhallow. All the nobles of Tener and Suhdra, whether they had raised arms against Malcolm, fought at his side, or stayed out of the war completely, came to honor his passing. Promises were made, and honors given, but they were just words, and Tenumbra was not a land of quiet peace for long.

On the morning after they buried his father, Ian stood in his rooms in Houndhallow and prepared for his new life. His sister, grown so much since the start of the war, found him there.

"They would crown you, you know," she said quietly. Nessie lingered at the door, watching as her brother filled a light pack. Their father's sword lay on the bed.

"They would. Which is why I'm leaving," he said without turning around.

"Mother does not want you to go."

"Mother has a duchy to govern, and a daughter to raise," Ian said. He had rearranged the items in his pack a dozen times, and would a dozen more if time allowed. But it didn't, and he was only making excuses now. "The two of you will do Houndhallow proud."

"You didn't fail him."

"I did."

"No, it was—"

"Nessie, please. I wasn't there, and he died. There's no changing that." Ian smiled weakly and shrugged. "Someday I may learn to carry that, but not here, not in these walls."

His sister fell silent for a while. Ian finally threw the pack over his shoulder, snatched a walking stick from the wall, and made for the door.

"The sword?" she asked. Ian paused.

"It's yours. You'll have better luck with it than I will."

"This isn't what he would have wanted, Ian."

"No. But it isn't his decision to make. It's mine. Take care of Mother, sis. She's just strong enough to break."

They embraced, and then he was gone, out the door and down the road, to disappear over the horizon.

Nessie watched him from the window of his room until he was a speck, and then nothing. Then she went to find her mother. There still had to be a coronation.

The inn was a narrow building, barely room for the bar and three stools. The innkeeper hustled back and forth, unusually busy even for a market day. Another customer came in, a nervous, stooped, skinny man in robes that might once have been black, but were now the color of the mud; it looked as if he had slept in them the night before. He made his way to the bar, ordered a beer and a room, and avoided all other eye contact. His feet were caked with dirt, as though he had been traveling for months. Or running for longer.

Night fell, and the tavern got louder and louder. The man stayed at the edge of the bar, nursing his thin beer and watching the other customers. One of them would have to do; he just couldn't decide which one. A stranger in a rural town like this would pass unnoticed, but a stranger in a town dealing with a murder would stand out like a sore thumb. Best to wait until morning, then. But he was so hungry. He hunkered down, cursing his luck and hoping one of them would slip.

So consumed with his hunger and dark thoughts was he that the stranger didn't notice when the bar went utterly silent. He was muttering into his beer when the chair next to him was pulled out, scraping loudly against the floor. He looked over and dropped his beer, gaping.

Henri Volent sat down next to the man. He was dressed in simple clothes, a chain shirt, his sword as plain as a butcher's knife. Volent laid a dagger on the bar and nodded to the innkeeper.

"Two more; one for my friend. Whatever you have that isn't complete shit," he said. His soft voice carried through the silent tavern. Patrons started filing out. Volent ignored them. The innkeeper brought their beers and then disappeared into the kitchen, leaving Volent alone with the man.

"You know, I've been looking for you for quite a while. Harder and harder to taste your lot in the wind. You might even be the last. Wouldn't that be something?" Volent asked. He took a deep drink of the beer, ignoring the thin swill, tasting only his own words. "The last one. Hm."

"I... I don't know—"

"Oh, let's be honest with one another. We can do that, at least." Without looking, Volent reached under the bar and twisted the dagger out of the man's hands, breaking his wrist in the process. He threw the blade away, set down his beer, and then started spinning his own knife on the counter. "Gwen did a mighty work. Tore most of you from the world completely. Even I felt it. That's when I knew. All this time, I was one of you, a fragment of your great work. Hilarious, isn't it?" The man didn't laugh, so Volent shrugged and continued in his quiet, echoing voice. "Sacombre must have known. Probably why he tried to kill me. But here I am, still alive, still infected. But after Gwen's sacrifice, I could still feel you, some of you. Distant, hidden... but there. And so I have been finding you, one by one, and putting an end to this little corruption."

"You're mistaken. You're mad. I'm not... I'm nothing. Nothing!"

"Yes, you are," Volent answered. "You know, I really think you're the last one. Once we're finished here, I can go away, someplace far, someplace I can't hurt anyone. That will be marvelous."

"Finished?" the man asked nervously.

"Yes," Volent said. He picked the knife up from the table. "Finished."

Years passed. The pain of Lucas's death haunted Elsa. They had found him sprawled on the floor in the Reaveholt, his soul driven from his body by her own blade, nothing but a shell of flesh and blood. But the church needed priests, and she was among the few to survive Halverdt's corruption with her faith intact. She returned to Heartsbridge, then the Lightfort and Cinderfell, when she found the warmth of Strife's embrace too bright, and now she roamed the forests of the north once again. No longer hunting. Things had changed.

She rode that old familiar road, thinking about how everything had started here. As she came over the hill, the town of Gardengerry spread out before her, peaceful and prosperous once again. The doma had been repaired, the nightmare of the hunter gheist driven from the minds of the people by a new shrine, and a new theology. Tenerrans no longer avoided this place, walking the streets openly with their shamans and their ink, even as the evensong rose from the doma. She wondered what had become of the girl, the one she and Lucas had met on their way here, so many seasons ago. She might never know.

"Hard to imagine," she said quietly. "So much has changed."

"And yet, so much is the same," Ian said. He rubbed his nose impatiently, his freshly shorn hair still glowing in the evening light. She looked over at him and laughed, causing him to wrinkle his nose. "What?"

"You'll have to learn how to cut your hair better than that," she said. "You look like a shorn sheep."

"Can we get on with the job?" he asked. "The elders will already have gathered. Wouldn't want the prayers to go on without us."

"Of course, of course. The impatience of youth, it will

damn us all," Elsa answered. She lowered the deep cowl of her black hood over her head, swallowing her face in shadow. "Look stern, young man. The villagers have certain expectations of an inquisitor and her vow knight."

Ian laughed, but by the time they reached the city gates, his face was placid. The setting sun glistened on his golden armor, and when the witches greeted him, Ian raised a sword of steel wrought in his own blood, runes of gold chasing up and down the blade. Elsa sat at his side, and remembered, and mourned.

They went into the village together, Cinder and Strife, to lay a memorial at the shrine of the hunter in the name of their friend, Gwendolyn Adair. Always to be remembered as the huntress, and never the heretic.

ACKNOWLEDGMENTS

ABOUT TEN YEARS ago, I called up my agent and said "I'm thinking about doing something a little different. Something rather epic." This series is the result of that conversation, and while it has gone through more revisions than even I would believe, The Hallowed War has lived up to that original premise. It is different than most fantasy, and yet is more than a little epic. It's strange to close a project that has consumed so much of your life, but I'm satisfied with it, more satisfied than I thought possible. I did what I wanted to do with it. And now it's done.

None of this would have happened without my agent, Joshua, my editors Steve and Sam at Titan, and the enduring love of my wife, Jennifer. Thank you all. And, as always, to God be the glory, and the honor. Amen.

ABOUT THE AUTHOR

TIM AKERS WAS born in deeply rural North Carolina, the only son of a theologian, and the last in a long line of telephony princes, tourist-attraction barons, and gruff Scottish bankers. He moved to Chicago for college, and stayed to pursue his lifelong obsession with apocalyptic winters.

He lives (nay, flourishes) with his brilliant, tolerant, loving wife, and splits his time between pewter miniatures and fountain pens.

Tim is the author of the Burn Cycle (*Dead of Veridon*, *Heart of Veridon*) from Solaris Books, as well as *The Horns of Ruin* (featuring Eva Forge) published by Pyr Books.

His website is http://www.timakers.net/.